GOD RESTRAINER

Christopher Mitchell is the author of the epic fantasy series The Magelands. He studied in Edinburgh before living for several years in the Middle East and Greece, where he taught English. He returned to study classics and Greek tragedy and lives in Fife, Scotland with his wife and their four children.

City Ascendant
Dragon Eyre Badblood
Dragon Eyre Ashfall
Dragon Eyre Blackrose
Dreams of Kell
God Restrainer
Holdfast Imperium

Brigdomin Books Ltd
First Edition, November 2022
ISBN 978-1-912879-76-2

For Sophie

ACKNOWLEDGEMENTS

I would like to thank the following for all their support during the writing of the Magelands Eternal Siege - my wife, Lisa Mitchell, who read every chapter as soon as it was drafted and kept me going in the right direction; my parents for their unstinting support; Vicky Williams and Marilyn Hopwood for reading the books in their early stages; James Aitken for his encouragement; and Grant and Gordon of the Film Club for their support.

Thanks also to my Advance Reader team, for all your help during the last few weeks before publication.

THE PEOPLES OF THE STAR CONTINENT

There are five distinct peoples inhabiting the Star Continent. Three are descended from apes, one from reptiles, and one from amphibians. Their evolutionary trajectories have converged, and all five are clearly 'humanoid', though physical differences remain.

1. **The Holdings** – the closest to our own world's *Homo sapiens*. Excepting the one in ten of the population with mage powers, they are completely human. The Holdings sub-continent drifted south from the equator, and the people that inhabit the Realm are dark-skinned as a consequence. They are shorter than the Kellach Brigdomin, but taller than the Rakanese.

2. **The Rakanese** – descended from amphibians, but appear human, except for the fact that they have slightly larger eyes, and are generally shorter than Holdings people. They are descendants of a far larger population that once covered a vast area, and consequently their skin-colour ranges from pale to dark. Mothers gestate their young for only four months, before giving birth in warm spawn-pools, where the infants swim and feed for a further five months. A dozen are born in an average spawning.

3. **The Rahain** – descended from reptiles. Appear human, except for two differences. Firstly, their eyes have vertical pupils, and are often coloured yellow or green, and, secondly, their tongues have a vestigial fork or cleft at their tip. Their heights are comparable to the Holdings and the Sanang. Skin-colour tends to be pale, as the majority are cavern-dwellers. Their skin retains a slight appearance of scales, and they have no fingerprints. They are the furthest from our world's humans.

4. **The Kellach Brigdomin** – descended from apes, and very similar to the Holdings, they are the second closest to our world's humans. Their distinguishing traits are height (they are the tallest of the five peoples), pale skin (their sub-continent drifted north from a much colder region), and immunity to most diseases, toxins and illnesses. They are also marked by the fact that mothers give birth to twins in the majority of cases.

5. **The Sanang** – descended from apes, but evolved in the forest, rather than on the open plains that produced the Holdings. As a consequence, their upper arms and shoulders are wider and stronger than those of people from the Holdings or Rahain. They are pale-skinned, their sub-continent having arrived from colder climates in the south, and they occupy the same range of heights as the Holdings and Rahain. The males bear some traits of earlier *Homo sapiens*, such as a sloping forehead and a strong jaw-line, but the brains of the Sanang are as advanced as those of the other four peoples of the continent.

DRAMATIS PERSONAE

Colsbury

Karalyn Holdfast, Dream Mage

Kyra Holdfast, Karalyn's Daughter (7 years old)

Cael Holdfast, Karalyn's Son (7 years old)

Shellakanawara, Custodian of Colsbury

Agang Garo, Sanang Retiree

Daphne Holdfast, First Holder of the Republic

Keir Holdfast, Storm Mage

Thorn Holdfast, Soulwitch

Corthie Holdfast, Wanted in Kell

Aila Holdfast, Demigod from City

Killop Holdfast, Corthie and Aila's Son (2 years old)

Konna Holdfast, Corthie and Aila's Daughter (9 days old)

Kelsey Holdfast, Blocker of Powers

Frostback, Kelsey's Silver Dragon

Lucius Cardova, Banner Officer

Caelius Logos, Banner Sergeant

Plateau City

Bridget, Empress; Holder of the World

Bryce, Bridget's Son and Appointed Successor

Brogan, Bridget's Eldest Daughter

Bedig, Bridget's Son from Triplets

Berra, Bridget's Daughter from Triplets

Bethal, Bridget's Daughter from Triplets

Daimon, Imperial Mage

Tabor, Holdings Vision Mage

Tabitha, Holdfast Housekeeper

Tilda Holdwain, Young Aristocrat

Ravibattanara, Rakanese Clay Mage

Nadia, Rahain Stone Mage

Olo'osso, Dragon Eyre Pirate

Broadwater, Sanang

The Matriarch, Ruler of Sanang

Pechtang, Matriarch's Brother

T'Lang, Matriarch's Brother

Aberfeld of Hold Terras, Holdings Vision Mage

Holdings

Weir, Deputy First Holder

Celine Holdfast, Hold Fast Estate Manager

Jemma Holdfast, Celine's Apprentice

Cole Holdfast, Keir and Jemma's Son (9 years old)

Dragon Eyre

Blackrose, Queen of Ulna

Maddie, Blackrose's Rider

Ashfall, Dragon from Lostwell

Alara'osso (Lara), Captain of the *Giddy Gull*

Oto'pazzi (Topaz), Master of the *Giddy Gull*

Atili'osso (Tilly), Captain of the *Sow's Revenge*

Vizzini (Vitz), Master of the *Sow's Revenge*

Ari'anos (Ryan), Carpenter's Mate

City of Salve

Emily, Queen of the City

Daniel, King of the City

Lady Aurelian, Daniel's Mother

Lady Omertia, Emily's Mother

Elspeth, Emily and Daniel's Daughter (1 year old)

Van Logos, Banner Commander

Quill, Blade Commander

Nadhew, Roser Lawyer

Naxor, Imprisoned Demigod

Jade, Guardian of the Salve Mine

Dawnflame, Guardian of the Salve Mine

Amalia, Former God-Queen

Kagan, Amalia's Mortal Partner

Implacatus

Austin, Demigod in Hiding

Salah, Austin's Mother

Sunnah, Austin's Aunt

Edmond, Blessed Second Ascendant

Bastion, Edmond's Lieutenant

At Large

Sable Holdfast, Mage

The Magelands
The Unknowable Ocean
Realm of the Holdings
Arakhanah
Sanang
Royston
Shield Mountains
Holdings City
Blackwater
River Holdings
Barrier Mountains
Plateau City
Beechwoods
Twinth
Broadwater
Mya
Tritos
Black Mountains
Inner Sea
The Plateau
Forbidden Mountains
Basalt Desert
Rainsby
Grey Mountain
Akhanawarah
Tahrana City
Jade Falls
Rahain Capital
Calcite City
Brig
Domm
Kell
Fire Mountain
Lach
Rahain Republic
N

The Plateau

Barrier Mountains
Colsbury
Plateau City
Amatskouri
Inner Sea
The Plateau
Westport
Black Mountains
Stretton Sands
Anamindhari
Forbidden Mountains
Rainsby
The
Grey Mountains
N

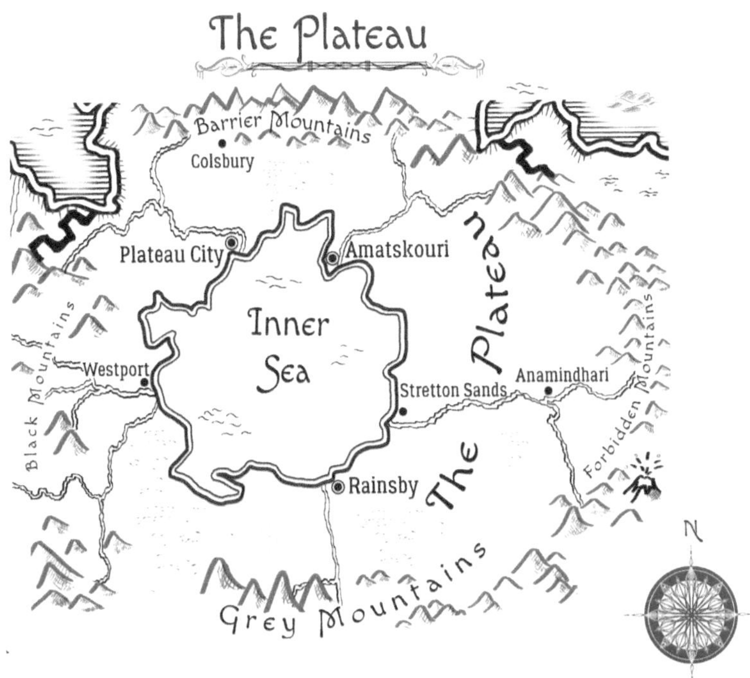

Dragon Eyre - Western Rim

Dragon Eyre - Eastern Rim

CHAPTER 1
SWALLOWED UP

Hold Cobb, Republic of the Holdings – 29th Day, Second Third Summer 534

Sable sat on the edge of the quarry, a lit cigarette in her right hand. Down to her left, the Greater River of the Holdings emerged from a mountain valley in a foaming torrent of rapids, its dull roar echoing across the steep hillside. The banks of the river were dotted with huge water wheels that turned without ceasing, powering the mills that cut the slabs and blocks of stone extracted from the quarry behind her. Sable glanced at the dozens of workers down by the rows of squat buildings. Shaped building stone was being loaded onto wagons by a paved roadside, the blocks hoisted by iron cranes, ready to be taken to Holdings City. Sable turned to her right, where the low, sprawling Hold Cobb mansion stood, its thick walls making it look like a fortress.

She wondered if she should turn away. Travelling to Hold Cobb had been a risk; there were too many people on the estate who might recognise her – old retainers she had known as a child, and house servants, whose memories of her as a girl might cause them to stare, before they fled in terror when they remembered what she had done as an adult. She removed the Quadrant from her shoulder bag, and studied the engravings. If she touched a certain combination, she could be back in

Dragon Eyre, but which combination? She knew how to travel to Implacatus, but not how to return to the world that she had devastated; the world that she longed to see again. The world where Lara lived.

One thing at a time, she thought. She might never get another opportunity to return to Hold Cobb. She placed the Quadrant back into her bag, and got to her feet. She walked along the lip of the quarry, away from the river. Centuries of digging for stone had eaten a huge bite out of the side of the hill. As a child, she had been saddened by the sight of the half-devoured mountain, brought low by the incessant labour of picks and shovels, its innards stripped and sent to build the mansions of Holdings City; but now, as an adult, she felt an affinity with the hollowed-out hillside. Her feet found the path that led down to the mansion, and she entered a patch of woodland, where the roar from the river receded, and she felt some respite from the blazing sun. The trees had been imported from Sanang, and were stunted in the arid conditions of the Holdings, their potential capped by the dry, rocky soil that clung to the side of the hills, and their leaves smeared in dust from the quarry.

Sable reached the rear of the mansion, where a protruding wing sheltered a small garden. She entered the garden through a tall, iron gate, and it was just as she had remembered. Neat gravel paths passed between ordered beds of flowers and shrubs, with a few trees for shade, under which sat iron benches. Sitting on one of the benches, alone, was an old woman, a cup of tea in her right hand. Sable's boots crunched on the gravel, and the old woman turned. Sable stopped, as their eyes met. The old woman stared at her for a moment, then, without saying a word, she patted the empty space on the bench next to her.

Sable walked over to where she sat, then joined her on the bench.

'I didn't think I would ever see you again,' the old woman said.

Sable nodded.

'Are you on the run?'

'I don't know,' said Sable.

The old woman smiled. 'That's unlike you. You used to know everything. You were the most headstrong child I ever knew; stubborn, and always right.' She laughed. 'Well, you always believed that you were right.'

Sable said nothing. She had been thinking about this meeting for a long time, but was starting to feel as though she had made a mistake. The past was over. She felt an urge to use the Quadrant, to escape the awkwardness.

The old woman took her hand. 'I missed you, daughter.'

Sable closed her eyes.

'I know that you have done... certain things,' the old woman went on; 'but, to me, you will always be my little Sable. I have prayed for you, every day. I ask the Creator to watch over you, to keep you safe, and, from the look of you, my prayers have been answered. You seem to be in good health, and you look younger than I had imagined. I thought that you might have been confined within a dungeon all these years, but that doesn't seem to be the case.'

'I've been far away, mother.'

The old woman's eyes welled up, and she lifted a silk handkerchief to her face.

'What happened to father?' Sable said.

The old woman shook her head. 'He passed some years ago, Sable. After what Karalyn Holdfast did to him, he was... never the same. He couldn't speak, or feed himself, and I think he lost the will to live. He and his brother, the former Holder Black, died within a third of each other, up on the Blackhold estate. It was a terrible time, but at least their suffering didn't last too long. Your cousin is the new Holder Black. He said that I could stay with his family, but I returned here, to my parents' home, a few days after your father passed. The Blackholds, and the Holdcobbs, were ostracised after your uncle's attempt to take the throne, and I was no longer welcome in Holdings City.' She squeezed Sable's hand. 'I know what happened. I know that your father and uncle were planning to have you executed.'

'He told me the truth,' Sable said. 'The last time I saw my father, he told me who I really was.'

The old woman frowned. 'I know who you are, Sable – you are my daughter, and you always will be. For your first sixteen years, who was it who cared for you? Who tucked you up in bed each night, and read you stories? I might not have given birth to you, but I am still your mother. I still love you.'

'Why did you never tell me?'

'I suppose there were a few reasons. Your father and I were sworn to secrecy. When Mirren and Guilliam brought you to our home, they told us about the affair between the Queen and Godfrey Holdfast. Guilliam was adamant that no one ever discover that his sister had given birth to a daughter, and I was only too happy to go along with the deception. And then, as time passed, I almost forgot, or, I made myself forget. You were mine, my beautiful little girl. Queen Miranda died, and Godfrey Holdfast knew nothing. Then Guilliam and Mirren died, and the circle of those who knew shrank to your father, your uncle, and me. When you were fourteen, and started to develop mage powers, I wondered if you would get suspicious, as there was never any trace of powers in either the Blackholds or the Holdcobbs, but you never mentioned anything about that, and so I kept quiet. You are not a Holdfast, Sable. Bloodlines are meaningless compared to years of nurture. That... family has no claim on you.'

Sable said nothing. She thought back to the times on Lostwell, and on Dragon Eyre, when she had called out for Daphne to help her. Not once had she ever sought the help of her adoptive mother. Guilt coursed through her; how could she have been so ungrateful?

'Are you staying long?' the old woman said. 'Where are your things? Did you come by carriage?'

Sable glanced down. 'I came to say goodbye.'

The old woman looked away. Her features hardened, but her eyes were lit with pain.

'I have a new home,' Sable said, 'far away. To get there, I need to visit the Holdfasts. I might never be back in the Holdings after that, and I wanted to see your face again.'

'Don't go to the Holdfasts, Sable. They will swallow you up.'

'I have no choice. If I want to go home, I'll need their help.'

'Sable, you are home.' She raised her left arm. 'This is your home. Hold Cobb was where you spent every summer. You used to play by the river, even when I told you it was too dangerous.' She shook her head. 'What am I saying? You didn't listen to me then; why would you do so now? What does this new home of yours have to offer that I can't?'

Sable's thoughts went to Lara. 'I think I've fallen in love.'

'Oh. Well, I can't compete with that. I hope he's a good man, Sable; someone strong enough to stop you walking all over him. Does this mean that you might have children of your own?'

'I don't think so, mother. I would make a terrible parent.'

'As long as he makes you happy, Sable.'

Sable thought about mentioning that Lara was a woman, but she didn't want to start a row.

'I am not the same person I used to be, mother,' she said. 'My hands are drenched in blood.'

'I already knew that. You were a spy, weren't you – working for the Rahain against the empire? The most wanted criminal in the world.'

'And yet you still want me to stay here?'

'Yes. I am your mother, Sable. No matter what you have done, that will never change. I will be sad if you leave, but happy that you have found someone. Be careful, though; the Holdfasts are snakes. Daphne might hand you over to the Empress.'

'She won't.'

'And Karalyn is worse. Remember what she did to your father. I know he was mistaken about many things, but did he deserve what she did to him? Death would have been less cruel. You cannot trust them.'

'I will be careful. I will take what I need from the Holdfasts, to ensure I can go home. But, all the same, I am one of them. I know it must pain you to hear it, but it's true. I am a Holdfast.'

'Then go,' her mother said, pulling her hand away.

Sable stood, and removed the Quadrant from her bag.

'Goodbye, mother,' she said.

'Goodbye, Sable.'

Sable touched her thumb to the surface of the Quadrant. The air shimmered, and she appeared on the banks of a lake, high in the Barrier Mountains. She eased the Quadrant back into her bag, and took a moment, wishing she had embraced her mother. Had it been worth it? She didn't know. She didn't seem to know anything about what she was doing, she realised. The world of the Star Continent seemed foreign to her, her past unrecoverable. She knew what she wanted – to return to Dragon Eyre – but, beyond that, everything else was vague and hazy.

She lit a cigarette and turned towards the island fortress of Colsbury, a few hundred yards to her left. The roofs of the Summer Palace, the Spire and the two keeps were glistening in the sunshine, and the air had a slight chill to it. She took a long breath, and started walking along the path that ran by the shore of the lake. She reached the small village opposite the island, and walked past the rows of stone cottages, nodding to the groups of locals who were out working. She paused when she got to the bridge, half-expecting Karalyn to appear, to tell her that she wasn't welcome, and doubts flooded her mind. Was she about to walk into a snare? The last time she had willingly entered Colsbury, she had been clapped in chains and pushed into an underground cell. But, instead of being executed, she had been taken to Lostwell. What would the Holdfasts do with her this time?

She set foot onto the bridge, and crossed the twin spans to the gatehouse that guarded the island. The tall, double doors were lying open, and two militia soldiers were standing by the entrance, watching Sable as she approached. She tossed her cigarette over the side of the bridge, and halted in front of the soldiers.

'Are you coming in?' said one.

'Do you need to check who I am first?' she said.

'No. The gates are open. Are you here to see someone?'

'Yes. Daphne Holdfast.'

'She's probably in the Great Keep,' said the soldier, moving to the side.

Sable nodded, then walked under the entrance arch and into the large internal courtyard within the curtain walls of Colsbury. On her left, dozens of workers were gathered round the burnt façade of the Summer Palace, carrying out repairs to the huge building, while the two massive square keeps sat on her right. Sable walked through the courtyard, and no one paid her any attention. She passed the entrance to the Great Keep, and kept walking, her ears picking up sounds of men working at the far end of the island. The courtyard turned to the right, and straight ahead of her was the ruined harbour, from where the voices were coming. Sable stayed back, watching for a moment. She recognised one of the men as Lucius Cardova, who had given her some of his life force in Plateau City. He seemed to be organising the others, who included Corthie.

'Good morning, boys,' she said.

The men turned to her, and Corthie's expression changed. He stared at her, then hurried from the harbour towards her.

'Sable?'

She placed a hand on her hip. 'Yes. How are you, Corthie?'

Her nephew shrugged. 'My head's a mess, to be honest. Never mind that; it's good to see you, but what are you doing here?'

'I came to talk to your mother. Is she on Colsbury?'

'They're all here, Sable. All of the Holdfasts are here.'

'They are now,' she said.

Cardova wiped his hands with a rag and stepped forwards. 'Good morning, ma'am.'

'Hello, Lucius,' she said. 'Are you repairing the harbour?'

'I like to keep busy,' said Cardova.

'It was his idea,' said Corthie. 'I think he wants to keep me occupied, so that I don't dwell on what happened.'

'And what did happen?' said Sable.

Corthie glanced down. 'I nearly killed Karalyn. Daimon... he, uh... I...'

'It's over with now,' said Cardova. He glanced at Sable. 'Did Daphne invite you here? I know she was hoping that you would make it in time for the conference.'

Sable raised an eyebrow. 'I wasn't invited, but then, no one knew where I was. I didn't come here for any conference, though. I want to ask Daphne if she'll send me back to Dragon Eyre.'

'You'll need Karalyn for that,' said Cardova. 'She controls the Sextant. Corthie, perhaps you should escort Sable into the Great Keep. We'll keep working here.'

'Alright,' said Corthie.

Sable noticed an air of suspicion in Cardova's demeanour. 'Are you still angry with me for killing all those Banner soldiers?'

'Yes, ma'am,' he said.

Sable smiled. 'At least you're honest.'

'How many are left on Dragon Eyre?'

'I don't know. Two hundred thousand, maybe? I don't intend to kill any more, not now that the gods have withdrawn. However, I still have to deal with the last of the Unk Tannic. To them, I will show no mercy.'

Cardova nodded. 'Then, ma'am, no offence, but I hope you go back to Dragon Eyre as soon as possible.'

He turned and walked back to the harbour, leaving Corthie alone with Sable.

'Let's go via the gardens,' said Sable, 'and enter the keep through the back door.'

Corthie nodded, his eyes still downcast, and they strolled towards the entrance to the walled garden.

'It wasn't your fault, Corthie,' Sable said, as they walked. 'Daimon is a dream mage; you had no choice.'

'How do you know about Daimon?'

'I've been reading people's minds since I got back, thirteen days ago. I didn't want to walk in here unprepared.'

Corthie muttered something.

'What was that?' she said.

'I am a beast,' he said, as they entered the gardens. 'A killer. It's all I know how to do.'

'Yes, but you do it so well, nephew.'

'Do you think it's funny?'

'No. It's a curse. All the same, there's no one I'd rather fight beside,

Corthie. The Ascendants fear me, but they're terrified of you. You give Edmond nightmares.'

'But I want to live in peace with Aila and the children,' he said. 'I don't want to kill anyone, not ever again.'

They paused by the rows of gravestones. Sable scanned the engraved lettering, until her eyes fell on the grave of Lennox. Fresh flowers had been placed by the headstone, and bees were flitting about above the petals.

'You poor bastard,' Sable said.

'Don't call him that,' said Corthie.

'Why not? Lennox was a good man until I got hold of him. I wish I could undo what I did, Corthie, but I can't. None of us can. We just have to live with the regret.'

Corthie glanced at her. 'I didn't think you regretted anything.'

'I don't regret much; it's true. Tell me, Corthie – do the Holdfasts all hate me?'

'Kelsey doesn't. I don't.'

'Well, that's two of you.'

'Aila likes you.'

'Does she? She's an eight-hundred-year-old god, Corthie, who fell for an eighteen-year-old mortal. I'm not sure she's the most reliable judge of character.'

He smiled, but Sable wasn't convinced.

They left the graves, and took a path that led to the keep, passing the spot where Karalyn had taken Sable and Belinda to Lostwell. The path went under the Lesser Keep, and they emerged on the ground floor of the Great Keep, where the air was still and cold. They ascended two flights of stairs, and Corthie took her to a doorway, which he pushed open. Sable glanced into the large chamber, and almost turned round and walked away. The room was full of Holdfasts, from three generations. Sable counted two babies and three small children, two nephews and two nieces, two adopted Holdfast women and two wives, and one half-sister.

Corthie entered the room. 'Sable's here.'

Every eye turned to her.

Sable remained in the doorway, wishing she was back in Hold Cobb.

'What's she doing on Colsbury?' cried Keir.

'Quiet, son,' said Daphne, getting to her feet.

'Am I a Holdfast?' said Sable.

'You are my sister,' said Daphne. 'You are welcome here.'

Kelsey jumped up, and ran to Sable. She threw her arms round her aunt, and a few of the others blinked in astonishment.

'Thank Pyre someone normal is here at last,' said Kelsey. 'This family is driving me crazy, Sable.'

Sable smiled at her niece. 'Then why are you still here? I thought you would have gone back to Salve City by now.'

'I asked everyone to stay,' said Daphne, hovering close by. 'We've been looking for you, Sable. I didn't want to proceed until all of us were present. Do you know everyone?'

'I think so,' said Sable, her eyes going over the people in the room. 'This is the first time I've met Celine, and Corthie and Aila's children.' She glanced down at where Aila was holding onto a two-year-old boy, and a days-old baby girl. 'They're demigods, aren't they?'

'They are,' said Daphne. 'Kelsey, dear, please release Sable from your grip. She and I need to talk.'

Kelsey edged away, her face flushing.

Karalyn shook her head at her sister. 'So, you do know how to hug? Mother, I want to be present for any discussion with Sable.'

'No,' said Daphne. 'We shall all be here for another few days; you will have plenty of time to catch up.'

'I don't want to catch up with her,' said Karalyn. 'I want to ensure your safety.'

Sable laughed. 'Anything I wanted to do to your mother, I could have done from a safe distance.'

'But Kelsey's here,' said Aila. 'Your powers won't work. Mine certainly don't.'

'Kelsey's presence doesn't stop my powers from working,' said Sable.

'Let them talk alone,' said Corthie. 'Sable saved mother from Rakana; we can trust her.'

'Thank you, Corthie,' said Sable.

Karalyn and a few others frowned, then Daphne led Sable back out of the room. They walked along a corridor, and entered a smaller chamber. Daphne threw open the shutters to let in the sunlight, then she and Sable sat across from each other. Daphne picked up a bottle of Severton whisky, and filled two glasses.

'How did you find me?' she said.

'You've been in Colsbury for days,' said Sable; 'it wasn't difficult.'

'That's not what I meant,' said Daphne. 'How did you find me in Rakana?'

'I was looking for you. I learned from someone in Plateau City that you had gone to Arakhanah City, and so I searched there. It took me a few days to track you down.'

Daphne nodded, then slid one of the glasses towards Sable.

'Why?' said Daphne.

'Why what?'

'Why did you rescue me?'

'Did you not want to be rescued?'

'Don't play games. Answer the question.'

'I can't. I'm too embarrassed.'

Daphne raised an eyebrow. 'That sounds a little unlikely.'

Sable faked a laugh, then took a sip of whisky. 'Got any gin?'

'Don't insult me. Of course I have gin. However, I have poured you a glass of whisky, so that is what you shall drink. Why would you be too embarrassed to tell me?'

'Because... it doesn't matter. Why were you looking for me?'

'You're a Holdfast, and the family is preparing to hold a conference. I wanted all of us to be here; even you.'

'Even me.'

'Yes. You are my little sister, after all, despite everything you have done. Karalyn has told me about Dragon Eyre. Very impressive, Sable. You would make a useful ally.'

'I'm not interested in being an ally. I want to go home.'

Daphne looked confused for a moment.

'I want to go back to Dragon Eyre,' Sable went on. 'I have unfinished business.'

'That's not up to me. Only one person here knows how to use the Sextant. However, Karalyn's feelings towards you are conflicted, to say the least.'

'I'm sorry for what I did to Lennox.'

'Why are you telling me this? It's Karalyn you should be speaking to. The Empress is also looking for you. You should be aware of that.'

'Then, aren't you breaking the law by sheltering me? Should the Herald of the Empire flout the commands of the Empress?'

'I am no longer Herald. I resigned. Hence the gathering of the Hold-fasts. This family is on the cusp of being declared outlaws.'

Sable frowned. 'May I read your mind?'

Daphne looked incredulous. 'You're asking my permission? Maybe you have changed.'

'I read your mind in Arakhanah.'

'It's called Rakana now.'

'I learned much from your memories,' Sable went on, 'but I feel I might need a little update.'

'Then proceed.'

Sable sent her powers out, and entered the mind of her half-sister. She scanned the memories from the previous few days, and saw what had occurred in the Great Fortress in Plateau City. She withdrew from Daphne's mind, and took another sip of whisky.

'Why would Daimon order Brannig to kill the Empress?'

Daphne shrugged. 'Did he? We don't know that.'

'Yes, but it's what you suspect.'

'How could we ever prove it? Keir killed the evidence.'

'You could have held this conference without me. I have no desire to get involved in the politics of this world. What do I care about the succession to the imperial throne? I have Unk Tannic terrorists to slaughter. One world is enough for me, and it isn't this one.'

'Aila and Kelsey have aired similar sentiments. Frankly, I don't care. You're here now, and so we shall convene, as a family. Each one of us will be permitted to have a say. Indulge me, Sable.'

Sable nodded. 'Alright. You know, I often dreamed about fighting you. I would have kicked your arse, of course, but now, it would feel wrong. Your balance would be off, due to you losing two toes. It would be unfair.'

'Don't push your luck,' said Daphne, a half-smile on her lips. 'Even with eight toes and one good arm, I would still knock you over in ten seconds. All the same, if the Ascendants were to invade this world, I would prefer that we fight side by side.'

'The Ascendants aren't going to invade,' said Sable. 'They're too scared of the Holdfasts. This is the last world they want to visit, believe me. You can thank me, Corthie and Kelsey for that. Lord Bastion cries himself to sleep every night just thinking about us.'

Daphne frowned. 'That cannot possibly be true.'

'I protect Dragon Eyre; Kelsey shields Salve City; and here you've got Corthie and Karalyn. If anything, we should take the fight to Implacatus. I still have to go back there, to fulfil a promise I made. We should bring down the Ascendants, and burn Cumulus to the ground. And then, we'll all be safe.'

'I have to sort out this world first.'

'How – by making an enemy of the Empress? I thought you were friends.'

'We were, although Bridget never really liked me. She tolerated me, but there was no affection. Killop was the glue that kept us together. Without him, we are merely two women who don't get along.'

'May I see the Sextant?'

'If you like,' said Daphne, standing.

Sable placed her glass onto the table, then followed Daphne out of the room. They went up a flight of stairs, and entered a large chamber. In the middle of the floor sat the Sextant, then Sable realised that it appeared to be hovering an inch over the floorboards, as it emitted a low hum.

'Why has it been left on?' Sable said. 'Is that not dangerous?'

'As I said, only Karalyn knows how to use it.' Daphne pointed at the hilt of a sword embedded into the side of the huge device. 'If you take that sword out, it stops working. At first, Karalyn kept the sword separate from the rest of the Sextant, but it proved to be too much of a nuisance, and she keeps it here now.'

Sable moved closer to the device, and examined the hilt of the black-bladed sword.

'Is there a Quadrant jammed in there, too?'

'Yes,' said Daphne. 'The Quadrant Karalyn obtained in Lostwell.'

'You mean the one she stole from Blackrose? Have you any idea of the trouble that caused me? What's it doing stuck in the side of the Sextant?'

'Karalyn needed it there, so that she could use the Sextant to appear on the salve world, and also so that she could rescue you. Before it was there, all she could do was look; she couldn't intervene.'

Sable nodded. 'How does Karalyn activate it?'

'She places her palm onto its surface.'

Sable straightened her back, then reached out with her left hand.

Daphne narrowed her eyes. 'What happened to your little finger?'

'A god cut it off on Lostwell,' Sable said.

'You were right about the fight – it wouldn't be fair. On you.'

Sable smiled at her sister, then placed her hand onto the Sextant.

What is your desire, Sable?

Sable jumped back. 'It spoke to me.'

Daphne's eyes widened. 'What did it say?'

'It asked me what I desired.'

'That's what it says to Karalyn.'

'How does she make it take her places?'

Daphne frowned. 'I think you should step away from the Sextant, Sable. Leave it to Karalyn.'

Sable put her hand back onto the surface of the Sextant.

What is your desire, Sable?

Take me to Dragon Eyre.

Silence.

Sextant? Are you there?

What is your desire, Sable?

Take me to Dragon Eyre. Now.

Silence.

Sable glared at the huge device. 'Why isn't it working?'

The door of the room swung open, and Karalyn entered.

'Get away from the Sextant,' she said.

Sable lifted her palm off the glass surface of the device. 'It doesn't belong to you alone, Karalyn.'

Karalyn turned to Daphne. 'How could you let her in here, mother? What were you thinking?'

'I would rather you didn't take that tone with me, dear,' said Daphne. 'I was merely showing Sable the Sextant. She wants to go back to Dragon Eyre.'

'I know,' said Karalyn.

'There's something else you should know.'

'What?'

'The Sextant,' Daphne said; 'it talks to her.'

CHAPTER 2
GATHERING

C olsbury Castle, Republic of the Holdings – 30th Day, Second Third Summer 534

'Are you sure you wish me to attend, ma'am?' said Caelius, as they walked through the garden. 'It sounds like a family affair.'

'Yes,' Daphne said; 'as an observer. You won't be alone – Cardova and Frostback will also be present, along with Shella and Agang. Not all of you will be allowed to vote in the proceedings, but it would be prudent to have witnesses.' She noticed Thorn waiting for her by the apple trees. 'Please excuse me, Caelius; I need to discuss a few matters with my daughter-in-law.'

Caelius smiled. 'Of course, ma'am. I will take my seat, and wait for the conference to begin.'

'Thank you,' said Daphne.

Caelius bowed his head towards Thorn, and slipped away through the trees. Daphne approached the young woman, who seemed nervous.

'Are you ready, Thorn?'

'I think so.'

'Remember, there are ten adult Holdfasts, and so there shall be ten votes on offer.'

'There will be nine. I can hardly be expected to vote for myself.'

Daphne smiled. 'True. Do you intend to abstain?'

'No. I shall vote for Lord Bryce.'

'Why?'

'Didn't you vote for Bridget, and she vote for you, when we last held such an occasion?'

'But Lord Bryce is not here to return the favour, dear.'

'All the same, it is what I shall do.'

'Be prepared for a few abstentions. Do not take them personally. There are some among us that wish to have nothing to do with the crisis brought about by the Empress.'

Thorn nodded. 'Are we doing the right thing?'

'What do you think?'

'I think we are.'

'Then hold on to that thought. Don't weaken. For years, we have been working towards this moment. You shall be Empress, Thorn. Bridget's mistake is our opportunity. If she had agreed to attend this conference, she could have brought Bryce, Brogan, Tabor and Daimon; perhaps even Ravi and Nadia. She could have weighted the scales until they tipped in her favour. Instead, she refused to even respond to our invitation, breaking the laws on the constitution that she helped to write. Such arrogance cannot go unchecked. Once this conference is over, the world will see the difference between tyranny and the law. I have every confidence that we shall prevail.'

'Keir doesn't want me to do it.'

'I don't care. As long as he votes for you, his feelings are immaterial.'

The air shimmered next to them, and Karalyn appeared.

'I've hidden the Weathervane,' she said.

Daphne frowned. 'Was that really necessary, dear?'

'Aye, it was,' said Karalyn. 'If Sable knows how to use the Sextant, then we're better safe than sorry.'

'It refused to take her to Dragon Eyre.'

'I know, but she'll figure it out, if she's given enough time to play with it. She shouldn't have told you that it spoke to her.'

'She trusted me.'

'Why not just let her go back to Dragon Eyre?' said Thorn.

Daphne and Karalyn turned to her.

'What are you hiding from me?' said the soulwitch.

Karalyn looked embarrassed. 'Well, I... uh, need Sable for something first. Returning to Dragon Eyre will be her reward.'

'Does Sable know this?' said Thorn.

'Not yet,' said Karalyn.

'Let's get today over with,' said Daphne, 'and then we can discuss our next steps.'

'This won't change if I become Empress, will it?' said Thorn. 'You two will always have your secrets.'

'I promise to tell you everything,' said Daphne, 'as soon as you secure the nomination.'

A shadow flitted overhead, and the three women gazed upwards to see Frostback soaring above the garden, her silver wings outstretched.

'Kelsey and her dragon appear to be back from their little flight,' said Daphne. 'We should go; I wouldn't like to keep a dragon waiting.'

'The most disturbing thing about yesterday,' said Karalyn, as they walked along the path, 'was Kelsey embracing Sable like that. I tried to hug Kelsey in the City of Salve, and she nearly punched me.'

'She does love to be contrary,' said Daphne.

'I sensed genuine affection,' said Thorn. 'Kelsey looks up to Sable, though why, I'm not so sure.'

'It's the same thing that binds Corthie to them,' said Karalyn. 'They've been away for a long time, living and fighting on other worlds. All of them feel dislocated, and they can sense it in each other.'

'Oh Corthie,' said Daphne. 'What am I going to do about that boy?'

'Let him go back to Kell, mother; that's what he wants.'

'He wants to sit in a prison cell for ninety days?'

'It's better that he's out of the way, before we plan... you know.'

Daphne frowned.

'He'll want to come along, mother,' said Karalyn. 'So, unless you're happy about that, Corthie needs to be far away.'

Thorn glared at Daphne and Karalyn. 'More secrets?'

'Actually,' said Daphne, 'it's the same secret as before.'

She looked up, and saw Frostback land in the largest clearing within the garden. Kelsey unfastened the straps keeping her on the harness, and jumped down to the ground, landing on the soft grass. In front of the dragon, several tables had been laid out by Shella's staff, arranged in a horseshoe. Shella had her own table, in the midst of the horseshoe, which she was sharing with Agang Garo.

Kelsey laughed when she saw her mother approach.

'You've even arranged the tables in the same shape,' she said.

'I did,' said Daphne. 'I considered holding the meeting in the same location as before also, but decided that the open air would be more suitable, so that Frostback could bear witness.'

'You have my thanks, Kelsey-mother,' said the dragon. 'Humans often overlook these things; I am gratified that you did not.'

Daphne smiled. 'Everyone, please take your seats. There are name tags by each chair. Caelius and Lucius, you will sit over by Frostback; Holdfasts, you shall be at the table.'

Jemma was already in her chair, at the far left end of the horseshoe, with Cole on her lap. To her right, Kelsey took her place, followed by Aila and Corthie, each clutching a child. Daphne's seat was next, in the centre of the horseshoe, then Sable's name tag sat next to an empty chair. To its right, Karalyn took her place, while her two children played on the grass behind her, then Thorn sat, followed by Keir. At the far right end, Celine took the final place.

'Has anyone seen Sable?' said Daphne.

'I'm here,' said Sable, walking along the path leading from the two keeps. She strode up to Karalyn. 'Why have you disabled the Sextant?'

Karalyn narrowed her eyes. 'To stop you using it.'

Sable put a hand on her hip. 'Do you think it belongs to you? It doesn't.'

'Sit, Sable; please,' said Daphne. 'This can wait.' She gestured at the chair to her right. 'You are next to me, at the head of the table.'

'This is bullshit,' said Keir. 'Why does Sable sit where Bridget sat in the Summer Palace? Do you think we're idiots, mother? We all know you've copied the same arrangements from the meeting when she abdicated. Why is Sable in the seat of honour?'

Daphne shrugged. 'Age and experience.'

'But Celine's the oldest person here.'

Celine frowned. 'Thank you for mentioning that, Keir.'

'I think I might be the oldest,' said Aila. 'Celine's an infant compared to me.'

Sable sat, and then Daphne did the same. She glanced at the waiting faces, pride filling her. All four of her children, and all five of her grandchildren – in the same place at the same time.

'Right, Holdfasts,' said Shella. 'Let's get this started. Agang and I will chair, I guess. Daffers has given us an agenda, but, as chair, none of you get to speak unless Agang or I allow it; right? Okay, over to you, Daffers.'

'Thank you, Shella,' said Daphne. 'It's not often that the Holdfasts are gathered; in fact, I can't remember the last time all four of my children were together. It fills me with joy to see you all, but that joy is tinged with sadness, as I know that, once this conference is over, some of us will travel our separate ways, and we shall be divided again. Kelsey will be going back to the salve world, while Corthie and Aila will be returning to Kellach Brigdomin with their children.'

'Aye, to go to prison,' laughed Kelsey.

'Wait for your turn,' snapped Shella.

'Sorry, o wise one.'

Daphne smiled. 'As we have established, these occasions are exceedingly rare; and this one coincides with a serious problem that we must face. A few days ago, Empress Bridget, Holder of the World, broke one of the fundamental laws of the empire, and declared that her eldest son should be her successor. She made this decision without consulting anyone, and without a free and transparent vote being held.' Her face grew sombre. 'The law is clear – the high mages of this world select its Emperor or Empress. Bridget had no right to act in this way. Bridget was elected in five-oh-seven. From the electors who were there that day,

Shella, Agang and myself are present here. The procedure was repeated in five-two-six, when Bridget abdicated. Again, we voted, and Bridget was chosen. If Bridget wants Bryce to be the next Emperor, then she should have followed the law that she herself helped create. She should be here today. She declined our invitation. More than that, however, she has also excluded the Holdfasts from any positions of power within the empire. Thorn, Keir, Shella, Caelius and I were locked in the dungeons under the Great Fortress, and, for a while, our lives hung in the balance. Therefore, I propose that we assume the right to convene a grand council, and select the next Emperor or Empress. Do you agree? Please raise your hand if you think we should press ahead.'

Daphne scanned the people at the table. One by one, hands were lifted into the air. Jemma, Kelsey, and Corthie on the left side, and Karalyn, Thorn, Keir and Celine on the right. Only two kept their hands down – Aila and Sable.

'The proposal carries,' said Shella. 'Seven to two.'

'Thank you,' said Daphne. 'The next stage is the nominations. I would like to nominate someone. Does anyone else wish to do the same?'

Thorn raised her hand.

'Speak, Thorn,' said Shella. 'Who do you nominate as successor?'

'I nominate Lord Bryce,' she said.

'And you, Daffers?'

'I nominate Thorn Holdfast.'

'Anyone else?' said Shella.

No one spoke.

'It is important to remember,' said Daphne, 'that we are not discussing Bridget's right to rule. Regardless of what happens next, Bridget is, and will remain, the Holder of the World. This will not change that. All we are deciding is who should come next.'

Shella lifted her hand. 'As Lord Bryce is not here, I want to ask Thorn to speak next, to tell us all why she should become Empress after Bridget.'

Thorn stood. 'Thank you, Shella.' She took a breath. 'I accept

Holder Fast's nomination, although I will be voting for Lord Bryce. If I am selected as the successor to the imperial throne, then I shall rule this world with courage, compassion and purpose. I may have been critical of Empress Bridget's rule in the past, particularly during the latter stages of the war against the archmages, but there is no doubt in my mind that Empress Bridget has been an exceptional peacetime leader. I will follow her policies as regards trade and prosperity, and will respect the constitutional arrangements of the component nations that make up the empire. What is at issue here is not so much the identity of the next person to sit upon the throne, but the manner in which that person is selected. I voted in five-two-six, and it was an honour to be present; just as today, I have been honoured as a nominee. I love the Star Continent, and, if elected, I will defend it to my last breath. I also pledge to you all that I will happily submit to a similar process, so that my successor will be elected in the same manner.' She gazed at the people sitting in the garden. 'I do not ask any of you to vote for me. You all know me, some more than others, and if you think I am unsuitable, then I will abide by your decision. If, however, you select me, I promise that I will live the rest of my life in service to the people of this world.'

Thorn sat. There was no applause, and no one spoke.

Kelsey raised her hand.

'Yes?' said Shella.

'Who knows this Bryce guy? I vaguely remember him from before I went to Lostwell, but what's he like now?'

Shella looked around, and Thorn got back to her feet.

'I know him quite well,' said Thorn. 'Lord Bryce is an exceptional young man. Devoted to his duty, conscientious, and wise for his years. He would make an excellent Emperor.'

She sat again.

Kelsey frowned. She glanced over to where Cardova and Caelius were sitting.

'Hey, Lucius!' she called out. 'Weren't you with Bryce in Kellach Brigdomin?'

Cardova stood. 'May I speak, Madam Chair?'

'Is he talking to me?' said Shella.

Agang chuckled. 'Yes, Lucius, you may speak.'

'Thank you,' Cardova said. 'I have no stake in what happens here; but I did spend some time with Lord Bryce, when we were hunting for Daimon. I agree with what Thorn said about him. He's a good man. He must be aware that what his mother has done is wrong, which is a shame, as he might have won a free vote. But, the law is the law.'

His eyes flitted over Karalyn, as if inviting her to add to what he had said, but Karalyn shook her head, and Cardova retook his seat.

'I think we're ready for the vote,' said Shella. 'As high mages, Agang and I will also vote, but only at the end, and only if our votes would make any difference to the outcome. I'll go round the table, and each of you will tell us who you are voting for, or if you have decided to abstain. Okay, Jemma; you're first.'

Jemma sighed. 'I'm not sure why I get a vote.'

'You voted in five-two-six, that's why,' said Shella. 'The precedent's been set.'

'Fine,' said Jemma. 'I abstain. I don't know Bryce, and I don't want to see Keir as consort to a new Empress. Sorry, Thorn.'

Thorn smiled, and said nothing, while Keir rolled his eyes.

'Kelsey,' said Shella. 'You're next.'

'I vote for Bryce,' said Kelsey. 'You know, just so no one will say that every Holdfast voted for a member of their own family.'

Shella nodded, as Agang wrote something down. 'Aila?'

'I abstain,' said the demigod. 'This has nothing to do with me.'

'Corthie?'

'I vote for Thorn,' he said, his gaze cast low.

Daphne puffed her cheeks in relief. 'I also vote for Thorn,' she said.

Shella pulled a face. 'Well, you nominated her. I wasn't even going to ask you, Daffers. Sable?'

Sable glanced up. She said nothing for a while, then lit a cigarette. 'I was going to abstain,' she said, 'but I have to say that I think you're all deluding yourselves if you imagine that this is going to end well. What will happen when the Empress refuses to acknowledge the outcome of this vote? Are you prepared to go to war? With what army? If all you're going to do is issue a polite complaint, then this is pointless. Otherwise, you have to take a moment to think – is this really worth starting a civil war over? How many will die in a War of Succession? There's only one answer that makes any sense, and that is to vote for Bryce. If this meeting selects Bryce, then the process will have worked, the Empress will be happy, and war will be averted.' She glanced at Thorn. 'This is nothing personal against you. You've saved my life twice – once when Nadia stabbed me, and again when I was starving to death. I'm grateful, Thorn, but not so much that I think this world should go to war over your ambitions.' She turned back to Shella. 'My vote is for Bryce.'

Agang wrote again on the document in front of him.

'Karalyn?' said Shella.

'Thorn,' Karalyn said, without hesitation.

'Thank you,' said Shella. 'Thorn?'

'I vote for Lord Bryce,' said Thorn.

'That's three apiece, with two abstentions,' said Agang. 'Keir?'

Keir frowned, his face displaying his unhappiness with the entire event. 'I guess I'll have to vote for Thorn.'

'Numpty,' muttered Kelsey.

'That's enough,' said Shella, pointing a finger at Kelsey. 'Stop bloody interrupting.' She turned to Celine. 'You're the last Holdfast; your turn.'

'I should be on the Hold Fast estate,' said Celine. 'I didn't vote in five-two-six, and I shouldn't be voting now. Therefore, I abstain.'

Daphne suppressed her anger. What was supposed to have been a smooth acceptance of Thorn was turning into something more fragile; something more dangerous.

'Well, well,' said Shella, nudging Agang. 'It looks like we're going to have to vote, too, monkey-boy.'

'You go first,' said Agang.

'Okay. I was also going to abstain, if it came to it, but I have to say that Sable has convinced me otherwise. What she said about the process, and about the possibility of a civil war; well, it hit home. If we pick Thorn, then all kinds of shit could happen. I don't want war, and

I'm too old for another damn siege of Colsbury. I vote for Bryce. Four votes each – I guess it's up to you, Agang.'

Daphne held her breath as she stared at the old Sanang mage. Daphne had spent no time trying to convince Agang to vote for Thorn, as she had assumed that his vote would not be required.

'What happens if I abstain?' he said.

'We take a break,' said Shella, 'then come back here in an hour, and do it all over again.'

Agang nodded. He was keeping his eyes lowered, to avoid catching anyone's glance, as everyone stared at him.

'I don't know Lord Bryce,' he said, 'although, from what certain people have said, it seems as though he would be a suitable candidate. However, I do know Thorn. She has her flaws. She's ruthlessly ambitious; who among us is not aware that she has harboured a desire to become Empress since her earliest days? Every move she's made throughout her life seems to me to have been coloured with the ulterior motive of attaining power. And yet, she is also a suitable candidate. With little to choose between the two nominees, it comes down to what Sable said. Do we appease the Empress by selecting Bryce; or do we inflame the situation by selecting Thorn? Like Shella, I do not want another war, but, if we go along with the Empress's choice, then there will be no more high mage conventions in the future. Bryce's offspring will inherit the throne. I choose Thorn.'

Daphne exhaled, her right fist clenching. She gazed up at the sky for a moment, oblivious to the sound of talking going on at the table.

'Thorn wins,' announced Shella, 'by five votes to four, with three abstentions. Thorn is therefore declared the next-in-line to the throne of the Empire. Daffers, over to you again.'

Daphne took a moment to calm herself.

'Congratulations, Thorn,' she said. 'You will make a fine Empress, when the day comes.'

'Thank you, Holder Fast,' said Thorn, her face a mask of serenity.

'I shall instruct the Holdings government,' Daphne went on, 'to issue a proclamation within the next few days, to the effect that the

Holdings does not recognise Lord Bryce as successor, and that they shall follow the vote carried out here today. The Holdings shall recognise Thorn Holdfast as the legitimate successor, and no one else. However, the Holdings alone is not enough. I therefore propose that Thorn and I travel to Sanang, to meet with the Matriarch, in order to press her to do the same. If we are successful, then the Empress will have to confront the combined might of Sanang and the Holdings. We shall also send a letter to the Clan Council in Kellach Brigdomin, although I have little hope of any success there. Bridget's own people will not desert her, and we would be foolish to imagine otherwise. As for the Empress herself, Karalyn has agreed to convey the outcome of this conference to her Majesty in person.'

'That's great,' said Kelsey. 'Can Frostback, Lucius and I go home now?'

'Tomorrow,' said Daphne. 'Karalyn has agreed to transport everyone to where they wish to be.'

'Everyone?' said Sable.

Daphne shook her head. 'I misspoke. Not everyone. Karalyn will not be taking you to Dragon Eyre, Sable. Not yet, at any rate.'

Sable stood. 'Why not?'

'I will take you back,' said Karalyn, 'but only after you do something for me first.'

'And what would that be?'

'Let me deal with the Empress,' said Karalyn, 'and then you and I can sit down and talk about it.'

Sable eyed Daphne. 'Do you know?'

'If you try to read her mind,' said Karalyn, 'I will block you.'

'This is bullshit,' said Sable.

'It's not,' said Karalyn. 'You owe me, Sable. You owe me for what you did to Lennox; and for rescuing you from that pit on Wyst. If you do this thing for me, then I will consider the balance between us settled. I think I'm being more than fair.'

Sable cursed under her breath, then her shoulders sagged. 'I can't argue with that, can I? I suppose I should feel honoured. It's presumably a dangerous task, with little hope of success, and I'm probably the only one here who could do it. Am I right?'

'Aye,' said Karalyn. 'You are exactly right.'

Sable smirked. 'Then I'll do it. Right, who wants to get drunk with their Aunty Sable?'

Kelsey laughed. 'Me!'

Aila nudged Corthie. 'You go as well. I'll watch the children.'

Corthie stood, looking as though he was bearing the weight of the world on his shoulders. Sable and Kelsey walked up to him, and led him off towards the Great Keep. Jemma also got up, and then she, Aila and Karalyn headed away, taking their children with them. Daphne watched them leave, feeling a strange sadness bubbling away in her chest. Would her children ever be together again? Keir's three siblings had barely looked at their brother, who was sitting alone, his face a picture of misery.

Thorn stood, then sat down in the seat Sable had vacated.

'That was closer than we anticipated,' she said.

Daphne smiled. 'I was worried for a moment or two, but this is the best possible result. There was no biased landslide, which would have looked terrible. Had one vote gone the other way, it would have been Bryce.'

Frostback reared up, then lowered her neck down to where Daphne and Thorn were sitting.

'My congratulations, Thorn,' the dragon said. 'This voting is a most undragonlike activity. Among my kin, you and Bryce would have fought each other to decide this matter.'

Thorn laughed. 'If we had done that, then I would have won by a greater margin. That would have been a very unfair contest.'

'It occurs to me,' said Frostback, 'that after tomorrow, we may never meet again. If that is the case, Kelsey-mother, then let me say that I approve of you. You are a strong leader, and you care deeply for your kin. Tell me; why would you not wish to be Empress?'

'Because Thorn would be better,' said Daphne. 'She is also half my age, and Bridget might be alive decades from now. Put those two facts together, and the conclusion is clear. I had my chance, eight years ago, and I felt nothing but relief when Bridget was re-selected. I have the Holdfasts to look after; that's enough for me.'

Shella walked over. 'Hi, Daffers. Sorry about voting for Bryce. Nothing personal, eh?'

Daphne raised an eyebrow. 'A close vote will give a better impression.'

Shella laughed. 'I'm glad you're seeing the bright side. I was watching you while Agang was talking; you looked like your head was about to explode. While you,' she said, glancing at Thorn, 'looked calm and fresh. Weren't you nervous?'

Thorn gave a gentle shrug. 'I had resigned myself to accepting the outcome, whatever that might have been.'

'It took guts to vote for Bryce when the tally was so close.'

'It was the honourable thing to do.'

'It certainly was,' said Frostback. 'Now, as Kelsey will be getting inebriated with her aunt and brother, I would like to offer you all a small gift, as a token of my respect for you. My harness can fit three people – would you like to fly?'

Daphne smiled. 'That sounds wonderful; thank you.'

Thorn's eyes widened, then a slight frown passed her lips, and she glanced over to where Keir was still sitting.

'Perhaps Keir should go, instead of me,' she said.

Keir stood. 'I'm not climbing onto the back of a winged gaien.'

'Find Kelsey and Corthie,' said Daphne, 'and have a drink with them.'

Keir snorted. 'No, thanks.'

They watched as he strode away.

'Allow me to apologise on behalf of my elder son,' said Daphne.

'There is no need, Kelsey-mother,' said the silver dragon. 'Climb up, and we shall soar over the mountains.'

Thorn clambered up the harness first, pulling on the leather straps, then she leaned over from the saddle, and helped Daphne up, as Frostback crouched low. Shella climbed up last, and then the three women fastened the buckles as the silver dragon extended her wings.

Shella let out a whoop of excitement as Frostback lifted into the air, carrying them above the small island of Colsbury. The dragon circled through the clear sky, then sped off over the still surface of the lake, the mountains reflecting off it like a mirror.

CHAPTER 3
SEPARATING

Colsbury Castle, Republic of the Holdings – 30th Day, Second Third Summer 534

'Aye, Corthie,' said Kelsey, a mug of ale in her hand, 'but ninety days? You're mad.'

Corthie shrugged. 'I've already served ten days, so they might knock that off the sentence. On the other hand, I escaped, so they might add on more time for that.'

Kelsey rolled her eyes. 'But why? Why would you want to go back to Kell, knowing that?'

'What else can I do?' said Corthie. 'I own a damn farm down there. I have to try to make it work. What's the alternative, that I just stay here in Colsbury, doing nothing? I'd drink myself to death within a year.'

Kelsey and Sable glanced at each other.

'If it's fighting you're after,' said Sable, 'then perhaps you should consider coming back to Dragon Eyre with me, whenever Karalyn finally allows it.'

'Come on, Sable,' said Cardova, who had joined them in the tiny village tavern. 'Corthie on Dragon Eyre? Are you serious?'

'I can't go to Dragon Eyre,' said Corthie. 'I have two children. Killop and wee Konna.'

'That's a funny name you chose for the girl,' said Kelsey.

'Aila picked it,' he said. 'It's a Salve City god-name, I guess.'

'Then it's apt,' said Sable, 'considering Konna is a god. In a thousand years from now, your children might still be around, Corthie.'

He nodded, then drained his glass of whisky.

'Another round?' said Cardova.

'Are you paying?' said Kelsey.

Sable threw a purse onto the table. 'Use this. I robbed a merchant in the River Holdings a few days ago.'

Kelsey laughed.

'Don't encourage her,' said Cardova, standing. He withdrew a few coins from the purse, and strode towards the bar.

'I don't think Lucius approves of me,' said Sable.

Kelsey glanced at her brother. He looked morose, and she felt pity for him. While she and Sable had found their places in life, Corthie seemed adrift, and without purpose.

'What about coming to the City?' she said to him. 'You know you'll always be welcome there. Emily would do a wee dance of joy if I brought you back with me.'

He glanced at her.

'There are greenhides to kill,' Kelsey went on. 'Not as many as before, not since the nests on either side of the City were destroyed, but there's still plenty of work to be done on the Western Bank around Jezra.'

'It's the killing that's the problem, Kelsey,' he said. 'If I went back to the City, I'd lose myself again. I need to fight, but the beast I have to slay lies within me.'

'Pyre's tits, brother; that's deep.'

'You're still young,' said Sable. 'Have a go at farming. Work hard in Clackenbaird, and see where you are in a year or two. I know what you mean about having a beast living inside you.' She took a drink of gin from her glass. 'I nearly lost control on Dragon Eyre. No, that's a lie. I lost control. I was so filled with thoughts of vengeance that I... I might have gone too far.'

Cardova returned to their table with a tray loaded with drinks.

'What did I miss?' he said.

Kelsey glanced at Cardova as he sat. Her vision clouded for a moment, then she saw out from his eyes. He was standing next to Karalyn, and both of them were frowning at Kelsey, who was laughing under a deep red sky. Kelsey blinked. The prophecy had lasted a mere fraction of a second, and she wondered what she was going to do in the future that would annoy Cardova and her sister. She kept her expression neutral, lifted her glass from the tray, and pushed her vision to the side.

'Sable was telling us about her mad rampage on Dragon Eyre,' she said.

Cardova frowned. 'I hope she turns her attention to the Unk Tannic when she gets back there.'

'I will,' said Sable. 'I intend to root them out from the Eastern Rim first, then attack their bases in the Home Islands.'

Corthie glanced up at her. 'Is that the only reason you want to go back? To kill?'

'No, it's not the only reason,' she said.

'Well?' said Kelsey. 'Spill it.'

Sable smiled. 'There might be someone there waiting for me.'

Kelsey let out a cheer. 'Yay! Sable's found a man.'

'Did I say it was a man?'

'Oh. Alright. Yay; Sable's found a woman. At least, I hope it's a woman; otherwise this conversation's about to get weird.'

'Her name's Lara,' Sable said. 'Alara'osso.'

Cardova almost choked on his drink. 'You're seeing one of the Five Sisters?'

Sable grinned. 'Yes. It was casual at first, but, towards the end, before I was captured by Wystians, it was starting to go somewhere. Lara gets me. And now, it's been five months since I saw her; I mean five thirds. Regardless, it's been too long.'

'Wait a moment,' said Cardova. 'That man we rescued along with you – wasn't he a member of the Osso family?'

Sable's eyes widened. 'Oh, shit. You mean I didn't dream that? Don't worry; I'll sort it. I'll check on him tomorrow.'

Cardova laughed. 'Does Lara have a ship?'

'The *Giddy Gull*,' said Sable. 'We spent a lot of time together in the cabin on board.'

Kelsey raised her hands. 'Please stop right there. I don't want to hear about that. You're my auntie, for Pyre's sake.' She glanced at Cardova. 'What about you, Lucius?'

'What about me?'

Kelsey winked at him. 'How did you get on with my sister, eh?'

'Fine.'

'Is that it? "Fine"?' She glared at him. 'I thought you fancied her? What happened – did she knock you back?'

'I didn't give her the chance to knock me back,' he said. 'I had a job to do, and I behaved like a professional.'

'You numpty,' said Kelsey. 'I had high hopes for the two of you. I thought you were going to work the old Lucius charm on her. You've completely blown it.'

Cardova shrugged. 'My duty was more important than my personal feelings.'

'So,' said Sable, 'you admit that you do like Karalyn?'

'Yes. I admit it, though don't tell her. We're going back to the City tomorrow, and our trip will be over. It's better if she doesn't know how I feel.'

'You're an idiot,' said Kelsey.

'Why, thank you, ma'am.'

'Can I ask something?' said Corthie.

'We're not having a damn conference, brother,' said Kelsey. 'You don't need to ask for permission to speak.'

He smiled, but Kelsey could tell it was forced. 'When I was under Daimon's control...' He paused, his eyes glancing downwards. 'When... he was trying to make me kill Karalyn, I could hear her voice in my head. She was trying to help me, but it all seems like a dream, and I don't know if what I remember about it is true.'

'Go on,' said Sable. 'What do you want to ask?'

'Well, Karalyn was telling me to be strong, and to resist. And then she told me, or at least I think she did, that Belinda was still alive.' He shook his head, his eyes almost closed. 'Is it true; do you know?'

'It might be true,' said Kelsey. 'There was a rumour about it on Implacatus. Caelius told me.'

'It's not just a rumour,' said Sable. 'Bastion confirmed it to me in person on Dragon Eyre. He said that Belinda was placed into a god-restrainer mask until she agreed to marry Edmond.'

Corthie put his head in his hands and started to sob. Kelsey glanced at Sable, then placed a hand onto her brother's shoulder.

Sable snapped her fingers. 'That's what Karalyn needs me for. It's obvious. She wants me to go to Implacatus and get Belinda. Why couldn't she and Daphne just be honest about it? What was the need for secrecy?'

'Umm,' said Kelsey. 'I think the reason is sitting right here with us.' She nodded towards Corthie.

Sable's eyes narrowed. 'They didn't want Corthie to know?'

'Clearly. Because if he did...'

'Then he'll want to come along?' said Sable. 'Oh.' She turned to Corthie. 'Why did I not know your feelings towards Belinda?'

'Probably because you never asked,' said Kelsey. 'Corthie was very close to her, after Karalyn scoured her mind.'

'I love her,' said Corthie, wiping his eyes. 'She feels like a third sister to me. If you're going to rescue her, then I'm coming, too.'

'No,' said Sable. 'Daphne and Karalyn are right, although they should have been more open about it. Going to Implacatus won't be the same as a straight fight between two armies in the field. In a battle, there is no one better than you, Corthie. Rescuing Belinda will take sneakiness and deception, and downright betrayal. It's quick Quadrant work, and there is no one better at that than me. Look at me, Corthie. If this is what Karalyn wants me to do, then I will do it.'

'It's insanity,' said Cardova.

'Which is why I would be perfect for the job,' said Sable.

'I can't argue with that.' He turned to Corthie. 'Leave it to Sable; that's my advice. Go back to Clackenbaird and live your life with your family. For now, let's just get drunk.'

———

Kelsey groaned as the shutters in her room were opened.

'Leave me alone,' she croaked, pulling the covers over her head.

'It's time to get up,' said Cardova. 'I've brought you a mug of fresh coffee.'

Kelsey peered out from under the blanket. 'Coffee?'

He nodded. 'With sugar.'

She reached out for it, and Cardova placed the mug into her hands. He sat, and sipped from his own mug.

Kelsey slurped some coffee, and sighed. 'I guess this is the last one of these we'll be having for a while.'

'I doubt that,' said Cardova. 'Daphne has prepared a huge haul of goods to be transported back with us to the City – as a gift from the Holdfasts to Queen Emily. And before you ask – yes, there's plenty of chocolate; and sugar, coffee, tea, as well as tons of raw materials – copper, iron, leather, and a stash of tobacco for me. Van is getting a shiny new sword, made from Holdings steel. There must be ten tons of stuff sitting in the courtyard in front of the Great Keep.'

Kelsey narrowed her eyes. 'Why are you so perky this morning? I watched you and Corthie demolish an entire bottle of whisky.'

'Thorn and Agang have been healing our hangovers,' he said. 'Obviously, there was no point in trying to heal you.'

'Bastards.'

Cardova laughed. 'Feeling a bit rough, are we?'

'Shut it, or I'll tell Karalyn that you fancy her.'

'She hates what I did in the Banner,' he said. 'It would never work.'

'She killed a hundred thousand Rahain soldiers. She's a damn hypocrite if she holds what you did against you.'

'Be that as it may, I'm going to do my best to forget about her once we're back in the City.'

'Don't give me your bullshit. "Be that as it may". Who says that crap?'

'Did you enjoy seeing your family again?'

'Some of them,' she said, sitting up. She pulled the blanket up to her neck. 'Some of them get right on my nerves. It was good to see Corthie and Sable, though; and Karalyn, too, I guess. My mother and Keir can piss off, but.'

'What have you got against your mother?'

'I guess I'm sick of being her least favourite child. She doesn't make any attempt to hide it. Just watch what happens later today. I bet she cries when Corthie leaves, but she won't shed a tear for me.'

'She's worried about Corthie; whereas you're happy with your new life.'

'Shut up, Lucius. You're not allowed to be right when it comes to my family. I wonder what Van's been up to. I hope he missed me.'

'Of course he will have missed you. We'll have to think about how to break the news to him that Caelius has decided to stay.'

'It occurs to me, Lucius, that since Karalyn can use the Sextant to travel back and forward whenever she pleases, there might be a lot more traffic between the two worlds. Emily has a Quadrant, aye? If Karalyn could show us how to use it, then Van could visit his father as often as he liked. And, eh, you could see Karalyn.'

'I don't know. It might be dangerous, seeing as how the Ascendants are trying to find both worlds.'

'Did you not hear what Sable was saying last night? The Ascendants are too scared of the Holdfasts to attack us. She said that I protect the City, while she protects Dragon Eyre, and the rest of the family protect this world.'

'Forgive me for saying this, but sometimes Sable's full of shit.'

Kelsey laughed. 'You're wrong. All her boasting, and her arrogance, it's because she can actually do the things she claims to do. She killed an Ascendant on her own. That makes her as good as me, because I've helped kill two Ascendants.'

'Frostback killed Simon.'

'Aye, but only because I was there. Same with Leksandr. Frostback, Deathfang and Halfclaw might have been the ones to turn him into ash, but, again, only because I was there. Two halves equal one whole. Did they not teach you to count on Implacatus?'

Cardova smiled. 'You get your arrogance from Sable, I assume?'

'Cheeky bugger. Come back to me when you've killed an Ascendant.'

Cardova got to his feet.

'I was only joking, ya daft bastard,' said Kelsey.

'No, you've mortally offended me,' he laughed. 'Get washed and dressed, and I'll see you on the roof. Karalyn's getting ready to take Corthie to Kell.'

Kelsey watched him leave, then she swung her legs out of bed. She downed what was left of the coffee, and groaned, her head throbbing. She reached for her clothes, swearing that she would never touch alcohol again.

Forty minutes later, Kelsey staggered up onto the roof of the Great Keep. She wandered over to where Corthie was standing with Aila and their two young children. Next to them sat a huge pile of luggage, and several chests of gold.

'Morning,' Kelsey mumbled.

'You look terrible,' said Aila. 'Luckily for us, Thorn healed Corthie's raging hangover at dawn. He was in an awful state before that. Late night, was it?'

'It might have been,' said Kelsey. 'I can't remember all that much.' She waved her hand at the luggage. 'What's all this stuff?'

'Mostly gifts from Holder Fast,' said Aila. 'Money, clothes, farming tools; things for the farmhouse. The Clawhammer is buried somewhere amongst it all, too.'

Kelsey smirked. 'Are you going to use it as a plough?'

Corthie laughed. 'I might.' He reached out to embrace her.

Kelsey stepped back, then sighed. 'Fine,' she muttered. 'Don't break my spine, you great oaf.'

Corthie hugged her for a moment, then Aila did the same.

'It's called human contact,' said Aila. 'Don't be scared.'

'You're a pair of right smartarses this morning,' said Kelsey.

Karalyn and Daphne approached from the side.

'Are you ready?' said Karalyn.

'Aye,' said Corthie. 'Can you take us to Clackenbaird Farm? I'll walk down the hill to Marchside from there, and hand myself in to Chief Kallie.'

Karalyn nodded. 'Sure.'

Daphne sobbed, and dabbed her eyes with a hanky. Kelsey shot a glance in Cardova's direction, and Lucius rolled his eyes and looked away.

'Don't worry about me, mother,' said Corthie. 'I'll be fine.'

'Where's Sable?' said Karalyn, her eyes narrowing as she scanned the roof. 'Mother, as soon as we've gone, could you go downstairs and make sure Sable isn't playing with the Sextant? I put the Weathervane back into it, in preparation for taking Kelsey to the City.'

'Of course, dear.'

Corthie raised an arm. 'Bye, everyone.'

'Take care, brother,' said Kelsey.

Corthie smiled, then he, Aila, Karalyn and the two children vanished, along with the huge pile of luggage.

'Why Kell, of all places?' said Daphne. 'Corthie can tell me not to worry, but I'm going to. I'd better go downstairs.'

'I'll come with you,' said Kelsey. 'The sun is making my headache worse.'

'That's what you get for drinking too much, dear,' said Daphne, as they walked towards the stairs.

'No,' said Kelsey; 'it's what I get for having stupid blocking powers that prevent me from being healed. Is it our turn next? Is Karalyn taking me, Frostback and Cardova home when she gets back?'

'She's going to take Celine, Jemma and Cole to the Hold Fast estate first.'

'And then us?'

Daphne sighed. 'Are you truly so desperate to escape, Kelsey?'

'I'm not desperate, but I miss Van, and I miss the City.'

'Are you going to marry this Van?'

'Aye; it's going to be a double wedding – me and Van, and Karalyn and Lucius Cardova.'

'Ha ha, Kelsey. I suppose you blame me for keeping them apart?'

Kelsey halted on the stairs. 'Why would I do that?'

Daphne glanced at her. 'I presumed that's what you were referring to.'

'What did you do, mother?'

'I merely reminded Cardova that he was on duty, and forbade him from trying anything with my elder daughter. I was perfectly within my rights.'

'Oh, for fucksake, mother.'

'Don't you speak to me like that!'

'Don't you want Karalyn to be happy?'

'Of course I do. That's why I acted. Now, you must not mention this to Karalyn; am I clear?'

'Or what? I'll be in the City, out of your reach. What are you going to do?'

Daphne stared at her daughter for a moment, then began descending the stairs again.

'Nothing, that's what,' said Kelsey, following her. 'There's nothing you can do. I'm not under your control any more; and you hate that, don't you? Never mind, you'll have Keir to dote on after I'm gone.'

They reached the bottom of the stairs, and went to the Sextant Chamber. Daphne opened the door, and shook her head. Sable was crouching by the side of the Sextant, a Quadrant in her hand. She glanced up, and saw Daphne and Kelsey enter.

'Good morning,' Sable said, standing. 'Now, where do you think my Quadrant might go? That's the key, isn't it? This Quadrant has been to Dragon Eyre, so if I can discover the correct slot where it fits, then the Sextant will also be able to take me to Dragon Eyre. I'm right, yeah?'

'I wouldn't know,' said Daphne, frowning.

'I have another question,' said Sable. 'What would happen if I took the Weathervane out, while Karalyn is on another world? Would she be able to get back? In other words, does she need the Sextant to be operational for her to travel between worlds?'

'You would have to ask her that. She guessed you would be down here, interfering with her Sextant.'

'It's not *her* Sextant,' said Sable. 'If it belongs to anyone, then it belongs to the Ascendants.'

'If that's true, then your Quadrant doesn't belong to you, either.'

Sable laughed. 'Good point. Look; I'll be happy to share the Sextant with Karalyn.'

'Were you using it before we came in?' said Kelsey.

'Yes, a bit. I could see Dragon Eyre. I saw Ulna, and the ships in the harbour of Udall. Lara is on one of those ships. She was so close, and yet completely out of reach. Very frustrating.'

'Karalyn had a similar experience when she was first trying to use the device,' said Daphne.

'And she needed to insert the Quadrant to enable her to travel to the City? But she also travelled to Dragon Eyre. How?'

Daphne shrugged. 'I don't know. Karalyn doesn't use these devices in the same way as the gods. Quadrants speak to her. Do they speak to you?'

Sable shook her head. 'I am a master of using a Quadrant; the best there is. But I use it the way it's supposed to be used, by touching the correct sequence of engravings. I have no idea how Karalyn does it. She doesn't even need a Quadrant to travel about on the same world. But I was asking about Dragon Eyre.'

'Be patient,' said Daphne. 'Karalyn will take you there, once you have completed a task for her.'

'You mean, once I've rescued Belinda?'

Daphne frowned. 'How did you know that? Have you been in my mind?'

'No. We worked it out in the tavern last night.'

'Oh. Does Corthie know?'

'Aye,' said Kelsey. 'Don't worry, though; we talked him out of wanting to go.'

'You should have been honest with him,' said Sable.

'Perhaps,' said Daphne. 'However, Corthie's mental state is a little fragile at the moment, as I'm sure you perceived last night. We didn't want him to worry.'

Karalyn walked into the room. She frowned at Sable, suspicion in her eyes.

'Did Corthie and the others arrive in Kell all right, dear?' said Daphne.

'Aye,' said Karalyn, 'and I've taken Celine, Jemma and Cole back to Hold Fast. Kelsey, you're next. Mother, guard the Sextant from Sable while I'm gone.'

Sable laughed. 'Why? What is it that you think I'm going to do?'

'Work out how to get to Dragon Eyre on your own.'

'I've worked it out. I only need to find the right place to fit my Quadrant. However, yesterday, at the conference, I told you that I would undertake the little task you have for me, and I don't go back on my word.' She gestured at the Sextant. 'This is just professional curiosity. What would happen if someone removed the Weathervane while you were on a different world?'

Karalyn glanced down at the Sextant. 'I don't know for sure. I think I might be trapped where I was.'

'Then, wouldn't it be safer to learn how to use a Quadrant properly?'

'I have an idea about that,' said Kelsey. 'Once I'm back in the City, what if we used Queen Emily's Quadrant to travel back and forth between this world and there? Then we wouldn't need to worry about the Sextant. Sable could show us how it works; I mean, how it's supposed to work.'

'Yes,' said Sable, 'but I don't know how to make a Quadrant travel between worlds. Apart from Implacatus; I know how to get there.'

Karalyn blinked. 'You do?'

Sable laughed. 'Yes. Which is just as well, isn't it, if I'm going to rescue poor old Belinda.'

'I didn't tell her anything about Belinda,' said Daphne. 'She worked it out on her own.'

'Alright,' said Karalyn; 'so now you know. Kelsey, let's go.'

'Are we leaving from the roof?'

'No, from the courtyard outside,' said Daphne. 'I've put together a few things for you to take to Queen Emily, as a gift...'

'...from the Holdfasts. Aye; I know,' said Kelsey.

Daphne nodded at her. 'Well, take care, dear.'

Kelsey had hardened herself in preparation for her mother's expected reaction to her departure, but she still felt like crying when she saw how nonchalantly she was acting.

She lowered her gaze, as an ache formed in her chest. 'You too, mother.'

Sable put a hand on her shoulder. 'I'm going to miss you, Kelsey. It was great to see you again. Punch Van on the arm for me.'

Kelsey nodded, then embraced her aunt. She pulled away before she could start crying, and followed Karalyn from the room. The tears came when they were halfway down the stairs. Karalyn glanced at her in surprise.

'Are you alright, Kelsey?'

'I'm so tired, sister,' she sobbed; 'tired of mother not loving me. What did I do to earn her contempt? She loves Keir more than me, and Keir treats her like shit.'

'Mother does love you.'

'Bullshit.'

'She believes you try to push her away, so maybe she keeps her distance.'

Kelsey clenched her fists and suppressed a howl of anguish.

'I love you, sister,' said Karalyn. 'I admit that I used to hate you, when we were younger, and I'm sorry for that; I'm sorry for a lot of things I did when I was young. But you are my sister, and I will always love you.'

Kelsey wiped her eyes. 'Thanks, Karalyn.'

They emerged into the sunlight, and saw Frostback and Cardova standing by an enormous heap of crates and sacks in the castle forecourt.

Frostback lowered her head.

'My rider; are you sad? You have been crying.'

Kelsey tried to smile. 'Just saying goodbye to everyone.'

'Is no one else coming?' said Cardova, glancing around.

'Wait!' came a voice.

They turned, and saw Thorn hurry out from the Great Keep.

'Have a safe journey,' Thorn said.

'Thank you, Empress-elect,' said the silver dragon. 'May your reign be fruitful.'

Karalyn nodded to Thorn, then the air shimmered. Kelsey blinked, and when her eyes reopened, she saw a deep red sky above her head. She grinned. They were standing at the top end of Princeps Row in Tara.

'I'll leave you now,' said Karalyn. 'I'll come back in a while, to talk about the Quadrants.'

'How long's a while?' said Kelsey.

'I'm not sure. Within a third, maybe? I have to take mother and Thorn to Sanang, and then organise going to Implacatus for Belinda.'

'Don't do it,' said Cardova. 'You've never been to Implacatus, and Sable has barely spent a few hours there. You don't know what it's like.'

Kelsey nodded. 'He's right, sister. It sounds like you'll need someone who knows Implacatus well. Now, who do we know that used to live in Implacatus?' She elbowed Cardova. 'I've forgotten his name. Who could it be?' She laughed, as Karalyn and Cardova frowned down at her. 'Oh, and by the way, Karalyn; Lucius fancies you, but mother made him promise not to try anything. Boys, eh?'

Karalyn's mouth opened, then she vanished.

Cardova glared at Kelsey.

'Oh, come on,' she said; 'it was funny.'

'I shall not pretend to understand this human nonsense,' said Frost-back, extending her wings. 'I shall seek out Halfclaw, and see you all later.'

The silver dragon ascended into the red sky, then soared off over the ruins of Maeladh Palace.

'Let's find Van,' said Kelsey. 'I owe him a punch on the arm.'

CHAPTER 4
RANSACKED

Colsbury Castle, Republic of the Holdings – 1st Day, Last Third Summer 534

'But I don't want to,' said Kyra, folding her arms.

'We have to, wee Kyra,' said Karalyn. 'You've missed lots of lessons recently. We need to finish this page in the book, and then we can play.'

'I don't want to play with you,' the girl said. 'I want to play with Kelsey and Frostback.'

'They're not here any more. They went back to their home.' She opened the book at the correct page. 'Now, if I have two apples, and you have three apples, how many does that make?'

'This is stupid!'

'Count on your fingers.'

Cael glanced up from the floor, where he was drawing. 'Five apples.'

'Thank you, Cael,' said Karalyn, 'but we did this page earlier, and I know that you know the answer. I want Kyra to tell me.'

Kyra smirked. 'Five apples.'

The door opened, and Agang peered into the room. 'I'm not interrupting, am I?'

Karalyn sighed. 'No. What is it?'

'The declaration has been finalised, and is ready to be sent to the Empress.'

Karalyn pushed some paper and crayons in front of Kyra. 'Draw for a while,' she said, then she stood. 'I won't be long.'

She walked out of the room with Agang, and they went to the chamber that Daphne had taken over. She had moved a desk and book-case into the large room, and the surface of the desk was piled high with papers. Thorn, Keir and Shella were sitting by the window, while Daphne was rooting through a sheaf of documents. Karalyn frowned at her mother.

Daphne glanced up, and raised an eyebrow. 'Why are you giving me an evil look, dear?'

'You know why, mother.'

Daphne shook her head. 'This can't still be about that Cardova busi-ness, can it? Is this what I get for looking out for my eldest child?'

'I can decide these things for myself; I'm not a child.'

'No, but you're my child. Lucius Cardova might have seemed like a charming young man, but I know what soldiers are like.'

'So do I, mother; I was married to one.'

'Is this why I'm here?' said Keir. 'To discuss why Karalyn can't get a boyfriend?'

Karalyn looked down at him. 'I don't know why you're here. If you don't like Colsbury, then leave.'

'I wasn't talking about Colsbury, but while we're on the subject, you know why I'm stuck on this damn island. Where else am I supposed to go? Jemma has taken my place as next-in-line to run the Hold Fast estate; and I would probably be arrested if I set foot in Plateau City. My life has turned to shit.'

'Now, now, children,' said Shella. 'Don't fight in front of mummy.'

'I called this meeting for two reasons,' said Daphne. 'Firstly, to present Karalyn with the documents that she will be taking to the Empress; and, secondly, to discuss our plans for going to Sanang. Kara-lyn, I trust you will be able to transport us to Broadwater without difficulty?'

Karalyn nodded. 'And how will you be getting home? After Rakana, I think we need to be more specific with the details.'

'I agree. As Agang has decided to accompany us, we think it would be advisable to travel back overland, so that we can visit the old Mya enclave. It's not just the Matriarch we need to persuade; there are many powerful merchants in Mya that need to be convinced that we are following the right course.'

'Alright,' said Karalyn. 'That fits with my plans to take Sable to Implacatus. I can't predict how long we'll be away for, so your return journey may have been in doubt, anyway.'

'Where is Sable?' said Thorn.

'She took off with her Quadrant this morning,' said Karalyn. 'She'll be back later today, or so she said.'

'What's she doing?' said Daphne.

'She didn't say, though I strongly suspect that she's on a supply run. She mentioned to me that she needed new clothes, armour, weapons, and so on.'

'Are we just going to let her disappear like that?' said Keir.

'Aye,' said Karalyn. 'Sable isn't our prisoner. She walked in here of her own free will, and she can leave in the same manner.'

'Quite,' said Daphne. 'Back to the Sanang trip. Caelius will also be coming.'

Karalyn smiled. 'Sorry, mother, but I forbid you from seeing him.'

Daphne frowned.

'Now, do you see how that feels?'

'Oh, it was your little joke, dear,' said Daphne. 'Most amusing.' She turned to Keir. 'As for you, I would like to ask you once more to come along with us. A trip to Sanang would be far better for your spirits than moping around Colsbury Castle.'

'No, thanks,' he said. 'Can I go now?'

Daphne glanced at Thorn, who nodded. Keir got up, and strode from the room. The others stood or sat in silence for a moment. Karalyn eyed Thorn, but she seemed unperturbed by her husband's behaviour.

'Now,' said Daphne; 'on to the documents.' She leaned over the desk, and picked up a thick envelope. 'In here are two sets of papers, Karalyn. The first is a copy of the constitutional law mandating the succession to the throne. It was drafted by Herald Calder, here in Colsbury, to formalise what occurred at the vote when Bridget abdicated. I have underlined the sections where Bridget has broken her own laws. The second set of papers has been drawn up by Agang, and they set out the vote that took place yesterday. We have another copy here, in case the Empress tosses them into the fire.'

She extended her hand, and Karalyn took the envelope.

'Be very careful, dear,' said Daphne. 'Transport yourself back here at the slightest hint of trouble. If it comes to it, present the documents to a courtier who will take them to the Empress; don't place yourself at risk.'

Karalyn nodded. 'When do you want to go to Sanang?'

'Shall we say in two days' time?' said Daphne.

'That sounds reasonable,' said Thorn. 'That way, we should be back here before the end of summer.'

'If that's everything,' said Karalyn, 'I need to continue the children's lesson.'

'Oh,' said Daphne. 'I was hoping you would travel to Plateau City without delay, dear. The sooner Bridget learns what took place here, the better.'

'Daimon has probably told her already, mother. The moment Kelsey left, he was free to spy on us again.'

'All the same, correct procedures must be followed.'

'Fine,' Karalyn muttered. 'Can someone else finish Kyra's lesson, please? We've been working on counting.'

Daphne, Agang and Shella all glanced at each other.

Thorn stood. 'I'll do it.'

Karalyn smiled. 'Thanks.'

'Is that why you voted for me? Because I looked after your children for four years?'

'Partly,' said Karalyn. 'Bryce is a nice guy, but you? I would trust you with anything, Thorn. I will never forget what you did for me. I also happen to think that you'll make a good Empress, so there was that, too.'

Thorn laughed, then left the room.

Karalyn glanced at her mother. 'See you soon.'

Outside the Great Fortress, Plateau City. Go.

The air shimmered, and Karalyn found herself in the shadows of an alcove, a hundred yards from the bridge over the dry moat by the northern gates of the Great Fortress.

You cannot see me.

A few passers-by, who had stared at her arrival, gazed around with puzzled expressions on their faces. Karalyn retreated into a side alley, close to the entrance to the massive open-air market. She waited until no one was around, then relaxed her powers. She passed the envelope into her left hand, and strode back out on to the main road, and joined the pedestrians walking towards the Great Fortress. She crossed the bridge, then two tall soldiers by the gates glanced in her direction.

You don't notice me.

She passed the soldiers, and walked into the fortress. Mindful of the fact that she was barred from entering the palace, she joined a queue of petitioners who were waiting to speak to a pair of courtiers sitting behind a desk by the left-hand wall of the large entrance hall. The queue moved slowly, but Karalyn was patient. Whenever any soldiers or officials appeared to take an interest in her, she quietly persuaded them with her powers to ignore her.

When she reached the front of the queue, the two courtiers glanced up at her. Their eyes widened.

'My name is Karalyn Holdfast, and I would like to speak to the Empress, if that's possible.'

'Karalyn Holdfast?' said one, his face paling.

'Aye. Could someone please tell her Majesty that I am here?'

One of the courtiers gestured to a squad of soldiers, who came over to the desk.

'Did you not see Karalyn Holdfast walk into the fortress, Sergeant?' the courtier shouted at the lead soldier. 'You and your squad were given strict instructions to deny access to any members of the Holdfast family.'

'Sorry, sir,' said the sergeant. 'Should we throw her out?'

'I'm only here to hand over some documents,' said Karalyn. 'That's all. I won't cause any trouble.'

I won't cause any trouble.

'Just documents, you say?' said the courtier, calming.

Karalyn held up the envelope for them to see. 'Aye.'

A side door opened, and two imperial officers strode into the hall. They scanned the area, and saw Karalyn. They glanced at each other, and walked over to the desk.

'Mage Daimon told us that we'd find you down here, Miss Holdfast,' said one. 'He sensed you using your powers to slip past the soldiers.'

'That's right,' she said. 'I bear important documents for the Empress, and I knew the soldiers would prevent me from coming in. May I go upstairs to speak to her Majesty?'

'We're here to escort you to the palace, miss,' the officer said. 'Come with us.'

The officers led Karalyn away from the desk. They passed through the doorway, and began to climb the stairs that went up to the palace levels.

'A word of warning, miss,' said one of the officers. 'Mage Daimon will block any attempt you make to enter the mind of anyone within the palace.'

'I would expect nothing less,' she said. 'I am only here to speak, and to hand over this envelope. I will make no attempt to use my powers, unless I am threatened.'

They reached the palace, and Karalyn was taken through the hallways to the Empress's small meeting room. One of the officers knocked on the door.

'Enter.'

The officer pushed open the door, and gestured for Karalyn to go inside. She walked into the meeting room, and saw Bridget sitting at the head of the table. By her left shoulder stood Bryce, and Daimon was standing to her right.

'Close the door,' said the Empress.

The officer saluted, backed out of the room, and shut the door behind him.

'Right, Karalyn,' said Bridget; 'I was expecting one of the Holdfasts to appear here. It makes sense that your mother would send you, I suppose.'

Karalyn held out the envelope. 'She asked me to bring you this.'

Bridget nodded to Bryce, who leaned forwards and took the envelope from Karalyn. He showed his mother the seal, then cracked it open with his thumb. He put his hand into the envelope, and pulled out the two sets of papers, each tied with a ribbon. As he was flicking through the pages, Karalyn glanced at Daimon. The young dream mage was smiling at her, but it wasn't a smile of friendship. She searched for any sign of his powers, but felt nothing.

'How are you, Daimon?' she said.

'Our new dream mage is settling in well,' said the Empress. 'He is proving to be very useful. For example, I already know the contents of that envelope, thanks to him. He gave me a full report of your conversation with Daphne, Thorn and Keir earlier this morning.'

'Were you spying on us, your Majesty?'

'Aye. Do you blame me?'

Bryce glanced at his mother. 'It's exactly as Daimon said it would be. The first set of papers outlines the old law of succession, and the second details the results of the Holdfasts' vote.'

'You would have won the vote, Bryce,' said Karalyn, 'if you had bothered to show up. You, Daimon and Tabor would have been enough.'

Bridget took a sheet of paper from Bryce, and read it.

'Kelsey voted for you, son,' Bridget said, laughing.

'Sable did, too,' said Karalyn, 'and Shella, and Thorn. The non-mages and Aila abstained. The vote was legitimate, your Majesty; fair and free. It was also within the bounds of the law, unlike your unilateral decision to appoint your own son as your successor.'

'What's your point, Karalyn?'

'I ask you to follow your own laws, your Majesty. Nothing more, nothing less. Accept the outcome of the vote, with grace, and the crisis in the empire will be over.'

'There is no crisis in the empire,' said Bridget. 'The only crisis that exists is within your mother's head. I have been training Bryce to take over for many years. He was born to be Emperor; whereas, Thorn was born to be a grasping, ambitious schemer. She only married Keir to join the Holdfasts. She saw that as her best route to the throne. By appointing Bryce as my successor, I will spare the Empire from her misrule.'

'I'll repeat what I said before,' said Karalyn; 'if Bryce and a few of your mages had turned up in Colsbury, then he would have won. The fact that you ignored the invitation, your Majesty, tells me that you know Thorn is a suitable candidate. You were frightened that she would beat Bryce, and so you flouted the law – the law that you and Herald Calder wrote.'

'That law has been superseded,' said Bryce. 'A new law of succession is now in force.'

Karalyn laughed. 'Oh aye? Since when?'

'Since two days ago,' said Bryce; 'the day before your little conference took place. Your attempts to usurp power have been in vain.'

'It is you who is usurping power, Bryce,' said Karalyn. 'You know this is wrong. Take a stand. Tell your mother that you want no part in her law-breaking. Tell her that you refuse to go along with this treachery against the Empire.'

Bridget raised her hand. 'Enough. I was prepared to talk to you, Karalyn, but it's like listening to Daphne. Did she feed you those lines? Did she write them down and make you memorise them? We have nothing more to say to each other, except this – anyone who decides to accept the outcome of your pathetic little vote will be deemed a traitor. The same goes for anyone who refuses to accept my son as next-in-line to the throne. Take that message back to your mother, and ask her where her army is. I have over two hundred thousand imperial soldiers under my command; how many does your mother have? A few Holdings militia, perhaps? If you want a war, you can have one, but I imagine that it would be over quite quickly. The balance of power has changed, Karalyn. I have my own dream mage now.'

Daimon smiled. 'Should I prevent her from escaping, your Majesty?'

'No. Let her go.'

Karalyn bowed her head. 'Your Majesty, if Daimon attempts to interfere with any of my family, then I shall retaliate.'

'And if you interfere with us, then Daimon will retaliate.'

'So be it. Farewell, your Majesty.'

Colsbury Castle. Go.

Her surroundings changed, and she found herself back in the same chamber she had left from. Daphne was sitting behind her desk, sorting through papers.

'Welcome back, dear,' she said. 'Feel free to smoke. Did it go as badly as we suspected it might?'

Karalyn sat, and lit a cigarette. 'Aye. I was right about them spying on us. They knew what was in the envelope before they opened it.'

'That settles it. You cannot go to Implacatus. Without you here, we would be defenceless.'

'But, mother, I can't leave Belinda there.'

'Then allow Sable to go on her own. She's the expert at this sort of thing.'

'I can't. Sable and Belinda hate each other. They bickered every moment we were on Lostwell together, and I ended up sending Sable away to stop them fighting. Belinda nearly killed Sable a little later, when they were reunited at Yoneath. If Sable arrives on her own, Belinda will most likely believe that she's there to kill her. Besides, I think this might be beyond even Sable's abilities, and if she encountered difficulties, then she would have the temptation to go back to Dragon Eyre dangling in front of her.'

'You don't trust her?'

'Can you blame me, mother? I think she has changed; and I know she feels regret over Lennox, but still – this is Sable we're talking about.'

'But, dear, if you and she were away for a considerable amount of time, then Daimon could destroy us. He could turn my powers off again, and Thorn's, and Keir's. How could we oppose him? Did you speak to the Empress about Brannig?'

'No.'

'Why not? She should know that we suspect Daimon of being behind that.'

'Without proof, it would have sounded as though I were making wild accusations. Bridget didn't demand that we send Keir back to Plateau City, so I assumed that she didn't want the subject brought up. I don't think she cares what Daimon has done in the past, as long as he obeys her now.'

'And will he?'

'I don't know. He seemed happy enough to be standing by her shoulder.'

'I wonder what his long term plan is.'

'He's sixteen; he probably doesn't have a long term plan. He's probably just amazed at how much his life has changed. One thing we can be sure of, though – he'll be angry and grieving over Dillon's death. He shares something with Bridget and her children. They've all had someone close to them killed by a Holdfast.'

'But Corthie didn't mean it, and Keir was trying to protect the Empress.'

'Aye. I know that; and you know that. Will it make any difference to how they feel about us?'

'All the more reason for you not to leave us, Karalyn. If you go to Implacatus, they will be free to seek their revenge.'

Karalyn flicked her cigarette into an ashtray, unable to think of an argument to counter her mother.

'We must protect Thorn, at all costs,' Daphne went on. 'Thorn, and the children.'

The door opened, and Sable strode in.

'Good morning,' said Daphne.

'Is it still morning?' said Sable. She swung a large bag from over her shoulder and set it down on the floor. 'Do you two have a minute? There's something you should see.'

'Where?' said Karalyn.

'Plateau City.'

'I was just there.'

'Did you visit the Holdfast townhouse?'

Karalyn shook her head.

Sable pulled the Quadrant from an inside coat pocket. 'You should stand up; otherwise you'll both fall on your arses when we arrive.'

Karalyn got to her feet, but Daphne frowned, and remained sitting.

'Perhaps I should stay here,' she said.

'Why?' said Sable. 'You're missing the entire point of having a Quadrant, Daphne. A Quadrant is power; the power to be wherever you want to be, and the power to escape from any trap.'

Daphne sighed, and stood. 'Are imperial soldiers ransacking the townhouse?'

'No,' said Sable.

She glided her thumb across the surface of the Quadrant, and the air shimmered. Karalyn glanced around, and saw the ground floor hallway of the Holdfast townhouse in Plateau City.

Daphne sniffed. 'Everything seems normal.'

'Did you use your thumb to get us here?' said Karalyn.

Sable nodded. 'I had to learn how to operate the Quadrant one-handed, so that I could carry a sword at the same time. It took a lot of practice, but I hardly even have to look at the Quadrant any more. I've memorised the engravings. East, west, up down; it's all pretty simple once you've grasped the basics.' She laughed. 'I had a habit of always arriving a few feet above where I intended, but I've sorted that out, after falling through the air about a dozen times.'

'That's very impressive,' said Karalyn. 'I still don't know how to use a Quadrant properly. How did you learn in the first place?'

'I read the mind of a demigod called Naxor, and then I practised. I wish you could have seen the way I captured the Ascendant I killed. It was pure poetry.'

'This is all fascinating,' said Daphne; 'but I assume we are here for a reason?'

Sable smiled, then pushed open the door leading into the townhouse's main living room. Inside, was a scene of destruction. Silver lamp fittings had been ripped from the walls, and the wooden cabinets had been turned over, the contents of their drawers scattered in piles across the floor. Sitting in a chair, her head in her hands, was Tabitha, the servant assigned to take care of the townhouse.

'Oh my word,' said Daphne. 'Tabitha, are you all right?'

The servant glanced up. She had tears in her eyes, and her wrists were covered in red weals.

'Holder Fast?' she said. 'I'm so sorry; I couldn't stop him. I tried, but he was too strong.'

Daphne marched into the room, her expression darkening. 'Who did this? Was it soldiers? Did the Empress send men to harass you?'

'No, ma'am; this had nothing to do with the Empress.'

'I found her tied to a chair,' said Sable. 'I gave her some food and water, and then left to collect you two. Some of the rooms upstairs are in a similar condition. I would guess that a large quantity of silver has been stolen – lamps, cutlery, dishes, and so on. We would need an inventory to be sure of everything that's been taken.'

Daphne stamped her foot on the floor. 'Who did this?'

'His name is Olo'osso,' said Sable. 'Karalyn rescued him at the same time she brought me here.'

'Oh, shit,' muttered Karalyn. 'That old guy?'

Sable laughed. 'That "old guy", as you put it, happens to have been the most notorious pirate on Dragon Eyre.'

'He was kind at first,' said Tabitha. 'He just seemed grateful to be alive. He was very polite, and asked me lots of questions about the city, and the Holdfasts. I did what was asked of me – I made sure he was treated as an honoured guest. Then, two days ago, I found him filling a sack with silver, and tried to stop him.' She sobbed. 'He tied me up. He's gone.'

Daphne turned to her daughter. 'And you let him stay here?'

'He was half-dead, mother. To be honest, I'd completely forgotten about him.'

'Sable,' said Daphne, 'where might he have gone?'

'My first instinct was to check the harbour,' Sable said. 'Olo'osso is a sailor at heart, as well as a pirate; but I couldn't find him. He could have exchanged the silver for coins, and booked passage on any number of ships crossing the Inner Sea. You probably don't need me to tell you how difficult it is to find someone on a ship at sea. He could be on his way to Rainsby, or Stretton Sands; anywhere.'

'We'll need to change the locks on the front door, in case he has a key,' said Daphne. 'I could send Keir down here, to clear up, and take an inventory. Something to keep him busy.'

Tabitha's eyes widened. 'Ma'am, I... um...'

'What is it, Tabitha?'

'She doesn't want to be alone with Keir,' said Sable. 'It's clear in her mind; I can see it.'

'If we forget your arrogant assumption that you can raid people's minds whenever you feel like it,' said Daphne, 'why would Tabitha not want to be alone with my son?'

Sable pulled a face. 'Do I need to spell it out for you in detail? She wouldn't feel... comfortable in his company.'

Daphne stared at her half-sister. 'My son would never behave inappropriately. He's a married man.'

Sable glanced at Karalyn.

'Why are you looking at her?' said Daphne.

'Sable's right, mother,' said Karalyn. 'I know you don't want to hear it, but Keir... He...'

Daphne snorted, and stormed out of the room.

Tabitha rubbed her bruised wrists. 'Lord Keir isn't coming here, is he?'

'If he does come,' said Karalyn, 'he won't be alone. I'll make sure of it. Did he ever hurt you?'

Tabitha shook her head. 'It was more the way he looked at me.'

Karalyn nodded. 'Sorry.'

'It's not your fault,' said Sable. 'You should think about turning off Keir's vision powers. He's been using them to...'

'I don't want to know,' said Karalyn.

'But you know he's been having an affair?' said Sable. 'A young woman by the name of Tilda Holdwain. She works at the Holdings Embassy.'

'No, I didn't know,' said Karalyn, 'because I don't go around reading everyone's minds.'

'Perhaps you should,' said Sable.

'Don't tell mother this. She would probably kill him. And not a word to Thorn.'

Sable shook her head, a look of incredulity in her eyes. 'Damn it, Karalyn; you are clueless. Thorn already knows.'

Karalyn stared at Sable. Could it be true? It sounded ridiculous to her ears, but Sable had no reason to lie to her.

'Maybe you should pay a little more attention to what's going on around you,' said Sable, 'instead of dreaming about Belinda and Lucius Cardova.'

Karalyn's temper bubbled to the surface. 'Have you been in Lucius's mind?'

'No,' Sable said. 'I didn't need to go in; he told me about his feelings for you. The more important question here is – why didn't *you* read his mind? Instead of dithering, you could have saved yourself a lot of trouble. You are the mightiest mage on this world; on any world! – and yet you haven't the slightest notion about what's happening around you.'

'Ma'am,' said Tabitha; 'should you be saying this in front of me?'

Sable raised an eyebrow, then she pointed a finger at the servant. Tabitha blinked, and gazed around.

'Don't worry, Tabitha,' said Sable. 'Everything's going to be fine.'

She walked to the door, and Karalyn followed her out into the hallway.

'Did you just wipe her memories?'

Sable nodded. 'Just the last part of our conversation; she'll remember everything else.'

'You abuse your powers.'

'So? You neglect yours. You could do anything, Karalyn. What do you think Bridget and Daimon are planning to do to us? Do you believe that they will allow their scruples to hold them back? Yet, here you are, unwilling to even go into my mind to check if I was telling the truth about Thorn knowing about Keir's affair. You need to get a grip, niece. You need to harden your heart and start acting like a proper dream mage. If you don't, Daimon will piss all over us.'

Karalyn lowered her gaze. 'I don't know if I can.'

'Then we shall lose. It's as simple as that. By voting for Thorn, the Holdfasts have picked a fight with the Empire; an Empire with thousands of trained soldiers. An Empire with a dream mage who will use his powers without hesitation. Where is the woman who had the guts and the ruthlessness to steal a Quadrant from a dragon? That's the Karalyn we need right now.'

Daphne appeared on the stairs coming from the upper floors.

'Upstairs is a disaster,' she said, as she reached the bottom step. 'The townhouse has been stripped of silver. I want this Olo'osso found, and I want him hanged.'

Sable smiled. 'That's the Holdfast spirit,' she said. 'Now, Daphne, I don't suppose you could pass on some of that to your elder daughter?'

CHAPTER 5
WITH THE MATRIARCH

Colsbury Castle, Republic of the Holdings – 3rd Day, Last Third Summer 534

'They need at least four hours of lessons every day,' said Karalyn, 'before they are allowed to play. Kyra is behind on her reading, and Cael needs to work on his arithmetic, so concentrate on that, if you can. And please, don't take them anywhere with the Quadrant. Oh, and try not to swear in front of them.'

Sable raised an eyebrow. 'You're only going away for two days, Karalyn. We'll be fine. Shella and I can handle a couple of kids.'

Daphne frowned. 'I'm not sure this is a good idea.'

'If Thorn could do it for four years, we can do it for two days.'

'Remember,' said Karalyn; 'Keir will be here if you need any help.'

Sable smirked. 'Shella and I are going to lock Keir in the attic while you're away.'

'Just make sure Colsbury is still standing upon our return,' said Daphne. She glanced at Shella. 'You're in charge.'

'Of course I'm in charge,' said the Rakanese mage. 'Colsbury belongs to me.'

'Well, to be strictly accurate,' said Daphne, 'Colsbury belongs to the Holdings government, Shella, although I've been thinking of purchasing it for the Holdfasts. The Hold Fast estate is too remote to be used as a family base.'

'You what?' said Shella. 'And you thought this would be a good time to tell me that; just before you leave?'

'We won't evict you, Shella,' said Daphne. She smiled. 'As long as you behave yourself.'

Caelius and Agang walked into the chamber.

'We're all packed and ready to go,' said Caelius.

'Excellent,' said Daphne. She glanced at Karalyn. 'Shall we?'

Karalyn crouched down, and hugged her two children.

'Will you be back for our birthday, mama?' said Cael.

'Of course I will,' said Karalyn. 'It's not till the end of the third – the last day of summer. Granny, Aunty Thorn, and Uncle Agang will also be back by then. We won't miss your birthday.'

Karalyn kissed the twins, then they left the room. Caelius led them to a larger chamber, where a pile of luggage sat. Daphne glanced at her travelling companions. Thorn looked regal in her sapphire-blue dress, though her eyes were betraying her irritation at Keir's refusal to attend their departure. Agang had also smartened himself up, while Caelius looked every inch the tough old veteran that he was.

'I'm a little nervous,' said Thorn. 'This will be the first time I'll have been to Sanang since I left nearly ten years ago.'

Daphne smiled, but said nothing. This would be her first trip to Sanang since she had crawled out of the forest, maimed and half-dead after escaping from Agang's clutches. That had been thirty years ago, before Thorn had been born.

'I was seventeen back then,' Thorn went on, 'and thought I knew everything. Now, I'm twenty-seven, and I'm not sure I know anything.'

'You never struck me as modest,' said Shella.

Thorn smiled. 'I'm sure it will pass.'

'Gather round,' said Karalyn.

'Do you remember when we used to have to hold on to each other to be transported?' said Daphne, as she strode towards her daughter.

'You did what?' said Sable, laughing.

Caelius and Agang moved closer to Daphne, Thorn and Karalyn.

'Have a good trip,' said Shella.

'We're breaking out the gin as soon as you've gone,' said Sable. 'The kids can eat chocolate until they're sick.'

Karalyn narrowed her eyes, then the air shimmered, and the five travellers found themselves standing on an unpaved road in a forest, their luggage piled next to them.

Daphne glanced at the trees around them. 'Why did you bring us here? Where's Broadwater?'

'We can't appear in the middle of a town, mother,' said Karalyn. 'It causes panic.'

'And how are we supposed to carry all of our things along this poor excuse for a road? Thorn's dress will get muddy. First impressions count, dear.'

'Fine,' Karalyn muttered. 'Let's do it your way. Just be prepared for screams.'

The air shimmered again, and their surroundings altered to that of a busy street, with wooden houses flanking the roadside. Carts and wagons were being pulled along, and dozens of the Sanang inhabitants of Broadwater turned to stare at the five people who had appeared in their midst.

Someone screamed, while others ran. A man and a woman, both armed with crossbows, aimed them at the new arrivals.

'We are here to speak to the Matriarch,' Daphne said. 'We would like to...'

'They don't speak Holdings, mother,' said Karalyn.

Daphne switched to Sanangka. 'My name is Daphne Holdfast, and this is high mage Thorn.'

Thorn stepped forwards, her eyes on the two militia soldiers, as reinforcements ran towards them. The street was cleared of civilians, though many were watching from windows and doorways.

'We have come from the empire,' said Thorn. 'We bear gifts for the Matriarch of Sanang. Please take us to the Citadel.'

One of the soldiers squinted at her. 'Thorn of Greyfalls Deepen?'

'Yes, it is I.'

Daphne heard a few nervous mutterings of *seulitch*, as the soldiers glanced at each other.

'It is true that I am a soulwitch,' said Thorn. 'The greatest soulwitch for a hundred years. Take us to the Matriarch.'

The soldiers from the town militia formed up around the visitors. One of them requisitioned a cart from a local tradesman, and their luggage was loaded onto its back.

'What was that about?' whispered Caelius. 'I don't speak the local language.'

'Nothing to worry about,' said Daphne. 'Just a few awkward introductions.'

Caelius scanned the street. 'There are no men my age here; no men over thirty, as far as I can see.'

'They were wiped out in the wars against the Creator,' said Daphne. 'The balance between men and women is only now starting to reassert itself.'

They set off as soon as the cart was full, and the militia soldiers guided them along the street, as the locals stared. They turned right at a crossroads and started to climb a gentle slope, up towards a thick palisade wall constructed from tree trunks.

'This used to be my home,' said Agang, in Holdings, as they strode up the hillside. 'I built this town.'

'Oh yes?' said Caelius. 'What happened?'

'Keira the fire witch happened,' said Agang. 'She took all the men, and marched on Plateau City.'

Daphne glanced at Karalyn. 'Are you ready to block the imperial vision mage?'

Karalyn nodded.

'There's a mage here?' said Caelius.

'Yes. Mage Aberfeld of Hold Terras. He's been posted here for several years, ever since Sanang became a full member of the empire. He will be under orders to report any unusual activity to Mage Tabor in

Plateau City, and I would imagine that our arrival might be considered unusual.'

'Hold Terras? Are they allies of Hold Fast?'

'Not particularly,' said Daphne. 'We've had our ups and downs.'

The wooden gates of the Citadel were lying open, and they passed through the entrance, coming into a large open space. Squat buildings sat to either side, while a large hall reared up in front of them, several storeys high. Some of the soldiers who had been escorting them strode up to the great hall, and spoke to others in low voices. An officer glanced at Thorn, then went into the building.

A few moments later, Daphne felt a pressure behind her temples.

Mother. Mage Aberfeld has just attempted to reach out to Plateau City with his powers. I stopped him.

Thank you, Karalyn. Where is the mage?

He's upstairs, in the Matriarch's personal quarters. Understandably, he is a little agitated. I don't think he liked me blocking his powers.

Who would, dear?

After a few minutes, a well-dressed young Sanang man emerged from the hall. He cast his eyes over the arrivals, then walked towards them.

'Greetings,' he said. 'The Matriarch has been informed that you are here, and she will see you shortly. I would recommend, for the future, that you let us know well in advance that you might be visiting.'

'Of course,' said Thorn. 'Circumstances have dictated the manner of our arrival in Broadwater.'

The young man glanced over Thorn for a moment, then nodded. 'Come with me. You can wait inside, and rest. I will ensure that your luggage is safely secured within the Great Hall.'

The small group followed the man into the building, while soldiers unloaded the cart. The interior of the hall was cool, with many of the side shutters closed to keep out the hot rays of the sun. In the dim light, Daphne saw long rows of empty tables, and a high platform at one end, where an unoccupied throne sat. They were shown to a table, and sat. The young man excused himself, and strode back outside.

'What do we know about this Matriarch?' whispered Caelius.

'Not very much,' said Daphne. 'She replaced her mother a few years ago. Her mother was the first Matriarch of Sanang, though I'm not sure how she was selected as leader.'

Thorn leaned in closer. 'The first Matriarch was trained as a blacksmith by Holdings artisans who came here when Agang joined the empire in five-oh-six. When Keira passed through, the Holdings who were here were all executed, along with every male blacksmith. The Matriarch escaped with her life, because none of the Sanang warriors would believe that a woman could be a blacksmith. After the war, she was virtually the only person left in Sanang with those skills. She set up a forge, and everyone came to her here, in Broadwater.'

'She was a blacksmith?' said Caelius.

'Yes. With no men left, she assumed command. No one selected her; she took power by the force of her personality. Her first act was to open up every female enclosure; at a single stroke, the women of Sanang were free.'

'I was supposed to rule Sanang after the war,' said Agang. 'But, when I returned here, the Matriarch had already taken over. In the end, I had to make do with the Mya enclave, to the east of here on the border with the Plateau. It was the new Matriarch who pushed me out of there. Mya is part of Sanang again.'

'Mya was always part of Sanang, Lord Agang,' came a voice from behind them.

They turned, and saw a young woman in a black gown, a silver tiara on her brow.

Agang got to his feet, and bowed low. 'My lady.'

The young woman smiled, as the others stood and did the same. To the woman's left was a small group of her courtiers, including a Holdings man, who looked angry.

The Matriarch approached the table.

'Greetings, Lady Thorn of Greyfalls Deepen,' she said.

'It is a pleasure to meet you, Matriarch.'

'And you must be Holder Fast, Herald of the Empire,' she said to Daphne. 'To what do we owe the pleasure of your company?'

'I have important issues to discuss with you, Matriarch,' Daphne said, in clear Sanangka. 'This is my elder daughter Karalyn Holdfast, and this is my companion, Caelius Logos, who does not speak the language of Sanang. May we go somewhere more private to talk?'

Mage Aberfeld took a step forwards. 'Matriarch, you should be aware that someone here has blocked my vision powers. I am unable to use them at present.'

The Matriarch smiled. 'And why would you wish to use your powers on our guests?'

'I wished to send a message to the Imperial Capital, my lady. We were not expecting a visit from the Herald of the Empire, and I wanted to seek advice from the Empress.'

'Your powers will return as soon as we leave,' said Daphne.

'You can leave them inoperable for longer than that, if you wish,' said the Matriarch. 'It makes a few of my courtiers nervous that there is someone living here who can read minds.'

Aberfeld scowled, but said nothing.

'Come,' said the Matriarch. 'Let us go into the meeting chamber at the rear of the hall. I'm sure Lord Agang remembers how to get there.'

She turned, the hem of her long black dress swishing over the swept flagstones of the hall. Her courtiers followed her, along with six burly Sanang soldiers, and the guests came last, escorted by more soldiers. They walked behind the high platform at the end of the hall, and passed through a doorway into a smaller room, where dark oak tables faced another throne. The Matriarch stepped up, and sat down upon the throne, and her courtiers arranged themselves on either flank. Thorn led the other guests to the front row of tables. The Matriarch gestured to them, and they sat.

'The usual procedure,' said the Matriarch, 'is to send advance notice of at least one third before any official state visit from the Empire, and yet you have arrived here unannounced. I do not wish to seem inhospitable, but perhaps refreshments can wait until I have heard the reason for your unexpected visit. Lady Thorn of Greyfalls Deepen, please stand and tell us why you are here.'

Thorn stood, her chin high.

'There is a crisis within the empire, Matriarch,' she said. 'Empress Bridget has broken the clear laws of succession, by appointing her own son as next-in-line to the throne. Despite official complaints and personal appeals, the Empress has refused to reconsider her decision. Therefore, with a heavy heart, the high mages of this world convened, and followed the law. A new successor was selected, following a free and fair vote. We have come here today to ask that you support our decision to uphold the laws, and to request that you give your full backing to the one who was selected.'

The Matriarch said nothing for a long moment, her eyes never leaving Thorn. To her right, the Holdings mage was growing more impatient, but he kept his silence.

'I see,' said the Matriarch. 'Tell me; who was selected by this convention to inherit the throne of the empire?'

Thorn's eyes caught the gaze of the Matriarch. 'I was.'

'The convention selected a Sanang woman?'

'Yes, Matriarch. I am to be the next Empress, the next Holder of the World.'

'Ah. Now I understand why you blocked the powers of our resident vision mage. Am I to assume that the Empress is hostile to the decision of this convention?'

'Her Majesty is very hostile. She has announced that any who refuse to accept her son as heir to the throne is a traitor to the Empire. However, she is mistaken. It is the Empress who is in breach of the law, a law that she helped write. She has thrown away the basis of collective decision-making that binds the differing nations together. If her Majesty has her way, then the throne will be occupied by the Kellach Brigdomin forever.'

'I assume you are aware that I inherited the position of Matriarch from my mother? We do not vote for our leader in Sanang.'

'I am aware of that, Matriarch. Each nation is permitted to govern themselves by their own laws, but the Empire as a whole is different. The Empire represents all of us. A Holdings man was the first Emperor, followed by a woman from Kellach Brigdomin.'

'Are you saying that it is the turn of the Sanang?'

'No, Matriarch. I was selected, but anyone could have been nominated.'

'If I decide to support your claim, will the Empress seek to punish Sanang?'

'This very day, the government of the Holdings Republic shall issue a proclamation in support of my right as imperial successor. If Sanang joins the Holdings, then it is hoped that the Empress will come to her senses before any unfortunate action is taken. However, there is a risk, and you should be aware of that. If her Majesty continues to refuse to see reason, then violence may ensue. I desire peace, but I will not hesitate to fight for what is right. The throne of the Empire does not belong to a single family, no matter where that family originates. The throne belongs to all of the nations, and it deserves better than to be hoarded by Empress Bridget's offspring, as if it were a possession. We are the Empire, and the Empire is us.'

The Matriarch sat back in her throne, her eyes dark. Behind her, several of her courtiers looked desperate to say something, but no one opened their mouths.

'I shall need to consult with my trusted advisors,' the Matriarch said, after some time had passed. 'Remain here. Refreshments will be brought to you.'

The Matriarch stood, and strode out through the doorway. Her courtiers hurried to follow her, and the doors were closed.

Thorn sat.

'Well done,' said Daphne.

'I'm not sure it was enough,' Thorn said. 'I forgot to mention the gifts we brought.'

'You covered the important points.' She turned to her daughter. 'Keep an eye on things, dear. The next few minutes will be crucial.'

'I'll watch what's going on,' said Karalyn.

'Be ready to intervene, if it looks as though they might decide to be hostile. Some of the Matriarch's advisors could be counselling her to hold us here as prisoners, or send us to the Empress in chains.'

Agang shook his head. 'They wouldn't dream of doing that.'

'I admire your confidence,' said Daphne, 'but after what happened in Rakana, I'm taking no chances. Why do you think we brought Karalyn along? It wasn't for her negotiating skills – it was in case we needed to flee in a hurry.'

'What will happen if they refuse to support Thorn's claim?' said Caelius. 'Without Sanang, the Holdings will be isolated.'

'There are a few options; none of which are appealing,' said Daphne. 'We could back down, and accept Lord Bryce as successor, or we could try to pull the Holdings out of the empire. It would become the main political argument of next year's election. Ultimately, the voters of the Holdings would decide.'

'Colsbury would no longer be safe for the Holdfasts if we lose,' said Karalyn. 'I would consider withdrawing from this world altogether.'

Daphne frowned at her daughter. 'Really? And where do you suggest we go?'

Karalyn shrugged. 'Dragon Eyre or the Salve City.'

'I will not leave this world,' said Thorn.

Karalyn glanced at her. 'Are you prepared to die for the throne?'

'I am.'

'Then you would be wasting your life.'

'In your opinion,' said Thorn, 'but I think that some things are more important than my life. If we fled, then we would be reviled, and then forgotten. I would rather be a martyr for what is right. If it comes to it, I will hold my head high on the gallows, knowing that I had justice on my side.'

Karalyn rolled her eyes.

'You voted for Thorn, dear,' said Daphne.

'I know,' said Karalyn, 'and I also stood up to the Empress when I handed over our proclamation. I told her that she was wrong to her face. But that doesn't mean that I think we should burn this world to the ground over a point of principle. Bridget asked me where our army was, and I had no answer. We would have to use mage powers to kill the soldiers of the imperial army; unleash Thorn, Keir, Sable, and Corthie, too. We would end up as the most hated people on this world. The Holdfast tyrants overthrow the beloved and popular Empress Bridget. Is that what we want?'

Daphne glared at her. She was about to respond when the doors opened, and a line of young men and women entered, bearing wooden platters. They queued up in front of the tables where the Holdfasts were sitting, and set the platters down, bowing their heads as they did so. Daphne and Thorn smiled at them, then the young Sanang servants departed, and the doors were closed again.

'What have we here?' said Daphne. 'Coffee, honey and chocolate cakes, smoked meat. There's enough to feed a few dozen people.' She picked up a coffee urn, and began pouring the hot black liquid into a row of small cups.

Caelius glanced at a tray of smokesticks. 'They've given us cigarettes?'

'There's no tobacco in those,' said Daphne. 'I would recommend holding back, unless you wish to spend the next few hours in a dreamweed daze.'

Agang placed a few weedsticks into a pocket. 'For Shella,' he said, when the others glanced at him.

The doors opened again, and Mage Aberfeld entered the chamber. He walked up to the Holdfasts, his eyes on Daphne.

'May I sit?'

Daphne gestured to a chair.

'Thank you, Holder Fast,' he said. He sat, and Daphne poured him a coffee. 'You have placed me into a rather tricky position,' he went on. 'I swore an oath to Empress Bridget, but I have also sworn oaths to the Republic of the Holdings. Whatever I do, I will be breaking my word.'

'I understand,' said Daphne. 'Therefore, you must do what you think is right.'

Aberfeld gave a grim chuckle. 'If only it was so easy.'

'How are the negotiations progressing?' said Thorn.

'The Matriarch is saying nothing,' said Aberfeld. 'She's listening to her advisors; asking them each in turn for their opinion. I excused myself. What was I supposed to say? A few of her advisors appear to be suggesting that they should ask for concessions.'

'What sort of concessions?' said Thorn.

'Trade and tax, mostly,' he said. 'Some of them seem to think that they should demand a massive cut in imperial taxes, in exchange for their support for you, Lady Thorn.'

'I'm afraid that is out of the question,' said Thorn. 'The Holdings government agreed to support my claim without requiring a crude bribe. If I were to offer these concessions to Sanang, then the Holdings would, understandably, be rather irked.'

Aberfeld nodded. 'I'm glad to hear that, my lady. However, to save face, the Matriarch will probably ask for something in return for her support. She has two younger brothers, both of whom have found it difficult to live in their sister's shadow. The Matriarch has been considering what to do with them for some time, and I suspect she may request that you allow them into your imperial court, my lady.'

Daphne smiled. 'Did you really excuse yourself, or did the Matriarch ask you to come here to sound us out?'

Aberfeld smiled. 'The two aren't mutually exclusive, ma'am.'

'I would be happy to allow close relatives of the Matriarch into my court,' said Thorn. 'Their presence would certainly give the Great Fortress a flavour of Sanang. However, I cannot guarantee that I will assign them positions of authority. I would need to reflect upon that.'

'I understand, my lady,' said Aberfeld. 'Might I ask – who would be your Herald of the Empire?'

'I would offer the position to Holder Fast.'

'And I would accept such an offer,' said Daphne; 'but only for a few years, until the new regime has found its feet.'

'I have one further question,' said Aberfeld. 'If the Matriarch lends her support to Lady Thorn, and the Empress mobilises for war, how would you respond? Is there a secret army lying within the Holdings, ready to defend your claim?'

Daphne shook her head. 'The Holdings has no army.'

Aberfeld sighed. 'It is as I thought. Holder Fast, while you may indeed be right about the legalities of the imperial succession, without an armed force at our disposal, our chances of success seem rather remote.'

'We have Karalyn,' said Daphne. 'You know what she did to Agatha's soldiers.'

Aberfeld glanced down, then took a sip of coffee. Karalyn looked ready to say something, her eyes tightening, but Daphne shook her head at her daughter.

Aberfeld got to his feet. 'Please excuse me. I shall see how things are with the Matriarch.'

The Holdings mage bowed then strode from the chamber.

'Can we trust him?' said Caelius.

'I think so,' said Daphne.

'Don't use my name like that, mother,' said Karalyn. 'I am not your weapon.'

'Perhaps not,' said Daphne, 'but you are a formidable deterrent. I will say this to you again – do not go to Implacatus. Send Sable, by all means. Send others with her, if you feel she requires support – but do not leave this world. Without you, we are vulnerable.'

'We've gone over this, mother.'

'And yet you still won't listen.'

Karalyn lit a cigarette and turned away, her eyes dark.

Daphne sighed, and selected a chocolate-covered honey and nut cake from a tray. If they had to wait, then at least they would eat well.

After several hours of sitting inside the meeting chamber, courtiers arrived to escort them upstairs to a set of rooms that had been prepared for them. Agang seemed excited to show them his old home, but there was a bitterness, too, that what he had worked so hard to build was now in the hands of someone else. More food was brought up to them, along with thick, sweet mead, but Daphne abstained, preferring to keep a clear head. Lamps were lit as the sun set in the west, then Karalyn, Thorn and Agang retired to bed, while Daphne and Caelius sat out on a balcony, watching the lights of the town of Broadwater in front of them.

'Is the whole of Sanang forested?' he asked.

'Almost,' said Daphne. 'The Mya region lost half of its trees in the Holdings invasions, and is now predominately farmland, thanks to Agang's stewardship.'

'I imagine that this country would be difficult to invade.'

Daphne smiled. 'Easy to invade; difficult to occupy.'

'Would the Empress send her troops here?'

'More likely, she would seal the borders. There's an old wall where Sanang meets the Plateau; just as there is on the frontiers of Rakana. The Empress would concentrate on the Holdings, I think, while ensuring that contact between my homeland and Sanang was impossible.'

Caelius kept his gaze on the dark forests beyond the limits of the town. 'Is it worth it?'

'I believe it is, Caelius. We might lose, but I would rather fight than meekly submit to Bridget's will.'

'The Ascendants would be laughing, if they knew how this world was on the verge of tearing itself to pieces.'

'Do you think I'm making a mistake?'

'Perhaps, although I cannot see the alternative. Whatever happens, I will stand by you.'

Daphne smiled. 'Even if we are forced to flee to Dragon Eyre?'

'At least I am familiar with that world. Or, I was, before Sable's recent campaign. If there are plenty of stranded Banner soldiers there, I might even feel at home.'

Daphne's eyes widened. 'Damn it; of course.'

Caelius glanced at her.

'Sable said that there were close to two hundred thousand Banner soldiers stuck on Dragon Eyre.'

Caelius nodded. 'Yes, she did say that.'

'Presumably,' Daphne went on, 'the native inhabitants would be pleased if someone were to remove those soldiers?'

'Indeed,' said Caelius. 'The men and women of the Banners will be hungry and desperate. Their contracts will have expired by now, but they'll have no way to get home.'

'So,' she said, 'we have a cause, but no army, while on Dragon Eyre there is an army with no cause?'

Caelius narrowed his eyes. 'What are you suggesting, ma'am?'

'Nothing. It's just an idea. And there's no need to call me 'ma'am', Caelius. I think we're beyond that now. You are my friend.'

The veteran nodded. 'I would like to be more than friends, Daphne.'

Daphne glanced at him. She was attracted to Caelius, but did she have time for what he was suggesting? Wasn't her life complicated enough? She realised that she had hesitated for too long with her response. Caelius nodded, and looked away.

'I'm sorry, Caelius,' she said. 'I can't think about this right now. I'm not saying no, but I am saying not now.'

There was a gentle tap on the balcony door as Caelius was about to reply.

'Forgive the interruption,' said Mage Aberfeld. 'The Matriarch would like to see you alone, Holder Fast.'

Daphne stood, and took a breath. 'I am at the Matriarch's service.'

'Follow me, please,' said the mage, and Daphne strode from the balcony. Aberfeld led her up a flight of stairs, and they entered the Matriarch's private suite of rooms. The young leader of Sanang was reclining on a long couch, surrounded by her courtiers. She smiled when she saw Daphne approach, and raised a hand to quieten the chatter.

Daphne bowed her head. 'Matriarch.'

'Holder Fast,' she said. 'Thank you for coming at this late hour. Are your rooms comfortable?'

'Your hospitality has been generous.'

The Matriarch smiled again, though her eyes remained sharp. 'Excellent. Now, I don't think we need to spend any more time on pleasantries. I asked you here to tell you the outcome of our deliberations. You have placed the Matriarchy of Sanang into an impossible situation, Holder Fast. We will be damned by half of the world no matter what I decide. The easy route would be to side with the Empress; she has the soldiers, and the gold. However, I long for a Sanang to become Empress. For too long my people have been looked down upon by the other nations of this world. We are seen as backward, as barely-literate savages; useful only for the goods that flow from our forests into the homes of those who live on the Plateau.'

'I will not lie to you, Matriarch. That is indeed how some people see the Sanang. However, I am not one of those people. I understand the potential that Sanang has to offer. If you were to raise an army, and train your soldiers with care, then Sanang would never be conquered.'

'If I support Thorn, will it come to war?'

'I cannot answer that. However, we must be prepared for such an eventuality.'

'If I raise an army, will the Holdings do the same?'

'Yes.'

'And the Holdings troopers currently serving within the imperial army – would they come over to our side?'

'Some might decide to; but others will remain loyal to the Empress.'

The Matriarch shook her head. 'It doesn't sound as though we can win this fight.'

'What if I were to tell you that another army exists? A well-trained, highly-disciplined force that could alter the balance of power on this world?'

'Then I would question your sanity, Holder Fast. What army are you talking about? The Empire has been most efficient in denying the nations their own armed forces. All Holdings and Kellach recruits work directly for the Empress, while Rahain lies in ruins. Sanang and Rakana possess small militias, but nothing that could possibly threaten the imperial forces. Even if I were to mobilise an army of my own, I would be fortunate to gather ten thousand soldiers, compared to the hundreds of thousands who fill the ranks of the imperial army. So, where is this secret army?'

Daphne smiled. 'Not on this world, Matriarch.'

A few of the courtiers glanced at each other.

'If I support you,' said the Matriarch, 'can you guarantee that this new army will be under your control?'

Daphne hesitated for a split second, then nodded. 'Yes.'

'Very well,' said the Matriarch. 'Holder Fast, you shall have the support of Sanang. I recognise Thorn of Greyfalls Deepen's claim to the imperial succession. A Sanang shall sit on the throne of this world.' She looked Daphne in the eye. 'And in return for my support, you, Holder Fast, shall supply the army.'

Daphne bowed her head. 'Thank you.'

'You may now leave my presence,' said the Matriarch. 'Sleep well.'

Daphne bowed again, then backed out of the chamber, her head spinning. What had she just promised? She made her way back down to the rooms that had been set aside for the Holdfasts, and found Caelius still on the balcony. She sat, and picked up a weedstick from a little tray.

'We're in business,' she said to Caelius, as she lit the weedstick. 'All we need to do now is work out how to transport two hundred thousand Banner soldiers here from Dragon Eyre.'

CHAPTER 6
WITH THE HOLDFASTS

Colsbury Castle, Republic of the Holdings – 5th Day, Last Third Summer 534

'Bark like a dog!'

Sable laughed. 'No thanks, Kyra; I don't think I will.'

The girl glared at Sable. 'I said – bark like a dog!'

Sable felt the suggestion roll through her senses. It was powerful, but nowhere near as powerful as Karalyn's skills, and Sable was able to shrug it off.

'How are you doing that?' said Shella. 'How are you able to resist the twins?'

'It's not fair,' said Cael.

'Life isn't fair,' said Sable, lighting a cigarette. 'Deal with it, little person.'

Shella chuckled. 'Your way with children leaves a lot to be desired.'

'You're one to talk,' said Sable. 'What time did you crawl out of bed this morning?'

'Agang is usually here to cure my hangovers. Don't tell him this, but I actually miss the ape.'

'Is anyone going to do our lesson today?' said Cael.

'Read my mind, and you'll see the answer to that,' said Sable, putting her feet up onto the table.

'So, they can read your mind?' said Shella.

'Oh, yes. They could probably scour it, too,' said Sable; 'if they were angry enough. The only thing they can't do to me is persuade me to bark like a dog, or anything like that. It must be because I share that particular power. It probably won't last, though; they'll get stronger as they get older.'

'Can you read their minds?'

'No. They're as closed to me as Karalyn or Kelsey. But, why would I want to read the minds of a pair of seven-year-olds? Do they know how to get to Dragon Eyre?' She glanced at the twins. 'Go and annoy Keir. Shella and I are nursing our hangovers.'

Cael glanced at his sister, then back at Sable. 'What can we eat?'

'Whatever you like,' said Sable. 'But, if you're sick, you'll have to clean it up on your own.'

The twins grinned and ran away.

'Karalyn's going to freak out when she gets back,' said Shella.

'Why?'

'Well, you haven't done any lessons for the children, and they've eaten enough chocolate to rot all their teeth.'

'So?'

Shella raised an eyebrow. 'I guess I'm not used to having to be the responsible adult. Karalyn and Agang are so serious, and as for Daphne? She hasn't relaxed in thirty years.'

'I can be responsible,' said Sable, 'but I don't feel like it this morning. Dragon Eyre is still occupying nearly all of my thoughts. What I lost there, and what is still waiting for me. It haunts me – all of it. I was an avenging god, and now I'm sitting here, looking after Karalyn's kids. I must be the most over-qualified childminder in history.'

'You're certainly not the most modest. Kelsey had to do it, too, you know; when Karalyn was searching for Daimon. She didn't like it, either.'

'I don't blame her. Is that all we are to Karalyn – babysitters? Kelsey and I could bring Implacatus to its knees, especially if she brought her dragon.'

'Karalyn said that you had a dragon, too. What happened to it?'

'He wasn't an "it", Shella. He...' She paused, finding it hard to put her feelings into words. 'I loved him, more than I've loved anyone else. Why do you think I went a little crazy on Dragon Eyre?'

'Was he killed?'

'Yes. By a god.'

'Did you get the god who did it?'

Sable nodded. 'I scraped his brains off the sole of my boot.'

'And you want to go back to this place?'

'Yes. I also have an ulterior motive for wanting to visit Implacatus; one that doesn't involve slaughtering gods or rescuing Belinda. I left a friend there. I was supposed to return to collect him, but I was captured by dragons.'

'Does Karalyn know about this?'

'I don't know. I mean, I haven't told her, but she could read it out of my mind if she chose to.'

'I don't think that's how Karalyn operates. When she first moved to Colsbury, I assumed that she would be in my head whenever she felt like it. It took me a while to realise that she wasn't remotely interested in reading my thoughts.' She glanced at Sable. 'I suppose it would be too much to expect the same from you?'

Sable smiled, but said nothing. She withdrew the Quadrant from a deep pocket and gazed at its surface.

'I could go to Implacatus any time I wanted,' she said. 'I even considered collecting my friend, with or without Karalyn's permission. But then it occurred to me – if I brought him back, I would have to bring him here, and with his powers, Karalyn would enrol him in the operation to find Belinda. Within a few days of his rescue, he would be heading back to Implacatus.'

'Is your friend a god?'

'Yes. Well, a demigod. His mother is a mortal. He has flow powers, like you, and also healing powers. He was an extremely useful accomplice. I guess he's safer where he is, for the moment at least. I just hope he forgives me when I finally turn up.'

'It sounds like there's a long list of people you hope will forgive you.'

'It's the story of my life, Shella. I hurt everyone I touch. Sometimes, I don't even mean to, but it happens all the same. Look at Karalyn; she hasn't forgiven me for Lennox, and probably never will.'

Shella shook her head. 'You don't deserve to be forgiven for that. You are exceedingly lucky that she's good-natured enough to let you keep your life. As for me, I still haven't forgiven you for what you did to Silverstream.'

'It was the Army of Pyre who destroyed Silverstream. I was merely there when it happened. Does anyone ever ask if Lennox should be forgiven for that? He was there, too.'

'You remind me of Keir. Is anything ever your fault, Sable?'

'Rainsby was my fault; capturing Thorn and burning down the hospital – all me. Killing Nyane – me again. Capturing Kelsey and Ravi – yes, that was me, too. Sending soldiers dressed as civilians into the marketplaces of Plateau City to cause carnage – all my idea. But I had nothing to do with Silverstream. Agatha broke her Quadrant, and they wanted a diamond mage to try to fix it for them. I'm going to tell you something else, something that I've never told anyone before. I could have won the war for Agatha. When the marines stormed Stretton Sands, Lennox and I were in the harbour, watching the ships come in. I ordered Lennox to destroy the fleet, and he refused. I could have forced him to do it, but I didn't. If Stretton Sands had held out that day, I would have taken Lennox and Thorn to Rahain, and presented them as a gift to Agatha. But I took a decision, and didn't force Lennox to burn the ships. That led Agatha to suspect me of treachery, and I realised then what her plan was; and I fled. It would be nice to occasionally be given credit for what I didn't do, as well as blamed for everything I've done.'

'Why didn't you do it? Why didn't you force Lennox to burn the ships?'

'I felt sorry for him. He was a mess after Rainsby; a pitiful mess. It might have broken his mind. I experienced a twinge of guilt, and then the moment passed, and we had to run for it. I was so angry with myself that a few minutes later I murdered Thorn's best friend for talking too loudly. Not my proudest moment.'

'You might be the most fucked-up person I've ever met, Sable.'

Sable smiled. She wondered why she found it easy to talk to Shella. There was something about the Rakanese mage – she was curious but non-judgemental.

'You've known my sister for a long time, haven't you?'

'Are you calling her that now?' said Shella. 'I remember when you used to be disgusted by your association with the Holdfasts. Anyway, yes is the answer. I met Daffers when she was pregnant with Karalyn. She was sick, day and night, for thirds. We hated each other, but it was a long journey from Akhanawarah to Plateau City and, by the end of it, we were friends. You know, she may not like you very much, but she respects you. You've proved how ruthless you can be, and Daffers can't help but admire that. Are you going to support her with the whole Thorn thing?'

'She hasn't asked me to.'

'And if she did?'

'I have another life waiting for me on Dragon Eyre.'

'A life of slaughter?'

'Yes, but also, just maybe, a life of love. The woman I want to be with is there.'

'A woman, eh?'

'Yes. Is that a problem?'

'No. I didn't know that you preferred women, that's all.'

'I don't; not necessarily. It's individuals I'm attracted to. Lara understands me, and accepts me for who I am. Nothing really scares me, but I'm a little nervous that she might have moved on. I haven't seen her in over five months.'

'I noticed Kelsey and Corthie talk about months as well. It's like you exiles have your own secret little language. So, what if you bring this Lara back here?'

Sable laughed. 'You sound as though you want me to stay.'

'Maybe I do. Maybe I think that you being here is good for Daffers. There were two seats at the head of the table when we voted for Thorn. Daffers was in one, and who did she choose for the other? Not Thorn, or any of her children. She chose you. If you return to Dragon Eyre, and never come back, then I think that she will miss you more than she could ever admit.'

Sable stubbed out her cigarette. 'I think you're exaggerating.'

'I know her better than anyone, Sable. She rarely speaks about her feelings, but I notice the little signs. I saw the effect it had on her when you swooped in and rescued us from Rakana. She was in pieces. You are the little sister that she never had. Her deranged, crazy, ruthless little sister who takes no shit from anybody.' Shella got to her feet. 'Anyway, I'm going for a hot bath, to try to wash this hangover off. Don't kill Keir while I'm away, yeah?'

'I can't guarantee it.'

Sable watched as Shella stumbled her way out of the room, then she stretched her arms. She sent out her vision, and checked on the twins. She couldn't sense their presence, but was able to see them by looking into each room. They were playing in their bedroom. Well, thought Sable, "playing" was a loose term. The twins seemed to have emptied the contents of their cupboards onto the bedroom floor, and were making a mess of gargantuan proportions. Sable shifted her vision along the hallway, then looked in on Keir. He was sitting by a table, his gaze on the view through a window. Next to him was a full ashtray, and several empty cups of coffee.

Hey, Keir, she said in his head.

What do you want, Sable?

Go and play with the twins. Show them that you aren't a complete arse-hole. Oh, and make them tidy their room while you're there; Karalyn's due back today.

Fuck off.

Sable flooded his mind with her powers. *Do what I say, Keir. Do it now; there's a good boy.*

She watched as Keir stood, his mind unable to resist her persuasive powers, then she got to her feet. She walked out of the living room and entered the Sextant chamber. The huge device was sitting in silence, Karalyn having removed the Weathervane prior to departing for Sanang. Sable crouched by the side of the Sextant, and examined the various slots and gaps. She saw where the Weathervane needed to go for the device to work, and tried placing her own Quadrant into a few places. She noticed the other Quadrant, but left it where it was. It belonged to Karalyn, and was none of her business. Her thoughts turned back to Lara. It occurred to Sable that perhaps she no longer cared about exterminating the fanatics of the Unk Tannic. Lara was the reason she wanted to go back to Dragon Eyre, so maybe Shella had made a good point. She sat, and leaned her back against the Sextant. Would Lara consider living on the Star Continent? Did Sable want to live there? Dragon Eyre held so many bad memories; did she really desire to relive them? But, if she stayed on the Star Continent, she would be consumed by the Holdfasts. There would be no way to avoid the looming struggle between the Empress on one side, and Daphne on the other. She tried to imagine what it would feel like to be loyal to her half-sister, to take Daphne's orders, and obey them.

She heard a yell of pain come from somewhere on the same floor of the Great Keep, and got back to her feet. She followed the sounds until she came to the twins' bedroom, and pushed open the door. Keir was writhing on the untidy floor, his hands covering his ears, and his eyes clenched shut. Next to him, the twins were standing, and Kyra had a finger pointed at his head.

Sable glared at Cael and Kyra. 'Release him now,' she said in a firm voice.

'But Keir was being mean,' said Cael.

'Then you should have come and told me or Aunty Shella,' said Sable. 'You have five seconds to let him go. Five, four, three...'

Kyra lowered her hand, and Keir's cries ceased. He gasped, and opened his eyes. He glanced at the twins, and began to shuffle backwards as fear crossed his face.

'They're evil,' he sobbed; 'pure evil, like their mother.'

'They're children, Keir,' said Sable. She crouched by Kyra. 'What you did was wrong. I want you to say sorry to Uncle Keir.'

'No.'

'Say sorry, Kyra, or you will be in serious trouble. I'm not joking. Believe me; you don't want to make me angry.'

Kyra shuddered, then lowered her eyes. 'Sorry.'

Sable turned to Keir. 'You too. Tell the twins that you're sorry.'

'What? I'm not apologising to those little maniacs. They were trying to scour my mind! They're dangerous.'

Say that you are sorry, or you'll see how dangerous I can be.

Keir's expression changed in an instant. His lower lip started to tremble, and his eyes welled.

'I'm sorry,' he said.

Sable smiled as she stood. 'Excellent. Now, twins, you have an hour to tidy your room. I want it spotless, with all of your clothes and toys cleared away in their proper places. And I will check, so do it properly. Once you've done that, you can go outside and play. Keir, come with me.'

The two adults left the room, and Sable closed the door. She turned, and headed towards the roof. After a few paces, she noticed that Keir wasn't following her, so she turned and gave him a look. His shoulders sagged, and he went after her. They climbed the stairs, and came out onto the roof of the keep.

'Why have you dragged me up here?' said Keir.

'I think it's time we had a chat, nephew.'

'What about?'

'About why you have decided to destroy your life. I know about Tilda Holdwain, and I know a lot more besides. Your mother would kill you if she found out, so why are you doing it?'

'You don't know me.'

'You're intelligent, handsome, and an extremely powerful mage. How old are you?'

'Twenty-five.'

'You should know better, Keir; you're not a child. So why do you act like one?'

'Shut up, Sable.'

'What do you want from life?'

'That's none of your business.'

Sable nodded. She knew she probably shouldn't intervene, but she was curious to see how far she could push him.

Relax, she said in his mind. *You can speak to me. You trust me, and want to tell me everything. Let it all out, and that's an order.*

'Do you like being in Colsbury?' she said.

Keir shook his head. 'I hate it. It's obvious that no one likes me. I'm treated like an outcast.'

'Your mother loves you.'

Keir snorted. 'Even wicked mothers love their children.'

'Where would you rather be?'

'On the Hold Fast estate; but Celine is now training that bitch Jemma to take over as estate manager, when the job was supposed to be mine.'

Sable nodded. 'Why do you think Jemma is a bitch?'

'Because she refuses to let me spend any time with Cole – my own son. And no one does anything about it. It's so unfair.'

'I see. Do you want to spend more time with Cole? You don't seem to enjoy spending time with the twins.'

'The twins hate me. Is it any wonder that I don't want to be around them? But now Cole hates me too.' He started to sob. 'The family think I'm nothing but a failure.'

Sable raised an eyebrow. 'Have you spoken to your wife about this?'

'Thorn doesn't love me any more,' he said, as tears streamed down his cheeks. 'She actually told me that. She threatened to tell mother about Tilda if I tried to divorce her. The Holdfast women are witches, and Corthie's too stupid to see it. Even Kelsey has turned against me; she used to be so loyal, like a little puppy that followed me around. Everything is Karalyn's fault; if she hadn't scoured my mind when I was a baby, then I wouldn't be this way. One day, I'm going to make her pay for what she did.'

'Perhaps you should stop blaming other people for your problems. No one forced you to sleep with Tilda Holdwain.'

'I want out of this family. The Holdfasts are suffocating me. I hate them.'

Sable leaned on the rooftop parapet, her gaze on the tear-shaped lake before them. Keir's expression changed, and he glanced at Sable with suspicion in his eyes.

'I don't know why I said all that. You're not even a proper Holdfast; you're illegitimate. You're a Blackhold, Sable.'

'I wanted to see if I could fix you, Keir.'

'Fix me? What are you talking about? You're the one who's broken.'

'Yes, I suppose I am. The thing is, though, I don't really care. I jump into things without thinking them through, much as you did with Tilda.'

'Are you comparing the two of us?' he said. 'I am nothing like you.'

'I realise that now. I own my mistakes.' She glanced at him. 'This conversation was one of them.'

Keir snorted, turned, and strode away. Sable turned back to the view. The sun was high in the sky, and a light breeze was causing the surface of the lake to ripple, distorting the reflection of the mountains. She tried to sympathise with Keir, but the only thing they had in common was their family name, and the fact that neither felt they belonged in Colsbury. She adored Kelsey and Corthie, and had a grudging respect and admiration for Karalyn, but Keir was like none of them. If treated carelessly, he might turn out to be a bigger enemy to the Holdfasts than Bridget or Daimon. She wondered if she should mention any of her concerns to Daphne, but what could she say? Excuse me, Daphne, but I think your son might be a danger to the Holdfasts? Daphne would be unlikely to keep her temper at such a suggestion. It would be better to say nothing; it would be better to pretend that their conversation had never taken place.

Sable closed the door of the twins' bedroom. She had told them a bedtime story about dragons and pirates, tucked them up in bed, and turned off the lamp. It had taken an hour of stubborn persistence to make them tidy their room, but Sable had refused to back down and, in the end, they had obeyed her.

She exhaled as she walked down the quiet hallway, marvelling at Thorn's resilience to have cared for Kyra and Cael for four years. In two days, they had tested Sable's patience to its limits, and she was feeling very happy that she had decided not to have children of her own. She came to the entrance to the living room, and saw Shella sleeping on a couch, her gentle snores echoing with the rise and fall of her chest. Sable frowned. With Shella asleep, the twins in bed, and Keir brooding on his own, Colsbury seemed enormous, quiet, and empty. She felt a tremor of anxiety pass through her. She needed company; otherwise, she would start to dwell on the things she had done in Dragon Eyre. Her mind flashed to an image of a young Banner soldier about to strike the explosive device strapped to his chest with a hammer, and she almost flinched. She paced the halls for a while, unsure what to do, the silence sounding louder in her mind than the roar of a hundred dragons burning Port Edmond to the ground.

She found herself back in the Sextant chamber, and wondered if her feet had unconsciously led her there. She lit a lamp, then placed her palm onto the surface of the dormant device.

'Lara,' she said; 'I know you can't hear me, but I miss you. I'm trying, I really am, but I feel so alone, surrounded by nothing but memories. It's not the Holdfasts; they have actually been kinder to me than I thought, but it's so hard to do this without you. I feel crushed by the weight of everything that I've done, and by everything that I'm still expected to do. Wait for me, that's all I ask. Don't give up on me, not yet.'

'What are you doing, Sable?'

She turned, and saw Karalyn standing by the doorway.

'Nothing,' she said. 'Just wishing Lara was here.'

'We need to talk.'

'Do we?'

'Aye, about my mother's latest insane idea. And about Implacatus.'

Sable placed a hand on her hip. 'I'm ready to go when you are.'

'Are the children in bed?'

'Yes.'

'Were they any trouble?'

'No. It was fine. They had Keir squirming about on the floor earlier today, but I'm pretty sure he deserved it. I made Kyra apologise.'

Karalyn nodded. 'Thanks for looking after them.' She frowned. 'You... um...'

'Yes?'

'Are you really feeling alone?'

'Do you care?'

'It's just that I've never seen you like that before. The way you were speaking, I mean.'

Sable walked out of the room. 'Then, you shouldn't have been listening.'

Karalyn followed her into a small study. Sable opened a drawer in a desk and pulled out a half-full bottle of Holdings rum. She filled a glass, then glanced at Karalyn, who nodded. Sable got another glass, poured a measure, then slid it across the table to Karalyn.

They sat. Karalyn seemed uncomfortable with the silence, but Sable said nothing.

'The trip to Sanang went well,' Karalyn said.

'That's good.'

'Of course, I offered to bring the others back with me, but they insisted on travelling overland to Mya.'

Sable lit a cigarette.

'So,' Karalyn went on, 'I was thinking that we should get the whole Implacatus thing over with before my mother and the others have time to get back to Colsbury.'

'I'm not sure you should leave the twins with only Shella and Keir here to look after them.'

'I don't intend to. First though, I wanted to tell you about my mother's idea. You are aware that we don't have an army to oppose the Empress?'

'Yes.'

'Well, she remembered something you said, about thousands of Banner soldiers being stranded on Dragon Eyre. Mother wants me to use the Sextant to…'

'Stop right there,' said Sable. 'You were right. This plan is insane.'

'You didn't let me finish.'

'I didn't need to; it's obvious. Daphne wants to hire two hundred thousand Banner soldiers to fight her war for her. There are several problems with that, the largest of which is that those Banner soldiers were fighting me – a damn Holdfast. Does Daphne believe that they'll suddenly decide to work for us? I killed tens of thousands of Banner soldiers, Karalyn. They all know my name.'

'Caelius doesn't think that's a problem. He said that Banner soldiers don't care about politics, as long as their contract is fair. Lucius Cardova mentioned something similar to me. Caelius believes that if we went to Dragon Eyre, and talked to the Banner soldiers, we could persuade many of them to sign up. We would also be doing Dragon Eyre a tremendous favour, by removing so many disgruntled, unemployed soldiers from their midst. Mother thinks you would be perfect for this job.'

'Me?'

'You have plenty of experience of Dragon Eyre, and you're a Holdfast.'

'Those are precisely the reasons why the Banner soldiers there hate me. And I would like to point out that I am already doing you a favour by helping rescue Belinda. You told me that once I had done that, then I would be free to return to Dragon Eyre, but not to enlist Banner soldiers.'

'Mother hopes that you'll stay here, and help Thorn's claim to the throne.'

Sable laughed. 'Does she, indeed? Why?'

'Don't be like that, Sable. You know why.'

'Do I? Enlighten me.'

'You're her sister.'

'So?'

'Does that mean nothing to you?'

Sable rubbed her face, a hand shielding her eyes from Karalyn's gaze.

'Are you a Holdfast or not, Sable?'

Sable said nothing.

'This family means nothing to you, does it? You're just as selfish as you've always been.'

'You have no idea what you're talking about,' Sable cried. 'You, Daphne, none of you understand what it's been like for me, stranded on Lostwell, then going slowly crazy on Dragon Eyre. If only you could have heard the times I called out for you to help me; the times I lay dying, begging for my sister to come to my rescue.' She started to cry, sobs wracking her body. 'I knew you couldn't hear me; I knew it was stupid, but you and Daphne were the only people I believed in. You gave me strength, even though you didn't know it. I kept thinking, if only I could make it back to the Star Continent, then I would be able to tell you how sorry I was, and how I regretted every stupid decision I've made; and then everything would be all right. I'm so sorry, Karalyn, for what I did to Lennox. It was the worst thing I've ever done, and the guilt eats me up every day. I ruined your life as well as his, and I can never make it better, no matter what I do. When I lost Badblood, I thought my life would end; I wanted it to end, but I was too cowardly to go through with it. I couldn't do it, not until I had asked you for forgiveness. But you'll never forgive me, will you? You hate me, and I don't blame you.'

She put her head in her hands and wept. A hand touched her shoulder.

'I don't hate you, Sable.'

Sable glanced up, and saw that Karalyn was also crying.

'I miss Lennox so much, it tears my insides,' Karalyn said, 'but I know that you're sorry, Sable. I believe you. I forgive you.'

'I don't deserve to be forgiven.'

'Who does? You know what I did. I slaughtered a hundred thousand Rahain while they slept in their beds.'

Sable nodded, and wiped her eyes.

'No one in this family is blameless, Sable Holdfast,' said Karalyn. 'All we have is each other.'

CHAPTER 7
THE STORMS OF SWEETMIST

Jezra, The Western Bank – 10th Namen 3423

The rain ran down the streets of Jezra, submerging the cobbles and paving slabs like a network of little streams. Above the damp buildings, the thick black clouds of Sweetmist crackled and boomed with thunder, the occasional sheets of lightning illuminating the town in eerie flashes, before it was swallowed back up into the shadows.

Kelsey gazed at the view from the window of the Command Centre as the rain battered off the thin pane of glass. Down in the harbour, every ship was tightly lashed to the quayside. The masts and sails had been removed and then stored in a squat brick warehouse by the ruined shoreline, along with anything else that couldn't be tied down, as the waves from the Straits crashed against the ancient settlement.

The humidity was oppressive, and Kelsey wiped a bead of sweat from her forehead with the sleeve of her tunic. She had taken a cold shower that morning, after she had awoken drenched in perspiration, and felt as though she needed another one.

'Are you missing home?' said Van, walking up to her.

'I am home, you numpty,' she said.

He put his arm round her waist and they kissed.

'I'm happy to hear you say that,' he said. 'I was worried that you wouldn't want to come back, especially knowing that Sweetmist was on the way.'

'I'd forgotten what month it was,' she said. 'When I left the Holdings, it was still summer; it was only when I got back that I realised it was only a few days before the rains were due to start. Maybe we should have chosen Tara for Sweetmist. I miss the mansion on Princeps Row.'

'We spent so long in Tara, it was time to give some attention to Jezra again,' he said, 'but I know what you mean. The facilities here are a little... basic, compared to what we were becoming used to in Tara. What are your plans for today? Are you going to brave the weather to visit Frostback?'

'No. She's pretty grumpy about the rain. If anyone's missing the Holdings, it's her. She loved the desert – it brought out her inner lazy dragon. She spent almost every hour of daylight basking in the sunshine. No; today I'm going to work on Mona's research again, which means hours of trying to decipher and transcribe her terrible handwriting. You would think a demigod would be able to write neatly; I mean, they've had centuries of practice. Do you think I could get some coal?'

'What for?'

'So I can try to recreate one of the experiments in her notes. Burn the coal, heat the water, and make the piston move the wheel. I only need a few tons.'

Van laughed. 'You do realise how tightly rationed coal is? I can't justify diverting that much, not when winter's on its way. If the dragons are able to locate a new source of coal when the rains clear, you can take as much as you like. But, until then, heating the homes of the citizens is the priority.'

Kelsey frowned. 'I'm sick of all the shortages. Is there anything we aren't rationing?'

Van gazed out of the window. 'Water?'

'Aye, great. You know, my idea was a good one. I'm disappointed Emily didn't agree. The Star Continent has an abundance of everything the City lacks.'

'Her Majesty didn't disagree; she said she would give it her utmost consideration.'

'Aye, but I know what that means.'

'Think about it,' said Van. 'Who in the City knows how to use a Quadrant? There isn't exactly a great list of candidates. Should we release Naxor from prison, and hand him the Quadrant? We both know what would happen next. And maybe it's a little too early to trust Amalia with it. Besides, neither of them knows how to get to the Star Continent.'

'Karalyn could show them; well, she could show Amalia. I agree about Naxor.'

'And then, we have an even bigger problem.' Van said. 'Let's say that your plan works, and we end up with a Quadrant that can take us back and forward to your home world – what then? The Star Continent might have plenty to trade with us, but what do we have to offer in return? Greenhides?'

She narrowed her eyes at him. 'You know what I think.'

Van sighed. 'The King and Queen will never agree to trading salve, Kelsey. It's the very substance that we want to keep under control. The Ascendants are still searching for this world.'

'But Sable said...'

'I know what your aunt said. However, the truth is that no one on Implacatus knows what happened to Simon. The gods might well be scared of the Holdfasts, but none of them know that you're here. They might suspect it, after you showed up in Serene, but they don't know. As far as they're concerned, this world is still at the top of their list of targets. I imagine that supplies of salve are running perilously low on Implacatus by now, and the Ancients will be terrified that they will begin aging again. It's too much of a risk to start sending salve to other worlds.'

'So we'll have to live with these shortages forever?'

'Not forever. It will take time for the City to recover, but in a few years, the number of greenhides will start to decline on both sides of the City, and that will give us a chance to expand. There has to be more coal and iron on this world, along with everything else we need; we just have to be patient.'

Kelsey stared at the rain. 'I'm not a very patient person.'

'There are other ways we could spend the next few years.'

'Like what?'

'Like, maybe, children?'

Kelsey groaned.

'Fine,' said Van, his eyes tightening. 'Excuse me for bringing it up. Am I foolish to imagine that we might have children one day? Look at all we've been through; and I mean us, not the City. We've split up and got back together more times than I can remember, but now we've finally managed to make it work. Kelsey, I can't imagine being with anyone else for the rest of my life. I want to marry you. I want to start a family.'

'My mother would be very happy to hear you say that.'

'I don't care about your mother, Kelsey; it's not her I want to marry.'

'Your father might.'

'What my father does is his own business. To be honest, I'm glad he's found somewhere he can be content; the City was always too small for him. And, if he finds love there, I won't begrudge him that.'

'Aye, but it's too weird. Your father and my mother? Together? It makes me queasy.'

'Then don't think about it. Think about us. Do you want children?'

'I don't know. Maybe? I wouldn't be a very good parent.'

'We won't know that unless we try.'

'And if we're terrible at it, it will be too late.'

He smiled. 'We could have a little Van junior.'

'No. My mother would disown me if we ever named a child that. She has rules – the name of each Holdfast child has to sound as though they could be from Kell. Even Aila had to bow before my mother's demands when it came to naming her two kids. Caelius would work, though.'

'Then we name him after my father. If that's what it takes, Kelsey, I can compromise.'

The door to the small room opened, and Cardova walked in.

'Thank Pyre you're here, Lucius,' said Kelsey. 'Van was trying to persuade me to have children again.'

Cardova nodded, his expression downcast.

'Oh, come on, Lucius; you can't possibly still be angry with me.'

'I'm not angry,' he said.

'Right. You're clearly ecstatic to be back in the City.'

'Did you need me for something, Captain?' said Van.

Cardova stood to attention. 'No, sir. I came to see if you needed anything.'

'You're on leave, Captain,' said Van. 'You should be relaxing.'

'He can't relax,' said Kelsey. 'He's too busy day-dreaming about my sister.'

'Don't tease him,' said Van.

'Why not? It's the basis of our entire relationship. We insult each other; that's how it works.'

'I'm not in the mood, Kelsey,' said Cardova.

'Take a seat,' said Van.

'May I smoke, sir?'

Van nodded, and they sat around a low table in the centre of the room. Cardova pulled out a packet of cigarettes and lit one.

'What's troubling you, Lucius?' said Van.

Cardova shook his head. 'I feel conflicted, sir.'

'Don't call me sir. You're on leave. This is us being friends. Why are you conflicted?'

'I love the Banner; you know I do.'

'But?'

'I came very close to breaking my contract on Kelsey's world.'

'From what Kelsey has told me, Lucius, you performed with honour and professionalism. Are you sure it's not just Sweetmist getting you down?'

'It probably isn't helping, if I'm honest. The truth is, though, that if Karalyn had asked me to stay in Colsbury, then I might not have come back. The guilt is weighing on me, I guess.'

'Shit, Lucius,' said Kelsey. 'You've got it bad.'

'And you didn't help,' he said; 'telling her what I thought about her, just as she was about to leave. I had been completely discreet up to that point; but now she knows, and I feel like a fool. I still remember the look on her face when you told her.'

'The look she gave you was of shock, Lucius, not contempt. She was just surprised.'

'And then she vanished.' He snapped his fingers. 'Gone.'

'But she told us that she was coming back,' Kelsey went on. 'If she said that, then she will.'

'It would be better if she didn't.'

Kelsey rolled her eyes.

Cardova raised his glance towards Van. 'Might I request that the rest of my leave be cancelled? I need to work, to take my mind off everything that happened on the Star Continent. I would be happy with anything you need me to do.'

'Well,' said Van, 'the cellars under the main Exiles apartment blocks are flooding, and I have a team down there, removing everything before it's ruined. You could help out there, but it'll be wet and pretty miserable work.'

Cardova nodded. 'I could do that. Thank you, sir.'

'Alright. You can take command of the operation, though you're a little over-qualified. I'll let the lieutenant know that you're on your way, and you can get started after lunch.'

Cardova smiled for the first time since entering the room, and Kelsey shook her head. She hated seeing him miserable; it seemed so out of character for him, and she missed the old happy, always-joking Lucius that she loved. When Karalyn arrived, she thought, something would have to be done.

He stood. 'I'll get changed into more appropriate clothing, sir, so that I'm ready.'

'I'll come with you,' said Kelsey.

'What about our discussion about children?' said Van.

She stood, then leaned down and kissed Van. 'I'll give it my utmost consideration.'

Cardova and Kelsey left Van's office. They walked a few yards down the dark corridor, then Kelsey prodded Cardova on the shoulder.

'Look,' she said; 'I'm sorry about telling Karalyn. I'd just been crying about my mother, and I was feeling a bit off. I sometimes say stupid things when I'm feeling like that. Still, I think it's better that she knows. It means that, when she comes back, she won't be as clueless as she usually is. She'll know, and then at least you might have a chance.'

'A chance for what – a holiday romance? You can't conduct a relationship from different worlds.'

'Then we follow my suggestion, and get Emily's Quadrant up and running. We could travel back and forward whenever we liked. Stop seeing problems, and think about how to solve them instead.'

Cardova sighed. 'You're right.'

'I'm always right, Lucius. That's why you love me.'

He smiled.

She reached up and pinched his cheek. 'That's more like it. If you spoke to Karalyn the same way you spoke to me, then she'd see that you're not as uptight as the way you acted on the Star Continent.'

'I wasn't uptight; I was being professional.'

'What's the difference? To the untrained eye, you seemed cold and unfriendly, when I know that you're not like that. Karalyn probably thought that you didn't like her.'

'That was kind of the impression I was trying to give.'

'And you wonder why you have no success with women? Pyre knows how many girls you've turned down since you arrived in the City, and when you finally meet someone you like, you act all weird. Listen; I know Karalyn pretty well. She's pretty weird too, if I'm honest, but, more than that, she really needs things spelled out for her. She's so wrapped up in her own problems that she's oblivious to anything but the blatantly obvious. She doesn't do subtle, and she certainly has no conception of how to flirt. You need to be honest with her, and direct;

no games, and no mixed messages. Tell her how you feel, then give her time to process it.'

'Will that work?'

'I don't know, but it's a damn sight better than doing nothing.'

'Alright; I'll give it a go.'

Kelsey grinned. 'Good. Now, you have my permission to wade about in freezing cold water in the apartment cellars. Try not to drown.'

He strode away, leaving Kelsey alone in the corridor. She thought about going back to Van's office, but couldn't be bothered having to go through another conversation about babies. She was only twenty-four; she had plenty of time to think about that. She turned, and made her way to the room where she and a few volunteers worked on Mona's research. It had been hard to find suitable people to help with the project, as the majority of the young Exiles were lacking the academic skills necessary to transcribe ancient documents. With three years at university behind her, Kelsey was one of the best qualified, but they had found an older Torduan man who had worked in the Governor's Residence in Old Alea as a clerk, writing letters and reports for the gods who had ruled Lostwell.

The Torduan was the only person in the chamber when Kelsey walked in. He glanced up from a desk, an old, battered pair of spectacles balanced on the bridge of his nose.

'Good morning,' said Kelsey.

'Morning, ma'am,' he said.

Kelsey took a seat, and glanced at the piles of papers in front of her. In one heap sat the original sheets of faded old parchment retrieved by Mona from under the ancient library, while the second heap contained Mona's own hand-written notes and commentary. In the final pile sat the team's completed transcriptions in plain, clear text. She picked up a sheaf of Mona's notes, and got to work.

A few hours later, Kelsey was so engrossed in an ancient treatise on steam power that she failed to notice that someone else had entered the room.

'Hey, Kelsey,' said a voice; 'where are the red skies I was promised?'

Kelsey glanced up, and her eyes widened. 'Sable?'

The aunt laughed. 'You are a damn hard person to find, do you know that? Karalyn and I have been in this rain-sodden dump for nearly an hour. Why didn't you tell me it rained so much?'

Kelsey's face split into a broad smile, and she stood. 'It's Sweetmist. A solid month of rain. After that, there's an entire month of fog to look forward to, and then the red skies come back.'

'I don't think we can hang around that long. Are you coming? Karalyn is upstairs with your man.'

Kelsey nodded. 'Sure. So, eh, why are you here?'

'We're getting ready to leave for Implacatus, and we needed to take care of a few loose ends.'

They walked from the room, then climbed the narrow stairs to the top floor.

'This building is so draughty,' said Sable, 'and it leaks.'

'Aye, well, it was built in a hurry. We had to keep the greenhides at bay, and there was no time to make anything more elegant. It's a different story on the other side of the Straits. There, you've got palaces and all sorts. Jezra is still a work in progress. So, how have things been?'

'Alright. I've been staying in Colsbury. Shella's a good laugh; Keir's miserable; and Karalyn and I have been getting on surprisingly well. Your mother and Thorn are still in Sanang, I think.'

They reached the door of Van's office, and Sable pushed it open.

'I found her,' she said.

They walked into the office, where Van was sitting on the edge of his desk, speaking to Karalyn. Next to Kelsey's sister were her two children, who were sitting on a couch, fidgeting while the adults talked.

'About time,' said Karalyn.

'Hi, sis,' said Kelsey, 'and hello to my wee nephew and niece. Did you come along for a little holiday? It's a pity about the weather, but that's Sweetmist for you.'

'I've summoned Captain Cardova from the cellars,' said Van. 'He should be here soon.'

'Why?' said Kelsey.

'Karalyn wants to speak to him.'

Kelsey cackled. 'I bet she does.'

Van frowned. 'She has requested that I grant the captain a period of leave, so that he can be part of the operation to locate Lady Belinda.'

'Oh. Is that true, sis? You want to take Lucius to Implacatus?'

'If he's willing to go,' said Karalyn.

'And if the Queen grants permission,' said Van. 'As I've already told your sister, the final decision regarding senior Banner officers lies with the crown. After all, we are under contract to Queen Emily, and she might have a need for the captain.' He glanced at Karalyn. 'However, in order to travel to Tara during Sweetmist, I'll need to ask for your assistance in transporting us there.'

Karalyn attempted a smile. 'I also need to ask you for another massive favour, Kelsey.'

Kelsey's eyes narrowed. She glanced at Sable, who shrugged, then at the twins.

'Fine,' she muttered. 'How long for this time?'

'I'm hoping to have completed the rescue operation within the next ten days, so that we're back in time for their birthday.'

'At least I'll get away from Sweetmist for a while.'

Karalyn shook her head. 'I intend to leave them here, in the City, if that's alright.'

'They'll be bored out of their minds in the constant rain.'

'But they'll be safe.'

Kelsey frowned. 'This is an inconvenience; I'm not going to lie. I have work to do. But, for you, Karalyn, and for the twins, I'll do it.'

'Can we see Frostback?' said Cael.

'Sure,' said Kelsey.

'Let's wait until we've been to Tara,' said Van. He turned back to

Karalyn. 'Would it be possible to send the Queen a message, so that she knows we're coming?'

'I'll do it,' said Sable. 'Think of the Queen's face for a moment.' She gazed into Van's eyes. 'Alright; got it.' Her own eyes glazed over.

Van raised an eyebrow. 'I thought that only Karalyn was impervious to Kelsey's blocking abilities.'

'Sable can do it, too,' said Kelsey. 'And she likes to show off.'

She sat down next to the twins, suppressing her frustrated annoyance that she had been called upon to look after them for a second time.

'I found the Queen, and have let her know that we are on our way,' said Sable. She smiled at Van. 'Did you know that Maddie still has your silver cigarette case?'

Van laughed. 'Does she? I'll pick it up next time I'm in Dragon Eyre, which will be never, I hope.'

'The place has changed a bit since you were last there,' Sable said. 'I changed it. Say, did you ever work out that it was me who made you accuse Felice of being a traitor in Old Alea?'

Van's smile faded. 'Yes; I worked it out. They killed me for that; Felice stabbed me in the heart, and then one of the other gods brought me back from the dead.'

Sable laughed. 'Oops. Do you remember when I took control of your body? That was fun.'

'Behave yourself, Sable,' said Karalyn. 'Van's taken.'

'What are you implying?' said Sable. 'Am I not allowed to be friendly?'

Kelsey squirmed in her seat as her sister and aunt glared at each other. The awkward atmosphere changed as the door swung open and Cardova entered, his clothes wet and streaked with mud. His eyes fell upon Karalyn, and he stared at her.

'Thank you for coming, Captain,' Van said.

'I was told it was urgent, sir.'

'We have guests, as you can see. Karalyn was about to take us all to Tara to visit the Queen.'

'He can't go like that,' said Kelsey. 'He stinks. Emily will puke when she catches a whiff of his clothes.'

Cardova gave her a look. 'I can get changed first, sir.'

'Unfortunately, we have already informed the Queen that we are on our way. I wouldn't like to keep her Majesty waiting.' Van rubbed his chin. 'Alright; you can stay here. Let me ask you, though – if the Queen were to grant you permission for a temporary release from your contract, would you be willing to accompany Karalyn and Sable to Implacatus to look for Lady Belinda?'

Cardova lowered his gaze and shook his head. 'It's an insane plan, sir.'

'Is that a no?'

Cardova glanced at Karalyn. 'No. I'll do it. When would we leave?'

'Tomorrow,' said Karalyn. 'Sable and I will stay here overnight, then go back to Colsbury in the morning.'

'While I get to look after the twins again,' said Kelsey, trying not to sound too disheartened in front of Cael and Kyra.

Cardova turned back to Van. 'In that case, sir, you and I should get drunk tonight, because I'll probably be dead in a few days.'

'You'll have two Holdfasts with you,' said Sable. 'We're going to kick some Ascendant ass.'

Cardova laughed. 'Do you see what I had to deal with on the Star Continent, sir? And we thought Kelsey was arrogant.'

'Pack your things, Captain,' said Van; 'and, if the Queen grants her permission, I'll see you back here this evening. I still have some whisky left over from the supplies you brought back last time.'

Cardova saluted, then strode from the room.

Kelsey frowned at Karalyn. 'You are unbelievable, sis. No, "Hello, Lucius, how have you been?" or, "It's nice to see you again". Honestly, if a stranger had just watched that exchange, they'd be convinced that you hated him.'

Karalyn stood. 'Let's go to Tara.'

'That's right; ignore whatever I have to say,' said Kelsey. 'That's the Holdfast way – Kelsey's opinions can be discounted.'

Karalyn glared at her. 'It's so easy for you; you say whatever pops into your head, and you don't care about the consequences. I had a whole little speech planned for what I wanted to say to Lucius, and then he walks in, and I clam up.'

'She's right,' said Sable. 'I overheard her rehearsing her speech. It was quite touching.'

'Shut up, Sable,' snapped Karalyn. 'You're as bad as Kelsey. Neither of you have the slightest inhibitions. You don't get embarrassed like I do.'

Van smiled.

'What are you smirking about?' said Kelsey.

'I just think it's nice to see the mighty Holdfasts argue like a normal family. It makes you seem more human.' He stood. 'Shall we go?'

Karalyn sighed, then the air shimmered, and the small group found themselves in the entrance hall of the Aurelian mansion on Princeps Row. A courtier was waiting for them, and he seemed only marginally surprised by the manner of their arrival.

They were led through the mansion to its largest room, which had been converted into an audience chamber. There were no thrones, but Queen Emily and King Daniel were sitting behind a long table.

Van bowed. 'Your Majesties; Karalyn Holdfast and her two children have arrived in the City; and may I present to you Sable Holdfast?'

Emily smiled. 'Sable has already introduced herself. She appeared in my mind a few minutes ago to let us know they were coming. Greetings once again, Karalyn; it's lovely to see you and the twins. Might I also take this opportunity to thank you for the extremely generous gifts you sent? The royal court in Tara has been in a state of constant uproar at the luxuries you bestowed upon us.'

'That was my mother's doing,' said Karalyn. 'I'll pass on your thanks when I next see her.'

'They wish to speak to you about Captain Cardova, your Majesties,' said Van. 'They would like to request that he be freed from his contract for a month, to allow him to accompany them on an operation.'

'I see,' said Daniel. 'What operation?'

Karalyn eyed the King. 'We're going to rescue Belinda from Implacatus.'

Emily and Daniel glanced at each other.

'Excuse me,' said Emily, 'did you say Implacatus?'

'Aye. That's where Belinda is, so that's where we're going.'

'Is that not a little risky?' said Daniel. 'Given that the Ascendants are searching for this world, and yours, is it wise to go to them? What if one of you is captured? Would the Ascendants be able to travel here?'

'We won't be captured,' said Sable. 'The entire thing will only take a few days.'

'I admire your optimism,' said Emily. 'Might I ask – why do you require Captain Cardova, if you are so confident of success?'

'He knows Implacatus,' said Karalyn.

'So does Caelius Logos,' said Emily, 'and I believe that he has decided to remain upon your world. Why not pick him?'

'I don't know Caelius well,' said Karalyn, 'but I know Captain Cardova. More importantly, I trust him.'

'It's too dangerous,' said Daniel.

'Even if we are captured,' said Sable, 'they won't be able to read my mind, or Karalyn's. And Cardova doesn't know how to use a Quadrant, so the Ascendants wouldn't be able to use him to find Salve City.'

'Is that what this world is being called – Salve City?'

Sable smiled. 'It's what I call it.'

'What does Captain Cardova have to say about this?' said Emily. 'I assume you have asked for his opinion, Major-General?'

'I have, your Majesty,' said Van. 'He is willing to go.'

'I see. And will you also be requiring Kelsey, Karalyn? Will she need to return to your homeland to care for your children?'

'Not this time,' said Karalyn. 'The situation on the Star Continent is unsettled at the moment.'

'Unsettled?' said Daniel. 'In what way?'

'The Holdfasts and the Empress have had a falling out,' said Sable.

'Aye,' said Karalyn; 'and the new dream mage is siding with the

Empress against us. I feel it would be safer to keep the children here, in the City.'

'I thought the children had the potential to be dangerous?' said Daniel. 'Aren't they also dream mages?'

Karalyn glanced down at the twins, who were on their best behaviour. 'They'll be fine, as long as Kelsey remains with them. I didn't want to drag my sister away from her home again.'

'I've agreed to do it,' said Kelsey. 'I can take them somewhere out of the way, and I can load up Mona's research, and take it all with us.'

'You are asking a lot of the City,' said Daniel. 'Not only do we have to lose one of our best officers, for a second time, but you are also asking us to take responsibility for two young dream mages. What powers do they have?'

'Is this between us?' said Karalyn. 'I'm not in the habit of divulging family secrets.'

'It will not leave this room,' said Emily. 'You have my word.'

'Alright,' said Karalyn. 'They can read minds, except for Kelsey's; and they can sometimes predict the future, though that's rare at the moment.' She hesitated. 'They can also persuade people to do things against their will. They have never done anything sinister, but they sometimes make the others in Colsbury bark like a dog, or grunt like a wild boar.'

Kyra giggled, then put a hand over her mouth.

'We do not have animals that go by those names here,' said Emily, 'but I think I understand. I would like something in return.'

'If it's more of the same goods that we brought last time,' said Karalyn, 'then that shouldn't be a problem.'

The young Aurelian Queen narrowed her eyes. 'Thank you, but I wasn't referring to that. It was more a pledge of mutual defence that I was proposing. What I would like from you is a promise that, if this world is attacked by Implacatus, the Holdfasts will not abandon us to our fate.'

Karalyn glanced at Kelsey.

'Why do you hesitate?' said Emily.

'I don't think Karalyn has the authority to promise that,' said Kelsey. 'Our mother would have to agree.'

'I cannot speak for all of the Holdfasts,' said Karalyn. 'As Kelsey has pointed out, only my mother, Holder Fast, could make such an alliance. However, I promise you both that I will come to your aid, in person, whether my mother agrees or not.'

Daniel smiled. 'I think we have ourselves an agreement.'

CHAPTER 8
THE WRONG REASONS

Tara, Auldan, The City – 10th Namen 3423

'Why are you going away again, mama?' said Cael, as Karalyn sat by his bed.

'To help a friend in trouble,' she said.

'I don't like the rain,' said Kyra, from the neighbouring bed.

'I know,' said Karalyn, 'but it won't be for long. Aunty Kelsey will take care of you. You like Aunty Kelsey, don't you?'

'Aye,' said Cael. 'She's funny.'

'I don't want Uncle Keir to look after us,' said Kyra.

'That's why you're here, wee Kyra,' said Karalyn. 'Granny is still travelling, so she won't be in Colsbury for a while. This is just like a little holiday, except with lots of rain.'

A rumble of thunder reverberated through the elegant mansion, and Kyra shuddered.

'Don't be scared of the thunder,' said Karalyn. 'It can't hurt you.' She smoothed down the blankets on the two beds. 'Settle down, and go to sleep. I'll be in the next room, with Aunty Kelsey and Aunty Sable.' She leaned over and gave each of the twins a kiss.

'Don't go away, mama,' said Cael.

'I won't be going until the morning, and then it will just be for a few days.'

'Will you be here for our birthday?'

'I won't miss it.'

'What if you do?' said Kyra.

'I won't, wee Kyra. I promise. We'll have a party for you.' Karalyn stood, and turned down the small oil lamp that hung from the wall. 'Sweet dreams, my little mages.'

She slipped from the room, and closed the door as quietly as she could. She remained outside the bedroom for a moment, listening by the doorway, but heard nothing. A grinding feeling of guilt hung over her at the thought that she was leaving her children again, but then she pictured Belinda suffering at the hands of Edmond, and she steeled herself. She walked down the carpeted hallway, and entered a small sitting room, where Kelsey and Sable were reclining on couches. The shutters were closed, but the sound of the rain pounding against the window echoed throughout the mansion.

'Are they asleep?' said Kelsey.

'They will be soon, I hope,' said Karalyn. She sat. 'Damn this weather.'

'It's bad timing,' said Kelsey. 'The entire City stays indoors during the two rainy seasons.'

'How long will it last?' said Sable.

'About another twenty days or so, and then the fog begins. It's to do with the way the cold air from iceward meets the warm air from sunward when summer changes into winter. The same thing happens, on a smaller scale, all year round in the Clashing Seas, where...'

'I don't really care,' said Sable. She glanced at Karalyn. 'Shouldn't we be discussing the plan with Lucius Cardova?'

Karalyn shrugged. 'Let's leave him to get drunk with Van.'

Sable shook her head. 'You should have brought Lucius here, rather than taking Van back to Jezra.'

'It's done now.'

'Can we talk about the Quadrants?' said Kelsey.

'Which ones?' said Karalyn.

'Well, we have two,' said Kelsey. 'No, is it three? There's one here, with Emily in Tara, and Sable has one. There's another, though, aye?'

'Aye. The God-King's old Quadrant is currently jammed into the side of the Sextant.'

'Right. Anyway, it occurred to me, you know, when you were promising to help the City if it got attacked, that we have no way to alert you if the Ascendants invade. I assume that you don't check the City every day through the Sextant, so how would you know? We need a way to tell you.'

Sable laughed. 'You really want to learn how to use a Quadrant, don't you? I remember you bringing this up in Colsbury.' She reached into her clothes and withdrew her Quadrant. 'It's pretty simple.'

'Can I hold it?'

Sable passed the copper-coloured device to Kelsey, who held it by its edges. She squinted at the engravings and the jewels that studded its rim.

'Is it talking to you?' said Karalyn.

Kelsey shook her head.

'Then you'll have to use it the normal way,' said Sable.

'Do you know how to make it take us to Colsbury?'

'Yes,' said Sable, 'but only because that was where I last used it. Before Karalyn brought us here, I transported myself inside Colsbury from one room to another; so that the Quadrant would remember the last place it was used.'

'I didn't see you do that,' said Karalyn.

'I was taking precautions,' said Sable. 'What if we got separated? I needed a way to get back. If I hadn't done that, then, no; I wouldn't know how to travel to the Star Continent. I don't know how to travel between worlds.'

'But you said you knew how to get to Implacatus.'

Sable nodded, then held out her hand, and Kelsey passed the device back to her. She pointed at a symbol.

'Touch here, and the Quadrant will take you to the last place it was used. Very handy, indeed. That's saved my life more than once.' She moved her finger. 'But here, it does something different – touch here, and the Quadrant will take you to the first place it was ever used. Implacatus, in other words.'

Karalyn leaned in closer. 'I see.'

'Hey,' said Sable; 'this lesson is meant to be for Kelsey's benefit.'

'So,' said Kelsey, 'if I could borrow one of the three Quadrants, and take it to Colsbury, then I could just keep using the "take me to the last place it was used" symbol?'

'Yeah,' said Sable.

'That's what Van did to rescue me from Implacatus, I think,' said Kelsey. 'I'd rather learn more, though. Just going back to the same place every time seems a bit limited. I don't suppose that there's a manual I could read?'

'No. You'll have to pick it up the same way that I did – trial and error, and tons of practice.' Sable glanced at Karalyn. 'You know, if you were to let me use the Sextant, and place my own Quadrant into it, then I reckon I could learn how to move between worlds in no time at all.'

'If I did that,' said Karalyn, 'then you'd run away to Dragon Eyre.'

'No, I wouldn't. I promised to help you find Belinda. Do you still not trust me?'

'I want to trust you, Sable.'

'Then trust me. It's easy. If I knew how to travel between worlds, then we could be more flexible when it comes to going to Implacatus. And, I could teach Kelsey how to get to anywhere on the Star Continent, rather than just the same spot in Colsbury.'

'And what would happen if you lost your Quadrant on Implacatus? The Ascendants would be able to use it to invade our two worlds.'

'I won't lose it.'

'You don't know that.'

'Perhaps you're being a little over-cautious, niece.'

'And perhaps you're being unduly reckless, aunt.'

Sable sighed. 'We're about to raid Cumulus, Karalyn – the home of the damn Ascendants, and you're worried about being reckless?'

'There's no point in taking unnecessary risks. I'm in charge of this operation.'

'You should let me lead. I have more experience of this sort of thing. I rescued a demigod from right under an Ascendant's nose; I know what I'm doing.'

'No,' said Karalyn. 'We're going to do this my way. If it was up to you, we'd attack Implacatus with a great wave of destruction and terror.'

Sable smiled. 'Yes. Let's bring the gods to their knees; teach them a lesson they'll never forget. And, of course, rescue Belinda at the same time.'

'This is not about teaching anyone a lesson. Belinda could be in great pain right now; that's why we're doing this.'

Sable glanced at Kelsey. 'What do you think?'

Kelsey blinked. 'You're asking for my opinion? Wait; let me remember this moment. Another Holdfast actually wants Kelsey's opinion.'

'Don't refer to yourself in third person,' said Sable. 'It makes you sound unhinged.'

Kelsey laughed. 'Alright. What do I think? Well, I think, firstly, that Karalyn should allow you to use the Sextant. It reduces the risk of something bad happening on Implacatus. Imagine that Karalyn gets hit by a crossbow bolt; you could be stuck there forever. But, if Sable can jump about from world to world, then you've got yourself a decent insurance policy. On the other hand, Karalyn's approach to the raid is probably the right one. Silent and sneaky sounds like it will have more chance of success than an all-out assault. One thing, though, that neither of you have mentioned is – what will Belinda think about this? Are we sure that she's an unwilling participant in her wedding to Edmond? What if she wants to stay in Cumulus? And, what do we do with her if we bring her back? Where will she go? Would she side with the Empress over the Holdfasts? If that's the case, then we've just handed victory to Bridget. Belinda's an Ascendant, with all of the powers that come with that, except, thanks to Karalyn, she's also immune to the powers of other Ascendants. She's the most powerful god in existence. Should that worry us? Anyway, that's what I think.'

Sable poured herself a gin. 'If Belinda doesn't want to come back, then we leave her there.'

'I refuse to believe that she's marrying Edmond willingly,' said Karalyn.

'I agree,' said Sable. 'Bastion was pretty clear about the situation. He told me that Belinda had been tortured with a restraining mask. Kolai confirmed it.'

'Kolai?' said Kelsey.

'The Ascendant I beheaded. He said that Edmond had done it out of love, if you can believe that. It's been a few years since Lostwell was destroyed. If she's been in that mask all this time, then there's a possibility that she might have lost her mind.'

'Yendra survived three hundred years in a restrainer mask,' said Kelsey.

'Yeah? And how was she after that length of time?'

'I didn't see her, but I was told that she was like a withered-up old husk, her life force almost drained away. It took lots of healing, and tons of salve, to fix her.'

'Maybe we need to take some salve with us,' said Sable.

'Emily won't agree to that,' said Kelsey. 'She doesn't want any more salve to leave this world.'

'Not even a small amount?' Sable shrugged. 'She wouldn't have to know. Where is it kept?'

'There's a salve mine two hundred miles east of here,' said Karalyn. 'It's protected by a dragon and a demigod with soulwitch powers.'

'Aye,' said Kelsey; 'Dawnflame and Jade. How did you know that?'

'I watched this world through the Sextant before I could travel here.'

Sable studied the Quadrant. 'Two hundred miles, eh?' She started to trace out lines on the surface of the device, her finger hovering just above the engravings. 'This marks distance, Kelsey; and over here marks direction. If you need to consider altitude, then you have to touch here as well.'

'Slow down a bit,' said Kelsey. 'I need to write this down.'

Kelsey jumped up and ran from the room.

'You could give her the God-King's Quadrant,' said Sable. 'You don't need it any more.'

'There's already a Quadrant in the City.'

'Yes, but what if Queen Emily doesn't feel like handing it over? It would give Kelsey independence, and power. It might be good for her.'

'You're forgetting one thing – Kelsey doesn't have vision skills. You and I, we can scan out locations before we travel there. Kelsey can't do that. She would be blind to where she's going.'

'Fair point, but Kelsey's smart enough to work round that. We should let her practice, at least. She's worth more to the Holdfasts than just a glorified babysitter.'

'It's more likely to get her killed.'

'She needs to know that we trust her with the important stuff. It's worth the risk.'

'Fine. Show her the basics, for all the good it will do.'

Kelsey strode back into the room, holding a quill, an inkpot, and a leather-bound notebook.

'Have you any idea how ridiculously expensive paper is here?' she said, as she sat down. 'If I had my way, I'd trade salve for essential goods for the City. We're short of everything at the moment. If we sold salve to the Star Continent, then we could really improve living conditions here.'

'What do you need?' said Karalyn.

'Where do I begin? Let's see – coal, iron, in fact, all metals; wood, paper, oil; stone for building, cotton, canvas, glass, tools...'

'Alright,' said Karalyn; 'I get it.'

'And that doesn't even cover the stuff that we don't have at all. All those little luxuries that sent Emily's court wild – coffee, chocolate, sugar, tea – we have none of that here. But hey, we have plenty of seaweed, and an abundance of concrete!'

Sable laughed. 'It sounds like you need to persuade Emily to reconsider her ban on salve exports. Or, I could change her mind for her?'

'Don't interfere,' said Karalyn. 'I'm open to a trading agreement, and I'm sure that mother would agree; but we can't manipulate the ruler of the City.'

'Alright. Let's do it your way. Do I have your permission to take some salve from the mine? I promise I won't kill its protectors.'

'You'd better not,' said Kelsey. 'Jade and Dawnflame are friends of mine.'

'This could be your first lesson,' said Sable. 'I could show you how to take us to the mine, and you could help me steal some salve.'

Kelsey nodded. 'Sure. Go over it slowly, and I'll write down each step.'

Sable leaned forward, and pointed at the Quadrant. 'Alright. Draw this little symbol, and remember it. It governs distance. The further you sweep your finger, the further you go. For two hundred miles, you would need to move your finger about an inch and a half, while touching the direction symbol at the same time.'

Karalyn watched as Kelsey started writing in the notebook.

'I'll leave you to it,' she said, standing. 'I don't want to know the details of your little raid on the mine. Take only enough to heal Belinda, and make sure you aren't caught in the act.'

'Wait,' said Sable. 'I'll need to know the precise location of the mine first; otherwise I could be searching for hours. Who knows where it is, who has a mind I can read?'

'Halfclaw knows,' said Kelsey, 'but I don't think he'd like you rummaging about in his head.'

'He won't feel a thing,' said Sable. 'I'm a master at reading dragons. How do you think I survived on Dragon Eyre? Right; Halfclaw it is. Give me a moment.'

Karalyn shook her head, and left the room.

Several hours had passed before Karalyn heard the sounds of laughter coming from the living room. She had been lying on top of her bed, going over her plan for Implacatus, when Sable's voice reached her ears. Karalyn got up from the bed, and walked through to the living room.

She stood by the doorway for a moment, watching as Kelsey and Sable laughed. Kelsey had the Quadrant, while Sable had a bag over her shoulder.

'The twins are sleeping,' Karalyn said. 'If you wake them up, you two are putting them back to bed.'

'That was amazing,' said Kelsey. 'You should have seen us; Jade and Dawnflame didn't even know we were there; and I brought us back. Alright, so I only touched the "go back to the last place it was used" symbol, but still – I used a Quadrant!'

'Time for some more gin, I feel,' said Sable, dumping the bag onto a table.

'I assume that's salve?' said Karalyn.

'You assume correctly. It's raw and unrefined, though. It would be nice to know how to concentrate it, so that we could just take a little vial with us to Implacatus.'

'Amalia knows how to refine it,' said Kelsey.

'Does she? And where does she live?'

'In a villa on Roser territory. Should we visit her?'

'It's the middle of the night,' said Karalyn, 'and you're still speaking too loudly. Go in the morning; we can make time for it.'

Sable sat. 'Gin it is, then.'

Kelsey grinned. 'Pour one for me, Auntie.'

Sable nodded, and got another glass ready. 'Do you want one, Karalyn?'

'No. If you two are staying here, then I might visit Jezra.'

'Why?' said Kelsey.

'I had a chance to think while you were both away,' she said. 'Maybe it's a mistake to request that Lucius comes with us. It's not fair on him. I put him into a position where he couldn't say no. He doesn't want to come; you could tell by the look on his face.'

Sable sighed. 'Who cares about the look on his face? Read his damn mind, Karalyn. If you want to know what he's thinking, then find out. If you're too queasy about it, then I'll do it for you.'

'Stay out of his mind, Sable.'

Sable shrugged. 'I was only making a suggestion. It doesn't matter to me if Lucius Cardova comes along. I assumed that you were only asking him because you wanted someone to keep you warm at night.'

'Of course that's why she asked him,' said Kelsey. 'Most people, if they fancy someone, ask them out for a nice meal, or perhaps for a stroll along the promenade. Not our Karalyn – she asks them to go on dangerous missions to god-infested worlds. It's her idea of fun.'

Karalyn laughed, despite herself. 'Maybe I've forgotten what "fun" means. Don't get too drunk; remember that the twins are in the next room along. See you later.'

Command Centre, Jezra. Go.

The air shimmered and darkened, and Karalyn found herself in a damp, brick-lined corridor. The sound of the storm outside was buffeting against the building, and every window and door was rattling in the wind.

You cannot see me.

Karalyn ghosted past several open doorways, where Banner soldiers and uniformed Exiles were resting. Many were repairing equipment and uniforms, while others were playing games with cards and dice in the flickering light of a few oil lamps. She went up three flights of stairs, and slipped past the guards posted close to Van and Kelsey's apartment. She persuaded them to turn a blind eye, and went through the entrance. Van and Cardova were sitting by a low table, where a half-empty bottle of whisky and a full ashtray stood, and, for a moment, Karalyn forgot that she was invisible.

'It's madness,' Cardova was saying, 'but the Holdfasts don't listen to a damn word I say.'

Van nodded. 'I still don't understand why they asked you to go with them. I mean, Belinda will be in Cumulus, not Serene. Have you ever been to Cumulus?'

'Never. Not once in my life. Have you?'

Van shook his head. 'As far as I know, you had to be a major in a Banner, or higher, before the Ancients would even look at you, let alone invite you up to Cumulus. So, why do they want you to go?'

'You must have a suspicion.'

'Well, yes. I know what Kelsey's told me, and I know that you have a thing for Karalyn. Tell me, as a friend, do you want to be with her?'

Karalyn stifled a groan, and wished she had walked into the room like a normal person would have.

Cardova shrugged. 'I don't know. I like her, and I missed her when Kelsey and I got back from the Star Continent. I would like a chance to see if it could work, but what chance will we have on Implacatus? It's hardly the most romantic of destinations. But, you know me. I'll do my duty, as always, and watch her back; well, at least until I'm killed.'

Van smiled. 'You never know; they might succeed.'

'Yeah.' He laughed. 'That would be almost as bad. Can you imagine how cocky Sable would be? We'd never hear the end of it.' He glanced at Van. 'What do you think of her?'

'Who, Sable?'

'No. Karalyn.'

Van took a sip of whisky. 'Well, she's too tall for me, for a start.'

Cardova laughed.

'I'm not sure,' Van went on. 'I'd be careful, Lucius; she seems to have a pretty serious past. I've never once seen her smile or laugh, and she seems to have the weight of the world on her shoulders. She's also been married before.'

'So have I.'

'Yes, but your wife wasn't murdered by a god. Karalyn killed a hundred thousand soldiers in retaliation. There aren't many Ancients who could match that level of revenge. And, she has two dream mages for children.'

'So?'

'I'm just pointing it out. What I'm saying, I guess, is that it probably won't be easy.'

'Do you think I should steer clear of her?'

'That's up to you, Lucius.'

Cardova nodded, his eyes cast downwards.

Karalyn relaxed her powers. 'Hello.'

The two men jumped in their seats.

'Holy crap!' cried Van. 'Gods above; I felt as though I was about to suffer a salve-induced heart attack. Maybe you should knock first, Karalyn.'

'I'll remember that for next time.'

'Have you just arrived from Tara?' Van went on.

'Aye,' she said, lying. 'I wanted to speak to Lucius about tomorrow.'

'Alright. Do you want me to leave? I could do with a trip to the bathroom, anyway.'

'Thanks,' she said.

Van got up, swayed a little, then smiled and headed out of the room. Cardova glanced up at Karalyn, waiting for her to say something.

She sat. 'You don't have to come to Implacatus if you don't want to.'

Cardova said nothing for a moment, and took a sip from his glass.

She frowned. 'Did you hear what I said?'

'I heard you. I was just trying to work out why you would say it.'

'I chose you for the wrong reasons, Lucius.'

He raised an eyebrow. 'What wrong reasons?'

'I was being selfish. I've thought about you a lot since you left the Star Continent, and I missed having you around. And what Kelsey said, when I brought you both back here... Well, I've been thinking about that, too. I wanted to spend more time with you, but I couldn't think of an excuse, so I decided to ask you to help Sable and I rescue Belinda. I shouldn't have. I'm sorry.'

'You did this because you want to spend more time with me?'

Karalyn nodded, feeling a surge of embarrassment wash over her.

'I want to spend more time with you, too,' he said; 'but Implacatus?'

'I'm a mess, Lucius. I think I've forgotten how to connect with people, if I ever knew how in the first place. I don't have any friends, not any more. People think I'm cold and unapproachable, and maybe I am. Anyway, I release you from your promise. You can stay here.'

'I'm coming,' said Cardova. 'I've seen the way you and Sable bicker; you'll need someone there to stop you from killing each other.'

'You don't have to say what you think I want to hear.'

'You know what I think of your plan.'

'You think it's insane.'

'Yes. I do. Our chances of success are low, but if anyone can pull it off, it's you and Sable. And if you do, then I want to be there. If we survive, it'll certainly be something to tell the grandchildren about.'

'But if you get killed, it will be my fault.'

'No, it won't. It'll be the fault of the god who kills me; and it'll be my fault for agreeing to come along. My choices are not your responsibility. Do you remember when we spoke in the *World's End*, about what I had done on Dragon Eyre? I told you then that I wanted to do the right thing for a change. If Belinda is being tortured and imprisoned, then rescuing her is the right thing to do. I don't want to go to Implacatus, but I would feel a whole lot worse if I stayed here and let you two maniacs go on your own.'

She smiled. 'Sable's the maniac.'

'That she is,' he said, laughing. 'Think no more of it, Karalyn. I want to come. I mean, I've already packed, and I can't be bothered having to unpack everything again. Did you say we were going to Colsbury first?'

'Aye, as soon as we've had breakfast. I want to show Sable how to do something with the Sextant, and then we'll leave for Serene.'

'I'll be ready.'

'Thank you, Lucius.'

He smiled. 'As Sable would say – let's kick some Ascendant ass.'

CHAPTER 9
TO FIGHT FIRE

Midfort, Sanang/Plateau Frontier – 20th Day, Last Third Summer 534

The carriage wheels rumbled over the cobbled road. Inside, no one spoke. Agang was looking mournful, his eyes on the new settlement on the Sanang side of the old Frontier Wall. When Daphne had last been there, the land had been a desolate waste of tree stumps and mud, and now there were streets, houses, and a bustling marketplace. The sections of the wall destroyed by Keira the fire mage had long since been cleared away, and in some places it was hard to tell where the exact line of the border lay, the new Sanang town mingling with the edges of Midfort. Merchants seemed to be everywhere – displaying their goods, carting them off on wagons, and governing the myriad transactions between Sanang and the rest of the Star Continent. Out of the Matriarch's domain flowed timber, coffee, spices, chocolate, and a hundred other items, while, heading in the other direction, came an abundance of metals, and goods finished in the workshops of the Holdings and the Plateau. Even whisky from Domm, the remotest part of the world, travelled through Midfort, and what had once been a heavily fortified border town was now the mercantile capital of the world.

Agang wiped a tear from his eye.

'Does this make you sad?' said Thorn.

'Yes,' he said, 'but also proud. I oversaw the building of the town on the Sanang side, and it was my home for many years before the Matriarch annexed Mya.'

The young Sanang man sitting opposite Agang rolled his eyes. As one of the Matriarch's two younger siblings, he was sharing the lead carriage with Agang, Thorn and Daphne, while his brother was in the rear carriage with Caelius and their luggage.

'I don't wish to sound disrespectful,' he said, 'but Mya has always been a part of Sanang. Your rule here, Lord Agang, was a temporary aberration. My sister did nothing more than restore Mya to its proper place.'

Daphne glanced at Agang, half-expecting his temper to flare. Instead, Agang merely nodded.

'You are right, of course, Pechtang,' he said. 'All the same, I worked day and night for years to transform what was a wasteland into what you can see today with your own eyes. It was the manner of the annexation that upset me, rather than its inevitability. The first I knew of it was when soldiers knocked at my door at dawn, and told me I had one hour to pack my things and leave.'

'It had to be planned in secret,' said Pechtang, 'so that the merchants wouldn't panic. By the end of that same day, Sanang officials were in charge of the border, and things carried on as normal.'

'Normal for everyone except me, I suppose. I was cast out of my home, and forced into exile.'

Pechtang narrowed his eyes. 'You left Mya as the richest man in the history of Sanang. You should be grateful my sister allowed you to take your wealth with you. There were several in her court who argued that it should have been confiscated. You now live a life of luxury among your Holdfast friends; a life unimaginable to the peasants and workers of Sanang.'

'Forgive me for interrupting,' said Daphne, 'but I am more concerned with what will occur here once the Empress is informed that Sanang will support Thorn's claim to the throne. Midfort has a garrison of imperial soldiers, who, if they remain loyal to Empress Bridget, could attempt to close the border.'

Pechtang laughed. 'Do you think this is the only border crossing, Holder Fast? The old wall is riddled with holes. If the imperial soldiers close the border here, then we shall cross into the Plateau by other means.'

'It is vital that we maintain the road links between Sanang and the Holdings,' said Thorn. 'This is where we are most vulnerable. The coastal road is long, and could be easily blocked by the forces of the Empress. What we need is a force of our own, to ensure that the road remains open.'

'I intend to scout the route as we travel along it,' said Daphne. 'Cavalry would be most suited to its defence, I think. Stationary garrisons would require too many soldiers. We need a force that can move up and down the road at speed; and the Holdings can provide such a force.'

'The Empress might perceive any deployment as a provocation,' said Agang. 'Her Majesty might believe that we intend to choke off supplies from Sanang to the Plateau, and she would send her own troops to guard the road.'

Daphne bit back her own response, and glanced at Thorn.

'Perhaps it would be better to avoid escalating the situation,' Thorn said. 'A cavalry force should be prepared, and held in readiness at the western gap in the Barrier Mountains. From there, they could deploy all the way down the coastal road to Midfort, if and when it becomes necessary.'

'I'll see to it,' said Daphne.

Pechtang laughed. 'You two are already acting like Empress and Herald.'

'Show some respect,' said Agang. 'Holder Fast and Lady Thorn are two of the world's most formidable mages.'

'Respect is earned, Lord Agang,' said Pechtang. 'I support the idea of a Sanang becoming ruler of the Empire, but I'll reserve my judgement until I see it happen.'

The occupants of the carriage quietened as they came to a halt on the road. Imperial soldiers were positioned across the street, guarding the line of the border between Sanang and the Plateau. They were allowing traffic to pass, but had stopped the two carriages containing Daphne and the others.

'What are those fools doing?' said Pechtang, leaning over to gaze out of the side window. 'How dare they stop us? We're flying the insignia of the Matriarch.'

'Daimon knows we're here,' said Daphne.

'Maybe not,' said Agang. 'Mage Aberfeld might have alerted the Midfort garrison.'

'Aberfeld would not have betrayed us so quickly,' said Thorn.

'He might have had no choice,' said Daphne. 'Daimon could have examined his mind and reported back to the Empress.'

'Contact Karalyn,' said Agang. 'She can extract us.'

'Let's not panic,' said Daphne. 'Everyone remain calm.'

An officer approached the lead carriage, flanked by crossbow-wielding Holdings soldiers dressed in the uniform of the imperial army. The officer rapped his knuckles against the side window, and Agang opened it.

'Good day,' said the officer, his eyes scanning the passengers. 'Greetings, Holder Fast. What brings you to Midfort?'

'We were visiting the Matriarch in Broadwater, Captain,' said Daphne. 'Are you here to provide us with an escort?'

The officer raised an eyebrow. 'Not quite, ma'am. Will you be staying in Midfort this evening?'

'We shall.'

The officer smiled and took a step back. 'Safe journey, ma'am.'

He raised an arm, and the two carriages began to move off again.

Pechtang snorted. 'What was that about? They stopped us just to wish us a pleasant trip?'

'They were checking to see who was in the carriages,' said Daphne. 'If they were going to try to arrest us, they wouldn't do it out here, not in front of these crowds.'

'Do you think they will attempt something tonight?' said Thorn.

'Perhaps.'

'All the more reason to contact Karalyn,' said Agang.

'I hope they try to arrest us,' said Pechtang. 'My brother and I can fight, and we have a soulwitch with us. The soldiers wouldn't stand a chance.'

'I would rather avoid a massacre,' said Thorn.

'We shall keep to our plan,' said Daphne. 'We shall stop for the night, and hire fresh horses, so that we can return these to the Matriarch. We don't want to give the impression that we are scared.'

'I'm not scared,' said Pechtang.

Daphne glanced at Pechtang. He had the broad shoulders and thick, strong arms of a typical Sanang man, and she had no doubt that he was as fearless as his compatriots. It had been so long since Keira had stripped the forests of Sanang males that the world had almost forgotten how well they could fight; and it seemed to Daphne that Pechtang was itching to remind them.

The streets became noticeably wider as the carriages rolled through Midfort, though the bustling marketplaces were the same as on the other side of the border. Sanang merchants mingled freely with those from the Holdings and further afield, while a few soldiers stood around, keeping order. The centre of the town had altered beyond recognition since Daphne's last visit, and it was hard to believe that an entire army had been annihilated by Keira when she had broken into the Plateau. Among the dead had been Daphne's brother Vince, incinerated along with thousands of others. Thirty years later, not a mark of that disaster could be seen anywhere in Midfort, the memories buried under the foundations of the new buildings, along with the rubble of the old.

***

They checked into a comfortable tavern as the sun was setting beyond the frontier wall to the west. As soon as the horses had been halted in the tavern forecourt, Daphne supervised their handling, giving strict orders to have them sent back to the Matriarch in Broadwater, then she and Caelius conducted an examination of the tavern from the outside, walking round it as the others got settled into their rooms.

'There are four ways into the building,' said Caelius. 'If soldiers come tonight, we might be able to fight our way out.'

'Thorn doesn't want a slaughter,' said Daphne; 'and I tend to agree with her. We have to assume that Daimon is watching us at every moment.'

'Yes; but what will he do? Or, more precisely, what will the Empress order him to do?'

'If it was me, I'd surround the building and set it on fire; make it look like an accident. They must know that if they storm the building, Thorn will kill them all.'

'Maybe they want a massacre. The soldiers round here all seem to be from the Holdings. If the Empress is ruthless enough to sacrifice a few dozen of them, then she could achieve a propaganda victory, by claiming that the pretender to the throne has carried out an atrocity at the border.'

'Bridget doesn't think like that.'

'Power does things to people; you know that. If the Empress is desperate, she might allow her baser instincts to take over.'

'Perhaps Agang was right. Maybe I should reach out to Colsbury, and summon Karalyn to bring us home.'

They entered the tavern, where a fire was burning in a corner hearth. They collected their room keys from the reception desk, then climbed the stairs to the upper storey.

Caelius pointed at a door. 'This is where I'm sleeping. Shall I see you downstairs for dinner in a little while?'

'We might not be here that long,' she said. 'Come into my room for now. You can keep watch while I contact Shella.'

She unlocked her door, and they stepped inside. The room was small but clean and comfortable, and Daphne's luggage was already sitting by the bed.

'Pour me a glass of water,' she said, 'and I'll send out my powers.'

She sat on the bed as Caelius walked over to a table by the shuttered window.

Daphne relaxed, and allowed her vision powers to leave her body. She sent her sight through the gaps in the shutters, then sped off in a north-easterly direction, leaving Midfort far behind. She followed the coastal road for a while, until she came to a junction where it split – the northward branch heading towards the Holdings, and the eastward towards Plateau City. Daphne turned towards the Barrier Mountains, and traversed the long miles to Colsbury. When she reached the island fortress, the Great Keep was almost in darkness, with just a handful of lights coming from a few windows. Daphne pushed her vision into the building, and passed through several empty rooms. She found Shella sitting alone in her living room, and entered her mind.

Shella, it's me. Where's Karalyn?

Shella jumped in fright, spilling her whisky onto the rug.

Damn it, Daffers! Are you trying to kill me?

I'm in a hurry. Where's Karalyn?

She's not here. She took her kids and Sable and left earlier today. It's just me and Keir here at the moment.

Where have they gone? I assume that Karalyn isn't rash enough to take her children to Implacatus.

I don't know where they went, and I didn't ask. She said they would be back in the morning. You might want to try again around breakfast time.

Damn it.

What's up?

We're in Midfort, on the border between Sanang and the Plateau. The moment that Karalyn gets back, tell her to look for us. There might be trouble brewing with the local imperial garrison. Tell her it's urgent.

Okay, will do. Does this mean I might see you tomorrow?

With any luck, Shella.

Daphne severed the connection and blinked. Caelius handed her a glass of water and a lit cigarette, and she took them.

'Did you find your daughter?' he said.

'She's not there. She and Sable are off doing something until the morning. I'm afraid we're on our own for now.' She took a long draw on the cigarette. 'I think we should gather within the same room, and have food sent up for us. We'll be safer if we stick together.'

'I can knock on their doors, and ask them to come here.'

'Thank you, Caelius.'

He stood, and left the room. Daphne set her cigarette down in an ashtray and opened one of her bags. She rooted about for a while, then pulled out a short sword. She slid the blade from its sheath and frowned. It had been a long time since she had used a sword to fight anyone, and she wondered how the loss of two toes would affect her ability to use battle-vision. She had been able to master walking without too much difficulty, but she hadn't trained with a sword in years. She would need to rectify that, if they survived the night.

Daphne awoke as a hand nudged her shoulder. She opened her eyes, and saw Caelius standing by the bed, a small lamp in his hand. The air in the room was thick with smoke, after the two Sanang men had indulged in several weedsticks throughout the evening. The Matriarch's siblings were sleeping on the floor of the room, while Agang was in an armchair.

Caelius put a finger to his lips, then beckoned for Daphne to join him by the window. She glanced over at Thorn, with whom she had been sharing the single bed, but she remained asleep. Daphne rubbed her eyes and got up. Caelius had opened the shutters a few inches, and she peered down into the street. Soldiers were moving through the night shadows, blocking off the escape routes from the tavern.

'What time is it?' she whispered.

'The midnight bell rang a while ago,' Caelius said, 'but I can't be more precise than that. Do you recall what you said you would do if you were leading the soldiers? I think they might be planning something like that.'

'They're going to burn the tavern to the ground?'

'Look over there,' he said, pointing towards a cart. 'Do those look like oil barrels to you? Some soldiers dragged them here a few minutes ago.'

'We need to get out of here. Now.'

Daphne rushed back to the bed, and shook Thorn awake, while Caelius did the same with Agang. Daphne then tried to awaken Pechtang and his brother T'Lang, but the two young Sanang men continued to snore, their minds dulled by alcohol and weed.

Thorn got to her feet as Daphne was about to slap T'Lang.

'Leave them be for the moment,' said Thorn. 'What is our plan?'

'We should get out of the tavern,' said Daphne.

'But all of our things are here – our luggage, and the gifts the Matriarch gave us.'

'The soldiers are going to burn us out,' said Daphne. 'If we don't run, then we'll have to kill them all. Is that what you want?'

Thorn and Agang walked to the window, and gazed down at the soldiers.

'Why would they burn us out?' said Thorn.

'Because, from the Empress's point of view,' said Daphne, 'it's the smart thing to do. If we all die in a fire, they could say it was a tragic accident. At one stroke, the succession crisis will be over.'

Agang's eyes narrowed. 'Bridget would murder us? I can't believe it.'

'We don't have time to debate the issue; we need to make a decision.'

'Let me think,' said Thorn.

Daphne glanced out of the window. The soldiers had reached their positions, sheltering in the shadows of the neighbouring buildings, while a handful stood next to the cart. Two of them lowered one of the barrels to the ground, then rolled it towards the tavern.

'I have an idea,' said Thorn.

She strode back to the bed, then rummaged around in a leather pouch that was lying next to Pechtang's head. She withdrew some matches, and glanced at Daphne.

'Throw some water over our sleeping companions, then stand away from the bed.'

Daphne glanced at Caelius, and he nodded. The veteran picked up a jug of water, and tipped it over the two sleeping Sanang. T'Lang spluttered, and clenched his fists.

'Is this a joke, old man?' he cried.

'Move away from the bed,' said Daphne, 'and get your boots on. We're leaving.'

The two Sanang men glared around the room, as if challenging the others.

'Do it,' said Thorn. 'We're going to start a little fire, before the soldiers outside have the chance to light a bigger one.'

'There are soldiers outside?' said Pechtang, leaping to his feet. He grabbed an axe from his bag and rushed to the window. 'Bastards!'

Thorn crouched by the bed, and struck a match. She held it out towards the blankets and sheets, and the flame slowly began to spread.

'Boots on, now,' said Daphne. 'Grab your things.'

Thorn lit another match, and touched it to the other corner of the bed, and, within seconds, the two little fires were taking on a life of their own.

She stood. 'Now we raise the alarm. Screams, shouts – the louder the better.'

Daphne shouldered one of her bags, then Caelius kicked the door down, breaking the lock.

'Fire!' he yelled. 'Everybody out! Fire!'

Smoke started to rise from the bed, and the room was soon dense with the grey fumes. T'Lang started coughing as he tried to pull on his boots, then his brother dragged him from the room by his shoulders. Thorn went next, running out after Caelius, and shouting at the top of her voice. Caelius was banging on every door he passed, and some guests who were staying in the tavern appeared, their sleepy expressions changing as soon as they caught a glimpse of the smoke belching out of the room where Daphne and the others had been sheltering.

'Fire!' cried Caelius, his voice booming. 'Get outside; everyone, get outside!'

A panic ensued. Guests scrambled to gather up their possessions and children, and the hallway on the upper floor became clogged with fleeing people, many in their underwear, or dressed only in a long coat. Daphne and her party slipped into their midst, as the nervous crowd hurried down the narrow stairs. At the bottom of the stairs, a Sanang man broke down a side door, and they spilled out into the street. Daphne watched as the soldiers glanced at each other, unsure of what to do. Three of them were standing by one of the oil barrels, as if about to pour its contents onto the side of the tavern, and they stared at the crowd with guilty expressions on their faces.

The tavern owner appeared amid the growing crowd, clad in a dressing gown.

'Is everyone out?' he cried.

The crowd turned, and gazed up at the building. Smoke and flames were streaming from the window of Daphne's room.

The tavern owner clenched his fists. 'If someone was smoking weed up there, I'll have their balls!'

Beyond the limits of the crowd, the soldiers started to pull back, slipping away into the shadows.

'Let's go,' said Daphne, 'before the soldiers try to find us.'

She took a hold of Thorn's arm, while Caelius and Agang shepherded the two young Sanang men away with them. Daphne led them from the vicinity of the tavern, as her mind tried to recollect the layout of a town she hadn't visited for thirty years. After a few streets, she realised that she was lost, but that seemed irrelevant next to the fact that they had got away with their lives intact. She kept the others walking, to give them confidence that she knew where she was going. They reached a small square, where the shops were all boarded up for the night, and they sat by a flowerbed.

Agang put his head in his hands. 'They tried to kill us. The Empress tried to kill us.'

'What did you expect?' said Thorn. 'I am the greatest threat to her rule.'

'But we aren't trying to overthrow Bridget,' he said. 'She is still the Empress to whom we all swore an oath. She is still our sovereign ruler.'

'She is,' said Daphne, 'but to her, we are now traitors and rebels.'

'But the rest of the world will be horrified to find out what she did this night.'

'The rest of the world will never find out,' said Thorn. 'An accidental fire in a tavern; that's how it will be explained.'

'You did very well, Thorn,' said Daphne. 'You kept your head, and thought our way out. Best of all, no one died. The Empress might have been trying to provoke us into carrying out a massacre, but we avoided that, and we also avoided being burnt to a crisp.'

'What now?' said Caelius.

'I shall scout for an empty apartment,' said Daphne. 'And then we wait for Karalyn. The sooner we get back to Colsbury, the better. I have a feeling that the coastal road might not be very safe for us to travel on.' She glanced up at the sky. 'If you're watching us, Daimon, you should know that we aren't frightened of you. Make sure you tell the Empress that.'

***

Daphne glanced down at the silent streets. Caelius had volunteered to take the watch, but she had insisted that he get some sleep. The warehouse she had found was cold and draughty, but no one had seen them enter the empty building, and they had enjoyed a few hours of peace and quiet. She turned to look at the eastern horizon, and saw a faint patch of light creeping up into the sky. Another two hours until dawn, she thought.

'Are you ready to go home, mother?'

Daphne smiled. She glanced to her left and saw Karalyn standing a few feet away.

'I wasn't expecting you until later, dear.'

'Sable and I got back to Colsbury just a few minutes ago. It was midmorning where we were, and here it's still the middle of the night.'

'Where were you?'

'I'm not going to tell you that, in case Daimon reads your mind.'

'Do you know about the fire?'

'Aye. There's an option you haven't considered, mother; that Daimon did it, but the Empress didn't know. Daimon's young and impressionable; perhaps he was trying to impress Bridget by getting rid of you and Thorn.'

'I'd like to think that was true. I confess that it hurts to imagine that Bridget could so easily throw our lives away, after everything we've been through together over the years.'

Karalyn nodded, her eyes scanning the others as they lay sleeping on the floor of the warehouse.

'The two young Sanang gentlemen shall be staying with us in Colsbury,' said Daphne. 'A gift from the Matriarch.'

Karalyn nodded. 'And Caelius?'

'What about him, dear?'

'You've been spending a lot of time with him.'

Daphne smiled. 'That's none of your business, dear.'

'I agree, mother. It's none of my business. You should know that I fetched Cardova from the Salve City. I'm sure you'll agree that his presence is none of your business, either, and that if you try to interfere again, then that would make you a hypocrite.'

Daphne said nothing.

Karalyn caught her glance. 'Let's go home.'

CHAPTER 10
QUADRANT PRACTICE

Colsbury Castle, Republic of the Holdings – 21st Day, Last Third Summer 534

Sable crouched by the Sextant, and placed her Quadrant into one of the many gaps.

'Karalyn will be back soon,' said Cardova, as he leaned against the doorframe.

'I know,' said Sable. 'That's why I'm doing it now – before she has a chance to come back and change her mind.'

She stood, and laid her palm onto the glass surface of the huge device.

What is your desire, Sable?

'Can you see my Quadrant?'

Yes.

Sable smiled. 'That wasn't too bad. It only took nine attempts. Alright, Sextant; display the Quadrant in my mind. I want to see it.'

Sable's vision filled with an image of the surface of her Quadrant. Engravings she had barely noticed before shone out, bright and clear, while the jewels along the rim glistened with a light of their own.

'Show me what I need to touch to get to Ulna on Dragon Eyre.'

Three of the engravings glowed brighter than the others, and Sable laughed out loud.

'Gotcha, you bastard,' she cried. 'Were you timing that, Lucius? Apparently, Karalyn's had this device for years, and I figure it out in seconds. Sextant, do the same thing, but for Tara in Salve City.'

A different combination of engravings glowed on the image of the Quadrant.

'Now Serene on Implacatus.'

Sable stared at the image, remembering everything.

'And now Colsbury on this world.'

The image changed again, and she embedded the details into her mind.

'You have to touch the Quadrant in three separate places to travel to another world, it seems,' she said. 'I'll need to practise doing that with one hand.'

'Are you running away to Dragon Eyre now?' said Cardova.

She laughed. 'What a terrible thing to suggest, Lucius. Have you such little faith in me? Let's try something more ambitious. Sextant, show me how to build a new world.'

The image of the Quadrant vanished, and was replaced by swirling chaos. Sable felt herself be pulled into the internal mechanism of the Sextant, where she was surrounded by a moving, flashing maelstrom of cogs and wheels, wires and gears, glass and steel.

'Stop!' she cried. She lifted her hand from the device, as dizziness made her stagger. 'Maybe that was a little too ambitious.'

Cardova laughed. 'Were you trying to make Sable-world?"

'What a world that would be,' she said, placing her hand back onto the surface of the device. 'Right; I'm going to see if I can talk to Lara. Sextant, show me Ulna.'

Her vision changed again, and her heart soared as she caught sight of the island of Ulna. She lowered her gaze, controlling the actions of the Sextant without any direct command, and homed in on the town of Udall. She saw the enormous palace that sat above the wide, brown river, and she turned to the harbour. Many of the buildings were still in ruins, but the harbour itself was up and running, and was busy with ships of all sizes. Berthed at the far end of the quayside was the *Giddy Gull*, its decks swarming with workers. The quarter deck had been rebuilt, and carpenters were sawing wood and hammering nails for the new captain's cabin. Sable stared at the people there, then she saw Lara, standing close to the aft hatch, overseeing the work that was going on. The sight of her made Sable hesitate. What if Lara had moved on? What if she had forgotten about Sable? Maybe it would be better to leave her in peace.

Bollocks to that, she thought, and entered Lara's mind.

Lara; it's me – it's Sable.

The pirate captain froze mid-sentence. The carpenters by the aft hatch glanced up at her, and a few raised their eyebrows.

'You were saying, ma'am?' said one.

'Never mind that,' Lara cried. 'I've, eh... got something to do.'

She ran to the bow of the ship, which was empty of sailors and workers. She glanced around, then sat down by the bowsprit, her hands shaking.

Am I dreaming?

No, Lara; it's really me.

Are you dead?

What? No; I'm fine. My niece rescued me from Wyst.

Lara started to cry.

Everything's fine, Lara. I'll be coming for you soon. I promise. We'll be together soon.

Where are you?

I am on another world. It's been hard to find a way to reach you, but I managed it.

I've missed you so much. These last few months... they've been bleeding awful. I feel like my heart's been ripped out of my chest. Nobody wanted to try to rescue you – not Blackrose; no one. I thought you were dead.

I nearly died, but Karalyn got to me in time. She also rescued your father.

My father's with you?

Not exactly, but he's on the same world as I am. He robbed a Holdfast mansion of its silver and took off.

Lara laughed as tears spilled down her cheeks. *That sounds like something he'd do.*

I have to help my family with something, in return for them rescuing me. As soon as I've done that, then I will be back in your arms. Can you wait a little longer?

I love you, Sable; of course I'll bleeding wait. It's so good to hear your voice.

I love you, too, Lara. See you soon.

Sable lifted her palm from the Sextant, and the image dissolved. Cardova reached over and passed her a hanky. She frowned, then realised that tears were rolling down her face.

'So, you do have a heart,' he said.

'If you ever tell anyone that you saw me crying, I'll break your nose.'

'Karalyn's back,' he said.

'Yeah?' she said, wiping her eyes. 'Did she come in here?'

'No, but I heard the sound of Holder Fast shouting downstairs. She's not too happy about something.'

Sable slid her Quadrant out of the Sextant's flank, and hid it within an inside pocket of her coat. She listened, and could hear the faint sounds of an argument coming from somewhere in the Great Keep.

'Let's see what the fuss is about,' she said.

'It might be none of our business.'

'There's only one way to find out. Besides, they might be arguing about us, in which case it most certainly is our business. How are my eyes? Can you tell?'

He shook his head.

'Come on,' she said.

They strode from the room, and descended a flight of stairs, as the sound of the argument grew louder. They walked along the hallway, and Sable pushed open the door of the main living room.

'You're being utterly irresponsible, daughter,' Daphne was yelling, her finger an inch from Karalyn's face. 'You're putting us in grave danger.'

'I have no choice, mother.'

'What's going on?' said Sable.

Agang glanced at her. 'Imperial soldiers attempted to kill us on the Sanang frontier,' he said; 'while you and Karalyn were away.'

'And she's intending to abandon us again!' Daphne cried. 'We'll be at Daimon's mercy if she goes to Implacatus.'

'I can't leave Belinda with Edmond,' said Karalyn, keeping her voice calm. 'If it was your friend, mother, you would do the same.'

'But Belinda betrayed us, right here in Colsbury. Have you forgotten that?'

'Of course I haven't forgotten,' said Karalyn. 'She made a mistake.'

'And so did you, by restoring all of her powers. If you bring her back here, she could kill us all.'

'You're being ridiculous, mother.'

Daphne glanced at her half-sister. 'Back me up, Sable. You know what Belinda's like.'

'I'm not getting involved in this,' said Sable.

'Why not? You stick your nose into everything else. You loathe Belinda; you always have.'

'Yes. I suppose that's true.'

'Then why would you want to rescue her?'

'Why did anyone want to rescue me?'

'Don't deflect; answer the question.'

'I told Karalyn that I would help. That's it. It's as simple as that.'

'Only because you want to go back to Dragon Eyre.'

Sable took out her Quadrant. 'I know how to get to Dragon Eyre. I could leave right now; in fact, I'm a little tempted to, if only to escape this pointless argument.'

Karalyn frowned. 'You've learned how to get to Dragon Eyre already? I was only away for fifteen minutes.'

'What can I say?' said Sable. 'I also learned how to travel to Implacatus, Salve City and the Star Continent. I'll show you later, when people aren't screaming at each other.'

'Tell me your solution, then,' said Daphne, her eyes narrow; 'if you're so damn smart. How should we protect ourselves from Daimon while you're on Implacatus?'

Sable shrugged. 'I can think of one solution.' She glanced at Karalyn. 'Take them all to the same place we took the twins.'

'Was it somewhere on this world?' said Thorn, her eyes narrow as she glanced at Daphne's sister.

Sable shook her head.

'Then no. I'm not leaving the Star Continent.'

'Maybe you should,' said Sable. 'Daimon would be clueless about your location. He wouldn't know that you had left; he'd probably think that we had Kelsey back with us.'

'No,' said Thorn. 'I need to be here, to react to anything the Empress does. I need to be visible. I need the people to know that I haven't deserted them.'

'I tend to agree,' said Daphne. 'The only solution is that Karalyn stays. Perhaps Sable and Lucius Cardova could conduct the operation on their own.'

Sable shrugged. 'Alright.'

'No,' snapped Karalyn. 'There's no way that's happening. Sorry, mother, but you're just going to have to manage on your own for a little while. I can't be everywhere at once.'

Daphne glared at her. 'You disappoint me, daughter. Don't be too shocked if you return to find our decapitated bodies dangling upside down from the battlements of the Great Fortress in Plateau City.'

Karalyn lowered her gaze, her rising temper evident in her eyes.

'I'm going to see Kelsey,' said Sable. 'Can I take her the God-King's Quadrant?'

'What?' said Karalyn.

'Remember we were discussing showing Kelsey how to travel here? I can do that now while you argue things out.'

Karalyn sighed. 'Fine. Don't be long; I want to leave in the next few hours.'

Sable glanced at Cardova. 'You coming, Lucius?'

'No. I think I will stay here.'

'No problem. Catch you all later.'

She swept her thumb over the Quadrant, and appeared in the Sextant chamber. She pulled the other Quadrant from the side of the device, then examined the engravings. She wasn't sure exactly where within Tara she would appear, and she hoped it wouldn't be a hundred feet above the ground.

She brushed a thumb and two fingers across the copper-coloured surface, and the air crackled. Her surroundings changed, and she was drenched in the rains of Sweetmist, the torrential downpour soaking through her clothes in seconds.

'Bugger,' she muttered, glancing around. She saw the ruins of the palace that sat at one end of Princeps Row, then ran down the street, avoiding the streams of water flowing over the paving slabs. She came to the mansion that Van used as his headquarters in Tara, and took shelter by the doorway, where two Banner soldiers were on guard.

'Is Kelsey here?' she cried over the sound of the rain. 'I'm her aunt.'

'She is, ma'am,' said one of the soldiers. 'Wait here; I'll tell her that you've arrived.'

The soldier ducked into the building, and Sable leaned against the wall, her clothes and hair dripping. She noticed the other soldier staring at her.

'Yes?' she said, raising an eyebrow.

'Sorry, ma'am, but are you holding two Quadrants?'

Sable smiled. 'Yes, I am. I'm a Holdfast; we always carry at least two Quadrants with us.'

The soldier frowned. 'Are you taking the piss, ma'am?'

She laughed. 'Tell me – do you not mind working for people that the Ascendants would classify as enemies?'

'A contract's a contract, ma'am. We don't get involved in politics.'

Sable nodded, her thoughts on the thousands of Banner soldiers stranded on Dragon Eyre. The other soldier emerged from the building and gestured for Sable to enter. Sable smiled at him, then strode into the mansion. Kelsey was waiting for her in the entrance hall.

'You look like a drowned rat, Sable,' she said. 'What's up? You only left an hour ago. Did you miss me already?'

Sable shook her hair, showering Kelsey with raindrops. 'Look what I'm holding in my hands.'

Kelsey glanced down, then her eyes widened. 'Is that the God-King's Quadrant? Did you steal it from Karalyn?'

'No. She agreed to let you borrow it. Do you have any spare clothes I can change into? Once I'm dry, I can show you how to use your new toy.'

'I don't have much in your style,' said Kelsey; 'but I'll take you to my room, and you can raid my wardrobe.'

'I was wearing one of Maddie's summer dresses when I fought Bastion; I'm sure I'll manage.'

An hour later, Sable was dressed in an ankle-length gown while her normal clothes dried in front of a roaring fire. Kelsey had filled several pages in her leather-bound notebook, and was staring at her new Quadrant.

'This is amazing, Sable,' Kelsey said. 'Thank you.'

'Make sure you don't misplace that notebook,' said Sable. 'We wouldn't want Naxor to find it.'

'Naxor's locked up with a bag on his head. He's going nowhere.'

'Are you ready to try out the Quadrant?'

'Where should we go? Jezra?'

'How about we find Amalia?' said Sable. 'We never got round to visiting her this morning, and I still want to find out how to refine salve.'

'The thing is, I don't know exactly where the old tyrant lives. I know she has a small villa somewhere in Roser territory, but the precise location is a secret.'

'I assume Queen Emily knows?'

'Oh aye. I think Van knows, too, but he's not allowed to tell me. Not that I particularly care.'

'Is Van in his office?'

Kelsey nodded.

Sable sent her powers out, and sped them through the mansion until she reached Van. She dove straight into his eyes, and remained silent as she rummaged about in his memories. She paused for a moment when she came across recollections of his addiction to salve, then she pushed on, locating the address where Amalia lived with her mortal companion and their young child.

'Right. Got it,' she said.

Kelsey frowned at her. 'I hope you didn't dig around too much in there.'

'Would I do a thing like that? Now, I'll need to scout out the address, to get the distance and direction.'

'Aye. That's something I'll never be able to do.'

'You'll just have to learn where everything is. Get hold of an accurate map, and measure out the distances. Back in a moment.'

She sent out her powers again, racing them sunward and east from Princeps Row. It took her a few minutes to find the correct villa through the torrential rain. She noted where it was, then cut the connection.

'Alright, Kelsey. Let's imagine that sunward is south for a moment. In that case, we'll need to go five-and-a-quarter miles, eight degrees south of east-by-south-east. It's roughly the same altitude as where we're sitting at the moment, but there's a slight chance we'll arrive a few feet above the ground. But hey, that's a lot better than a few feet below the ground. I used to always over-compensate for that, and I often fell through the air when I first started practising.'

'Is it exactly five-and-a-quarter miles away?'

'No; it's a little less than that, but let's not get too ambitious. If you try to arrive inside the villa at this stage, we'll probably end up in a wall.

Five-and-a-quarter miles will get us into the garden, and that should do for now.'

'You know, you could probably just read Amalia's mind from here.'

'I know, but where's the fun in that? I want to see you use the Quadrant before I head back.'

'But... Amalia?'

'Are you scared of her?'

'She doesn't like me very much. She held me and Aila hostage on Lostwell.'

'That was ages ago. I think I'd like to meet her. I mean, she was the God-Queen of the entire City.'

Kelsey frowned. 'If you insist.'

'I do. Grab an umbrella, and we'll go.'

Kelsey glanced down at the twins, who were playing on the rug. 'What about them?'

'They'll be fine,' said Sable. 'We'll only be a few minutes.'

Kelsey got up, and selected a large umbrella from a rack by the door. She opened it, then Sable stood, and pulled on her half-dry coat.

'Um, could you hold the umbrella?' said Kelsey. 'I'll need both hands free for this.'

'Sure.'

Kelsey passed her the umbrella, then she peered at the surface of the Quadrant in her hands.

Sable smiled. 'Whenever you're ready.'

Kelsey exhaled, then she drew her index finger over the surface of the Quadrant. The air shimmered, and they appeared close to a giant hedgerow, the rain pelting down onto them. They dropped a few inches, and landed on the sodden turf. Sable saw the villa fifty yards from where they stood, and she patted Kelsey on the back. Kelsey grinned, then she placed the Quadrant into her shoulder bag.

They ran across the grass, the umbrella flapping in the wind, then Sable banged her fist on the front door. After a few moments, an eye appeared through the small spy-hole in the centre of the door.

'Who is it?' said a man's voice.

'It's just a couple of Holdfasts,' Sable yelled over the noise of the storm. 'Rather wet Holdfasts.'

'What do you want?'

'To be warm and dry would be nice,' Sable said.

'Who is there?' came a woman's voice.

'Two Holdfasts,' said the man. 'One of them is Kelsey, but I don't recognise the other.'

The woman sighed. 'Let them in.'

Several bolts and locks were loosened and turned, then the door swung open. The man was eyeing Sable and Kelsey with suspicion, while the young-looking woman had her arms folded over her chest.

'Are you here to kill me?' said the woman.

Kelsey snorted. 'What?'

'Can we come in?' said Sable, pushing past the man and entering the villa. 'I'm Sable Holdfast. I was in Lostwell, though we never met.'

Kelsey backed into the entrance, then folded up the umbrella. The man closed the door, and the roar of noise subsided.

'My name is Amalia, and this is Kagan,' said the woman; 'although I presume you already knew that. How did you find out where we live?'

'I read someone's mind,' said Sable. 'Don't worry; I won't tell anyone.'

'You won't be able to use your powers on me,' said Amalia; 'not while Kelsey is here.'

Sable smiled, but said nothing.

'Kagan, boil a kettle, and we shall prepare some tea for our guests.'

'You have tea?' said Kelsey. 'Real tea?'

'Yes. A gift from Queen Emily. Well, from the Holdfasts, if I'm being strictly accurate. It somewhat pained me to drink it, knowing who supplied it, but it's better than the local alternatives. The City was always lacking a few decent little luxuries.'

She led them into a comfortable room, with thick carpets and wall-hangings, where the shutters were firmly closed against the weather. Kagan picked up a small boy from the floor, and left through another door.

'Sit, please,' said Amalia, gesturing toward a long couch.

'We have news about Belinda,' said Kelsey, once they had taken their seats.

Amalia's eyes sharpened. 'You do?'

Sable frowned. 'Do you know Belinda?'

'They were old friends from long ago,' said Kelsey.

'Belinda was my best friend for centuries,' said Amalia. 'Tell me; what news?'

'She's on Implacatus, and she's being forced into marrying Edmond.'

Amalia stared at Kelsey, the colour draining from her face.

'Bastion mentioned that she had been put in a restrainer mask,' said Sable.

'No,' gasped Amalia, her eyes welling.

'But here's the good news,' Sable went on. 'Karalyn and I are going to rescue her.'

Amalia raised a hand. 'Slow down. You spoke to Lord Bastion?'

'Yes,' said Sable; 'right before I kicked his arse. Kolai told me the same; just before I sawed his head off.'

'Lord Kolai is dead?'

Sable nodded.

'By your hands?'

Sable nodded again.

'And now you and... Sorry, what was her name?'

'Karalyn.'

'You and Karalyn are going to Implacatus?'

'That's right. Today, in fact. As soon as I get back to the Star Continent.'

'You came all this way to tell me?' said Amalia. 'Thank you.'

'I had another reason,' said Sable. 'I have a large bag of raw salve, and I would quite like to know how to refine it.'

Amalia waved a hand. 'Oh. That's easy. I could write down some simple instructions for you. Naxor always treated it as a state secret, but there's nothing to it, really. Let's go back to Belinda. She will most likely be in Cumulus. Have you ever been there?'

'No. I've been to Serene, once, but not Cumulus.'

'And has Karalyn been? Who is this Karalyn, by the way? I assume that she is yet another Holdfast.'

'She's my big sister,' said Kelsey.

'And she's the most powerful mortal mage in existence,' said Sable. 'We'll manage.'

'You'll get killed, you mean. The Ascendants and Ancients of Cumulus routinely wear protective eye-guards. Did you know that? They're always worried that someone will read their minds. How are you going to overcome that? Why aren't you taking Corthie?'

Sable frowned.

'I used to live in Cumulus,' Amalia went on. 'Everyone is paranoid that the others are trying to undermine their power and authority, and no one trusts anyone else. Edmond's palace is the greatest fortress ever constructed. It was designed to be almost impossible to Quadrant into, and whole areas are protected by screens of gauze that prevent anyone from using vision powers to scan what's going on inside. Were you aware of any of this, Sable Holdfast?'

'No. I wasn't.'

Kagan walked back into the room carrying a tray.

'Darling,' said Amalia, 'I might have to go away for a short time.'

'Go away?' said Kagan. 'Where?'

'One of my dearest friends is in serious trouble, and I am going to help her.'

'What?' said Kelsey.

'I think you heard me, Miss Holdfast. It seems clear to me that this rescue mission is destined to fail without my assistance. I don't think Queen Emily will mind if I leave the City for a while.'

Kelsey glanced at Sable. 'Say something.'

'It's not up to me,' said Sable. 'Karalyn is in charge of the operation.' She smiled at Amalia. 'But, I'm liking where this conversation is going. An extra god with soulwitch powers could be very useful. I'll have to warn you, though – Karalyn will probably want to read your mind first, before deciding. You know, to make sure you're not a homicidal maniac.'

Kelsey snorted. 'Good luck with that.'

'How do you intend to travel to Implacatus?' said Amalia.

Sable tapped her coat pocket. 'I have a Quadrant; and the Holdfasts have possession of the Sextant that was on Lostwell.'

'You want to go to Implacatus?' said Kagan. 'That sounds dangerous.'

'It will be dangerous, darling,' said Amalia; 'but needs must. Perhaps if I assist in the rescue of Belinda, she might finally forgive me. I would give a lot to be her friend again.' She stood. 'I'm going to pack a few things, but I travel light, so I won't be long.'

Amalia strode from the room, the hem of her dress swishing off the carpet.

'This is a dreadful mistake,' said Kelsey. 'One giant ego on the trip was enough; now there will be two.'

'You had better not be referring to me,' said Sable.

'Of course I'm referring to you. Let's face it, Sable, you aren't exactly modest. Within ten seconds of meeting Amalia you'd already told her that you'd beaten up Bastion and beheaded Kolai. The only reason I put up with your bragging is because I know you can back it up. You actually have done all the shit you say you have. Oh, and by the way, Amalia *is* a homicidal maniac.'

'Was,' said Kagan. 'She may have been a killer once, but she's changed.'

'Not too much, I hope,' said Sable. 'We could do with another killer on the team.'

Kagan scowled at her.

'You might as well head on home to the twins, Kelsey,' said Sable. 'I'll take Amalia to Colsbury, and we'll speak to Karalyn. And thanks for mentioning Belinda; it hadn't occurred to me to do that.'

'I did it as a polite conversation opener, not because I thought she'd want to tag along,' said Kelsey, taking out her Quadrant. 'Well, good luck and all that. I was never a great admirer of Belinda, but she did alright on Lostwell. I hope you find her.'

Kelsey's fingers touched the surface of the Quadrant, and she vanished.

'She forgot to stand up,' said Sable. 'Right now, she's falling on her arse.'

'Will the Holdfasts take good care of Amalia?' said Kagan. 'Maxwell's young, and he needs his mother alive.'

'She's thousands of years old, yeah? And you're a mortal – how did you two end up together? I thought Corthie and Aila's relationship was weird enough.'

'I didn't know she was a god when we met.'

'Yeah, but she knew.'

'That's none of your business,' said Amalia from the door. She had changed out of her dress, and was wearing clothes more suited for travelling. By her feet was a packed bag. 'I've kissed Maxwell goodbye,' she went on, 'and told him that I will be back in a few days.'

'And will you?' said Kagan, getting to his feet.

'That's the plan,' said Sable.

Amalia glanced around the room. 'Where did Kelsey go?'

'We've loaned her the God-King's Quadrant,' said Sable. 'She's gone back to Tara.'

'So, the Quadrants that Malik and I brought here have returned to the City? Apt, I suppose.' She glanced at Kagan. 'Well, darling; it's time to go. Take care, and I'll see you soon.'

They embraced, then kissed.

'I don't like this,' said Kagan. 'I don't trust the Holdfasts.'

'Neither do I, darling, but Belinda is the priority. It is my duty to help her; to save her from the vile clutches of Lord Edmond. What kind of friend would I be if I abandoned her to that fate?' She glanced at Sable. 'I am ready.'

Sable got to her feet, and took out her Quadrant.

'Where did you obtain that?' said Amalia.

'It used to belong to the governor of Dragon Eyre.'

'You were in Dragon Eyre?'

Sable smiled, then brushed her fingers over the surface. The air crackled, and they found themselves in the Sextant chamber in Colsbury. Karalyn and Cardova were also in the room, and the Banner soldier's mouth fell open.

'What have you done, Sable?' he said. 'Why is Amalia here?'

Karalyn narrowed her eyes. 'Amalia? You mean this is the former God-Queen of the City?'

Amalia smiled. 'I'm so glad that my reputation precedes me.'

'I don't know which sight is more surprising,' said Cardova; 'Amalia, or Sable in a gown.'

'I forgot that it was a little wet in the City,' said Sable. 'I'll get changed in a moment. Are we ready to go? Where's Daphne?'

'Sulking,' said Karalyn. 'Why is Amalia here?'

'Isn't it obvious, my dear Holdfast?' said Amalia. 'I'm here to prevent you from making complete fools of yourselves in Cumulus. I know Cumulus – I used to live there. More importantly, Belinda is the best friend I ever had, and I would like to offer you my assistance. You have but one chance of success, and that is if you permit me to come along.'

Cardova groaned.

'I want to read your mind first,' said Karalyn.

'Sable said you might. Please proceed. Everyone in the City knows what I have done; the Holdfasts might as well know, too.'

Sable strode from the room as Karalyn stared into Amalia's eyes. She went to her bedroom, pulled off the gown, then dressed in her more usual travelling clothes. She picked up her packed bag and swung it over a shoulder, then checked her appearance in the wall mirror. Her hair was a bit messy from the wind and rain, so she gave it a quick brush, then walked back to the Sextant chamber.

'I'm ready,' she said. 'Is Amalia coming?'

'Aye,' said Karalyn.

'Did you read her mind?'

Karalyn nodded. 'Her love for Belinda is genuine. I don't care about the things she's done in her past; each one of us standing here has committed acts that we're not proud of.'

Amalia smiled.

'How are we getting there?' said Sable. 'Sextant or Quadrant?'

'Let's use the Sextant,' said Karalyn. 'That way, we can be more precise with our arrival point. Where should we start?'

'Allow me,' said Sable. 'I know a safe place, where we can plan our attack.'

'But...'

'Trust me, niece.'

Karalyn sighed, but did nothing to prevent Sable from striding up to the Sextant. She placed her hand onto the glass surface of the device.

What is your desire, Sable?

'Show me Serene,' she said, and an image of the city in the mountains appeared before her. She scanned down to one of the lower levels and scouted for a few moments, until she located the right place.

'Found it,' she said.

'Where?' said Karalyn.

'You'll see. Sextant, take all four of us to the location I can see.'

The air crackled, then Sable, Karalyn, Cardova and Amalia appeared in a grimy kitchen, lit by a smoking oil lamp. A young man and two older women jumped up from the table where they had been eating dinner.

Sable smiled at the young man.

'Hi, Austin. Sorry I'm late.'

CHAPTER 11
INTO THE SUNLIGHT

Tara, Auldan, The City – 11th Namen 3423

Kelsey appeared back in her rooms in the mansion on Princeps Row, and fell onto the rug with a thump.

'Not the most dignified of arrivals,' she said.

The twins glanced at her from where they were sitting on the floor.

'Where were you, Aunty?' said Kyra.

Kelsey slipped the Quadrant into her shoulder bag. 'I was taking Aunty Sable to see someone. I was only gone for five minutes. I hope you didn't get up to any mischief.'

'Can we see Frostback now?' said Cael.

'Soon. I'd better tell the Queen what just happened.'

'We will stay here,' said Kyra.

'No,' said Kelsey, as she got to her feet; 'you'd better come with me.'

'Why? You left us here on our own when you disappeared with Aunty Sable.'

'Aye, but that was only for a few minutes. This will take longer.'

'But I don't want to walk in the rain.'

Kelsey grinned. 'We won't have to.' She took out her Quadrant. 'See? I have one of these now. No more walking about in the rain for us. Now, I just have to work out the distance to the inside of the Aurelian mansion. Twins, which one of you can check to see where Queen Emily is?'

Cael's arm shot up in the air. 'Me! I can do it. Let me do it, Aunty Kelsey.'

Kyra smiled. 'I've just done it. Queen Emily is in the kitchen eating toast.'

'That's not fair!' cried Cael.

'It's not my fault you're too slow.'

Kelsey stared at the surface of the Quadrant. The Aurelian mansion was probably about a hundred and fifty yards away, but she started to doubt herself. Was 'probably' good enough? Could she risk taking the twins if there was a danger that they might appear in the middle of a stone wall? She needed to practice in an open area, but none would be available until the end of Sweetmist, and then there was the Fog of Balian to get through.

'Bollocks,' she muttered. 'Maybe we should walk.'

Kyra reached out with a finger, and touched the Quadrant. The air shimmered, and they appeared in the kitchen of the Aurelian mansion.

Kelsey and Emily jumped at the same time, and the Queen dropped her toast.

'How did you do that?' Kelsey asked Kyra, who smiled in return.

'How did *you* do that?' said Emily. 'Where did you get that Quadrant?'

'Um, it's the God-King's,' said Kelsey. 'Sable popped back for a bit, and gave it to me. Karalyn's letting me borrow it, whatever that means. Sable showed me how to travel to the Star Continent, and then back here again. I was deciding whether to use it or not, when Kyra touched it, and, well, here we are.'

Kyra shrugged. 'I just told it to bring us here; that's all. It was easy.'

Emily leaned over and picked up her toast from the wooden floorboards. She narrowed her eyes at it, then tossed it into a bin.

'It could be very useful,' Kelsey said.

'I'm not so sure about that,' said Emily. 'What if, say, Amalia or Naxor got hold of it? They would be able to go to your home world.'

'Well, no; they wouldn't. Not unless someone showed them where to press, and I don't plan on doing that any time soon. Besides, Amalia's gone. Sable and I visited her, to learn about refining salve, and Amalia decided to go with Sable to Implacatus to help rescue Belinda. The former God-Queen of the City is no longer in the City.'

'Lady Amalia is supposed to ask for permission before she leaves her villa, never mind the entire City. Did she leave Kagan and Maxwell behind?'

'Eh, aye. I assume so. I wasn't actually there when they left.'

Emily pursed her lips. 'We should let Daniel know. He probably won't be pleased about this, but he needs to know.'

The Queen gestured towards a door, and Kelsey ushered the twins along. They walked down a wide corridor, and past two Banner soldiers, who bowed their heads. A courtier opened the doors to the audience chamber, and they walked in. Daniel was seated with a few advisors, and he glanced up as Emily approached.

'We need to speak with Kelsey alone, dear,' she said.

Daniel glanced at his advisors, and they bowed, and left the chamber.

'What's this about?' Daniel said.

'There have been two rather important developments,' said Emily, taking her seat next to the King. 'Firstly, it appears that Lady Amalia has left this world. Sable Holdfast has spirited her away, so that she can travel to Implacatus with them.'

Daniel nodded. 'Is it too much to hope that she doesn't come back?'

'You might be missing the point, darling. Amalia knows how to get to the City. If she is captured on Implacatus, she could tell the Ascendants.'

'Karalyn will probably block her mind, so that vision powers won't work on her,' said Kelsey.

'I'm not sure that matters,' said Emily. 'If she is threatened with torture, do you honestly believe that she will keep her mouth shut?'

'Aye, I do. She won't want to lead them to Maxwell.'

'I sincerely hope you are right.'

'What was the other thing?' said Daniel.

Emily frowned. 'Kelsey is in possession of the God-King's Quadrant. The one that Princess Yendra gave Blackrose, so that they could travel to Lostwell.'

Daniel shrugged. 'So, now we have two useless Quadrants?'

'Not quite. Sable Holdfast has taught Kelsey how to use the device.'

Kelsey grinned. 'Think of the opportunities this gives us. The City is short of everything, right? While the Star Continent has all that we lack. With a Quadrant, I could pop back and forward, and bring us whatever we need.'

'Yes, but in exchange for what, Kelsey?' said Emily. 'The only surplus goods or products that we have consist of concrete, or seaweed. Somehow, I don't think the Star Continent will be lacking in those.'

'You know what I think,' said Kelsey.

'No. What do you think?' said Daniel.

Emily frowned. 'She wants us to export salve, dear.'

'Why not?' said Kelsey. 'It makes sense. Not only does the Star Continent not have anything like it, it would be in great demand. The City could charge a fortune for a few tons of the stuff. Imagine, we could import all the coal and timber we need, not to mention coffee and all of the other luxuries that exist on my home world. What about cows and pigs? The recent troubles almost wiped out the herds in Gloamer and Evader territory; we could restock them. And horses, too. And chocolate, Emily; think about the chocolate.'

'There's another problem,' said Daniel. 'Even if we decided to agree to this, Kelsey, with whom should we trade?'

Kelsey raised an eyebrow. 'What?'

'Didn't Karalyn and Sable tell us that the Holdfasts are now enemies of the sovereign ruler of the Star Continent? We should not get involved in this dispute, but we shall, if we pick one side or the other to trade with.'

'I wouldn't say that they are enemies. Yet.'

'So, Daphne Holdfast would have no problem with us supplying salve to the Empress? That could give her a considerable advantage in any coming conflict.'

'And it would also give the impression that we are snubbing the Holdfasts,' said Emily. 'The same Holdfasts who were so generous with their gifts. The same Holdfasts who have promised to help defend the City if we are attacked. We would look remarkably ungrateful.'

'Then, trade with the Holdfasts,' Kelsey said.

'And bypass the appointed ruler of your home world?' said Daniel. 'The Holdfasts are rebels, are they not? As sovereigns of the City, Emily and I can only deal with other sovereigns; and not with rebels.'

'The Holdfasts aren't rebels,' said Kelsey. 'We just happen to disagree with one particular decision that the Empress has made.'

'Then you should have no concerns about us treating with the Empress,' said Daniel. 'We would need to establish a point of contact before any trade could commence. Perhaps we should send a delegation to the Star Continent to request an audience with Empress Bridget.'

'And offer them what?' said Emily.

'I'm afraid I am starting to agree with Kelsey regarding salve,' said Daniel. 'Think of the difference we could make to the City if we could exchange a few tons of salve for all of the items we so desperately need. As things stand at the moment, we do not have enough reserves to heat the homes of the City's inhabitants this coming winter, and it will be years before we have a plentiful supply of wood again. I miss the old news sheets that used to be printed daily in Ooste; without them, we have no reliable way to pass on information to the citizens. The salve that lies in the Eastern Mountains could resolve all that; furthermore, its trade would bring our two worlds closer together.'

Emily lowered her gaze. 'I don't know. Selling salve seems to go against every instinct in my body.'

'But, we would be selling to our allies. That feels very different to being forced to hand it over to Implacatus. Many of our citizens are dispirited. After the greenhide incursion, and then Simon's depredations, they could do with something to lift their morale. Imagine the effect that all those little luxuries will have on the common people, once they start to appear in the markets of the City.'

'I'll need more time to consider it,' said Emily. 'Tell me, Kelsey – what is Van's opinion on this?'

'We should ask him,' said Kelsey.

'I can fetch him,' said Kyra. 'I know where he is.'

Kelsey glanced down at the girl, who was holding out her hand for the Quadrant.

'I'm not sure that's a good idea.'

Kyra shrugged. 'You can get wet if you want, Aunty. Or, you can count to ten, and I'll be back here with Van.'

Kelsey crouched down next to her, the Quadrant in her hands. 'How would you do it?'

'I'd say, "Take me to Van", and then I'd say, 'Take us back to Aunty Kelsey".'

Kelsey glanced at the window, where the rain was pelting against the glass.

'Let her do it,' said Emily. 'She got you here, after all.'

Kyra grinned, and her smile reminded Kelsey of Sable. She handed over the Quadrant, and the girl vanished. Kelsey started to count, but she had only got as far as three when Kyra reappeared, a bewildered-looking Van standing next to her.

Cael laughed at the expression on Van's face, then Kyra curtsied, and passed the Quadrant back to Kelsey.

'Well done, Kyra,' said Emily, smiling. 'Perhaps we should loan the God-Queen's Quadrant to the twins.'

Van narrowed his eyes. 'I hope someone is going to explain to me what is going on.'

***

Kelsey stared at the map lying on the table in front of her. She had a ruler in one hand and a pencil in the other, and she was taking notes of the distances between Tara and Jezra.

Kyra looked up from the chair where she was sitting. 'Let me do it, Aunty.'

'No. I need to learn on my own.'

'Why don't you have vision powers, Aunty?' said Cael.

'That's a strange question. Why don't you have two heads?'

Cael laughed. 'But the other Holdfasts have vision powers.'

'Uncle Corthie doesn't,' said Kyra.

'He's got battle-vision. That's a kind of vision.'

'The only thing I'm good at,' said Kelsey, 'is blocking other people's powers. Except, you know, I can't turn it off and on like your mother can. Right. As far as I can judge, the foundations of the ruined palace in Jezra are three-and-a-third miles away. It's a big, open space; so we should be fine if I've made a mistake.'

'Are we going to get wet?' said Cael.

'Aye.'

Kyra tutted.

'Don't give me your cheek,' said Kelsey.

'I didn't say anything.'

'No, but you made a loud tutting sound, and that counts as cheek.'

'I wasn't being cheeky,' said Cael.

'No,' said Kelsey; 'you weren't. You...' Her voice trailed off as she looked into the boy's eyes. Her vision clouded, and she saw the interior of a room. It wasn't anywhere she recognised; but, judging by the blood on the walls, violence had swept through it not long before. Heavily-armoured soldiers were standing in groups, while Daphne was crouching before Cael, her hand enclosing his. Daphne was smiling at her grandson, but her eyes betrayed the fear and pain she was feeling.

'Be brave, Cael. Everything's going to be all right,' Daphne said, then the vision vanished, and Kelsey found herself staring at the young boy.

'Why are you looking at him like that, Aunty?' said Kyra.

Kelsey blinked. 'What? No reason.'

Van opened the door and walked into the room. 'Are you still here? I thought you were going to visit Frostback and Halfclaw in Jezra.'

Kelsey shook the vision from her mind. The events it foretold could be years away, and were ambiguous. Besides, what could she do about it?

Van peered at her. 'What's wrong?'

'Nothing,' said Kelsey. 'I just needed to double-check the distance. Too short, and we'll end up drowning in the Straits; too far, and we'll be entombed in the side of the cliffs.'

Van nodded, then took a seat by the table. 'I've agreed to lead the trade delegation to the Star Continent.'

'That's nice.'

'Their Majesties want you to come as well.'

'To see Bridget? Is that a good idea?'

'The Queen is concerned that the Empress's new dream mage might try to use his powers to his advantage.'

'And how am I supposed to stop that? My powers won't work on him.'

Van frowned. 'But didn't Karalyn use your powers to hide the twins?'

'Aye, but that's completely different. Daimon can't find me with his powers; but he won't need to if I'm standing right in front of him. I can't stop him using dream powers on other people, just like I can't stop Karalyn doing the same thing. I'll be able to block any ordinary vision mage who happens to be there, but not Daimon. Apart from Karalyn, the only people who could conceivably do that are the twins.'

'Can we come?' said Cael.

'Your mother is trying to keep you safe from Daimon,' said Van. 'I don't think she'd be happy if we took you to see him.'

'I'm not afraid of Daimon,' said Kyra.

'And we wouldn't tell mama,' said Cael.

'Can we go, please?' said Kyra.

Kelsey shook her head. 'Do you two hate the rain that much?'

'Aye,' said Kyra. 'Every time I look out of a window I feel sad.'

'I can fix that; at least, for a while.'

'Are you taking us back to Colsbury?' said Cael, his eyes lighting up.

'No, but I'm ready to go to Jezra.'

'But it's raining in Jezra.'

'You aren't the only ones who are sick of Sweetmist,' said Kelsey. 'Stand up, and we'll go. Get ready to run towards the entrance to the cave where the dragons live.'

The twins got to their feet. They eyed each other, their expressions suspicious.

'What will I tell their Majesties?' said Van.

'I don't know,' said Kelsey. 'I guess I could go to Plateau City with you, but I won't be of any use.'

Van nodded. 'Alright. See you later.'

Kelsey swiped her fingers over the Quadrant. The air wavered, then the torrential rain hit her and the twins as they appeared on the stone foundations of the ancient palace in Jezra. Kyra shrieked, then they started running towards the cliff face, jumping over the enormous puddles that lay on the crumbling stonework. Lightning flashed somewhere ahead of them, and the grey skies turned silver for a moment. Kelsey herded the twins under the cover of the entrance to a huge cavern that had been excavated from the side of the cliff, and the smell of dragons struck her nostrils. They stood there for a moment, their clothes and hair dripping, as the storm raged outside; then they turned, and Kelsey led the children into the dark interior of the cavern.

Hello!' she cried out.

Two dragon heads emerged from the gloom.

'My rider,' said Frostback. 'Have you come to relieve the misery of this dreadful weather?'

'I've got something to show you,' she said. She held the Quadrant aloft. 'Look at my new toy.'

Frostback's eyes glowed. 'Has the Queen given you her device?'

'No. This is the God-King's Quadrant; well, it was. Sable brought it, and then she taught me how to use it. Do you want to get away from the rain for a while?'

'And go where?' said Halfclaw.

'I was thinking of the sunward desert,' said Kelsey.

'My beloved rider,' said Frostback. 'How I yearn to feel the sun's rays upon my scales and wings. That is an excellent suggestion.'

'Are you able to take both of us?' said Halfclaw.

'Aye; that's easy. It's distance and direction I'm having problems with, but it should be fairly simple to find the desert. How many miles away would you say it is?'

'The marshlands peter out after one hundred and fifty miles,' said Frostback.

'Alright. I'll take us a hundred and seventy, just to be on the safe side. Then we can get airborne, and look for an oasis.'

Kelsey glanced down at her Quadrant, and planned out what she needed to do. Kyra reached out to touch the device, but Kelsey lifted it away.

'I have to do it, Kyra,' she said; 'otherwise, I'll never learn.'

She swept two fingers over the surface of the Quadrant, and the air shimmered, then brightened; and they found themselves standing on a sand dune. The sun was blazing down from a blue sky, and Kelsey felt its fierce heat bear down upon her. The two dragons stretched their wings and arched their long necks.

Kelsey laughed. 'Is that better?'

'Much better,' said Frostback. 'Climb up, and we shall fly.'

The silver dragon lowered herself close to the scorching sand, and Kelsey helped the twins clamber up the harness straps and onto the saddle. She climbed up last, and made sure the twins were securely fastened to the harness.

Frostback turned her head, then, seeing that her passengers were ready, she lifted into the air. Halfclaw did the same, and they circled over the desert for a moment, then sped off towards iceward. The air was warm, but the speed of the dragons made it feel cool and comfortable to Kelsey as they soared over the flat, baked wasteland. After a few minutes, Frostback caught sight of a tiny patch of green, and they veered to the west. They swooped low over the oasis, then landed close by.

'This is perfect,' said Kelsey. 'A pool, and some trees for shade; it's beautiful.'

'And all the more welcome after so many days of unceasing rain,' said Frostback. She watched as Kelsey unbuckled the straps holding her and the twins to the harness. 'One thing I loved about the Holdings, rider, was the weather. I loved the mountains there, too, and the long, green valleys that ran between the snow-capped peaks.'

Kelsey jumped down to the sand. 'It sounds as though you prefer it to here.'

'I do,' said the dragon. 'I would rather live there than here; as long as you and Halfclaw were with me.'

Kelsey frowned. 'Seriously? You'd rather stay on my home world?'

'How cold does the Holdings get in the winter?' said Halfclaw.

'About as hot as it gets each summer in the City,' said Kelsey.

The two dragons glanced at each other.

'So,' said Halfclaw, 'the best the City has to offer compares with the worst of the Holdings?'

'I guess so, if all you're interested in is the weather.'

'Frostback, my beloved,' said Halfclaw; 'perhaps we should give some serious consideration to moving to the Holdings. Everything you have told me about it makes it sound like the perfect environment for dragons.'

'Hey!' said Kelsey. 'I happen to like living in the City.'

'Even in Sweetmist, rider?' said Frostback. 'And what about Freshmist – do you enjoy that, too?'

'Well, no; but that's only four months of the year. The rest is fine.'

'Winter in the City may well be sunny,' said Halfclaw, 'but it is too cold for a pleasant life.'

'We can talk about this later,' said Kelsey. 'I need to get the twins into the shade before they fry.' She nudged Cael and Kyra towards the trees.

'Can we swim in the pool?' said Cael.

'Sure,' said Kelsey.

Cael yelled out in joy and sprinted towards the small pool of water, where he pulled off his outer clothes and jumped in. Kyra chose a more dignified approach, walking with Kelsey until they were under the shade of the trees, before folding her clothes into a neat pile and stepping into the pool. Kelsey unlaced her boots and sat with her feet in the cool water, her eyes on the children as they splashed and played.

'Think of the benefits,' said Frostback, from over Kelsey's shoulder. 'You would be close to your family.'

'Is that a benefit?' she said.

'Do you not love your family?'

'Sometimes.'

'I know you pine after all of the little things that cannot be obtained in the City.'

'We could have those things here if the trade delegation is successful.'

'Would you consider,' said Halfclaw, his head poking through between two trees, 'that we could live in the City each summer, then travel to your world to avoid Sweetmist and Freshmist?'

'That would be an acceptable compromise,' said Frostback.

Kelsey scowled at them. 'You would abandon the City, just like that?'

'We did not ask to come to this world,' said Halfclaw. 'Belinda sent us here. We have worked hard to defend it, and we have laboured long to help the Exiles rebuild Jezra. But, we have never seen this world as our home; not our permanent home.'

'What?' said Kelsey. 'Why have you never mentioned this to me before?'

'Because, my rider,' said Frostback, 'we knew of no way to get off this world. That situation has changed. You are in possession of a Quadrant, and you know how to use it to transport us to Colsbury Castle. Halfclaw and I wish to start a family, but we have delayed doing so, because we do not feel that a rough cavern in Jezra is a suitable place to raise our young.'

'I didn't know that.'

'Before you obtained the Quadrant, it would have sounded like futile complaining, and so we chose not to mention it to you.'

'What about Van? Do you expect me to leave him here?'

'Of course not, rider. Van would follow you anywhere. If you leave, then so will he.'

'The truth is,' said Halfclaw, 'that Frostback and I are Lostwell dragons, reared by the lava pools of the Catacombs. We are not accustomed to the cold and wet.'

'The same could be said about me. I come from the hottest, driest part of the Holdings. I don't know about this. I'll need to think it through.'

'But...' Halfclaw began.

'My rider has spoken,' said Frostback. 'Let her mull it over for now. It will do no good to continue prodding her. I, for one, would like to rest in the sunlight while the children play.'

Halfclaw tilted his head. 'So be it.'

The two dragons stretched out across the golden sands, and settled down to sleep. Kelsey kept her eyes on them, a mixture of anger and sorrow sweeping through her. She loved living in the City, despite the shortages, and the lack of space; and even despite having to endure Sweetmist and Freshmist every year. It was the independence that she loved; the freedom of having struck out on her own, away from the cloying embrace of the Holdfasts upon her home world. If she returned to the Holdings, she would revert to being the ignored and undervalued sibling of the family, forever in the shadow of Karalyn and the others. That wasn't Karalyn's fault; she realised that now, after many years of blaming her elder sister for her problems; but that knowledge didn't make her want to return to the way she had lived before.

Kelsey turned back to the children, who were paddling by the edge of the pool, then she closed her eyes, and tried to think of something else.

Kelsey was jolted awake by the sound of a child's cry. She opened her eyes, and saw Cael and Kyra staring out into the desert. Kelsey squinted her eyes from the glare. The sands around the oasis were moving, like ripples on the surface of a disturbed pond. A claw emerged from the depths of the undulating sand, then another, and another, as greenhides pulled themselves out from where they had burrowed under the surface of the desert. Sand spilled from the thick leathery armour that protected the creature's insect bodies, and a hundred sets of claws clacked together.

Frostback's eyes shot open, and her head reared up. She opened her jaws, and sparks leapt across the rows of teeth, but the twins were too close to the greenhides, and no flames roared out. Kelsey leapt to her feet. The greenhides were shrieking at the sight of the humans and dragons, and several dozen were charging towards the oasis. Kelsey whipped out the Quadrant and stared at the engravings. If she triggered it, she might bring back many of the greenhides with them, but if she did nothing, then the twins would be ripped to shreds within seconds.

Kyra screamed as a greenhide raised its claws above her. Halfclaw lunged forwards, and his flanks were assaulted by more greenhides emerging from beneath the hot sands. Halfclaw grabbed one of them, and tore it in half, but others were scrambling up onto his back.

Cael raised a hand. 'Stop!'

Every greenhide around the oasis froze. The beast that was inches from Kyra lowered its claws, as the girl stared at it in terror.

'Go away!' Cael shouted. 'Leave us alone!'

The greenhides scattered, racing away across the golden dunes in every direction. Those on Halfclaw's back dropped to the ground. Some started burrowing beneath the sand, while others fled, their hind legs carrying them away from the oasis.

Kelsey reached Kyra, and put her arms round the sobbing child.

'It's alright, Kyra; we're safe.'

'Take us back to Jezra, rider,' said Frostback, 'before the greenhides return.'

'They won't come back,' said Cael, turning to face them. 'I told them not to.'

'How?' said Kelsey. 'Did you go into their minds?'

'Aye,' said Cael. 'It's not nice in there.'

'This world is poison,' said Halfclaw, as blood dripped from a dozen small wounds across his green flanks. 'Even the good places, like this oasis, have been corrupted by the evil that dwells here.'

Kelsey kept her attention on Kyra.

'Halfclaw is right,' said Frostback. 'The desert is not safe for us, not if the vile greenhides use it to shelter from the rains of Sweetmist.'

Kyra reached out with a hand, and touched the Quadrant. The air shimmered, and they found themselves back in the dark and draughty cavern, the roar of the rain outside sounding almost comforting.

'I want mama,' sobbed Kyra.

Cael started to cry, too, as the enormity of what had almost happened seemed to hit him. Kelsey crouched by the twins, her arms round them both.

'I miss mama,' said Cael, as tears filled his eyes.

'I know,' said Kelsey.

Outside the cavern, the storm raged, drowning out the sound of their tears.

CHAPTER 12
REFINEMENT

Serene, Implacatus – 10th Tuminch 5255

The city of Cumulus was unlike anything Karalyn had ever seen before. Serene was strange enough, but it still resembled a city, and many of its streets and houses wouldn't have looked out of place in one of the great underground cities of Rahain before its collapse. Cumulus, on the other hand, reminded Karalyn of a forest in thick fog, except that the tree trunks were towers and castles, and the fog was cloud. Slender stone bridges and walkways connected some of the tall towers, but many stood alone, their rocky foundations lost in the grey murk that clung to the mountainside. There were no streets that Karalyn could discern, just the massive fortresses and keeps of the gods.

Edmond's fortified palace was easy to recognise. It was set apart from the other towers, and loomed above them – a windowless behemoth of dark, smooth stone, its pinnacles and spires cutting through the clouds like sharpened fingernails. Karalyn had searched for a way into the interior, but she had located only one gate in the structure, and it was closed. The sealed entrance overlooked a deep ravine, with no visible means to cross over to the rest of Cumulus. She had also found a couple of isolated skylights, high up in the tallest towers, but they were protected by several layers of gauze – a thin wire mesh that blocked her vision.

She cut the connection, and glanced around the living room of Austin's shabby apartment. It had been small for three people, and now seven were sheltering within its walls – two Holdfasts, an ancient god, a young demigod, a Banner officer, and two former slaves.

'Well, Karalyn?' said Amalia. 'Was Cumulus exactly as I described?'

Karalyn nodded. 'We may have to rethink our strategy.'

'There is no "may" about it,' said Amalia.

'I've also had a good look,' said Sable. 'I couldn't see into Edmond's palace, but we should be able to Quadrant directly inside.'

Amalia laughed. 'You foolish mortal. Weren't you listening to me?

Sable glared at the god, but said nothing.

'Nine-tenths of Edmond's palace consists of nothing but solid rock,' Amalia went on. 'The interior chambers are small, and randomly dispersed within the fortress. If you attempt to use a Quadrant to go there, there would be a very high probability of you arriving encased in stone. I dare say that there are many corpses buried within those walls, from previous, unsuccessful attempts.'

'Then, how do we get in?' said Cardova.

'Simple,' said Amalia. 'We request an audience. Well, to be precise, I shall request an audience. I was a rebel, many millennia ago, and the Blessed Second Ascendant has a reputation for savouring the grovelling apologies of former rebels. He will see me. Once inside the palace, Karalyn can then extract Belinda while Edmond is listening to my humble and heartfelt denunciation of the rebellion.'

'What about the rest of us?' said Sable.

Amalia smiled at her. 'It appears that you are superfluous to this operation.'

'Aren't you forgetting something, Lady Amalia?' said Austin. 'Lord Bastion will read your mind as soon as you arrive. They won't let you in until they are sure of your intentions. Remember that I also lived there for years. I know how cautious the Ancients and Ascendants can be.'

'You are a mere child,' said Amalia. 'I have long learned how to bury my thoughts deep within my subconscious. By the time Lord Bastion and the Blessed Second Ascendant learn the truth, Karalyn will have rescued Belinda, and retrieved me from the situation.'

'This plan will never work,' said Sable.

'What do you suggest?' said Cardova.

'We strike Cumulus hard, from several different directions at once, to distract them. Then, we use a huge quantity of explosives to blow a hole in the side of Edmond's palace, and storm the place. That way, we'll kill as many of the bastards as possible.'

'Killing gods is not our objective,' said Karalyn.

'It should be,' said Sable.

'Would anyone like more tea?' said Salah.

Karalyn glanced at Austin's mother. 'Aye. Thank you. And thanks again for letting us stay here. I know it must be an inconvenience for you.'

'It's no problem,' said Salah. 'It's nice to have visitors.'

'What about the wedding?' said Sable.

Karalyn turned back to her aunt. 'What do you mean?'

'Why don't we wait for that, and strike then?' said Sable. 'I presume it will take place out in the open, so that as many people as possible will be able to see it. That means Belinda will be moved out of Edmond's palace for a while, and we can snatch her.'

'Do we know when it will take place?' said Cardova.

Austin leaned over a low table, and sorted through a few newspapers.

'I think I saw the date being mentioned somewhere,' Austin said. 'I'm sure the wedding is due this month.'

'It's on the twenty-second,' said Salah, as she set down a few mugs of steaming tea onto the table. 'In twelve days' time. The gods have declared that day a public holiday.'

'That's too long to wait,' said Karalyn. 'I promised the twins I would be back in time for their birthday.'

Amalia smiled. 'Then the way ahead is clear. You and I, Karalyn –

we should infiltrate Cumulus together, just the two of us. The Ascendants would never expect us to be so bold.'

Karalyn said nothing for a moment, then she nodded. 'Alright.'

'This is bullshit,' said Sable. 'What are we supposed to do? Do you expect me and Lucius to sit here while you're in Cumulus?'

'Aye,' said Karalyn. 'That's exactly what I expect. We may need you if things go wrong.'

Sable shook her head. 'I might as well take Austin and his family to Dragon Eyre.'

'No,' said Karalyn. 'You will remain here; ready to act if I call upon you. Dragon Eyre will be our meeting point, but only if we are chased out of Implacatus. Lucius, do you have a problem with that?'

'I will do whatever you ask, ma'am,' said the soldier. 'This is your operation.'

Austin glanced up from the newspapers. 'Your arrival here might have been noticed by one of the many gods living in Serene. If that's the case, then this apartment might not be safe.'

'I won't leave you unprotected,' said Karalyn. 'I can block your minds from vision powers.'

Austin raised an eyebrow. 'Would that not be likely to attract even more attention? If the gods detect us, and are unable to access our minds, then they'll deduce that at least one Holdfast has returned. You should remember that it's not so long ago since Kelsey was here. Your sister's presence greatly upset the gods. So much so, in fact, that Lord Bastion was here in person, searching Serene for her.'

'Was he?' said Sable. 'When was this?'

'Back in Duninch,' said Austin. 'About four months ago.'

'So, after I kicked his arse on Dragon Eyre?' said Sable. 'Shit. Maybe Ashfall and the others were right; maybe I should have killed him when I had the chance.'

'Why didn't you?' said Amalia.

'I put a block into his mind, to make him terrified of ever returning to Dragon Eyre. I'm sure that aspect worked, but there's probably more I could have done.'

'The Ascendants have been silent about Dragon Eyre for months,' said Austin. 'A large batch of Banner soldiers returned at the same time as Lord Bastion, but none have come back since. It's as though the gods are pretending everything is normal; however, I've also noticed that no new reinforcements have been sent, either.'

'The families of the Banner soldiers will know that something is wrong,' said Cardova. 'If the usual rotation of regiments has stopped, then it's only a matter of time before they start demanding to know where their relatives are.' He glanced at Sable. 'It looks as though your block may have worked. Have the gods really given up on Dragon Eyre?'

'I don't think they can afford to do that,' said Austin.

Cardova frowned. 'Why not? I admit that I've never understood why the Ascendants wanted to get their hands on that world, but they've been fighting for it for nearly three decades.'

Austin and Sable shared a glance.

'We know why Implacatus invaded Dragon Eyre,' Sable said.

'Then tell us,' said Amalia.

'This world – Implacatus,' said Austin, 'is almost entirely uninhabitable. Below the cloud is nothing but a toxic desert wasteland. The gods have destroyed Implacatus, and only Serene and Cumulus are left.'

Cardova snorted. 'That's not true. There are farms and forests at ground level. Everyone knows that.'

Sable smiled. 'Have you ever seen these farms?'

'Well, no,' said Cardova; 'not with my own eyes. I've seen paintings, and I remember what we were taught at school. Millions of peasants live down there.'

'It's all a lie,' said Austin. 'The Ascendants and Ancients have been lying about the truth for centuries.'

'That wouldn't surprise me in the slightest,' said Amalia. 'My own home world of Yocasta is also a dead wasteland. The Ascendants have a habit of destroying everything they touch.'

'And now they want to take over Dragon Eyre,' Austin said, 'because this world is dying.'

Cardova laughed. 'No. I can't accept that.'

'Why not?' said Austin.

'Because millions of people live in Serene,' said Cardova. 'Are you telling me that they are all doomed? It would take a colossal effort to transport the gods from Cumulus to a new world, never mind the mortals of Serene.'

'I didn't take you as naïve, Lucius,' said Sable. 'The gods don't care about the mortals of Serene.'

'Maybe not, but they need us to clean, build, and grow food.'

'The settlers and enslaved natives of Dragon Eyre would easily replace them.'

Cardova narrowed his eyes, then he turned to Karalyn. 'Are they telling the truth? Have you looked below the clouds?'

Karalyn shook her head. 'No, but I can, if you wish. I can show you all. Do you want to see?'

'I don't need to see it,' said Austin. 'I've been down there. It nearly killed me.'

'Can you show me?' said Cardova.

'I would also like to see the truth for myself,' said Amalia.

'Very well,' said Karalyn. 'The three of us shall look together. Lucius, Amalia – look into my eyes.'

Karalyn waited until they were both gazing at her, then she pushed her dream powers out of her body. She went into Cardova's consciousness, gathered it up, and led it from his mind; then she did the same with Amalia.

Can you both hear me?'

Yes, said Lucius.

This is a novel experience, said Amalia. *How are you doing this?*

You will see things through my eyes, said Karalyn. *Are you ready?*

She sensed their agreement, then led her sight out through the slats in the shuttered window. She navigated the streets of Serene until they reached a wide, open terrace, where the sun was shining down onto a park and gardens. The thick clouds were only a hundred yards below the steel railings that guarded the edge of the terrace, and Karalyn led Cardova and Amalia down, passing several other levels of the city. They entered the dense clouds, and passed a few more levels, where dungeons and storage facilities were located, then the city petered out, replaced by the dark rock of a cliff face. The clouds seemed to go on forever, and Karalyn was wondering if they would ever end, when they broke through into clear sky. She heard Cardova gasp. The landscape below them was brown and barren, and devoid of life. Not even a scrubby bush clung to the side of the mountain; just bare rock. Karalyn sped her vision away from the mountainside, but, no matter in which direction they gazed, everything was the same. Sandstorms were lifting clouds of dust above the scorched, dry ground, which spread out for dozens of miles.

Have you seen enough? Karalyn said.

I can't believe it, said Cardova, his voice barely a whisper. *What have they done?*

The land is poisoned beyond repair, said Amalia. *Nothing can survive down here. This looks just like Yocasta – destroyed by endless wars. Is it any wonder that we rebelled against Edmond's misrule? Theodora would never have allowed this to happen.*

Karalyn severed the connection and their consciousnesses returned to their bodies.

'Well?' said Sable.

Cardova said nothing. He looked stunned for a moment, then he stood, and walked off without a word.

'It was just as you and Austin told us,' said Karalyn. 'I wonder if this means that other worlds are at risk. If you placed a block in Bastion's mind regarding Dragon Eyre, won't the Ascendants look for another world?'

'You're not thinking like a god,' said Amalia. 'Edmond and Bastion are aware of the powers of the Holdfasts, but they also know that you are mortal – and mortals die. There is nothing to stop them waiting a century for you and Sable, and Kelsey and the others, to perish. When you are all dead and gone, they will be free to restart their invasion of Dragon Eyre.'

Sable laughed. 'You don't know about Corthie and Aila's children, do you?'

'I was aware that my granddaughter was pregnant, and that Corthie was the father,' said Amalia, wrinkling her nose. 'Has Aila had more children with that brute?

'Two so far,' said Sable. 'And guess what? They're both immortal. The Holdfasts have started giving birth to gods.'

Amalia shook her head and sighed. 'I had a tiny suspicion on Lostwell that the child within Aila had self-healing powers, but it should be impossible. As far as I know, no demigod has ever successfully fathered or mothered a child with self-healing powers; not if their partners were mortals.'

'They have now,' said Sable. 'I've just realised that this makes us related. My nephew's kids are your great-grandchildren.'

Amalia's face paled. 'My great-grandchildren are Holdfasts? Oh my. Swear you aren't trying to trick me. Are both children really immortal?'

'Aye,' said Karalyn. 'I can't explain it, but I think it has something to do with the family's dream powers.'

'Would Aila allow me to see them?'

'We can ask her when we return from this operation. I'm going to find Lucius. The rest of you should work out how we can refine the raw salve that Sable brought with us. I want it reduced to the size of a small vial.'

'I shall get to work,' said Amalia. 'We may need to go out into a market to purchase some essentials.'

Karalyn nodded as she stood. 'Make a list.'

Karalyn left the room, and found Cardova in the tiny kitchen. He was sitting by the small dining table, a lit cigarette grasped in his fingers.

'Are you all right?' she said.

'No.'

'I guess it must have been a shock.'

'Everything I ever thought was true is a lie. The mighty Implacatus, the home world of the gods – rich, fertile, beautiful; it's all a deception.

A bedtime story to soothe the mortals of Serene. In reality, we're more like the City of Pella, Tara and the damn greenhides – surrounded by wilderness, and alone.'

Karalyn sat down next to him by the table.

'I don't know why I'm so surprised,' Cardova went on. 'I have seen what the gods have done to other worlds – why would Implacatus be any different?'

'If this world is dying,' said Karalyn, 'then we need to find out how long it has left. The end might still be centuries away. Do you have family here? If you want, we could move them to a safer place.'

Cardova glanced at her. 'Where?'

'My world. The Plateau has always been under-populated, and the war with Agatha didn't help matters. The combined population of Sanang and Kellach Brigdomin doesn't reach a million. Or, I could look for another world with the Sextant. I've barely scratched the surface of the worlds that were created by that device. There could be dozens of them out there; worlds that have been cut off from Implacatus for thousands of years.'

'Do you know how to transport masses of people with the Sextant?'

'No, but I haven't tried. If Belinda could move thousands of folk from Lostwell to the City, then saving the population of Serene is possible. Don't despair, Lucius.'

He cast his gaze downwards. 'Are you sure about this plan of yours? Can you trust Amalia?'

'I've looked into her mind.'

'That doesn't answer my question.'

'Amalia is guilty of many things, but her love for Belinda is genuine. I might not trust her, but I trust that she will do her best to help free Belinda from Edmond.'

'She might betray you in order to do that.'

'I won't allow that to happen. Come back to the living room; I want to give you all some protection from the gods.'

They got up from the table, and walked into where the others were discussing the intricacies of refining salve. Austin was scribbling notes on to a sheet of paper, while Amalia was talking about the boiling point of pure alcohol.

The former God-Queen of the City paused when she saw Karalyn and Cardova re-enter the room.

'There you are,' she said. 'We have put a list together, with everything we need to proceed. However, one of us shall have to leave the apartment, in order to purchase the items on said list.'

'We'll decide that in a moment,' said Karalyn, as she and Cardova sat down. 'First, I'm going to enter each of your minds in turn, to prepare some defences. Austin was correct earlier. If I simply block your minds against vision powers, then the gods may become suspicious. Therefore, I will do two things to each of you. I will block your minds, but then I will also create a space, a safe space, accessible to the gods, where they will see what I want them to see. If any of them try to read you, they will believe that their attempt has been successful; none of them will understand that they have been led to a place in your minds of my creation.' She glanced at the others. 'When I said all of you, I should have excluded Sable from this. I will leave her as she is.'

'Good,' said Sable. 'I would rather not have my mind manipulated; unless you are able to shield it from Daimon?'

'I can't do that,' said Karalyn. 'I wish I could, then I would have protected my mother and the rest of the Holdfasts in Colsbury.'

Sable nodded. 'Can you tell me if I'm at all resistant to Daimon's powers? I heard that Corthie was able to resist him to a certain extent.'

'No. I couldn't have predicted Corthie's success by looking into his head. I'm sorry, Sable, but the only way we'll know is if Daimon tries to manipulate you.' She turned to Austin. 'You first.'

She entered the demigod's mind, and set about erecting blocks around his consciousness and memories. Once that was done, she created a banal place inside his head – a place that any god with vision powers would be able to see; and she filled it with soothing, non-threatening emotions and desires. She made him appear loyal to the Ascendants; someone who would never dream of rebelling against them. She also made him appear boring to the point of mediocre dullness; not somewhere any god would wish to linger.

'Ow,' Austin said, rubbing his head.

Karalyn smiled. 'You're done. Sable and I will still be able to read your true thoughts and memories, but none of the gods will.'

'How long will it last?' he said.

'At least a hundred years. If you were mortal, then I would say for the rest of your life.' She glanced at Sunnah, Salah and Cardova. 'The blocks I will put in your minds will endure until you die.'

'Do it,' said Cardova, his eyes still grim. 'It will be a relief to know that none of those bastards will be able to find out what I really think of them.'

Karalyn nodded. She entered the mind of the Banner officer, then Austin's mother, and his aunt. She did the same to each mind as she had done to Austin's, taking care to vary their backgrounds so that the secure space inside their minds wouldn't appear too similar to any god who took an interest in them.

'Your turn,' she said to Amalia. 'With you, I intend to do something more subtle. I will allow the gods to inspect the majority of your memories; after all, you are known to them, and they will definitely want to give your mind a thorough examination. However, I will block your more recent memories, and hide your true intentions from them.' She paused. 'What should be your motivation for surrendering to the Ascendants?'

'I want to be on the winning side,' said Amalia. 'Let's not ascribe anything more noble than that – it would only make them suspicious. Let them think me amoral and selfish; it's what they would expect.'

'Alright,' said Karalyn. 'Do they know that you were friends with Belinda?'

'I'm not sure. I made the acquaintance of the Third Ascendant when I fled to Lostwell with my husband Malik. Other rebels may have perhaps mentioned my friendship with Belinda, but I cannot be certain.'

'Lady Belinda herself may have told them,' said Austin.

'I will make your friendship with her seem shallow and self-serving,' said Karalyn.

Amalia sighed. 'There is another factor which we may have to consider. I was here, on Implacatus, only a few short months ago.'

'What?' said Sable. 'This is a fine time to be telling us this.'

'What were you doing here?' said Austin.

'She delivered the headless body of Simon, the Tenth Ascendant,' said Cardova; 'along with a demigod called Lady Silva.'

'Silva is an honourable woman,' said Amalia. 'She wished to return here to search for Belinda, her great-grandmother, while I needed to return to the City to face Queen Emily. Silva is utterly devoted to Belinda, and would lay down her life for her. If she has been captured by the Ascendants, then they will have read her mind. If that is the case, they will not only know about the fate of Simon, but they will also know of my part in his downfall.'

'You should have told me about this,' said Karalyn. 'This complicates matters.'

'Should we search for this Lady Silva?' said Austin.

'The opposite is more likely,' said Amalia. 'Silva has a specific set of powers – she can sense the locations of certain immortals. If she's in Serene, there's a good chance that she will have noticed my presence here. With Silva, it is always easier to wait for her to come to you, rather than the other way around.'

'Can she read minds?' said Karalyn.

'No.'

'Alright. I'll make your feelings about Silva seem as self-serving as your friendship with Belinda.'

'That pains me, but make it so.'

Karalyn nodded, then entered the mind of the former God-Queen.

'I don't like Amalia,' said Sable, 'and I don't like your plan.'

Karalyn opened a packet of cigarettes, and handed one to her aunt.

Sable lit her metal lighter, and touched the flame to each cigarette, then the two women leaned closer to the open kitchen window, allowing the smoke to escape out into the dark street.

'It was your idea to bring Amalia along,' Karalyn said.

'I know, and I'm regretting it. She's an arrogant bitch, who thinks that her opinion outweighs that of everyone else.'

Karalyn smiled. 'It sounds as though you might be describing yourself.'

'I suppose I deserve that. However, did you see me lose my temper when she called me a foolish mortal? I wanted to punch her in the face, but, for the sake of this operation, I restrained myself. Anyway, forget her; it's your plan that concerns me more.'

'I know you'd prefer to launch an all-out attack, but give me some credit. I stole Agatha's Quadrant from under her nose; and I can do the same with Belinda and Edmond. Amalia's role is simply to get me into the Second Ascendant's palace.'

'And my role? I mean, apart from taking up space in this horrible little apartment.'

'As soon as I've freed Belinda, I intend to bring us back here. Be ready. Take us all to Dragon Eyre as a first step, and then I can take Belinda back to Colsbury. Do you have somewhere on Dragon Eyre to hide? How about that ruined temple on Haurn?'

Sable smiled. 'You know about Nan Po Tana, do you?'

'I occasionally looked in on you, to see what you were doing.'

'I wish I had known that at the time. Nan Po Tana would be perfect; it still has stocks of food supplies, along with a few other items which might turn out to be useful. When are you and Amalia leaving?'

'At dawn.'

Cardova entered the kitchen. 'You should close the window.'

'Why?' said Sable.

'Because Amalia and Austin are stinking out the apartment with the fumes from their little salve refining project. If the smell reaches the people out on the street, some might get suspicious.'

Karalyn nodded, then pulled the window shut.

Sable glanced from Cardova to Karalyn. 'I think I'll leave you two alone. Good luck tomorrow, Karalyn. You know where I'll be if you need me.'

Karalyn watched as Sable left the kitchen, then she turned to Cardova.

'I shouldn't have brought you here,' she said.

'There's no point regretting things like that,' he said. 'I'm here now, and that's what matters. It's frustrating though, knowing that you'll be going to a place where I won't be able to protect you.' He shook his head. 'I'll try to sit here patiently, but I'll be worrying about you, every moment that you're away.'

She smiled. 'You don't need to worry about me.'

'You can say that, but it doesn't make it true.'

She gazed up into his eyes then, surprising herself, she kissed him. He froze for a second, then kissed her back, his hands reaching down to her waist and pulling her closer. She felt a twinge of guilt over Lennox, then he kissed her neck, and she lost herself. His lips brushed her left ear, and she felt desire course through her.

'Whatever happens,' he whispered, 'stay alive.'

CHAPTER 13
A LITTLE CUNNING

Colsbury Castle, Republic of the Holdings – 23rd Day, Last Third Summer 534

'It's selfish, that's what it is,' said Daphne, as they walked through the orchard. 'Utterly selfish.' She glanced at Caelius. 'You're being very quiet.'

The old veteran nodded. 'I don't want to get into another argument with you.'

'And why would stating your opinion lead to an argument between us, Caelius? Do you disagree with what I am saying? Do you think Karalyn's abandonment of us is a good thing?'

'Not necessarily, ma'am.'

Daphne frowned. 'Don't call me ma'am. It makes you sound weak.'

'Sorry.'

'And don't apologise. Explain what you mean by "not necessarily".'

Caelius glanced away, as if interested in the fruit growing on the branches of the apple trees.

'Well,' he began, 'there are two sides to this, aren't there? It seems to me that Karalyn had a choice – abandon us temporarily; or abandon her friend forever.'

'You do realise that this "friend", as you put it, is a damned Ascendant? One of our sworn enemies? She's not some helpless mortal trapped in the clutches of the wicked gods – she's one of them. Not only that, but she opened the gates of this very fortress to Agatha and her army of Rahain, thereby proving that she cannot be trusted. Karalyn has always had a weak spot for Belinda. She was always blind to the fact that Belinda could turn against us at any moment; and when she did turn against us, what does Karalyn do? She forgives her. Of course she does. One day that girl's foolish notions of morality will get her killed. Her irresponsibility in leaving us here undefended might get us all killed.' She shook her head. 'Two sides, indeed. What nonsense.'

Caelius's eyes darkened a little, but he said nothing.

'I also take exception to your use of the term "forever",' Daphne went on. 'A decade means nothing to the gods of Implacatus – it's the merest blink of an eye to those who cannot age or die. What was stopping Karalyn waiting until the Daimon situation had resolved itself? It's not as if Belinda is getting any older. Karalyn could have easily remained here to deal with Bridget's pet dream mage, and then she could have embarked upon her silly little rescue mission. But no; she deserts us in our hour of need, taking Sable with her. She'll only have herself to blame if she returns to find Colsbury a heap of smouldering ruins.'

They paused in front of the garden's central fountain. A light breeze was sending wisps of water into the air, which glistened in the late summer sunshine. Some of the trees had leaves that were starting to turn a dozen shades of red, orange and brown, and Daphne shuddered at the thought of the approaching autumn.

'I should be in Holdings City,' she said. 'How can I be expected to run a country from here?'

'I thought that you were in daily contact with the Holdings government?'

'Yes. I vision to them every morning, but that's hardly the point. The election is a little more than six thirds away, and the campaign will be commencing shortly. I should be there in person, to coordinate everything; instead, I am trapped here.'

'There's nothing stopping you from travelling to Holdings City by road,' said Caelius.

Daphne narrowed her eyes. 'Have you forgotten what happened the last time we travelled by road? Soldiers tried to burn us out of a tavern. If Karalyn were here, then she could transport me directly to the residence of the First Holder and back again; twice a day if necessary. What did I do to be cursed with such ungrateful children? Just a short while ago, all of them were here, and now three have deserted me. At least Keir hasn't abandoned me; I should be glad I have one child who understands the meaning of loyalty.'

Caelius gazed at the fountain. 'Corthie and Kelsey are grown up; they have their own lives to lead.'

'Corthie is delusional. He seems to think that if he and Aila breed like rabbits, then he won't have to face up to his problems. I wonder if he's enjoying his life in a prison cell, the silly boy. As for Kelsey, she just likes to be contrary. She lives on another world to spite me.'

'Kelsey is in love with my son.'

'Then why doesn't Van move to this world? Is the defence of one city more important than the defence of an entire continent?'

'It pained me when Van left home, especially after his mother was killed; but I couldn't stand in his way. Children grow up, if we're lucky, and I couldn't be prouder of what Van has achieved. He's the major-general of an entire Banner, contracted to the ruling monarchy of a world at war with the gods. I would never ask him to give that up just to keep his old man happy.'

Daphne glared at him. 'Are you saying that I am the one who is being selfish? I, who have sacrificed a life of quiet comfort and wealth, am being selfish because my children do not understand the meaning of family? I have given up everything for the sake of the Holdfasts, yet I am being selfish?'

Caelius sighed. 'There's no point in talking to you today. No matter what I say, you'll find a way to criticise it.'

'If I'm being critical, it's because your arguments are foolish and illogical.'

'Tell me; did you speak to your husband in such a tone?'

'Don't bring Killop into this. Killop was twice the man you'll ever be.'

Caelius closed his mouth, turned, and strode away, leaving Daphne standing alone by the fountain. She remained where she was, her anger simmering. What was the point of Caelius being in Colsbury if he wasn't prepared to take her side? Was a little loyalty too much to expect? A slight pang of regret ran through her as she recalled her last comment to him, then she suppressed it. Caelius would never be Killop. Daphne had fallen in love with Killop from the first moment she had seen him locked up in a cage in Rahain; such things happened only once in someone's life, if they happened at all. If she and Killop had been destined to be together, then what place could Caelius ever take in her heart?

She sat down on a wooden bench, and ejected Caelius from her mind. She knew that it wasn't the old veteran who had made her angry; it was her irresponsible eldest child. How dare Karalyn choose Belinda over her family? Her thoughts went to Daimon, and she imagined the dream mage and the Empress laughing at her. Bridget had never liked her, not really. She had always held a grudge, blaming Daphne for Karalyn scouring Killop's mind in Slateford, and for luring him away from the Severed Clan. Neither of those events had been Daphne's fault. She hadn't asked Killop to follow her; he had left the clan of his own volition, choosing her over his best friend. Was that Daphne's responsibility?

She noticed Shella approach down one of the paths that wound through the gardens.

'Hi, Daffers,' the Rakanese woman said. 'I thought Caelius was with you.'

'No,' said Daphne.

'Oh. Anyway, you need to come back into the Great Keep. Thorn and Keir are at each other's throats.'

Daphne frowned. 'You came all the way down here to tell me that?'

'No. I came down here to get away from it. Listening to your son and daughter-in-law argue is not my idea of fun.'

'What are they rowing about?'

Shella shrugged. 'I'm not going to say, because I know how you'll react.'

'I could read your mind, I suppose.'

'If you like. Or, you know, you could go upstairs and act like a parent.'

'I'm going to choose to ignore that little insult, Shella,' Daphne said, as she got to her feet. 'After all, what do you know about parenting?'

Shella chuckled and shook her head. 'I know that you're still annoyed about Karalyn leaving, but was there any need for that?'

'I'm not annoyed; I'm livid. And disappointed, very disappointed. I shall do as you suggest, and bring some peace back to the Great Keep. Are our two Sanang guests also upstairs?'

Shella nodded. 'They're smoking my weed again. If they don't stop taking it without asking, I'm going to hide it.'

Daphne sighed, then began retracing her steps towards the two large keeps that dominated the centre of the island. She passed through an open gate, then entered the Great Keep, the air cooling within the thick stone walls. She ascended the stairs, and heard voices raised in anger before she had reached the main level where they lived. She paused outside the living room door, listening.

'I'm so sick of you nagging me!' Keir was shouting. 'I'm not a child!'

'Then grow up, because you're acting like a child,' Thorn cried back to him. 'All I asked you to do was to stop sitting on your arse all day in your dressing gown, drinking and smoking. We have work to do.'

'What work? Pretending that you're going to be Empress one day isn't work – it's a fucking delusion.'

'Don't swear at me, Keir.'

'Or what? Are you going to use your soulwitch powers on me? You would like that, wouldn't you? You probably fantasise about killing me and raising me from the dead, so that I would be more obedient; so that you could control me better.'

'I don't need to do any of that,' Thorn said. 'All I have to do is whisper a few words to your mother about what you were up to in Plateau City.'

Daphne frowned as she listened.

'You set me up,' Keir shouted. 'You planned the whole thing, just so you could blackmail me.'

Daphne pushed the door open. Thorn and Keir both turned, falling silent as they watched Daphne stride into the room.

'I could hear your voices from halfway up the stairs,' Daphne said.

'Apologies,' said Thorn. 'Things got a little heated. I shall go back to work.'

'No, you won't,' said Daphne. 'You will stay here and explain to me how you are blackmailing my son.'

Thorn raised an eyebrow. 'No. I don't think I will.'

'Are you defying me, Thorn?'

'Keir and I are married, Holder Fast. With all due respect, our argument is our business.'

Daphne glanced at Keir, who was standing in his dressing gown, his face unshaven for several days.

'Son,' she said, 'do you wish to tell me anything?'

Keir dropped into an armchair, shook his head, then picked up a half-smoked weedstick from an ashtray.

Thorn smiled, then walked towards the door.

'If you leave this room,' said Daphne, 'I shall withdraw my support of your claim to the throne of the Empire.'

Thorn blinked. 'You would allow Bridget to break the law because you overheard me arguing with your son?'

'No. I would do it because how can I trust someone to be Empress, if they won't tell me the truth?'

'The truth has nothing to do with you, mother,' said Keir.

Daphne smiled. 'Well, I'm glad to see you both agree about something, at long last. However, my point remains. Neither of you is going anywhere until you tell me what information Thorn has that she was threatening to tell me.'

'I don't care if you stay here,' said Keir. 'I'm not going anywhere. And, I don't care if you stop supporting Thorn's insane quest to become Empress. In fact, I'd laugh if you did.'

'Thorn is your wife, son. Your lack of support for her is disheartening, to say the least.'

Keir shrugged. 'I knew you'd side with her. The witches of the Holdfast family always stick together.'

Daphne narrowed her eyes, then she turned back to Thorn. 'I'm waiting.'

'For what?' said Thorn.

'For you to tell me the truth. If you don't, then I shall signal our submission to the Empress in Plateau City.'

Thorn smiled. 'You're bluffing.'

'Am I? In some ways, it would be a relief. Bridget and I could make amends, and the Holdfasts would be able to live here in peace, without worrying about what Daimon might do to us. You have ten seconds, Thorn.'

The Sanang woman shook her head. 'This is irrational. You would give up our dreams because Keir and I had a row?'

'Our dreams, Thorn? Don't you mean *your* dreams? Haven't you always desired to be Empress? I recall many people telling me that you only married my son to gain our family name. Oh, and your ten seconds have passed. Excuse me for a moment, while I send out my vision to the Plateau.'

Thorn's eyes widened. 'Wait.'

Daphne smiled. 'Have you something to tell me, Thorn?'

Thorn glanced at Keir, whose sullen expression had been replaced by a look of sheer terror.

'This is the last time I'll ask you both,' said Daphne.

Thorn exhaled, her eyes gazing at the floor. 'Keir... was, well, he was...'

'Yes?'

'Your son was having an affair in Plateau City with Tilda Holdwain.'

Keir made a strange choking sound, his eyes wide.

Daphne frowned. 'Ridiculous. Do you expect me to believe that, Thorn?'

Thorn gave a gentle shrug. 'You asked for the truth. I told the truth.'

Daphne glanced at Keir. 'Son, are you just going to sit there while your wife utters such brazen lies about you?'

Keir said nothing, his wide eyes staring at the two women in front of him.

'If you don't believe me,' said Thorn, 'send your vision to Plateau City. But, instead of contacting the Empress, divert your powers to the Holdings Embassy. Tilda Holdwain works on the first floor. Her desk is outside the office of the ambassador's secretary.'

'I know the Holdwains. The last time I saw Tilda, she was a mere girl.'

'And that mere girl has grown into a young woman,' said Thorn. 'An impressionable, rather immature young woman, but a woman nonetheless. If you delve into her memories, then you will be able to see if I am lying or not.'

'You are going to look very foolish in a few minutes,' said Daphne. 'I will do as you suggest, and visit young Tilda with my powers; if only to prove you wrong.'

Thorn smiled. 'You must do as you see fit, Holder Fast.'

Daphne glared at her, then prepared her powers.

'No!' cried Keir.

Daphne glanced at her son.

Keir pointed at Thorn. 'This is all her fault! She orchestrated the whole thing, mother; you have to believe me.'

'I did nothing of the kind,' said Thorn. 'Are you suggesting that I forced you into Tilda's bed?'

'Silence,' said Daphne. 'Keir, tell me the truth – a simple yes or no will suffice. Is Thorn's accusation true? Did you betray your marriage vows with that Holdwain girl?'

'No!' cried Keir. 'Thorn's making it up. She hates me, mother.'

Thorn laughed.

'You have to believe me, mother,' said Keir. 'Thorn's been threatening to make up lies about me, and then to tell you; but I knew you wouldn't believe her. I would never have an affair. I know I'm not perfect, but I would never break my marriage vows.'

'Thank you, son,' said Daphne.

'Wait,' said Thorn, her laughter fading. 'Do you actually believe him?'

'I know my own son, Thorn. He would never lie to me. You, on the other hand? Part of the reason I selected you as a suitable successor to the throne was due to your... well, let's call it cunning, for want of a better word. However, I never dreamt that you would stoop so low.'

'Oh, Daphne,' said Thorn; 'how can I answer that?'

'Well, you could apologise, for a start.'

Thorn looked Daphne in the eye. 'I'm sorry; sorry I married your son. If you wish, I shall divorce him, or allow him to divorce me, if you would prefer that. Shall I pack my bags?'

'I think that would be a good idea.'

Thorn tilted her head a little, smiled, then strode out of the room.

Daphne frowned, then turned her attention back to Keir.

'What just happened?' said Keir. 'Is my marriage over?'

'It certainly appears that way, son. It's sad, but perhaps it's for the best. Who would wish to be married to a wife who makes up wicked lies about their husband?'

'But...'

'Hush. I shall need to think deeply about this. Thorn's outrageous behaviour this day has altered everything. She is clearly unfit to rule the empire. What a humiliation this is. I shall have to go crawling back to the Empress on my hands and knees. Or, perhaps we should stage another vote – only this time, I shall nominate Lord Bryce, and instruct the family to support him. Either way, I will have lost a great deal of face by the end of this day. And damn it, I will have to inform the two Sanang gentlemen currently residing in Colsbury that the entire thing has fallen through. The Matriarch will switch from being an ally to my enemy in the blink of an eye. What could have possessed Thorn to behave so despicably? I just don't understand it.'

Keir stared at her, but kept his mouth closed.

'You're clearly in shock, son,' said Daphne. 'Try not to be too upset. Would you like a cup of tea?'

Keir nodded.

'I shall fetch you one,' said Daphne. 'Poor boy. Now I have an inkling of what you have been putting up with in recent years. I'm so sorry that I trusted Thorn over you. I'll make it up to you; I promise.'

She left the room, and walked down the hallway to a small kitchen. She filled a kettle with water, and placed it onto a stove that was kept warm. She prepared two mugs, and added an extra spoonful of sugar to Keir's. Her thoughts went to Tilda Holdwain. Not only had Thorn tried to besmirch Keir, she had attempted to ruin that poor girl's reputation at the same time. A small voice at the back of Daphne's mind wondered if she should check with Tilda, just to make sure. But that would suggest that she thought Keir might be lying to her; and Keir wouldn't lie to his own mother. Would he?

'Are you making one of those for me, Daffers?'

Daphne turned, and saw Shella standing by the doorway.

'Sometimes, Shella, I think you follow me around Colsbury.'

'I came back upstairs as soon as the shouting stopped.'

Daphne nodded, and prepared another mug for her friend.

'I passed Thorn and Keir's room on the way,' Shella went on.

'Did you, indeed?'

'Yeah. Um... why is Thorn packing a bag? She was stuffing her clothes into it, and, eh... well, she was crying. An unusual sight, I must admit. I assumed that Thorn had had her tear ducts removed at birth.'

'Perhaps she is reflecting upon the error of her ways.'

'Is she leaving Colsbury, or just switching rooms?'

Daphne sighed. 'I'm not entirely sure, Shella. It seems that she has been fabricating ridiculous lies about Keir. I may have made the biggest mistake of my life in supporting her candidacy for Empress. I'm too embarrassed by the whole thing to think clearly at the moment.'

Shella walked into the kitchen. 'Are you serious? What about the vote? We all voted – and Thorn won. You went all the way to Sanang. You staked your entire reputation on supporting Thorn. You...'

'I know all that,' Daphne snapped. 'I doubt I could feel any more stupid, but thank you for trying.'

'What lies was she making up?'

Daphne closed her eyes. 'She claimed that Keir was having an affair in Plateau City.'

'And Keir denied it, did he?'

'Of course he denied it.'

'Do you believe him?'

Daphne glared at her oldest friend. 'What kind of question is that? Why does everyone always assume the worst about Keir? If he had been having an affair, and Thorn discovered this, then why didn't she divorce him? Why would she keep that knowledge to herself? If only I could read their minds. But no, my foolish daughter blocked me from accessing their thoughts. Yet another colossal misjudgement on Karalyn's part. Oh, Shella, what I am going to say to Bridget? It's a pity you don't have stone powers, then you could trigger an earthquake that could swallow me up.'

'If I say something that you don't want to hear, will you fall out with me?'

'You're going to tell me that you believe Keir is capable of having an affair.'

'Well, yeah.'

Daphne sighed. 'Why does no one like Keir? I don't understand it. I know he has his flaws, but who doesn't? He can be immature at times, and rude, but he's trying his best. Look at the trouble he got into when he tried to save Bridget from Brannig. Everyone blamed him then, except for me; but he was completely innocent.'

'I know he was,' said Shella. 'Isn't there any way you could check who is telling you the truth?'

'Thorn gave me a name. I could read the girl's mind, but then I would know in my heart that I had doubted the word of my own son.'

'You need to do it, Daffers. If Thorn is lying, then you'll feel vindicated; otherwise, you'll always have that little nagging doubt. You'll always wonder if you made a mistake. This is no longer just about your son's marriage. The entire Empire is now involved. Are you going to sit back and allow Bridget to pick her successor, just because you refused to confirm the details?'

Daphne cursed inwardly, unable to counter Shella's logic.

'Fine. I'll do it. Could you please take a cup of tea to Keir when the kettle finally boils? And don't mention what I'm doing to him.'

'Sure.'

'I'll be in my room. It shouldn't take too long.'

Dispirited, Daphne trudged from the kitchen, feeling guilty that she would even consider questioning her son's integrity. Still, Shella was right. The future of the Empire was more important than her moral qualms. She slipped into her room, and opened a shutter. She gazed out of the south-facing window, and released her vision powers, speeding them over the foothills of the Barrier Mountains, and down onto the plains of the Plateau. The miles flitted by in a blur, then she approached the great city lying on the northern shores of the Inner Sea. She decided that, if Thorn had been lying, her next stop would be the Great Fortress, where she would grovel in front of the Empress, and beg her forgiveness.

She steered her powers to the Holdings Embassy, and entered through a window on the first floor. She knew where the office belonging to the ambassador's secretary was located, and saw a desk sitting outside the door. Seated behind the desk was a pretty young woman. The last time Daphne had seen Tilda Holdwain, she had been a girl of thirteen or fourteen, but Thorn had been right. Tilda was no longer a girl, but a young woman. Daphne took a breath, then entered Tilda's mind.

It didn't take long.

Images of Keir were scattered throughout Tilda's memories, and Daphne felt her resolve crumble into dust. She severed the connection before she could see anything that might live with her forever, then began to weep. Tears rolled down her cheeks, then her sorrow gave way to anger. She clenched her right fist, and stood. She left her room, and walked to where Keir was still sitting.

He glanced up at her as she entered, the cup of hot tea in his hands. Without a word, Daphne strode up to him, then struck him across the face with the back of her hand, powering her battle-vision as she did so. He cried out, dropping the cup as blood trickled from his nose.

'You stupid little bastard,' she hissed, then she turned her back to him and walked away.

She strode to the room shared by Thorn and Keir, and stood by the open entrance, watching for a moment as a tearful Thorn packed her things.

'I believe you,' Daphne said; 'and I'm sorry.'

Thorn turned her head, then wiped her eyes. 'Did you check with Tilda?'

'Yes.'

Thorn started weeping again, then rushed to the door and embraced Daphne. 'Thank you.'

'You are now my daughter, Thorn,' Daphne said, 'if you want to be. Even if you decide to divorce my son, you will still be a Holdfast, if that is what you desire.'

'I do,' Thorn said.

'I should never have doubted you.'

'You were just being a good mother.'

'And now I shall try to be a good mother to you, Thorn. Don't unpack. We'll find you a room of your own. I... I'm sorry about my son's behaviour. And... I love you, Thorn.'

Thorn smiled at her. 'I love you, too, mother.'

CHAPTER 14
INDECISION

Sable watched Amalia and Karalyn stride down the stairs of the tenement block, then she closed the front door of the apartment.

'Stupid bitch,' she muttered.

Cardova eyed her. 'I'm going to assume that you weren't referring to Karalyn.'

'You assume correctly, Lucius,' said Sable. 'At least I can relax, now that Amalia's gone.'

They walked into the small apartment's living room, where Austin was sitting with his mother and aunt.

'They've gone,' said Sable; 'off on their mission to pluck Belinda from Edmond's sweaty grasp. If we're fortunate, they'll be successful. If we're really fortunate, Amalia will bravely sacrifice her life in the attempt.'

Sable and Cardova sat down by the low table.

'You were very restrained while Amalia was here,' said Cardova.

Austin laughed. 'She was, wasn't she? She was very well behaved; not at all like the Sable I knew on Dragon Eyre.'

'I was just being polite,' said Sable. 'This is Karalyn's operation, and it appears that I'm only here to make up the numbers. If Karalyn hadn't been here, it would have been a different story.'

'I was wondering if you were scared of her,' said Austin.

'Who, Karalyn?' said Sable. 'Considering that she is probably the only being alive who could melt my brain with a thought, then, yeah: I guess I am a little scared of her.'

'I meant Amalia,' said Austin.

Sable snorted. 'Eh, no. She might have once been the God-Queen of an entire city, but she's just another arrogant god. If I'd met her on Dragon Eyre, I would have chopped off her head without a second thought.' She glanced at Cardova. 'I thought you were pretty restrained, too. I mean, you think the same about Amalia's so-called plan as I do; and yet you sat there saying nothing while we were discussing it.'

'That's what I was trained to do while on duty,' he said. 'If you think a superior's plan is bad, then you stay silent, unless asked a direct question.'

Sable smirked at him. 'Even when the woman you are besotted with is walking into extreme danger?'

'As you said – it's Karalyn's operation. She's in charge. I just hope that she knows what she's doing.'

'I notice you didn't deny that you are besotted with her. Oh, and by the way; you're a very loud kisser. We could hear the two of you all night.'

Sunnah frowned. 'I didn't hear anything.'

'Well, I did,' said Sable. 'It didn't help that we were all sleeping in the same room. The noise kept me awake.'

'Don't exaggerate,' said Cardova. 'Practically nothing happened. We were well aware that others were sharing the same room. And anyway, I don't care what you think. I've waited a long time to kiss Karalyn... and now I just have to hope that I'll see her again.' His gaze fell, and he shook his head. 'I can't believe that they're just going to walk into the Second Ascendant's fortress-palace. You know, I would prefer to be with them, rather than have to sit here waiting.'

'How long will they be, do you think?' said Austin.

Cardova shrugged. 'At least a day; maybe longer.'

'That doesn't sound too bad,' said Sunnah. She glanced at her sister. 'Perhaps we should pack our things, so that we're ready to go.'

Salah nodded. 'Let's have breakfast first. I suppose that we shouldn't go to work today.'

'We'll all stay here,' said Austin. 'I've probably lost my job, after not turning up yesterday.'

'What were you doing?' said Sable.

'I was working in a tavern kitchen,' he said. 'Washing dishes and mopping floors; that kind of thing.'

Sable nodded. 'Had you lost hope that I was ever coming back for you?'

'Not entirely,' he said, 'but I came close.'

'Austin had faith in you, Sable,' said Salah. 'He was always saying that you could do anything. We were more worried that you had been killed on Dragon Eyre. Just think – we could be there tomorrow.'

Sable's mood soured. 'I might have to take revenge upon the Wystians when we get back. I can't have them thinking that they can abduct me and not get punished for it. A dozen explosive devices placed into a few caverns ought to do the trick.'

'But, Sable,' said Austin, 'I thought we were going to live in peace.'

'You can,' she said. 'You've done your part, Austin. I still have work to do.'

'Forget the Wystians,' said Cardova. 'If you feel the need to draw blood, then go after the Unk Tannic.'

'What about Lara?' said Austin. 'I genuinely believed that you were going to settle down with her.'

Sable put her head in her hands. 'I want to. I spoke to her before we came to Implacatus. At that moment, all I wanted was to be with her; nothing else on Dragon Eyre was of the slightest interest to me. But after coming here, I'm not sure I'll be able to rest. What if the Unk Tannic try to take control of the Eastern Rim? What if Wyst invades Ulna?'

Austin leaned over the table. 'Sable; listen to me. You and I will be on Ulna. No one would dare try to invade – not the Unk Tannic, and not the Wystians. Blackrose will be delighted to see us.'

'Will she? Did you know that Blackrose did nothing to try to free me from Wyst? Nothing. She would have let me rot in that filthy pit.'

'That doesn't sound right,' said Austin. 'Why wouldn't Blackrose help you?'

'She was worried that it would start a war,' said Cardova. 'I was there, with Karalyn in Ulna. Queen Blackrose sympathised about Sable's plight, but she knew that Wyst would be able to overpower her realm with ease. There must be thousands of dragons living on Wyst. How many does Blackrose have? A few hundred?'

'And whose fault was that?' said Sable. 'If you and your Banner friends hadn't slaughtered so many of them, then Ulna wouldn't be so heavily out-numbered.'

Salah glanced at Austin. 'Are you sure that Dragon Eyre is a safe place to live?'

'It's safer than here,' said Sable. 'Besides, Austin has Ashfall waiting for him on Dragon Eyre.'

Salah glanced at her son. 'Who is this Ashfall? You didn't tell me that you had a girl waiting for you.'

Austin half-smiled, half-grimaced. 'Ashfall's a dragon, mother. She and I became close when we were fighting the occupation forces.'

'Close?' said Sable. 'She adores you, Austin.'

'She's probably forgotten about me. It's been months since I saw her.'

'Dragons don't forget things like that,' said Cardova. 'Are you her rider?'

'No,' he said.

Sable started to feel sick. She had been longing to return to Dragon Eyre ever since she had arrived back in the Holdings, but now that it seemed imminent, the old burdens were beginning to weigh upon her again. All the blood and death, the pain and exhaustion, the grief, and the never-ending rage. Her breathing became ragged, and she could feel her heart pounding behind her ribcage.

'Are you alright?' said Austin.

'Not really,' she said.

'She's got the Dragon Eyre shakes,' said Cardova. 'It was quite common among Banner soldiers who were about to return to that lizard-infested world.'

Sable swung her fist and punched Cardova in the face.

'Holy shit, Sable,' Cardova cried, his hand going to his bloody nose.

'If you ever call Badblood a lizard again,' Sable shouted, 'I will beat you to a pulp; do you hear me? Banner scum!'

She jumped to her feet and ran from the room, then realised that there was nowhere to go but the kitchen or the bathroom. She chose the kitchen, and fell into a chair as the tears started. She held her hands to her face as she wept. What was she doing on Implacatus? She should have gone to Ulna as soon as she had the ability to do so, and swept Lara up in her arms. Lara would understand. And then what? Would she try to live in peace, or would her need for blood push her into another rampage? Dark thoughts swirled round her head. How could she rest when the Unk Tannic would be making every effort to regain the world they had once dominated? They had to die – they all had to die.

She felt a hand touch her shoulder, and she pushed it away.

'Sable,' Austin whispered. 'Everything's going to be fine.'

'Is it?' she cried. 'Are we insane, Austin? What do you think will happen to me if we go back? This last month, since Karalyn rescued me from Wyst, I've been living as if nothing was wrong, as if my life on Dragon Eyre had been a bad dream. I don't want to go back, Austin. I'm scared of what I'll do there.'

'Don't think about that – think about Lara. And Millen and Maddie, too. You have friends who love you in Ulna.'

'How could I even look at Millen and Maddie? They know what I've done. I disgust them. I disgust myself. I'll never be able to live in peace, Austin – it was nothing but a stupid dream. My hands, they're covered in blood.'

'I'm sorry,' said a voice from the door.

Sable glanced up, and saw Cardova leaning against the doorframe, a handkerchief held to his nose.

'I forgot that you lost a dragon you loved,' he said. 'I shouldn't have called them that.'

Several cruel responses ran through Sable's mind, but she said nothing.

Cardova attempted a smile. 'That's twice I've caught you crying now.'

'Shut up,' she said. 'Light me a cigarette, you Banner halfwit.'

The soldier walked over, and sat down next to Austin and Sable by the kitchen table. He took out a packet of cigarettes, and gave one each to the others. Sable wiped the tears from her eyes, and wished she was able to shield her emotions as well as Daphne could.

'I'm a wreck,' she said, as Cardova lit her cigarette.

'You're recovering from a traumatic experience,' said Austin.

'I don't think I can go to Ulna,' she said. 'Except for Lara, of course. Maybe I could sail about on the *Giddy Gull* for the rest of my life.'

'Can I ask you something?' said Austin. 'You and Karalyn seemed to be getting along well. Did you speak to her about all that stuff you mentioned? About her husband?'

Sable nodded.

'And?'

'She forgave me. Karalyn's a better person than I'll ever be. In fact, most of the Holdfasts treated me well. Even Daphne. I think they might prefer it if I stayed there, with them in Colsbury – can you believe that?'

'That's great, Sable. I know how much you wanted to reconcile with them.'

'Then why do I feel like screaming?'

'That'll be Dragon Eyre,' said Cardova. 'I may have misspoken before, but the symptoms are real. I knew many men, hard, strong men, reduced to tears by the thought of returning there. It affects me, too. I hate that world with a passion, and I will be going back there along with the rest of you. Yes, Sable – even Banner scum have feelings.'

'I might have over-reacted earlier,' she said. 'I miss Badblood so much; I can't help it. If it wasn't for Lara, I don't think I could ever set foot on Dragon Eyre again.'

Cardova frowned. 'Why don't you take Austin, his family, and Lara to the Holdings? Damn it, even the City would be better than Dragon Eyre; but Colsbury would be ideal.'

'What's it like?' said Austin.

'It's beautiful, and peaceful,' said Cardova. 'Picture a castle on a small island, in a lake set amid the mountains.'

'It sounds nice,' said Austin. 'I would need to ask Ashfall, and then there's Blackrose to consider. I wouldn't want people to think that I was abandoning them.'

Salah appeared at the door, her expression lined with worry.

'I don't wish to alarm you,' she said, 'but a lot of soldiers have gathered outside the building.'

Cardova got to his feet and went to the kitchen window.

'What do you see, Lucius?' said Sable.

'Soldiers from the Banner of the Swift Arrow,' he said; 'commanded by at least three gods. An entire company has been kitted out in steel armour – they're going to storm the building.'

Salah's eyes widened. 'But why?'

'Could they have captured Karalyn already?' said Austin, standing.

'Everyone stay calm,' said Cardova. 'Salah, bring your sister into the kitchen.'

Sable remained at the table as Salah hurried away.

'Should we flee?' said Austin.

Cardova turned to face Sable, but the Holdfast woman said nothing.

A few shouts rang out from the street, then the sound of the tenement's front door being kicked down reached Sable's ears. Boots pounded on the stairs leading up to the apartments, but Sable remained frozen to her seat. Salah re-appeared in the doorway with her sister, their expressions fearful.

'Are we leaving now?' said Salah. 'I think we should leave now.'

Sable closed her eyes. The Quadrant was tucked into her clothes, so why wasn't she activating it? A strange sort of lethargy seemed to take hold of her mind, as the sound of the soldiers' boots on the tenement stairs grew louder.

'Sable!' said Cardova, shaking her shoulder. 'Get up.'

Sable didn't respond.

'What's wrong with her?' said Austin.

The front door of the apartment was kicked down, and Sunnah shrieked.

'We want Amalia!' called a voice from the hallway. 'Do not resist!'

Austin raised his hand in the direction of the kitchen door, as his mother and aunt moved behind him. Two armoured soldiers appeared in the doorway, their oblong shields raised high, while others could be seen crowding the hallway behind them.

'Don't come any closer!' Austin cried. 'Amalia isn't here!'

'Get up, Sable,' Cardova repeated, 'or I'll slap you across the face.'

Sable sensed Cardova's hand flash out, and she whipped her arm up, blocking the slap, her battle-vision pulling her out of her stupor. She got to her feet. She glanced into the eyes of the two soldiers, and wiped out a huge chunk of their memories.

Defend us, she commanded them. *Attack the other soldiers.*

The two armoured soldiers stared at her for a moment, then they turned, and began slashing out with their swords, cutting down their nearest colleagues amid cries and screams.

Sable took out the Quadrant, and gazed at the copper-coloured surface. The only location that she had learned how to travel to on Dragon Eyre was Ulna – a place that she did not want to see again.

She brushed her fingers over the device, and the air crackled. They arrived by the ground floor entrance to the bridge palace in Udall, next to the banks of the wide brown river. Before anyone could speak, she touched the Quadrant again, and they re-appeared within the walled temple complex on Haurn. The sun was high in the sky, and Sable felt its warmth against her skin. She stared at her surroundings. Some of the temple buildings had been damaged in the attack mounted by Bastion and Kolai, but most were still standing, including, she noticed, the large out-building where she had stored the explosive devices.

'Is this Dragon Eyre?' said Salah, her hands trembling.

'Yes, mother,' said Austin. 'This is where Sable and I stayed for a while. We're on an island called Haurn.'

'A greenhide-infested island called Haurn,' said Cardova.

'The walls surrounding the complex keep them out,' said Austin. 'We should be safe here.' He glanced at Sable. 'Can I speak to you in private?'

Sable glanced at him, then tucked the Quadrant back into her clothes. She turned, and strode into the ground floor of the temple, where she had lived for over two years. She gave a half-smile when she saw that most of her things were still there. The rooms had been ransacked, but nothing seemed to be missing.

Austin followed her inside.

'Why did you bring us here?' he said.

'I'd prefer to avoid Udall for now. I have no wish to speak to Blackrose.'

'Is there going to be trouble between you and the Queen of Ulna?'

'She refused to help me when I was imprisoned on Wyst. Even so, I would rather stay out of her way. I don't think anyone saw us arrive by the bridge palace, and we were only there for a second or two.'

'Back in the apartment,' he said, 'you seemed to freeze. Are you all right?'

Sable shook her head, then she leaned down and righted a chair that had been knocked over. 'I'm back on Dragon Eyre, Austin. It was the one place I wanted to return to, but, when it came to it, I panicked.'

'I would prefer to be in Ulna, Sable,' he said. 'It will take a lot of effort to get the temple's farms up and running again, and my mother and aunt aren't farmers. I told them they would be living in a palace, not in the half-ruined buildings of Nan Po Tana. And I want to see Ashfall.'

Sable picked up a table, and set it down onto its four legs.

'Are you listening to me?' he said.

'Haurn is where we're supposed to meet Karalyn.'

'No. We were supposed to meet her in my apartment in Serene, and then come here.'

'But this is where she'll come, after she realises that the apartment has been compromised.'

'Then we leave her a note, here, in the temple, telling her that we're in Ulna.'

'We should go back to Implacatus,' said a voice by the door.

Sable glanced up and saw Cardova by the entrance. 'This was a private conversation.'

'We're supposed to be assisting Karalyn in her operation to rescue Belinda,' the soldier said. 'We can't do that from Dragon Eyre.'

Sable picked up another chair. 'You just don't want to be on this world.'

'You're right; but that's not the point. We shouldn't abandon our posts.'

Sable laughed. 'The apartment was over-run, Lucius.'

'I know plenty of places where we can lie low in Serene.'

'What, and wait for the Banner soldiers to find us there? We were only in Serene for a couple of days before they kicked the door down.'

'They were looking for Amalia,' Cardova went on. 'Didn't you hear what they said? One of the gods must have sensed where she was. They weren't looking for Austin, and they wouldn't have been able to sense you, or Karalyn for that matter. We'll be safe if we go back.'

'I'm not going back,' said Austin. 'I've waited for months to get the chance to escape Implacatus; and I'm certainly not going to tell my mother and aunt that they have to return to Serene.'

Cardova glared at the young demigod. 'Fine; you can stay here. You're under no obligation to help us; but Sable and I promised to obey Karalyn's orders.'

Sable continued to tidy up the mess left by the soldiers.

'You need to make a decision,' said Cardova.

'Are you talking to me?' said Sable.

'Yes. You're next in command.'

'Does that mean you have to do as I say?'

'It does. My duty is to remind you of our obligations. Karalyn trusted us, and yet here we are, on another world.'

'Karalyn will come to us.'

'And what if she needs help? We're the back-up. If she gets into trouble and calls upon us, we won't be in a position to assist her. Here's what I suggest – take Austin, Salah and Sunnah to Ulna, and we can speak to Queen Blackrose. Then, you and I should return to Serene.'

Sable narrowed her eyes. 'You tried to slap me.'

'Yes. You were the only person who could save us from the soldiers, and you were unresponsive. I'm not going to apologise for that. Your indecision nearly got us all killed.'

'If you ever try that again...'

'Yes. I know. You'll beat the crap out of me. Sable, you're behaving as if this is a dream; wake up. Stop clearing up the mess in here, and think for a moment. You're supposed to be a professional at this sort of thing – act like one.'

Sable sat on a chair, and put her head in her hands. She closed her eyes, but could still smell the scents of Haurn – the orange blossom, and the salty tang in the air coming from the vast ocean that crashed against the nearby cliffs. If she allowed her mind to wander, she could almost pretend that the previous six months hadn't happened; that Badblood was outside, basking in the sunlight, while Deepblue was catching fish for their dinner from the little bay. She could almost hear Millen's voice, chatting to Meader, and to the locals who worked in the farms and groves of the temple.

'Sable?' said Cardova.

'Give her a moment,' said Austin. 'I think she's feeling a little fragile.'

'Fragile?' snapped the soldier. 'She's bloody useless.'

'Don't say that.'

'I heard she had a reputation for ruthlessness and daring. She's burned out, Austin; I recognise the look in her eyes – I've seen it on the faces of countless Banner soldiers over the years.'

'She was fine until we started talking about coming back to Dragon Eyre.'

'I know. That's what triggered her. I was damn near triggered myself.' Cardova sighed. 'Is there any food around here? Maybe we should get something to eat. I don't think we're going to get much out of Sable for a while.'

'There are probably some stores in one of the out-buildings. Should we take a look?'

'Yes. Show me.'

Austin put a hand onto Sable's shoulder. 'We'll make some breakfast. Perhaps you'll feel better if you eat something.'

Sable listened as the two men left the temple building, then she opened her eyes and glanced around. She got up from the chair, and began tidying again, as if everything would be all right if her old room looked the same as it had done when she had lived there. She made her bed, folding and tucking in the sheets and thin blanket, and plumping up the soft pillow. She heard a noise behind her, and saw that Salah and Sunnah had entered the temple, and were helping to clean it, without saying a word. Salah had a broom, and she was sweeping the dust and broken fragments of pottery from the wooden floor, while Sunnah was picking up scattered items of clothing.

'Thank you,' said Sable.

Salah smiled, but said nothing.

'Is this our new home?' said Sunnah.

'No. This is my old home,' said Sable. 'It's the only place that has ever felt like home. I was happy here, once.'

'You can be happy again,' said Sunnah. 'Even though we were living in poverty in Serene, every day I would be glad that my sister and I were no longer slaves. You reunited us with Austin, and freed us, Sable. Our happiness is thanks to you.'

'Austin never lost his faith in you,' said Salah. 'He looks up to you.'

'I turned him into a murderer,' said Sable.

'You gave him something to fight for; something to believe in,' said Sunnah.

'Don't you have a girl waiting for you in Ulna?' said Salah. 'Perhaps she could make you happy.'

'I don't want to ruin her life. I hurt everyone I get close to. I love Lara too much to do that to her.'

'Why sentence yourself to a lonely life of misery?' said Sunnah. 'You're lucky to have someone who loves you. And you're still a young woman, Sable.'

'Young? I'm thirty-one.'

'Exactly,' said Sunnah. 'You have much of your life before you, and there's so much that you could achieve.'

'You make it sound easy. I have done some terrible things, and I have lost so much.'

'My sister and I were slaves for decades,' said Salah. 'We were used, beaten and humiliated on a daily basis. If we can find renewed happiness, then you can, too.'

Sable stood. She gazed around her old room; her refuge. She could hide there, forever, isolated and alone; or she could force herself to confront the fact that she was back on Dragon Eyre. Austin and Cardova appeared in the doorway, each carrying a box of supplies.

'We're going to Ulna,' Sable said.

'Now?' said Austin.

'Yes. Now. I'm ready.'

She took out her Quadrant, and brushed her fingers over its surface. The air shimmered, and they reappeared by the entrance to the bridge palace in Udall, next to the brown river. This time, several people witnessed their arrival, and a few townsfolk gasped.

'It's Sable Holdfast!' someone shouted. 'She has returned!'

More people stopped what they were doing to look, and a crowd gathered around the small group. Many were cheering, with wild expressions of joy on their faces.

'Give us some room!' Cardova shouted. 'We are on our way to see the Queen.'

A chant of 'Sable, Sable' arose from the growing crowd, and a dragon swooped down to see what was causing the noise.

'We'll never get through these crowds,' said Cardova.

Sable nodded, and activated the Quadrant. The air shimmered again, and they appeared within the main reception hall of the palace, where half a dozen dragons and over a score of humans were gathered.

Maddie shrieked. She jumped down from a low platform, and ran towards Sable and Austin. She threw her arms around the Holdfast woman, and started to cry.

'Sable Holdfast,' cried Blackrose.

The tumult in the hall stilled.

Sable raised her eyes towards the black dragon. 'Hello, Blackrose.'

'I see that, despite all my warnings, Karalyn Holdfast saw fit to release you from captivity.'

'I'm glad someone did,' said Sable. 'I hear you ignored my plight.'

'If I had attempted to intervene, then Wyst would have destroyed my realm. It pained me, Sable, but I had to place the welfare of the entire population of Ulna over the rescue of one individual. Such are the responsibilities of leadership.' She turned her red eyes to Austin. 'Greetings, demigod.'

Austin bowed his head towards the Queen. 'Where is Ashfall, your Majesty?'

'I am here, Austin.'

They turned, and saw the slender grey dragon by the entrance to the hall. She pushed her way through the other dragons, then lowered her head to Austin's level, her eyes drinking him in. Austin lifted his arms, and embraced the dragon's face.

'I missed you, my rider,' Ashfall said. 'Your absence has been like a knife in my heart. Have you been on Implacatus all this time?'

'Yes. Sable came for me, after she was released from Wyst.' He gestured to Salah and Sunnah. 'This is my mother, and my aunt.'

Ashfall glanced at the two older women, then fixed her eyes on Sable. 'Thank you, Holdfast.'

'You are all welcome to stay in Ulna,' said Blackrose. 'Even you, Sable; if you can forgive me.'

'I don't know what I want,' said Sable. 'No, actually, that's not true. We can talk later. I want to see Lara.'

'And then you and I are going back to Implacatus?' said Cardova.

'I don't know, Lucius.'

She swiped her thumb over the Quadrant, and appeared on the long quayside by the harbour of Udall. In front of her, dozens of people were working on rebuilding the upper decks of the *Giddy Gull*, and the air was filled with the sound of saws and hammers. To the left of the *Gull*, Tilly's ship, the *Sow's Revenge* was sitting, and along from that was *Patience*, and the *Flight of Fancy*. Sable walked up the gangway onto the main deck of the *Giddy Gull*, and several workers quietened as they watched her pass.

She strode up onto the new quarter deck. Topaz was standing there, talking to two young sailors with his back to her, then the cabin door opened, and Lara and Tilly walked out.

Sable and Lara stared at each other.

Sable smiled. 'I'm back.'

CHAPTER 15
HAGGLING

Kelsey led the twins through a door and into a well-lit, comfortable chamber on the upper floor of the Aurelian mansion. Emily's mother, Lady Omertia, was sitting on a long couch, watching Elspeth as she crawled on the thick rug.

'Good morning, Lady O,' said Kelsey.

Lady Omertia smiled at Kelsey and the twins. 'Good morning.'

'Did anyone tell you that we were coming?' said Kelsey.

'Yes. I was informed just after breakfast that you would be leaving your sister's children with me for a few hours.'

'Good. Thanks for this. Van and I shouldn't be away for too long. Did you hear about what happened in the desert?'

Lady Omertia nodded. 'I did. Those poor children; they must have been terrified. I think I would have screamed if a hundred greenhides had suddenly crawled out of the ground.' She glanced at Kyra and Cael. 'You were very brave.'

'What are we going to do today?' said Cael.

'Would you like to help me bake some cakes?' said Lady Omertia. 'Then you can have one each when they're finished. For now, though, why don't you take a look at the picture books in the little cupboard by the window?'

Lady Omertia stood as the twins rushed away to examine the books.

'Is there anything I should know about them, Kelsey? Anything they like or dislike?'

'They're quite picky with their food,' Kelsey said; 'but they'll eat cakes. And, uh... they can also read your mind.'

'I see.'

'They're not supposed to, of course, and they've both been told that. But, you know, they're kids. If you catch them doing it, then tell me, and I'll think up a suitable punishment.'

'I presume each twin can read the other's mind also?'

'Aye. They're always at it. Whenever they're being quiet, watch them. They'll probably be talking to each other inside their heads. Or, they might even be talking to each other inside your head.'

'I'm sure I can handle that.'

'You don't seem all that surprised.'

'Nothing about the Holdfasts has the capacity to surprise me any longer, Kelsey,' said Lady Omertia. She leaned down and plucked Elspeth from the rug. 'I'll put this little one down for a nap, and then the twins will have my full attention.'

'See you later, Lady O. And thanks again.'

Kelsey walked from the room, then descended a flight of stairs. Van was waiting for her on the landing, and they walked down another set of stairs to the ground floor.

'Did you tell her?' Van said.

'Tell her what?' said Kelsey.

'About the twins' powers?'

Kelsey scrunched up her face. 'Um... I told her some things. I told her they could read minds.'

'And what about their ability to make you do things against your will?'

'I might have missed that bit out. I didn't want to alarm the old girl. It's not easy finding a babysitter for them, and it would be nigh impossible if I was completely honest about their powers. And yet, I can hardly take them with us to Plateau City. I'm supposed to be keeping them safe from Daimon, not delivering them into his hands.'

'Seems a little risky.'

'It was a calculated risk. If we come back to find Lady O mooing like a cow, or running naked through the storms of Sweetmist, then we'll know that I was wrong.'

Van shook his head. They entered the royal reception chamber, and found Emily and Daniel with Lady Aurelian and Commander Quill from the Bulwark.

'Good morning, your Majesties,' said Van, bowing.

'Good morning, Major-General,' said Daniel. 'Are you all set to travel to the Star Continent?'

'I think so, your Majesty. We shall be travelling light, as we intend to be back after a few hours.'

'We have decided that Commander Quill shall be accompanying you today,' Daniel went on. 'We felt that two senior officers would be better than one.'

'I certainly have no objections to the Commander of the Bulwark joining us,' said Van.

'I'm quite excited to be going, sir,' said Quill. 'I've wanted to see another world ever since I learned from Corthie and the dragons that other worlds exist.'

Kelsey took the Quadrant out of her shoulder bag. 'I'm ready now, if everyone else is.'

'Are you clear on what you need to say?' said Emily.

'I'll be letting Van do all the talking,' said Kelsey.

'Please remember to give our best regards to the Empress of your world.'

'Aye, no bother,' said Kelsey. She gestured for Quill to come and stand closer to her, then she examined the surface of the Quadrant. She had studied her notebook for hours the previous night, memorising the steps needed to transport them to the Star Continent, and she felt a twinge of nerves.

'Alright,' she said. 'Here goes. See you all soon.'

She swept her thumb and forefinger over the device, and the air crackled around them. Their surroundings altered, replaced by the Sextant chamber in Colsbury Castle. Van eyed the huge device, an eyebrow raised, while Quill walked to a window and looked out.

'I don't want to sound disappointed,' said Quill, 'but I'd always imagined Plateau City to be bigger; and I didn't know it was in the middle of a lake.'

'We're not in Plateau City,' said Kelsey. 'We're in Colsbury Castle. When Sable taught me how to travel to this world, she showed me how to get here; but don't worry – I can quickly work out how to shift us south to the Imperial Capital.'

'Ah, so this is Colsbury?' said Quill. 'That makes more sense.' Her eyes lit up. 'Will Corthie be here? I'd love to see him again.'

'Corthie's thousands of miles away, in the arse-end of nowhere, sitting in a prison cell.'

'What?' said Quill. 'Corthie's been imprisoned? Shouldn't we rescue him?'

Kelsey laughed. 'He gave himself up. He beat up a few guys, and got ninety days. He escaped on his own, but then he felt guilty about it, and went back willingly. The numpty. He wants to be a farmer.'

'Oh.'

'Each to their own,' said Van. 'I hope the lad finds happiness, no matter which path he chooses.'

'Come on,' said Kelsey; 'let's say hello to Caelius and my mother while we're here. It'd be rude not to.'

Kelsey slipped the Quadrant back into her bag, then they left the Sextant chamber. They walked down a long passageway, then Kelsey opened a door. Inside, Daphne, Thorn and Shella were talking in hushed tones around a low table.

Shella glanced up. 'Look who it is, Daffers.'

Daphne turned, and her eyes widened, then welled up. She leapt from her chair and rushed towards her daughter.

'Kelsey! Thank the heavens that you're here! You have no idea how happy I am to see you.'

Kelsey blinked. 'What? Are you crying, mother, because of me?'

Daphne wiped her eyes. 'We are safe at last. With you here, Daimon won't be able to touch us.'

'Um... We're not here for that, mother. We're just passing through on our way to Plateau City.'

Daphne's expression changed in an instant. 'Why are you going to Plateau City?'

'Let me make some introductions first,' Kelsey said. 'This is Commander Quill, an old friend of Corthie's. She's now in charge of the defences on the Great Walls – the first mortal ever to hold that position. And, eh... this... this is Van.'

'I see,' said Daphne, narrowing her eyes.

Van bowed. 'It is an honour to finally meet you, ma'am. Is my father here?'

'Not at present,' said Daphne. 'He is with Agang Garo.'

'Corthie and Kelsey have told us much about the Holdfasts, ma'am,' said Quill, also bowing her head.

Daphne frowned. 'I'm sure they did.'

Kelsey sighed. 'Why don't I make the other introductions, too, as it seems to have slipped my mother's mind.' She pointed at Shella. 'This is Princess Shellakanawara, a Rakanese mage, and midwife to the Holdfast babies.'

Shella stood. 'That's the first time you've ever referred to me as a princess.'

Kelsey shrugged. 'I'm just trying to impress our guests. Don't worry; I won't do it again.' She pointed at Thorn. 'And this is Thorn Holdfast. She's married to my brother. Not Corthie. The other one. Where is Keir, by the way?'

'Your brother is in his room,' said Daphne, 'where he shall be remaining.'

'Eh? What's he done now?'

'Never mind that,' said Daphne. 'It's a private family matter. I notice that you didn't answer my earlier question. Why are you going to Plateau City?'

'We are here to attempt to negotiate a trade deal with the Star Continent, ma'am,' said Van. 'The King and Queen of the City were very grateful for the gifts you sent, and their Majesties are hoping to obtain more of the goods and raw materials that we require.'

'If you want a trade deal,' said Daphne, 'then you can speak to me. I would be more than happy to offer generous terms to the rulers of the City.'

'Their Majesties would prefer that we negotiated with the sovereign ruler of this world, ma'am.'

Anger flashed across Daphne's face. 'You mean that after I donated all those gifts, you have decided to trade with the Empress behind my back? An Empress who has given you nothing? Does that not smack of ingratitude, at the very least? The Holdfasts are powerful and wealthy enough to trade with a single city. What do you need? Iron? Coal? Timber? I would rather give it to you free of charge than have you barter with the Empress.'

The atmosphere in the room chilled. Thorn got to her feet.

'Let's not argue with our guests,' Thorn said. 'It is understandable that any foreign entity would wish to deal with another nation's legitimate ruler, and Empress Bridget does remain our imperial sovereign. I wish you all the best of luck with securing a fair and equitable deal. Might I ask – what does the City have to sell?'

Van glanced at Thorn for a moment. 'Salve, ma'am.'

Thorn frowned. 'I am unfamiliar with salve. I recall Sable referring to your home by the name of Salve City, but I don't know what salve is.'

'It's a mineral found only upon the world of the City, ma'am. When refined, it can be used as a healing balm. It has much the same effect as that of a god with healing powers.'

'Thorn has healing powers,' said Kelsey.

Van nodded. 'That's what it does to mortals. On gods, however, it has a different effect. It rejuvenates them, restoring them to their youth. Take Lady Belinda, for example. She is over thirty thousand years old, and before the discovery of salve, she had the appearance of an exceedingly old woman. After taking some doses of the substance, she now looks about twenty-one. The City started exporting salve to Lostwell some three hundred years ago, and now the gods can't get enough of it. That is why they are hunting for the world of the City. Their stocks will be running low by now, and they will be panicking about starting to appear old again.'

'And you intend to offer this substance to the Empress?' said Thorn.

'Yes, ma'am; in exchange for raw materials and other items.'

'I'm not particularly interested in what it does to gods,' said Daphne, 'but it worries me that Bridget will get her hands on something that could heal any injuries to her soldiers. This will give her a decided advantage if it comes to open conflict.'

'Back when supply was plentiful on Implacatus,' Van said, 'salve was routinely distributed to Banner soldiers, in little glass vials. They would take some if they were wounded; but it also heightens aggression, and many soldiers would take a small sip before battle.'

'I do not want the Empress to obtain any salve,' said Daphne. 'If you promise to keep it from her, then I will supply what your City needs, at no cost. The only other condition I would request is that the City enters into a defensive alliance with the Holdfasts. This is a very generous offer. The City would get to keep its salve, and receive all of the raw materials and finished goods it requires. Deal with me rather than the Empress, and I shall make it so.'

Quill narrowed her eyes. 'Just to be clear, ma'am,' she said, 'you would effectively donate thousands of tons of coal, iron and timber, along with sugar, coffee, and so on; just to stop us supplying the Empress with salve?'

'And for an alliance between the City and the Holdfasts,' said Daphne. 'A treaty of mutual defence.'

'What if it came to war between the Empress and the Holdfasts, ma'am?' said Van.

'Then I would expect your assistance,' said Daphne. 'Similarly, if your world is assailed by the gods, then we would mobilise our forces to help you. That, after all, is the nature of a defensive alliance.'

Van and Quill glanced at each other.

'We should talk alone,' said Kelsey. 'Mother, would you please excuse us for a moment?'

Daphne smiled, and gave a slight nod.

Kelsey led Van and Quill out of the room, and they went back to the Sextant chamber.

'I don't understand,' said Quill. 'Is Daphne Holdfast bluffing? How could she possibly afford such an agreement?'

Kelsey sighed. 'Perhaps I was never completely clear about just how rich my family is. This is going to sound arrogant, but my mother could buy up the entire City ten times over. We're the richest family in the world.'

Quill's eyes widened. 'Where does their money come from?'

'Property, mostly. We own vast tracts of land all over the Holdings, and some large estates in the northern half of the Plateau as well. There are also the trading companies that ship goods over the Inner Sea – that brings in a lot. The Holdings hasn't got much coal – they get most of it from Kellach Brigdomin, and the Holdfasts have a significant stake in the mining operations down there. Then there are the horses – we supply nine out of ten horses on this world; sugar cane, weed, gold mines... You name it, the chances are the Holdfasts own it.'

Quill glanced at Van. 'What should we do, sir?'

'The King and Queen were quite clear about our role here,' said Van. 'They ordered us to deal only with the Empress.'

'But, sir, this new deal would be far more beneficial to the City.'

'And what if war breaks out? The Holdfasts would expect us to send soldiers to assist them.'

'That's one thing the family lacks,' said Kelsey; 'an army. The Empress controls the only substantial armed force on the Star Continent.'

Van nodded. 'The City doesn't have the capacity to defend its borders from the greenhides, and to divert forces to this world at the same time.

Every Blade, every Banner soldier, and every Brigade worker is already fully employed. If anything, we're short of people. A defensive treaty with the Holdfasts would be a commitment we would not be able to honour.'

'What should I tell my mother?' said Kelsey.

'Tell her that we are very grateful for her generous offer, but that we are required by our own leaders to approach the Empress. Tell her this, too – tell her that we will not finalise any agreement with the Empress until we have returned to the City to consult with the King and Queen. That way, we can present both options to their Majesties, and they can take the final decision.'

'I concur,' said Quill. 'This will leave our options open.'

Kelsey nodded. 'Alright. If you hear screaming, come and rescue me.'

She left the others in the Sextant chamber, and returned to the room where Daphne, Shella and Thorn were sitting. They quietened as she walked in.

'I have an answer,' said Kelsey.

'I assume it's bad news,' said Daphne; 'otherwise why have you come alone?'

'It's not good or bad, mother. I'll be honest with you – we're under strict orders only to deal with the Empress. The King specifically told us not to strike a deal with the Holdfasts, so that the City doesn't get involved in a civil war. However, your offer has melted the brains of Quill and Van, and so they're promising not to agree to anything with the Empress before the King and Queen have had a chance to hear your offer as well. But, we'll still have to visit old Bridget.'

'That sounds fair,' said Thorn.

Kelsey squinted at the Sanang woman. 'I'm not used to you being the most sensible person in the room. When did this happen?'

Thorn laughed. 'We all grow up eventually. Even you, Kelsey.'

'I'm counting on you, daughter,' said Daphne. 'When you return to the City, I expect you to promote my deal, and to discredit anything the Empress has to offer.'

'I'm not your spy, mother.'

'No. You are my daughter, Kelsey. Do your duty to the family, for once in your life.'

'Why are you angry with me?'

'She thought you'd come here to protect Colsbury,' said Shella. 'With Karalyn away, we're a little concerned that Daimon might try to harm us.'

'Karalyn will be back in a couple of days. I'm sure you'll cope until then.'

Daphne gave her a hurt look, mingled with a little anger.

'Do you want me to pass on a message to Bridget?' said Kelsey.

'Yes,' said Daphne. 'Ask her if she would kindly refrain from trying to kill us again.'

Kelsey frowned. 'Has she already tried once?'

'Some soldiers attempted to set fire to our tavern,' said Thorn; 'just after we had crossed the border from Sanang into the Plateau. We're not sure who was behind it.'

'I have a damn good idea, though,' said Daphne. She sighed. 'You'd best be on your way, Kelsey. I would be obliged if you could let me know the outcome of these negotiations as soon as possible.'

Kelsey nodded, then left the room. She walked back to the Sextant chamber, feeling deflated, as she often did after talking to her mother. Van and Quill were examining the Sextant as Kelsey walked into the large room, then she sat down and took out the Quadrant. She got back to her feet after a moment, and strode over to where a large map of the Plateau was hanging from a wall.

'How did she take the news?' said Van.

Kelsey shrugged. 'Better than I'd expected, I guess. Now, shut up, while I work out how to take us to Plateau City.'

She gazed at the map, and hoped it was accurate. She calculated the distance and direction to Plateau City, but that was as much as she was able to do. Attempting to arrive within the walls of the Great Fortress was far too ambitious; arriving within the walls of the city would be a feat. She decided to play it safe, and aimed for a location just to the north of the city's limits.

'Alright,' she said. 'Let's hope this isn't a complete disaster.'

She swiped her fingers across the Quadrant. The air shimmered, and they arrived five feet above the ground, only a few yards from the edge of the Inner Sea. They fell through the air, and landed onto a rocky beach, the walls of the city visible to their left. Van groaned, and pulled himself to his feet.

'Don't complain,' snapped Kelsey, from where she lay on the sand. 'I'm still learning.'

Quill glanced at the waters of the Inner Sea as she got up. 'It could have been a lot worse.'

'I know,' said Kelsey. 'With just the tiniest flick of my finger, we could have ended up a mile from shore.'

Van reached down with an arm, and helped Kelsey stand.

'That looks more like the kind of place I was expecting,' said Quill, pointing towards the high walls in the distance.

The three of them stood and stared at the edge of the city.

'What are we seeing?' said Van.

'Well,' said Kelsey, 'those are the northern walls of Plateau City. Its western side runs along the shores of the Inner Sea, and there are harbours and so on by the mouth of a river. We're quite close to the main road coming from Sanang and the Western Holdings; well, I think we are. If we walk east from here, we should come to it soon; and then we can enter the city by the Royal Gates. They used to lead to an enormous palace, but it was destroyed by my aunt before I was born. The new palace is on the upper floors of the Great Fortress, which is in the centre of the city.' She shrugged. 'An hour's walk, maybe?'

Quill glanced up at the sun. She pointed at its position in the sky, and smiled.

'You know,' she said, 'I don't think I ever quite believed Corthie when he told me that the sun here rises in the east and sets in the west. I think I might have accused him of talking bullshit.'

Van laughed, then they started walking towards the road.

Almost two hours later, Kelsey, Van and Quill were sitting in a quiet waiting room within the Great Fortress. The guards had taken exception to Kelsey's presence when they had appeared at the main gates of the palace, as all Holdfasts were formally barred from the building; but, after a few discussions with their superiors, the delegates from the City were allowed to enter. They had been led upstairs into the palace, and then asked to wait.

'I had no idea this world was so wealthy,' said Quill. 'Some of the houses we saw on our way here wouldn't have looked out of place in Princeps Row.'

'We walked through the most affluent part of the city,' said Kelsey. 'There are poorer areas to the south of the Great Fortress, though there's nothing as bad as the Circuit.'

The door opened, and a courtier walked in.

'Please,' he said, 'follow me.'

Kelsey, Van and Quill stood, and left the room behind the courtier.

'Unfortunately,' the man said, 'her Majesty Empress Bridget is indisposed at the present time, and will be unable to greet you. Perhaps if you had made an appointment, then you would not be disappointed.'

Kelsey snorted. 'How are we supposed to make an appointment from another world?'

'That is not my area of expertise, Miss Holdfast. Lord Bryce, the Herald of the Empire has kindly agreed to see you all for a few minutes. He's a very busy man.'

'That would be wonderful,' said Quill. 'Thank you.'

The courtier knocked on a door, then pushed it open. They entered a comfortable study, where two men were standing by a desk, while a third sat in a large chair behind it.

'Lord Bryce,' said the courtier, bowing; 'may I please introduce Major-General Van Logos, Commander Quill, and Miss Kelsey Holdfast. They have travelled... far, to be here in Plateau City.'

The man sitting behind the desk smiled. 'Thank you. You may leave us.'

The courtier bowed again, then walked from the room.

'Hello, Kelsey,' said Bryce. 'It's been a while.'

'What, seven years?' said Kelsey.

'Something like that. I am told that you have come from another world?'

'Aye. That's right. This is Van and Quill, senior officers in the military of the City. We're here to talk about a prospective trade deal.'

Bryce narrowed his eyes for a moment, then smiled again. He gestured to the two men standing by his shoulders. 'This is Mage Tabor, and Mage Daimon.'

'I remember Tabor from Rainsby,' said Kelsey. 'And this is the new dream mage, eh? How's he working out for you?'

'We are very happy with Mage Daimon's work, Kelsey; very happy indeed. Now, tell me more about this idea of yours. You wish to trade between our worlds? How would such a thing be possible?'

'With a Quadrant,' said Kelsey. 'You can transport tons at a time with a Quadrant. I'll hand over to Van – he knows more about the specific details.'

Van bowed his head. 'It is an honour to meet you, Lord Bryce. I shall be brief, as we were informed that you are extremely busy. In short, the world where we live is lacking a wide selection of raw materials. We suffer from shortages of timber, metals, coal, and a hundred other items. We three delegates have been authorised by King Daniel and Queen Emily of the City to negotiate a satisfactory agreement, whereby we could purchase some of these items from this world.'

Bryce smiled. 'I see. In principle, I cannot see any reason why we couldn't reach some sort of deal; but this is where I need to confess something. I already knew the reason for your visit here, and I know about the existence and properties of salve. Also, I am aware that you have been negotiating with the Holdfast family, and that, in fact, you have just come from Colsbury.'

'Spying on my family, are you?' said Kelsey.

'Taking necessary precautions, Miss Holdfast,' said Bryce. 'Mages Daimon and Tabor both felt that I should hide the extent of our knowledge from you, but I prefer a straightforward, honest approach. Did you think for a moment that we wouldn't be keeping an eye on the activities of your mother? Such an oversight would border on negligence. But, let us return to the matter at hand. The City has salve to offer, and the Star Continent has more than adequate supplies of everything the City needs. A deal can be made that would be mutually beneficial to both of our worlds. However, we shall not bargain with those who make deals with rebels.'

Van, Quill and Kelsey glanced at each other.

'The offer made by Daphne Holdfast must be rejected,' Bryce went on. 'It is nothing but a trap as, unfortunately, a conflict between the Holdfasts and forces loyal to the Empress seems all but inevitable. Daphne wishes to draw your world into the coming struggle, as she lacks an armed force of her own. I do hope your King and Queen are sensible enough to recognise this. Our terms will also be generous, and we will not insist on any kind of defensive alliance. Ours will be a strictly business arrangement, with no double-edged clauses that might require you to send forces to this world.'

Kelsey frowned. 'Why do you think a conflict is inevitable?'

'Due to the behaviour of your mother, and that of Thorn Holdfast,' said Bryce. 'If they had remained sealed up in Colsbury, then we would have been prepared to turn a blind eye to their various complaints and protests. However, as you know, they travelled to Sanang in order to split the empire in two; and this cannot be tolerated.'

'Did you send soldiers to try to kill them as they crossed the frontier?'

Bryce blinked. 'I'm sorry?'

'At the border between Sanang and the Plateau,' Kelsey said; 'did you send soldiers to burn down the tavern where my mother and Thorn were staying?'

'I don't know what you're talking about. Neither my mother nor I have authorised any hostile activity against your family, yet. We would not stoop to such tactics as assassination attempts. If war comes, it shall be openly declared.'

'Could Daimon have done it without your knowledge?'

Bryce laughed. 'Is this a crude attempt to divide us, Kelsey? I could just as easily state that your mother has fabricated this tale to sow division. I presume that Daphne has no evidence to support her claim?'

'You presume correctly.'

'Then I would give it no more thought, if I were you.' Bryce turned his gaze to Van. 'It would be wise for the City to remain neutral and aloof from any coming internal conflict that may sweep across the Star Continent. Tell me; were you authorised to negotiate with rebels?'

'No, my lord,' said Van. 'We were instructed by the sovereign rulers of the City to deal only with the legitimate leadership of the Star Continent.'

'That's good news,' said Bryce. 'I trust that you will obey the commands of your superiors?'

'We intend to present both offers to their Majesties upon our return to the City,' said Van. 'It would be a dereliction of duty to ignore the offer made by Daphne Holdfast, my lord. The final decision must be in the hands of King Daniel and Queen Emily, and in order to make the best judgement possible, they must be given all the facts.'

Bryce nodded. 'That is regrettable, but understandable; and I do not envy the difficult position into which the Holdfasts have placed you. Do you have a list of all the supplies the City needs?'

Van nodded to Quill, who withdrew a sealed sheaf of documents from an inside pocket. Mage Tabor extended a hand, and Quill passed him the bundle of papers. Tabor showed the seal to Bryce, then cracked it open, and unfolded the documents. Daimon leaned over to take a look, and the three men studied the papers for a few moments.

'We shall need some time to fully digest this list of requirements,' said Bryce, glancing back up at the delegates, 'but I think I can safely say that we can meet all of your demands. Therefore, on behalf of my mother, the imperial sovereign of this world, we are prepared to offer all that you need, for the price of one ton of refined salve every third, or month, as you name them. Our only condition is that you deal solely with us, and no one else.'

'Thank you, my lord,' said Van. 'We shall be sure to report your offer to the King and Queen of the City.'

'We should set a date for a further meeting,' said Bryce. 'I would like you to return here with a small sample of salve. In exchange for this courtesy, we shall gift the City ten tons of iron ore, twenty tons of coal, and fifty tons of timber; as a gesture of our goodwill. Shall we say ten days from now?'

'That would be acceptable, my lord,' said Van.

Bryce smiled. 'Excellent. We shall also be expecting your decision when you return. I desire that our two worlds forge a bond of cordial friendship and mutual respect, and I feel that we have made a good start this day. Now, if you would please excuse me, I have much work to get through.'

'Thank you for your time, my lord,' said Van, as he and Quill bowed their heads.

Kelsey took out the Quadrant, and she noticed Daimon's gaze focus on the copper-coloured device, his eyes narrow as he stared at it. She raised an eyebrow at him, and he looked away.

'Get ready for the rain,' Kelsey said to Van and Quill. 'We're going to be arriving smack in the middle of Princeps Row, so we'll have to run.'

She swept her fingers over the device. The air crackled, and they vanished.

CHAPTER 16
THE LIES OF AMALIA

Serene, Implacatus – 12th Tuminch 5255

'Well?' said Amalia.

Karalyn severed the connection to her dream powers. 'Soldiers are still searching the apartment. There's no sign of Sable or Cardova, or of Austin and his family.'

Amalia paced up and down the room. She paused by the open window, and glanced out at the clouds.

'They were looking for you,' Karalyn said.

'I'd guessed that,' said Amalia. 'Silva, or someone with similar powers, must have informed the gods that I had arrived in Implacatus. If I have endangered Belinda by my presence, I shall never forgive myself.'

Karalyn sat down onto the floor of the bare room. 'We should have realised that you would be valuable to the gods. Not just as a rebel, but as someone who knows the location of the Salve City. It's no wonder that they're looking for you.'

'And you're sure they won't be able to find me again?'

'Aye. I'm smothering your self-healing powers. No one will be able to detect you.'

'Should we turn back?' said Amalia. 'If we cross over into Cumulus, it will be too late to retreat. This is the only chance we have to slip away.'

'We can't turn back. We'll just have to adjust our plan. We're going to have to assume that Sable transported the others to safety when the soldiers raided the apartment, and carry on without them.'

Amalia lowered her glance. 'If we plan to keep going, then we have but one option – I should surrender myself willingly to the authorities; and then you can rescue Belinda while the gods are occupied with my interrogation. I assume that you have hidden my knowledge of how to travel to the City?'

'The Salve City? Aye. I've buried that knowledge behind impenetrable barriers. It's not good enough, though, is it? They won't believe that you have no memories of how to travel to the Salve City. It'll only make them more suspicious. This is something else I'll have to fix. Tell me – did you originally arrive in Salve City on your own?'

'No. I came with Malik, my husband, who was also a rebel at the time. We each had our own Quadrants; we needed two in order to open up a portal.'

'Why did you need to open a portal?'

'So that we could introduce greenhides into the world of the City. Don't look at me like that. We had a perfectly rational reason for doing so, or at least we thought we did at the time. As I'm sure you know, it didn't turn out the way we had planned. We lost control of the greenhides, and they ran wild, spreading across the world with lightning speed.'

Karalyn glared at the former God-Queen. 'Were there other cities on that world before you unleashed legions of greenhides upon it?'

'No. There were no cities whatsoever. But, there were scattered communities of hunters, and a few villages where farming had commenced. Where the City now stands, there was only a small collection of walled towns – Tara, Pella, Oostc and Dalrig. Malik and I chose that area to build our City, as it contained the largest concentration of humans who were still holding out against the greenhides.'

'And how did you discover salve?'

'Are these questions necessary?'

'They are, if I wish to build a convincing story that will fool Edmond and Bastion. When they read your mind, I want them to see this story, and believe it.'

Amalia nodded. 'The mortals of what was to become the City were already aware of salve, and its healing properties, when we arrived. At first, we took little notice of it, but Malik remembered something that Nathaniel had once said, back when he had been using the Sextant to create that world. The Fourth Ascendant had mentioned his desire to create a substance that could rejuvenate the gods, and, so, we each tried some. The effects were immediate, and obvious. Malik and I had appeared middle-aged, and suddenly we were taken back to our youth. It was a little startling, I will admit.'

'And now you look twenty-one.'

'I do, but that is a recent development. I allowed myself to slowly age again, especially after Malik and I had children. I wished to appear a little older than them, so I settled for a look that would put me into my early thirties. It was only when I returned to the City after Lostwell, and I needed to disguise my appearance, that I took another dose of salve.' She shrugged. 'There are worse things than looking twenty-one for a century or two.'

'Is that how long it will take for you to age again?'

'The rate at which an immortal ages varies from god to god. Some of the weaker demigods age faster than, say, an Ancient does. Aila, for example, ages more quickly than I do, because her mother was mortal.'

'So, in theory, an Ascendant wouldn't need to take salve very often?'

'That is correct. However, thousands of gods and demigods live in Cumulus and Serene, and that number requires a lot of salve to keep them all looking young. Edmond needs the salve to keep flowing not so much for him, but to keep his subjects happy. That is why he is so desperate to find my world.'

'One more question for now – why did you decide to begin selling salve to Lostwell? You must have realised that it would attract the attention of Implacatus.'

'It was Malik who made that particular decision. He and I had separated after the end of the Civil War, and I had moved into Maeladh Palace in Tara. Unbeknown to me at the time, Malik then commissioned Naxor with the task of selling salve to Lostwell in exchange for warriors. He loaned him his Quadrant for the purpose, and Naxor got to work. I was annoyed when I found out what was going on, but there appeared to be no ill effects from the trade. Naxor, as you might know, can be quite devious and cunning, and he did a fine job of keeping the trade secret. And the City got its champions, one of which was, of course, your brother.'

'And Blackrose.'

'Yes, her also, although she refused to help us. Buckler was altogether a greater success. Mortal mercenaries came and went, but Buckler was the greatest of all the champions. We also occasionally imported skilled engineers to work on repairing the Great Walls, with the promise that they could leave the City after the end of their contracts. Needless to say, none of them ever saw their homes again; it would have been too risky to send them back to Lostwell.'

'Do you need to know how to operate a Quadrant properly to open a portal?'

'No. If the other Quadrant is linked to it first, then it is a very simple procedure that requires no other knowledge of how a Quadrant actually works.'

'Alright. I'm going to enter your mind, and start constructing a believable narrative. It was Malik who knew how to travel to the City, not you. Malik learned it from Nathaniel. The only role you had was to help open the portal. Malik deliberately kept the location of the City a secret from you, and only Naxor was party to this information. To get from Lostwell back to the City, you used the "go to the last place the Quadrant was used" method, which means that you didn't use the Quadrant while you were on Lostwell. Does that all fit with events?'

'Well, I did use the Quadrant on Lostwell.'

'I can bury that information. This is a complicated process, and what I'm about to do to your mind might wear off after a while; but it should last a few months at the very least. Are you ready?'

Amalia sat down on the floor opposite Karalyn and nodded.

Karalyn got to work. She delved into the god's mind, and began sealing off different areas of her memories, and constructing new links, and new thoughts. Amalia groaned in pain, as perspiration appeared on her brow, but she made no complaint. Scanning backwards through her memory, Karalyn reached the point when Amalia and Malik arrived on the world of the City. She saw Malik vanish, and, seconds later, Amalia opened up a portal. Greenhides poured through. A few turned to attack Amalia, but she struck them down with death powers until heaps of corpses were piled up around her. After that, the other greenhides ignored her as they flooded the land. A giant queen lumbered through the portal, and then another, and Karalyn shuddered at the sheer cruelty of the former God-Queen's actions. She moved forward in time, and saw Malik and Amalia arriving in the small walled town of Tara, where they were welcomed with jubilant cries of joy. Malik put on his armour, and strode out from the gates of the town, a huge black-bladed sword in his right hand. As he cut through swathes of greenhides, Amalia appeared on the battlements, and raised her hands into the red sky. Greenhides screamed in agony, and began falling in their hundreds, then thousands, as the citizens of Tara watched open-mouthed from the town walls. Karalyn moved forward to Lostwell, and smothered all memories of Amalia using the Quadrant to travel around that world. She caught a glimpse of Kelsey and Aila chained up in a fortress by the ocean then, finally, she watched as Amalia returned to the City in shame, a fugitive in hiding.

Karalyn rubbed her head. 'It's done.'

Amalia lowered her gaze. 'That was a rather unpleasant experience.'

'As unpleasant as bringing thousands of greenhides to an innocent world?'

Amalia sighed. 'You have me there. My life is littered with mistakes, Karalyn; introducing the greenhides was just one of them.'

'You're not as arrogant as you were when we were with the others.'

'Sable riles me; I freely admit it. There's something about her that makes me want to slap her across the face. It may seem childish, but I derived some pleasure from putting her in her place.'

'I was surprised that she didn't try to slap you. When we meet up with them again, try to restrain yourself.'

'If we are successful, I will be too busying paying attention to Belinda to worry about Sable.'

'You should know that Sable and Belinda don't particularly like each other.'

'That doesn't surprise me. After meeting Sable, I would doubt that she has many friends.'

'Like you, Sable has also made many mistakes. And, like you, she is now trying to redeem herself.'

'Where did Sable flee, do you think?'

'I don't know. Possibly Dragon Eyre, as that was the next place we were due to go after here. Are you ready to be arrested?'

'I suppose I am. We should make our way to one of the terraces that connect to Cumulus. I would rather not be interrogated in Serene, not if our objective is getting all the way to Edmond's palace.'

'Are there bridges that span the gap between the two cities?'

'Not permanent ones. Ancients with stone powers are based on each of the terraces, and they create the bridges as and when necessary. Some terraces are for Banner officers, but we shall go to one that is exclusively for the use of immortals. You will be invisible, yes?'

'To everyone but you.'

'Remember that those powers won't work on any god wearing eye-guards. They will see you as clear as day.'

'We shouldn't encounter that problem until we're in Cumulus. I will slip away once we are there, and allow you to be interrogated, but I will be watching, to ensure that you come to no harm.'

Amalia smiled. 'And to ensure that I don't betray you?'

'You're not going to betray me. We have to trust each other; otherwise Belinda will remain a prisoner.'

You will not betray me.

Amalia nodded, then they got to their feet.

No one can see me but Amalia.

They opened the door and emerged out into a clean, white-painted corridor, with dozens of identical doors running along both walls. Amalia set off with a purpose, and Karalyn kept up, remaining a little to her rear. She continued to shield Amalia's self-healing powers as they walked, unwilling to risk her being detected too early. They reached an enormous stairwell, surrounded by huge sheets of glass, where a trio of statues rose all the way up from the ground floor, their heads almost touching the glass dome above them. Karalyn gazed at what she was seeing. The stairwell covered a multitude of different levels, and hundreds of civilians were either ascending or descending, while gods and Banner soldiers guarded the main landings.

'There she is,' said Amalia; 'my old friend Belinda.'

Karalyn glanced up at the faces of the statues, and saw one depicting an old woman with features that she recognised.

'Pre-salve, of course,' said Amalia. 'The others are Edmond and Theodora. Theodora died long before salve became known, and she never had the chance to look young again.'

'Am I supposed to feel sorry for her?'

'You should. Theodora was a kind and wise ruler, and her death changed everything. With Edmond in charge, Implacatus transformed into a crueller, more selfish place. If she had lived, there would have been no need for a rebellion.'

They came to a steel railing that ran around the rim of the stairwell, and Karalyn glanced down.

'What level do we need for the terrace?'

'We need to ascend two floors,' said Amalia. 'There will be checks, so that no unauthorised mortals manage to pass through.'

Amalia pointed upwards, and Karalyn followed the direction of her finger. Two levels above them, several gods were standing guard by an arched entrance, along with a few dozen soldiers, all wearing brightly-patterned stone armour.

You cannot see Amalia.

'You are now also invisible,' Karalyn said. 'We'll ghost past those guards, and then I'll make you visible again once we're through.'

Amalia smiled. 'I am invisible? What about our voices? Can anyone hear us?'

'No. No one can hear us.'

Amalia shook her fist in the direction of the statue of Edmond.

'You utter bastard!' she yelled. 'I hope you die in excruciating agony, as maggots devour your intestines, and crows pick at your eyeballs.' She smiled at Karalyn. 'That was quite therapeutic.'

They walked round the circular landing, then slipped past a group of soldiers by the base of a set of stairs. They passed another squad by the second flight, then crept through the group of gods, each careful not to touch anyone. Ahead, the archway was clear, and they hurried into the shadows, leaving the gods and soldiers behind them. They emerged into a beautiful garden under a blue sky, where the sun was shining in the east. Avenues of fruit trees ran next to pools and gravel paths, and a few gods and demigods were sitting on benches, enjoying the sunshine.

Karalyn and Amalia lingered in the shadows by the thick, high wall that bordered the garden.

You can see Amalia, and sense her powers.

'You're visible again,' said Karalyn, 'and any god with Silva's powers will be able to detect you, if they're looking.'

Amalia nodded, then swallowed. 'Let's get this over with.'

She set off along a path, and Karalyn followed, remaining a pace or two behind the former God-Queen. A few gods and demigods glanced at her as she strode between the lines of trees, but no one said anything. At the far end of the garden, the ground fell away into a sheer cliff, and beyond, the cloud-wreathed spires and castles of Cumulus were visible in the distance. A stone tower sat on the edge of Serene, its seven storeys rising into the sky like a sharpened pencil. A few soldiers were gathered around the gates of the tower, along with two robed gods.

'One of those immortals is an Ancient,' Amalia whispered, as they approached the tower. 'It shall be to him that I will surrender.'

The two gods by the gates began to pay attention to Amalia as she strode forwards, then the eyes of one widened.

'Halt!' cried the god, raising his hand.

Amalia stopped on the path. 'I am Amalia of Yocasta, Lostwell and the City,' she said in a loud voice, 'and I surrender to the authorities of Implacatus. I wish to prostrate myself before the Blessed Second Ascendant, and beg for his divine mercy.'

The Ancient by the gates signalled to the soldiers, and they rushed forwards.

'Be careful,' he said. 'She has death powers.'

Amalia kept her hands lowered by her sides as the soldiers surrounded her. Her wrists were pulled behind her back, and bound together.

The Ancient glanced at the other god by the gates. 'Instruct the Banner forces to call off the search. I shall escort the prisoner to Cumulus.'

'Yes, my lord,' she said, bowing.

The Ancient strode forwards. He gazed at Amalia, and Karalyn sensed his vision powers penetrate the former God-Queen's mind.

'So, Amalia; you have finally dared to set foot upon the holy ground of Implacatus?'

Amalia smiled. 'I thought it was about time. I can't say that I think much of Serene, if I'm being honest.'

Behind her, Karalyn gasped. Had Amalia been lying about her past? She cursed herself for not reading the god's mind more thoroughly. She had read everything about her time in the City, and on Lostwell, but hadn't gone back further. And now it was too late. Amalia had tricked her into bringing her along, and like a fool, Karalyn had fallen for it.

'Perhaps you shall find the dungeons of Cumulus more to your liking,' said the Ancient. 'Follow me.'

The Ancient walked to the edge of the precipice, as the soldiers bundled Amalia after him. The Ancient raised his hands into the air, and the stone on the cliff face beneath him started to ripple. It climbed and grew, the rock twisting and morphing as it stretched out across the gap between Serene and Cumulus. Karalyn edged forward, keeping close to the soldiers, while she tried to think through the ramifications of Amalia's confession that she had never been to Implacatus before.

Why would she lie? If she had wished to betray the Holdfasts, there were easier ways to have done it. It must be Belinda, Karalyn thought. She had detected strong feelings of love and affection within Amalia regarding her old friend – had she lied to Karalyn and Sable in order to assist with her rescue? If she hadn't claimed intimate knowledge of Cumulus, knowledge that she must have received from Malik, Karalyn would have refused to allow her to accompany them. Despite her anger, Karalyn felt a twinge of respect for the former God-Queen to have taken such a risk to help her friend.

The end of the bridge disappeared into the clouds that shrouded the city of the gods, and the Ancient lowered his arms. He glanced at Amalia, then gestured for her to step on to the bridge. Amalia acquiesced, shoved along by soldiers wearing steel gauntlets. The Ancient walked on to the bridge after Amalia and the soldiers, then Karalyn did the same, keeping behind the Ancient. She followed them across the narrow structure, trying not to look down as she did so. There were no side rails, and any misstep would send the victim hurtling down into the fathomless abyss. The rock was smooth under her feet, as if the stone had melted and re-formed, and she nearly slipped a few times. They entered the bank of cloud, and Karalyn grew dizzy as she lost sight of Serene behind them, and concentrated on walking in a straight line.

Ahead of them, through the gloom and murk, huge battlements reared up, formed of solid granite. The end of the bridge had touched down onto a lip of rock, where more gods and soldiers were waiting. Amalia was pushed down into a wide courtyard that lay in front of a massive pair of steel gates that led through the fortified wall. The Ancient followed her into the courtyard, and summoned the other gods who were there, as Karalyn slipped into the shadows.

'Amalia has surrendered herself,' the Ancient cried. 'The last rebel wishes to beg for mercy.'

'Execute her!' shouted a robed god.

'She has begged for the opportunity to plead for mercy at the feet of the Beloved and Blessed Second Ascendant,' said the Ancient. 'Take her in for questioning, and send a message to the Most Noble Lord Bastion that she is here. They shall decide what is to be done with the prisoner.'

The huge steel gates of the fortress were pushed open, and armoured gods dragged Amalia across the threshold, as dozens watched. Karalyn sheltered among the crowd, and followed them through the open gates into an inner forecourt, where a granite keep sat, its smooth, high walls reflecting the light of the sun. Karalyn saw more gods appear by an entrance, and she dived into the shadows as she realised that one of them was wearing eye-guards. She lost sight of Amalia amid the press of gods and soldiers, and hid in a shallow alcove. A door slammed, the steel gates were closed, and the forecourt fell into silence.

Karalyn glanced around. Amalia was gone, taken within the keep to be interrogated. She looked up at the tall walls, and saw soldiers high up on the battlements. She needed to get her bearings, and find a way for her vision powers to penetrate the building.

***

It took Karalyn over an hour of creeping around the fortress before she found a secure place where she could hide and see what was going on inside the keep. She had discovered the purpose of the fortress – to defend the western side of Cumulus from an attack from Serene, and to hold anyone who managed to cross without permission. There was no way to reach the palaces and elegant towers of the gods without first passing through the fortress, and it was garrisoned by a large number of heavily-armed Banner soldiers in stone-plated armour. Karalyn hadn't witnessed any others wearing eye-guards, so she was assuming that the god she had seen by the gates of the keep was the commander of the fortress.

She wriggled around in the confined space. She had found a gap between the roof beams and the stonework of a corner turret, and had wedged herself in. It was uncomfortable, but it was also out of sight. Twenty yards away was a narrow slit window. It was protected by a fine wire mesh, but there were tears in it that hadn't been repaired, and she was able to push her powers into the interior of the keep.

Once inside, it hadn't taken long to find Amalia. She had been strapped to an upright metal grid, her hands encased in thick gauntlets, and her head half-enclosed in a steel muzzle. Protruding from her chest and torso were several knives, buried up to their hilts to keep her subdued. In front of her sat over a dozen gods, including the one that Karalyn had seen wearing the eye-guards, while a handful of soldiers were standing by Amalia, holding a variety of metal implements of torture in their hands. Blood was staining the front and sides of Amalia's clothes, and she had her eyes closed.

'Do you expect us to believe your sorry excuses, Amalia?' said one of the gods, a giant of a man in full body armour. 'You were on the salve world for over three thousand years, and yet you claim to have no knowledge of its location.'

'That's right,' Amalia gasped. 'It was Malik who knew. My husband.'

'And where is Malik?'

'He's dead. He took too much salve, and it rotted his mind. I released him from his agony. It was his death that persuaded me to surrender myself.'

'How did you get to Implacatus?' said a female god, wearing dark red robes that fell to the polished, blood-spattered floor.

'With a Quadrant.'

Several of the gods sat up straighter at this.

'And where is this Quadrant?' said the red-robed god. 'It was not in your possession when you were arrested.'

'Don't you have it?' said Amalia.

'Explain that comment. How could we have it?'

'I left it in the apartment, where I had been hiding for a day. I know you raided it after I'd left. Didn't you find it?'

A few of the gods turned to one of their number who was dressed in uniform.

'There was no Quadrant in the apartment, my lords and ladies,' said the uniformed god, 'and it has been thoroughly searched. The soldiers who were there claim to have seen two men and three women inside, after they had forced entry. They also claim that these five people vanished. They must have taken the Quadrant with them.'

'Where did your colleagues go, Amalia?'

'I don't know.'

'You're lying.'

'I wasn't there, was I? How could I know where they have gone? We didn't imagine that the apartment would be raided so quickly, and so we had made no contingency plans.'

The armoured god banged his fist on the table. 'Cut her tongue out.'

'Yes, sir,' said one of the soldiers standing by the metal rack.

'Wait,' said the god with the eye-guards. 'How is she expected to speak if she has no tongue? Take an ear instead.'

The soldiers bowed, then one lifted a knife, and began slicing through Amalia's right ear. She screamed as the sharp blade cut through her flesh, then the soldier lifted the severed ear to show the gods.

'Let's try again,' said the armoured god. 'Amalia, where did your colleagues go? Are they still in Serene?'

'They might have gone to Dragon Eyre,' Amalia gasped, her voice ragged.

'Dragon Eyre?' said the red-robed god. 'Why would they go there?'

'To hide,' said Amalia.

'I want the names of the five people who were in the apartment.'

'The three women were all former slaves,' Amalia said. 'It was their apartment. The two men had accompanied me from the City…'

'Which city?' said the armoured god.

'I think she is referring to the salve world, my lord,' said the red-robed god.

'I see. Go on.'

'The two men came with me,' Amalia whispered. 'They were soldiers. One of them knew how to use a Quadrant, and so I left it with him.'

'If they came with you, why wouldn't they return to the salve world?'

'They might have; I don't know.'

'Then why did you mention Dragon Eyre?'

'We talked about Dragon Eyre as a possible refuge, if things didn't work out here.'

'Where upon Dragon Eyre, exactly?'

'I don't know. I came here to surrender. All I want to do is beg forgiveness at the feet of the Blessed Second Ascendant.'

'Then you should have brought a suitable gift, such as the location to the salve world. If you had done so, then we might have been prepared to allow you into the Blessed Second Ascendant's presence. As things stand, however, you are useless to us.' The armoured god turned to the one wearing eye-guards. 'We should throw her from the cliffs, my lord.'

Karalyn, who had been watching with growing alarm, plunged her powers into the mind of the red-robed goddess.

You should allow Amalia to grovel in front of the Second Ascendant. Edmond would enjoy it.

'I disagree,' said the red-robed woman. 'We all know how much the Blessed Second Ascendant likes to receive rebels who wish to debase themselves at his feet. Having this worthless creature grovel and beg in front of his Sacred Majesty might please him. I say we send her to the Palace of the Almighty.'

The god with the eye-guards chewed his lip for a moment.

'I would not want to risk the Most Noble Lord Edmond's wrath,' the red-robed god went on. 'If his Sacred Majesty discovers that Amalia was here, and that we disposed of her, he may be aggrieved.'

'Very well,' said the eye-guard-wearing god. 'Hood her, gag her, and keep her strapped to the rack; then take her to the Palace of the Almighty. Has word been sent to Lord Bastion?'

'It has, my lord,' said the armoured god. 'We have not yet received a response from his offices.'

'Inform him that Amalia is on her way. Soldiers shall escort her to the gates of the Palace of the Almighty, and transfer her there into Lord Bastion's custody.'

Karalyn severed the connection to her powers, glanced around, then began to clamber from her hiding place.

Two hours later, Karalyn was hiding by the side of a deep gully. To her left were the towers and castles of the gods, but on her right, across a bridgeless chasm, was the largest building she had ever seen in her life. She had scouted it a few days before, but now that she was a mere fifty yards from it, she could appreciate its vast, overwhelming size. Directly opposite her was a gate that led into the Palace of the Almighty, and hanging above it, nailed to a protruding crossbeam, was a withered old corpse.

The sound of approaching boots made her duck her head down, despite the fact that she was invisible. She watched as a squad of Banner soldiers appeared. Two of them were leading a cart being pulled by four white horses, and upon the back of the cart was the metal rack, with Amalia's body strapped to it. The soldiers reached the edge of the gully, and came to a halt. The gates of the Palace of the Almighty glided open without making a sound, and a wide stone bridge arced out over the gap. The soldiers fell to their knees, their heads bowed, as a line of gods in full armour emerged from the palace. They took possession of the cart, and led the horses over the bridge.

Karalyn hesitated, her heart pounding. She thought about her beloved twins, and the rest of her family. They would think her mad for what she was about to do, but she had no choice. She leapt up from the rocky bank of the gully, just as the cart was being led through the gates, and sprinted over the bridge. It began to disappear under her feet, pulling back into the bedrock, and she leapt the final yard, landing on her knees on the marble floor just beyond the entrance. She stifled a cry, then turned, and watched as the enormous gates clanged shut behind her.

She had made it. She was inside Edmond's palace. The easy part was over.

CHAPTER 17
OWNERSHIP PAPERS

Colsbury Castle, Republic of the Holdings – 29th Day, Last Third Summer 534

Daphne walked into the kitchen as dawn was breaking over the island of Colsbury. The sun was still behind the mountains to the east, but the sky was turning blue, and Daphne paused at the open window, savouring the cool breeze. The surface of the lake was rippling in the wind, while along the path that wound by its banks, the leaves on the trees were starting to turn shades of red and brown.

'Good morning, Daphne,' said a voice behind her.

'Good morning, Agang. Did you sleep well?'

'Yes, thank you. Any sign of Karalyn today?'

'Not so far.' Daphne filled a kettle and placed it onto the warm stove. 'Would you like a cup of coffee?'

'Yes. Thank you.'

Agang sat by the little table, his eyes heavy. 'It's the twins' birthday tomorrow.'

'I know.'

'Karalyn said that she would be back before...'

'Yes. I know what she said.'

'Do you think something has gone wrong?'

'How should I know?' she snapped. 'I am holding on to a slim hope that my errant daughter might be already back, and is with her children in whichever place she hid them; but the simple fact is that she could be dead in a ditch on Implacatus, along with Sable, Cardova and that god they brought from Salve City.' She took a breath. 'Apologies. I realise that I have been rather short-tempered in recent days, but with everything that's been happening, it's a wonder my head hasn't exploded.'

'I appreciate the apology, but none is necessary,' Agang said. 'You haven't been rude; well, not to me.'

Daphne turned back to the stove. 'But I have been rude to others?'

'I've been spending a lot of time with Caelius Logos, Daphne. He would never admit it, but I can tell that he's feeling uncomfortable. The only reason that he decided to stay here was because of you, and you seem to be pushing him away.'

'Has he been complaining to you about me?'

'Not at all – as I said, he would never admit his feelings to me, but I'm not completely oblivious to his mood. He's a good man, Daphne. If you don't want him to be here, then you should tell him.'

'That seems a little cruel.'

'It would be better than allowing him to believe that he has a chance.'

Daphne watched the kettle as it started to warm up. 'If I did tell him, where would he go? He's alone on this world.'

'He's resourceful. He would probably go on a tour of the Plateau, or maybe further afield. He's curious to learn more about this world. However, he doesn't want to leave Colsbury, in case you need him here.'

'I might need him here. He knows a lot about military tactics, and that might prove to be useful.'

Agang shook his head. 'He and I have also been spending time with Pechtang and 'I'Lang, and we've heard a few of his stories about the Banner campaigns. You're right – he does seem to know much about the military life. All the same, I think he might prefer that you wanted him here for a different reason.'

'My life is too busy and complicated for romance, Agang. Daimon could attack at any moment, and he's probably spying on us every day. On top of that I have Karalyn and Sable to worry about, and then there's Keir.' She paused. 'I can hardly express how disappointed I am with my elder son. How dare he treat his wife like that? Is it partly my fault? I tried to drum into each of my children the need to be loyal to the ones you love, but perhaps I didn't do a very good job with Keir.' She glanced at Agang. 'It seems you boys have been banding together – have you spent any time with Keir?'

'No. He's barely left his room in days, as far as I know. If you like, Caelius and I can try to include him more.'

'I would appreciate that. Perhaps he needs other men around him at a time like this. He referred to me, Thorn and Shella as a coven of witches the other day, as if he were the victim of a female conspiracy. I wish he could be more like Corthie, but, alas, he is not.'

Agang nodded. 'Can I ask – did you say something in particular to Caelius a few days ago? He seemed upset, but I couldn't draw the reason from him.'

Daphne cast her glance downwards just as the kettle boiled, and she lifted it from the stove.

'I might have mentioned something,' she said, as she poured hot water into a coffee pot. 'I told him that Killop was twice the man he would ever be.'

Agang groaned. 'Oh, Daphne. Why would you say such a thing? No wonder he was upset. Did you mean it? Actually, that doesn't matter. Even if you did mean it, you shouldn't have said it.'

She stirred the contents of the pot with a wooden spoon.

'You should apologise to him,' Agang went on.

Before Daphne could reply, Pechtang and T'Lang shuffled into the kitchen. They looked ill, and both fell into the chairs around the small table.

'Are you making coffee?' groaned T'Lang.

'I take three sugars and no milk in mine,' said Pechtang.

Daphne turned away from them and rolled her eyes. 'Of course,' she said. 'No problem.'

'Feeling a little hungover, lads?' said Agang.

'I feel like a goat shat in my mouth,' said T'Lang, 'then stomped on my head.'

Agang chuckled, then he leaned over, and touched T'Lang's hand. The Sanang man shuddered, then grinned, and stretched his arms.

'Thanks, Agang!' he cried.

'Me next,' said Pechtang, holding out his arm.

Agang placed a finger against Pechtang's thick arm, and, moments later, the young Sanang man was laughing.

'I feel like I'm ready to start drinking again,' he said.

'Perhaps you should try to make yourselves more useful,' said Daphne, as she poured coffee into four mugs; 'instead of smoking weed and drinking all day.'

'We're guests here,' said T'Lang. 'Do you want us to work?'

'Much of Colsbury still lies in a state of disrepair,' said Daphne. 'The Summer Palace, the Spire, the harbour, the gatehouse. I am currently making arrangements to purchase the title deeds to the entire island for the Holdfast family, and I intend to renovate all of the buildings. If you would like to work, then there is plenty to do.'

She placed the mugs down onto the table, sat, and lit a cigarette.

Pechtang and T'Lang glanced at each other.

'We're not trained to do that kind of work,' said T'Lang.

'Oh?' said Daphne. 'Tell me; what kind of work have you been trained to do?'

'Not much,' said Pechtang. 'We've always had servants to do everything for us.'

Caelius appeared in the doorway. 'Morning all,' he said, though he kept his glance averted from Daphne.

'Morning, Caelius,' said T'Lang. 'Agang's handing out free healings if you're suffering.'

Caelius laughed. 'You lads were so drunk last night that you didn't notice that I was still sober. I fancy a walk down to the village on the shore, to see if they have anything new in the market.'

Agang drained his mug of coffee. 'I'll come.'

'I think we'll stay here, mate,' said Pechtang. 'If you see any whisky, buy some. We finished the final bottle last night.'

'Will do,' said Caelius.

Agang got to his feet, and walked to the doorway.

'Caelius,' said Daphne; 'could I have a quick word?'

'Of course, ma'am,' he said.

'In private?'

Pechtang nudged his brother with an elbow, and winked. Daphne ignored them, and stood.

'I'll just be a minute or two,' Caelius said to Agang.

'I'll wait for you here,' said Agang, sitting again.

Daphne walked from the kitchen, and Caelius followed her. She led him into the empty living room, and opened a couple of shutters to let in the light. Then, she took a breath and faced him.

'I owe you an apology, Caelius,' she said.

'You do?'

'Yes. What I said to you a few days ago, when I compared you to Killop – it was uncalled for, and rude. I'm sorry.'

Caelius nodded. 'Was that all?'

'I didn't mean what I said. I was angry with Karalyn; I still am.'

'Thank you. I accept your apology. See you later.'

Daphne watched as Caelius strode from the room. A moment later, she heard him talk to Agang, then their footsteps faded into the distance.

Daphne cursed. She had taken Caelius's affections for granted, and had assumed that he would come running as soon as she called. Instead, he seemed to have resigned himself to the fact that she wasn't interested in him, and was moving on. She realised that she had missed his company over the previous few days, and that she would miss him even more if he left Colsbury. It was true that he was no Killop, but did that mean she was destined to forever be alone? She thought back to the time they had spent together in the prison cells of Rakana. She had felt close to Caelius at that moment, closer than she had felt to anyone since Killop's death. Her thoughts turned to her eldest child. Karalyn had also been widowed, only at a far younger age than Daphne had been – did she expect her daughter to never meet anyone else? She had tried to prevent Lucius Cardova from pursuing her, but why? That tactic hadn't worked; if anything, it had driven Karalyn closer to the Banner soldier. Had she been projecting on to her daughter how she thought a respectable Holdings widow should behave?

Forget respectability, she thought; she wanted Caelius to stay. She wanted to feel the way she had felt when they had kissed, without all of the pain that had accompanied that moment. She would sit him down and have a proper conversation with him when he and Agang returned from the market, she decided; and she would ask him to stay.

A servant appeared at the door, holding a bundle of letters.

'The post has arrived, ma'am,' he said, bowing.

'From Holdings City?'

'Yes, ma'am.'

He extended his hand, and passed her two letters.

'Thank you,' she said, then the servant bowed and left the room.

Daphne sat, and glanced at the thick envelopes. Each had been sealed with a wax stamp displaying the insignia of the legal department of the Holdings government. She opened the first. It was a letter from the property commission, acknowledging Daphne's bid to purchase the entire island of Colsbury from the government. The bid had been accepted in principle, and the commission was awaiting the transfer of funds to finalise the purchase.

Daphne smiled. Colsbury had come with an expensive price tag, but it would be worth every penny. Once the renovations to the Summer Palace had been completed, Thorn would be able to move in, so that she would have a home that befit the legitimate successor to the imperial throne. They would need to hire more servants, of course – cooks, gardeners, guards, tailors, dress-makers, carpenters, as well as a multitude of other professions; and Colsbury would be bustling by the time she was through with it. She needed to let Shella know that her home would shortly be owned by the Holdfasts; but first, she opened the second letter.

It was from the committee in charge of the census, and was a short note stating that Thorn's official adoption into the Holdfasts had been duly registered. Such things usually took thirds to formalise but, as First Holder, Daphne was used to having her requests prioritised.

She gazed at the brief statement. Even if Keir and Thorn divorced, Thorn was now her legal daughter; a Holdfast through and through.

Daphne got to her feet, her right hand clutching the two letters. She made her way to Shella's bedroom, and knocked on the door. There was no response, so Daphne eased the door open, and peered inside. Shella was sleeping in her enormous bed, her snores echoing through the darkness.

Daphne closed the door. Shella would have to wait for her news. Daphne walked further along the hallway, and knocked on Thorn's door.

'Come in,' came the reply.

Daphne opened the door and stepped into the large bedroom. Sunlight was coming in through an open window, illuminating a series of embroidered wall hangings. Thorn was sitting at her dressing table with a white towel wrapped round her hair, applying make-up with a small brush.

Thorn turned her head and smiled. 'Good morning.'

Daphne took a seat close to the dressing table. 'I have something to show you.'

She leaned forward and held out the letter from the census committee. Thorn put down the brush, and unfolded the note. Her eyes began to well as she read the words on the sheet of paper.

'This means more to me than I can say,' said Thorn. 'It has been nine years since my mother was taken to Rahain by Sable; nine long years. When my sisters died, I could mourn them, but the loss of my mother left an absence in my life I thought I would never be able to fill. And now I am part of a family again. Thank you.'

Daphne smiled. 'You're welcome. We can now openly discuss a certain topic that I have been avoiding.'

Thorn folded the letter in half, and passed it back to Daphne. 'What topic have you been avoiding?'

'That of your marriage to my disloyal son. If you wish to divorce him, then I will not stand in your way.'

Thorn nodded. 'I see.'

'Well?'

'I don't think now is the time to be displaying our divisions for the world to see.'

Daphne frowned. 'Oh.'

'I will not lie to you,' said Thorn; 'I am no longer in love with Keir, but I am prepared to maintain our marriage in public, if we agree that to do otherwise would be detrimental to our cause.'

'Might I intrude on a more personal matter?'

'I am your daughter; we should have no secrets.'

'It has always been in the back of my mind,' said Daphne, 'that you and Keir were unable to have children. If you were to divorce him, then that… condition would no longer apply. You would be free to court other men, including Sanang men, with whom you could, if you so desired, start a family.'

Thorn smiled. 'Is that something you would like me to do?'

'We're not talking about what I want, Thorn. What do you want?'

'I don't know. Ever since I met Keir, I knew that we wouldn't be able to have children; and I suppose that I have always tried to avoid thinking too deeply about it. Regardless, it's too soon for me to consider such things.'

'I understand. As long as you know that I will not impose any conditions or expectations upon you. You are free to live your life the way you see fit. However, if you ever decide to divorce Keir and remarry, your new husband would have to accept that he would join the Holdfasts.'

'I'll bear that in mind. Has there been any news of Karalyn?'

Daphne shook her head.

'The twins' birthdays are tomorrow.'

'Yes.'

'I don't understand. How long could it take to snatch Belinda? If Karalyn can come and go anywhere she pleases, then it shouldn't have taken this long.'

'I know.'

'Sorry. You must be full of worry, and my silly questions aren't making it any better. Have you tried to see Implacatus through the Sextant?'

'Nothing happens when I place my palm on to its surface. I hear no voice in my head. As far as I know, only Karalyn and Sable seem to be able to get anything out of that blasted device.'

Thorn nodded. 'You could ask Keir to try. Perhaps his Holdfast blood will allow him to use the Sextant.'

'This will sound terrible, but I'm not completely sure that I would trust my son with the Sextant. Not right now, at any rate; not while he has such a dark cloud hanging over his head. Besides, if I talked to him, I would be liable to start shouting.'

There was a gentle knock upon the door.

'Is Holder Fast in there?' came a voice.

Daphne got to her feet and opened the door. A servant in the hallway outside bowed.

'Sorry to trouble you, ma'am, but a carriage has arrived in Colsbury, and the gentleman passenger was requesting to speak with you.'

'Where is he now?'

'He is currently waiting in the castle forecourt, ma'am. Should I send him up?'

'Did he give you his name?'

'Yes, ma'am. He said he was called Olo'osso.'

Daphne frowned. 'Do *not* let him into the keep. You did the right thing making him wait outside. I shall go down and speak to this reprobate.'

'Is there a problem?' said Thorn.

'Nothing to worry about,' said Daphne. 'Finish getting yourself ready, and I'll see you soon.'

Daphne left Thorn's bedroom. She began to follow the servant towards the stairs, then she halted.

'One moment, please,' she said. 'I think I might bring along a couple of sturdy young men, in case Olo'osso decides to make a scene.'

The servant nodded, and Daphne went back to the kitchen where she had made coffee. Pechtang and T'Lang were still sitting there, smoking something that smelled like keenweed.

'Boys,' Daphne said, 'could I ask a small favour?'

The two Sanang men glanced up at her.

'Does it involve work?' said T'Lang.

'Not quite. You're both of an impressive size, physically, and I would quite like to intimidate a certain gentleman who has arrived unexpectedly in Colsbury. I would require you to glare, and to look mean and threatening. Can you do that for me?'

Pechtang laughed. 'Sure thing. Are we allowed to beat him up if he steps out of line?'

Daphne smiled. 'We'll see.'

The two young men got to their feet, and followed Daphne out of the kitchen. They went down the many flights of stairs to the ground floor, and emerged into the morning sunshine. A large carriage was parked between the Great Keep and the Summer Palace, and a muscular man with greying hair was waiting there, his shoulders draped in fur robes. He turned, and a broad grin split his features.

'Daphne Holdfast?' he cried. 'It is my considerable honour to meet you, my lady.' He bowed with a flourish, and the gold chain round his neck clinked and rattled.

Daphne stared at him, while the two Sanang men glowered by her shoulders.

'You are a thief, and a cad,' said Daphne. 'You abused the generous hospitality of my family, and I do not take such insults lightly.'

'I heartily agree with you, my lady,' said Olo'osso, straightening his back. 'I behaved abominably, and have no excuses.' He gestured to the carriage. 'I am here to repay what I stole from the Holdfast townhouse.

Inside that carriage lies a chest, full of gold, equal to the value of everything I took from you.'

He snapped his fingers at his driver, and the man climbed down to the cobbles, and opened the carriage door.

'Bring out the chest,' Olo'osso said.

'Stop,' said Daphne. 'If this gold is someone's stolen property, then I do not want it.'

Olo'osso looked shocked and aggrieved. 'My lady,' he cried, 'it pains me to the core that you would suggest such a thing. The gold is the result of hard work, and hard work alone.'

'How exactly did you earn it?'

'I invested every last penny that I took from you, and bought a sloop, and then I hired a crew to man said sloop. I have been at sea for a month, shipping cargo from Plateau City. We sailed to Westport, Rainsby, Stretton Sands and Amatskouri. Doing the circuit, as the sailors of the Inner Sea call it.' He smiled again. 'It was reasonably profitable.'

'Have you forsaken piracy?'

'I'll be honest, my lady; that wasn't my intention. However, the Inner Sea is too well-policed by imperial warships to allow any act of simple piracy. If I had tried it, I would have been hunted down within days. The Inner Sea is too small to evade any pursuers, and there is no open ocean in which to hide. And I must confess that I have not yet come to grips with the lack of moon and stars in the sky of this world. Sailing by night remains all but impossible for me at present. All of these factors were enough to persuade me that piracy on this world would be a mistake.'

'So, it wasn't a moral decision?'

Olo'osso slapped his thigh and burst into laughter.

Daphne narrowed her eyes at him and the laughter stopped.

'Sorry, my lady,' Olo'osso said. 'I thought you were joking.'

'Where is your sloop now?' she said.

'I hired a new captain, and sent it round the circuit again. They'll be halfway to Westport by now. I said that my voyage was profitable; I didn't say it was enjoyable. Being a respectable shipping merchant holds little allure for me, especially upon such a tiny, little sea. Still, it will keep the money rolling in, until I can work out how to get back to Dragon Eyre. Tell me; does a certain young Sable Holdfast reside here?'

'Sable isn't in Colsbury at present,' said Daphne. 'Here's what we're going to do, Mister Olo'osso. You say you bought your vessel with my silver; well, then I say that the sloop belongs to me. The Holdfasts already own a dozen or so ships that ply the waters of the Inner Sea, and I'm sure your little sloop will be a valuable addition to our fleet. You may keep the rest of your profits, and invest them as you see fit.'

Olo'osso's nostrils flared. 'But, my lady, I have the gold here; ready and waiting for you.'

'I don't want the gold; I want the ship.'

Olo'osso folded his arms across his wide chest. 'Tough. You ain't getting my ship. The *Spirit of Olkis* belongs to me; and I have the papers to prove it.'

'Can we beat him up yet?' said T'Lang.

Olo'osso eyed the two Sanang men. 'Your thugs don't frighten me, Lady Holdfast. To think that I came here to make amends, and now you're threatening me? If you refuse to take the gold, then I shall still consider my debt to you repaid in full.'

Daphne kept her eyes on the pirate. She didn't need another ship, but she wasn't about to let a criminal from Dragon Eyre dictate to her what she should do.

'Give me the sloop,' she said.

'No.'

'Do I need to call upon the castle guards, and have you arrested?'

Olo'osso snorted. 'On my world, we do not ask guards to deal with such matters. On my world, I would fight anyone who tried to take one of my ships.' He looked her up and down. 'Of course, I am too much of a gentleman to strike a lady.'

Daphne narrowed her eyes. 'I would be happy to fight you, if only to wipe that smug expression off your face. If you win, you keep the gold and the ship. If I win, you hand over the ownership papers to me.'

'Forgive me,' said Olo'osso, 'but I don't think I have ever heard such a ridiculous notion in my life. You are a woman.'

'I am aware of that.'

He gestured towards her left arm. 'And you appear to have a crippled limb.'

'I am also aware of that. Are you too cowardly to fight me?'

Anger passed over his features. Daphne took off her outer jacket and handed it to Pechtang.

'Hold this for me,' she said. 'I doubt this will take long.'

'You're right about that,' said Olo'osso. He removed the fur robes from his shoulders and passed them to his driver. 'Ten seconds should suffice, I'd imagine.'

Daphne watched as Olo'osso clenched his fists, and took up a fighting stance.

'This is your last chance,' he said. 'I would usually never strike a woman, but if you insist upon a fight, then I shall not hesitate to...'

Daphne powered her battle-vision, clenched her right fist, and slammed it into Olo'osso's jaw, almost breaking her hand in the process. Qlo'osso's head flinched back, as a tooth flew through the air. Daphne punched him in the stomach, then kicked him as hard as she could in the nether regions.

Olo'osso's hands went to his crotch, his eyes bulging, then he sank to his knees. The two Sanang men fell about laughing as Daphne stepped forwards. She raised her fist again.

'Enough!' cried Olo'osso.

'Do you yield?' said Daphne.

Olo'osso gazed at her with a wild anger in his eyes, then he slowly nodded.

Daphne lowered her fist.

'That was fucking hilarious,' said T'Lang.

'Language, boys,' said Daphne. 'If you must swear, then please refrain from doing so in my company.'

'My testicles feel as though they are somewhere in my chest,' gasped Olo'osso. 'Praise be to the gods that I have already fathered five children, because I don't think I'll be having any more.' He rolled over onto the cobbles, and lay still for a moment.

'The papers,' said Daphne.

'I have one condition,' Olo'osso said from the ground.

'I don't think you're in a position to bargain, but let's hear it,' said Daphne.

'Whenever I buy or sell a ship,' he said, his eyes closed, 'I always have a drink with the person I am dealing with. Call it an Olkian tradition. I'll give you the papers, but only over a damned drink.'

Daphne laughed. 'You have a deal.'

She reached out with her right hand, and helped Olo'osso to his feet. The two Sanang men watched the pirate captain stagger towards the entrance to the Great Keep, then they assisted him up the many stairs, and into Daphne's little office. She went to a drawer in the desk, and withdrew two sticks of dreamweed.

She handed them to the two Sanang men. 'Thank you, boys.'

'Any time,' said Pechtang, as he and his brother walked back towards the kitchen.

Daphne closed the door as Olo'osso lowered himself gently into an armchair. She returned to the desk and extracted a bottle of brandy from the drawer where she kept her alcohol. She glanced at it, then put it back, and selected a bottle of whisky that she had managed to keep hidden from Pechtang and T'Lang. She filled two small glasses, and then sat down opposite Olo'osso.

'Where did you learn to fight like that?' he said, a finger rubbing the gap in his jaw where the tooth had been. 'You reminded me of Sable. Are all the Holdfast women warriors?'

'No; just Sable and me. One of my sons is rather talented in that regard, but my three other children are hopeless at fighting.'

Olo'osso picked up his glass. 'So, you have four children, eh? One fewer than I do. All of mine are girls.'

'Did you want a son?'

He shrugged. 'Not in particular. I wanted sailors. Girl or boy; it didn't matter to me. All that mattered was that they were able to captain a ship. In that, I feel I was successful.'

He took a sip of whisky, then narrowed his eyes at the glass. 'What is this?'

'It is Severton twelve-year-old,' she said. 'Do you like it?'

'Why, do you own the distillery?'

'Funnily enough, it was my money that paid for its construction, but I have never made a claim for any ownership. Now, how about those papers?'

Olo'osso sighed, then he put a hand into his tunic, and withdrew a bundle of documents. He put his glass down onto a table, and sorted through the papers.

'Let's see,' he said. 'Ah; here they are.' He stared at them for a moment, his eyes filled with sorrow, then he passed them to Daphne. 'You will allow me to keep the gold, yes?'

'Yes,' she said. She placed the ownership papers for the *Spirit of Olkis* onto the desk behind her without looking at them. 'You can always buy another ship with it.'

'I don't think I will. As I said, the Inner Sea is too well-organised and patrolled for piracy to flourish there. On Dragon Eyre, chaos thrives, and the Sea Banner has never been powerful enough to drive us from the ocean. Here, I felt as though I was paddling about upon a little lake.'

'You seem to have adjusted rather well to being transported to another world.'

He laughed. 'You should have seen me during my first few days, while I was living in the Holdfast townhouse in Plateau City. I have never felt more confused or disorientated. I kept waiting for someone to come for me, but no one did. Still, anything would be better than the misery I endured while I was held in a pit in Wyst. After a few days in the townhouse, I began to calm down, and then I made my move.'

'You tied Tabitha to a chair and left her there, alone, without food or water.'

Olo'osso nodded. 'Is she alright?'

'Yes, no thanks to you.'

'I tried to slip out at night, so she wouldn't hear me, but she awoke, and attempted to prevent me from leaving.'

'She attempted to stop you making off with my silver.'

'Yes, she did. She was brave, but foolish. I warned her, but she wouldn't listen.' He smiled at Daphne. 'Is that why you kicked me so hard?'

'Partly.'

'Then I would say that we are even. You have my ship, and you bested me in a fair fight.' He looked into her eyes. 'Are we even, Lady Holdfast?'

Daphne smiled, and sipped from her glass. 'We'll see.'

CHAPTER 18
TRIPLE DATE

Udall, Ulna, Eastern Rim – 17th Tuminch 5255

Sable lifted the mug to her lips and drained the last of the wine. The sun was low in the western sky but the day was clinging on to its warmth, and a gentle breeze was sweeping across the quarter deck of the *Giddy Gull*. Next to her, Lara was reclining on a deck chair that had been positioned so that it was almost flat, a cushion propping up her head. Maddie, Topaz and Tilly were sitting along from them, while Vitz was carrying another bottle of wine from the half-built captain's cabin. Planks of wood lay in neat piles by the port side railings, along with a barrel of bitumen and several tools; and the scent of sawdust was in the air.

'This is like we're on a triple date,' said Maddie. 'We should do it more often.'

'As long as Vitz is doing all the work,' said Tilly, 'that's fine by me.'

Lara waved an unlit cigarette at Vitz. 'Light this for me, servant.'

'Only I get to call him that, sis,' said Tilly.

Vitz crouched by the deck chairs and opened the bottle of wine. He glanced at Tilly. 'I thought I was your master, not your servant.'

'Hey!' shouted Lara. 'Vitz made a joke. Who said that settlers have no sense of humour, eh?'

'I doubt the settlers on Gyle are laughing at the moment,' said Topaz.

'Don't bring the bleeding mood down,' said Lara.

'I'm just saying,' said Topaz; 'while we're sitting here relaxing and drinking wine, half of Dragon Eyre is still in flames.'

'Yeah, the western half,' said Tilly, as Vitz squeezed on to the deck chair next to her, his arm round her shoulder. 'The Eastern Rim's been peaceful for months. And, now that Sable and Austin are back, it's likely to stay peaceful.'

'That would depend on whether Sable's staying or not,' said Topaz. 'I was speaking to that Banner officer that arrived here with her. He was demanding that she takes him back to Implacatus.'

'Yeah, but he's Banner,' said Lara, 'so who gives a flying toss what he thinks?' She glanced at Sable. 'You're not thinking about going back to Implacatus, are you? I mean, I've been wanting to ask you for a few days, but I was worried what you'd say.'

'My sister has an idea about the Banner soldiers who are stranded here,' Sable said, changing the subject. 'She's thinking about transporting them all to my home world.'

Topaz frowned. 'Why?'

'So she can build an army. A Holdfast army. The Banner of the Damn Holdfasts, or something like that. Would that be a good thing for Dragon Eyre?'

'Damn right it would,' said Tilly. 'There are hundreds of thousands of the bastards stuck on Dragon Eyre. Removing them would fix a shit-load of problems.'

'Can she not take all of the settlers, too?' said Lara. She smirked at Vitz. 'Apart from you. We might let you stay, if you light my bleeding cigarette like I asked.'

Sable leaned over with her metal lighter, flicked it open, and lit Lara's cigarette.

'Why does your sister need so many soldiers to build an army?' said Maddie. 'I mean, it would be great for Dragon Eyre, but it sounds like bad news for your world. Blackrose told me that loads of the Banner soldiers have gone rogue, and have formed into groups of bandits; while others have raided food stores on Gyle and other places. They're starving and desperate; what good would they be?'

'If their discipline has broken down,' said Sable, 'it will be because they've been left leaderless and alone, with no means to buy food or find work. Their discipline should return if they're looked after properly, and offered a fair contract.'

'Yeah, maybe,' said Maddie, 'but why does your sister need them?'

'Is there trouble on your home world?' said Topaz.

'Not yet, but it might be coming. My family has asked me to help.'

Lara narrowed her eyes. 'And what did you say to them?'

'I didn't say anything. I was too busy thinking about having to go to Implacatus. I don't suppose you fancy living on my home world for a while?'

'Are you asking me to come back with you?'

'I haven't decided what I'm going to do next. If I stay on Dragon Eyre, then I'm going to have to do something about the Unk Tannic. I didn't go through all that pain and misery just to let them take over. Or, I could go back and help my sister put her daughter-in-law on the throne.'

'Her daughter-in-law?' said Maddie.

'Yes. That's what the trouble is about. The Empress wants to appoint her own son as successor, but the Holdfasts voted for someone else. I voted for the Empress's son, but, I lost. Still, I was surprised that the others allowed me to take part in the election.'

'Let's say for a moment that I agree to go to your world,' said Lara.

'What?' said Tilly. 'You can't be serious, sis.'

'I'm just asking,' said Lara. 'I want to know where we'd live, and what we'd do. Our father is stuck on that world. He might need our help, or he might be desperate to come home. This might sound silly, but are there ships on your world, Sable?'

'There's a sea in the centre of the continent,' said Sable, 'but it's small compared to the ocean here. A fast boat can sail from one end of the Inner Sea to the other in about eight days; or, it takes about a month to sail round the entire shore. A huge amount of trade is sent across the sea every day, from spring to the start of winter.'

'That sounds promising,' said Lara.

'Not for pirates,' said Sable. 'The imperial fleet patrols the Inner Sea, and there are no safe ports to sell stolen goods. The Empire is currently at peace, and any pirates would be hunted down and captured. If Olo'osso has tried to recreate his life here, then he'll already be in chains.'

'That's that, then,' said Tilly. 'There's no point in going to Sable's world.'

'What about father?' said Lara.

'Maybe Sable can bring him back?'

'I'd need to find him first, Tilly,' Sable said. She glanced at Lara. 'If you came back with me, then we'd be unlikely to live at sea, not unless you were happy with becoming a peaceful, law-abiding merchant. Besides, my sister wants me to help her, and that would involve living on land.'

Lara glanced away, her eyes troubled.

Topaz placed his empty mug onto the deck. 'Piracy is all but over in the Eastern Rim, Captain. We all know what Queen Blackrose thinks of it – she'd come after us if we broke the oaths she made us swear. She wants us to hunt pirates, as if the Five Sisters were her personal navy. If we wanted to go back to our old lives, we'd have to go all the way to the Western Rim, where we'd end up fighting ex-Sea Banner vessels turned renegade. Personally, I'd rather stay here, in Ulna.'

'Thank Malik for that,' said Maddie.

'We should talk to Ann about this,' said Tilly. 'She's the head of the Five Sisters, now that father's marooned on a different world. Whatever we decide to do, we should stick together.'

Sable got to her feet, and took out her Quadrant.

'Where are you going?' said Lara.

'Haurn,' she said. 'I want to check the temple to see if there's any sign of Karalyn. She's been gone for longer than we had expected, and I know that Lucius Cardova will be pestering me for information.' She glanced down at the two captains. 'You have three choices – stay in Ulna and serve Blackrose; return to the Western Rim, and get involved in a vicious fight with the remnants of the Sea Banner; or you could go to my world, and see if you like it there. Have a think, and we can talk about it later.'

Sable swiped her thumb over the Quadrant, and appeared, alone, in the temple complex of Nan Po Tana. She looked around at the derelict buildings, but saw no signs of movement. The notice that she had nailed to the front door of the temple was still there. She had left a simple message for Karalyn – *Gone to Udall, Sable* – in letters large enough to be read from the middle of the courtyard.

Sable frowned. Where was Karalyn? It was possible that her niece had rescued Belinda, and had then returned to the Star Continent, bypassing Dragon Eyre completely, but Sable was convinced that Karalyn would have sent her a message. She strode through an archway, and emerged on to the shores of the ocean, next to the little bay opposite the whitewashed ruins of the village of Pot An, where she had first learned how to control greenhides. She sat down on the bench in the shade of the ancient olive tree, and watched as the tide rolled against the rocks below her.

She had enjoyed the peace, freedom and companionship of the last few days in Ulna, but even so, she still felt a desire to seek out solitude, and had been using Karalyn as an excuse to travel to Haurn, where she could be alone with her thoughts. At the same time, no matter how long she had sat there on her own, she was no closer to arriving at a decision about her future. Dragon Eyre had Lara, and the beauty of the islands, but it was also a place that had scarred itself into her mind; a place that gave her nightmares. If she begged Lara to return with her to the Star Continent, then she was sure that the pirate captain would agree; but would Lara be happy there? Sable doubted it. Then there was Cardova, with his insistence that they return to Implacatus; and Daphne, who had been almost as insistent about her desire to have Sable fight alongside her in the coming struggle against the Empress. It was impossible to please everyone, so she had chosen the easiest option

– lingering in Udall with Lara, and spending her days in blissful indolence. But with every day that passed without any message from Karalyn, the more Sable was beginning to worry about her niece.

She stood, and activated the Quadrant. The air crackled, and she found herself inside the Sextant chamber within Colsbury castle. She tucked the Quadrant into her clothes, and left the room. She heard raucous laughter coming from her sister's office, so she walked down the hallway, and opened the door.

Daphne and Olo'osso were sitting in armchairs, drinking whisky. Sable raised an eyebrow.

'Good afternoon,' she said. 'Of all the things that I thought I might see here, this wasn't one of them.'

Daphne and the old pirate turned to see who was speaking, and Daphne jumped to her feet.

'Sable!' she cried. 'Are you and Karalyn back? What happened?'

'I came to see if Karalyn was here,' said Sable.

Daphne's face fell. 'What?'

'I assume that she hasn't come back?' said Sable.

'There's been no sign of her since you left together. I was hoping that she was safely with you. Did you get separated?'

'Yes. She left us, to go with Amalia to Edmond's palace in Cumulus. We can't get in there; not with vision powers, nor with a Quadrant. We've been waiting on Dragon Eyre for her.'

'Have you seen my daughters?' said Olo'osso.

Sable glanced at him. 'Yes. They're worried about you. When did you arrive in Colsbury?'

'At dawn this morning,' he said.

'What happened to your face? Did someone punch you?'

'No. I fell.'

Sable raised an eyebrow. 'Alright. Do you want me to take you back to Ulna?'

Olo'osso hesitated. He looked from Sable to Daphne, then slowly shook his head.

'I think I'll stay here for a while longer.'

Sable frowned. 'Why?'

Olo'osso shrugged. 'I am enjoying myself here. I was concerned about the girls, but if they are all right, then you can tell them that they don't need to worry themselves any longer on my account. Lady Holdfast has been the perfect host.'

Daphne's features flushed a little.

'I see,' said Sable. 'Tell me; where is Caelius?'

'He's gone for a walk to the market with Agang,' said Daphne.

'And Daimon? Has he tried anything?'

'I might have over-reacted a little,' said Daphne. 'The Empress has made no moves against us. Are you going to look for Karalyn? It's the twins' birthday tomorrow. Is it possible that she might be with them?'

'I can check.'

'Please do so, Sable. I'm sick with worry.'

Sable nodded, while noting that her sister hadn't seemed particularly worried when she had arrived.

'I'll do what I can,' Sable said.

'Thank you,' said Daphne.

'Right. I'll leave you to… do whatever it is you're doing. With any luck, Karalyn will be back soon.'

Sable left the room, and walked back to the Sextant chamber, shaking her head as she went. When she reached the chamber, she approached the huge device, and placed her palm onto its glass surface.

What is your desire, Sable?

'Show me Salve City.'

Her vision blurred, then re-focussed on a view over the bay where Tara, Pella and Ooste lay. She homed in on the row of mansions on Princeps Row, and found Van working in the Banner headquarters. She went from room to room, until she discovered Kelsey, who was attempting to give a reading lesson to Cael and Kyra, who looked miserable and uncooperative.

Sable swore, then lifted her hand from the Sextant. She had been hoping that her visit to Colsbury would have relieved some of her anxiety but, instead, she felt worse. She took out her Quadrant, swiped her fingers across its surface, and re-appeared in Udall, next to the base of the bridge palace. She touched the Quadrant again, and found herself back on the quarter deck of the *Giddy Gull*.

'That was quick,' said Lara, who was still reclining on her deck chair in the sunshine. 'Any luck?'

Sable shook her head, then noticed that one of the deck chairs was empty. 'Where's Maddie?'

'She got a message from the palace,' said Tilly. 'Blackrose wanted to speak to her.'

'What about?'

Tilly shrugged. 'No idea, but the summons was for you, too.'

'I need to go to the palace anyway,' she said. 'I bumped into your father while I was gone.'

'He's on Dragon Eyre?' said Lara, sitting up.

'No, he's getting drunk with my sister in Colsbury. He's fine.'

Tilly and Lara shared a glance.

'I offered to bring him here,' Sable went on, 'but he declined. He seemed to be enjoying himself. So did my sister.'

'That dirty old bastard,' said Lara. 'You should tell your sister to be careful. Father might be hunting for wife number four.'

'I'd rather not think about that,' said Sable. 'I'll come back after I've been to the palace. See you soon.'

She swiped her thumb against the Quadrant, and appeared within the bridge palace, just outside the entrance to the main reception hall. Raised dragon voices were echoing through the vast chamber as she entered, and she saw Blackrose, Shadowblaze, Ashfall and Greysteel in the midst of an animated debate; while their riders stood close by.

Austin caught her eye, and beckoned her over.

'What's going on?' said Sable, as she strode across the floor.

The dragons turned to glance at her.

'Thank you for coming,' said Blackrose. 'It is well that you are here, as the news we have received concerns you, Holdfast.'

'And how does it concern me?'

'There's been a raid in the north of Ulna,' said Maddie.

'What kind of raid?'

'We have been led to believe that a remote farming community has been practically wiped out,' said Greysteel. 'A surviving dragon has returned, and Austin had to heal his many wounds. The survivor said that he thinks dragons from Wyst were responsible.'

Sable frowned. 'I thought there were patrols over Enna? How could Wystians get past without being seen?'

'They could have flown far out into the ocean to avoid being detected,' said Blackrose. 'We should visit the site, and discover for ourselves.'

'We should fly at once,' said Shadowblaze.

'Why fly, when we can go by Quadrant?' said Sable. 'Gather round.'

Sable did a quick count as the others moved into positions around her. There were four dragons, and, including her, four humans.

'Who knows where the farming community was situated?' she said.

'I do,' said Greysteel. 'I visited the location some time ago, when the farms were being reoccupied. Some thirty humans had moved there, along with three dragons.'

Sable entered Greysteel's mind, and gleaned what she needed. The farms were about twenty miles north of Gliden, on the banks of a river. She nodded, then brushed her thumb over the surface of the Quadrant.

The air shimmered, and they appeared next to the slow-moving river. Smoke was rising from a dozen buildings that spread out between newly-ploughed fields. Sable glanced up into the blue sky, but caught no sign of any dragons flying. They walked along a farm track towards the largest cluster of buildings, and passed a burnt-out barn.

'Gods above,' cried Ahi'edo, his eyes wide as he pointed.

The others turned, and saw a pile of human corpses in the middle of a little square, their remains ripped to shreds. Smoke was pouring from every building surrounding the square, and flames were raging through the broken windows. Maddie ran towards the pile of bodies, then pulled up, her hands going to her mouth.

Blackrose growled. 'I will kill those responsible for this outrage.'

'There should be two other dragons here,' said Greysteel.

'I see one over there,' said Austin, pointing at the river.

They left the square, and found the corpse of a dragon, half-submerged in the waters of the river. His throat had been ripped out, and blood was coating the grass by the water's edge.

'Spread out,' said Shadowblaze, 'and look for any survivors.'

Sable accompanied Maddie as they walked down the paths of the small farming settlement.

'I can't believe this is happening,' said Maddie, her eyes welling. 'These people were innocent farmers. I thought the war was over.'

Sable said nothing, her anger growing with every step. They found no more human bodies, but they saw that every house had been systematically destroyed. A cry came from behind them, and they turned. Ashfall had her head raised, and was calling for everyone to come to her position, next to a burning barn.

Sable and Maddie hurried back, and squeezed between Shadowblaze and Greysteel. A dark red dragon was lying next to the burning barn. His wings had been torn to ribbons, and his face was a bloody pulp, the eyes ripped from their sockets.

'He lives,' said Ashfall. 'Austin, do what you can.'

The demigod ran forward, and pressed his palms to the side of the dragon's head. The beast shuddered, and cried out, then lay still.

'He is too weak for me to do any more just now,' Austin said, 'but his life is no longer in danger.'

Blackrose lowered her head to the maimed dragon. 'Suntide,' she said; 'can you hear me? This is your Queen speaking.'

The dark red dragon groaned, and sniffed the air. 'I am blind.'

Sable felt a wild rage grow in the pit of her stomach at the sight of a blinded red dragon, and she tried to control her breathing as memories of Badblood threatened to sweep her away.

'You are safe now,' said Blackrose. 'Tell us what happened.'

'The Wystians came, your Majesty,' Suntide whispered. 'They slaughtered the humans, but they left me alive. They wanted me to bear a message.'

'What message, Suntide?'

'War is coming to Ulna,' the dark red dragon gasped. 'The Wystians know that Sable has escaped, and they blame you, your Majesty. They told me that, unless Sable is handed over to them, they will do to Enna and Ulna what they did to this village. They say that you have broken your vows, your Majesty; and they have sworn revenge. Their legions are gathering. Ulna has until the end of the month to return Sable to their custody, or they shall invade.'

'Damn them!' roared Shadowblaze. 'Those Wystian cowards!'

'What shall we do, your Majesties?' said Greysteel.

Blackrose eyed Sable. 'What I feared has come to pass. Your escape from the Wystians has brought my realm to the brink of destruction, Holdfast.'

'It's not her fault,' said Maddie. 'Sable didn't try to escape – her niece rescued her.'

'That will make little difference to the Wystians,' said Blackrose.

'You can't be thinking of handing her over to those monsters.'

'Did I say that, rider? Sable, take us back to the palace in Udall. Suntide, you shall be coming with us. Austin will continue to heal you.'

'I can't guarantee that I shall be able to restore his sight,' said the demigod; 'but, whatever is in my power to achieve, I shall do.'

Sable took out the Quadrant as the others stared at her. She triggered the device, and they reappeared in the reception hall inside the bridge palace.

'Suntide needs to eat and rest before I can heal him again,' said Austin. 'I shall organise food for him.'

'I shall assist you,' said Ashfall.

Sable waited until Austin and Ashfall had left the hall, then she turned to Blackrose.

'What's the plan?' she said.

Blackrose lowered her gaze. 'I am at a loss to see any peaceful way out of this. Shadowblaze, what are your thoughts?'

'I fear I am too angry to think rationally, my beloved,' said the grey and red dragon. 'My thoughts are filled with notions of revenge, but how can we possibly prevail against such overwhelming odds?'

'We can't,' said Greysteel. 'The Wystians outnumber us ten-to-one.'

'But we have Austin and Sable,' said Maddie.

Blackrose glanced at her. 'And will they commit to fighting for us? Austin desires nothing but peace, and Sable's heart is being torn in many directions.'

'If you want me to kill Wystians,' said Sable, 'then I shall annihilate them.'

The hall quietened.

'You all know what I am capable of achieving,' Sable went on. 'If you direct me against Wyst, then I shall make them suffer.'

'Make who suffer?' said a voice from the entrance.

Sable turned, and saw Cardova walk into the vast hall.

'Hello, all,' the soldier said. 'Might I ask who you are talking about?'

'The Wystian dragons,' said Maddie. 'They slaughtered the inhabitants of a village up north, in revenge for Sable's escape.'

Cardova's eyes tightened. 'The Wystians? Not even Sable could kill them all.'

Sable snorted. 'That sounds like a challenge.'

'There are thousands of dragons living in Wyst,' said Cardova; 'and isn't there something else we should be doing? Karalyn is still on Implacatus. The woman who saved you from the Wystians in the first place needs our help, or had you forgotten?'

'I was in Colsbury an hour ago,' said Sable.

Cardova blinked. 'And? Is Karalyn safe? Is she back?'

Sable shook her head. 'She's not there, and she's not where her children are, either.'

'Then why are we still standing here?' Cardova cried, his eyes betraying his anger. 'Karalyn could be suffering right now, and you're talking about annihilating Wystians? Have you lost your mind?'

'Cool your temper, Banner soldier,' said Greysteel.

Cardova raised a finger and pointed at Greysteel. 'You can't tell me what to do – I'm not under your authority. Sable, take us back to Implacatus, today. I am tired of listening to your excuses.'

Sable's own temper boiled over. 'And what do you think we could do if we went back to Implacatus? We can't use the Quadrant to get inside

Edmond's palace, and my vision powers cannot penetrate solid walls. Going back would be suicide.'

'No, fighting the Wystians would be suicide, but you are too pig-headed to see it.'

'You are in the presence of the Queen of Ulna,' said Shadowblaze. 'Show some respect, Banner soldier, or you will be ejected from this chamber.'

'I don't take orders from dragons,' said Cardova. 'I am contracted to the Holdfasts, not to you.'

Shadowblaze's amber eyes glowed, and he raised his claws.

'Enough,' said Blackrose. 'Lucius Cardova, calm your emotions. I understand your pain, but Ulna is facing a grave threat. If the Wystians invade, they will slaughter thousands. Sable's incarceration was the only thing keeping the peace; now that she is free, the entire Eastern Rim is at risk.'

'I couldn't care less about the Eastern Rim,' said Cardova.

Sparks exploded round Blackrose's jaws. 'Sable, remove this man from my presence before I do something I will regret.'

Sable nodded, then brushed her thumb over the Quadrant. The air shimmered, then she and Cardova appeared on the quarter deck of the *Giddy Gull*.

'Hello,' said Lara, from her deck chair. 'I should warn you both; I'm quite drunk.'

Cardova ignored her. He prodded a finger towards Sable. 'You are betraying Karalyn by remaining here. If she dies, it will be your fault.'

'Hey!' Lara cried. She got to her feet, then staggered. 'No one talks to Sable like that, especially not some jumped-up Banner asshole. I'll bleeding well knock you out. Marines! Where are my bleeding marines?'

Topaz gazed at her, his eyes wide. 'Should I fetch them, ma'am?'

'There's no need,' said Cardova. 'I'm going. The last place I want to be is on the deck of a Five Sisters ship.'

The soldier strode away, and Lara collapsed back down onto her deck chair.

'I showed him,' she muttered. 'Dipshit Banner piece of crap. He ain't making any friends in bleeding Ulna, that's for damn sure.'

Sable sat down next to her, but said nothing.

'What now?' said Topaz.

'Now?' said Sable. She took a breath. 'I guess it's time to wipe out a few thousands Wystians.'

The others stared at her.

'First, though,' Sable went on, 'I'm going to need some more wine.'

CHAPTER 19
EARLY RELEASE

Tara, Auldan, The City – 19th Namen 3423

Emily sighed as she glanced around the table. 'It seems we are no further forward.'

'I am of the opinion that we have but one choice,' said Lady Aurelian, who was sitting to her son's left. 'Under no circumstances should the City get involved in a struggle taking place upon another world. The City has survived shortages before, and it can do so again. To commence trading with either the Holdfasts or the Empress would be folly.'

'With all due respect, my lady,' said Van, 'you have sufficient wealth to get through the next few years. The situation in the Circuit is fast becoming a disaster, and the unrest there will spread as the shortages take hold. We have barely enough food to feed the citizenry, and we are in the midst of a severe housing crisis. The people are cold, wet and hungry.'

'What nonsense,' said Lady Aurelian. 'The rains will stop in ten days or so.'

'And then it shall be winter,' said Van, 'and we don't have enough fuel to heat the homes of the poor.'

'Is Tarstation operating at full capacity?' said Daniel.

'Yes, your Majesty,' said Van, 'but supplies were badly interrupted during Simon's reign, and it will take some time before we have enough oil. The City usually falls back on coal and wood during such times, but we have none of either resource.'

'Isn't the Western Bank covered in forests?' said Lady Aurelian. 'There is plentiful wood to be had on the far side of the Straits.'

'The Western Bank is also covered in greenhides, my lady,' Van went on, his irritation becoming evident. 'In order to get supplies of timber, Brigade forces will have to risk their lives; and all of the wood gathered there is urgently needed to shore up the local defences.'

'Should we consider abandoning Jezra?' said Commander Quill.

'Absolutely not,' said Emily. 'Jezra is the key to the future. In time, the settlement on the Western Bank will provide everything the City requires. To ensure this, all we need to do is have our dragons eliminate the young greenhide queens that escaped the destruction of the nest. Once this has been achieved, in ten years from now, there will be no greenhides on the Western Bank, and our supply difficulties will end.' She glanced at the others seated around the meeting table. 'Ten years – that's all we're talking about. If we can get through the next decade, we will be secure. However, if we do not trade with the Star Continent, there is every chance there will be no City left ten years from now. Major-General Logos is correct; the supply situation is too severe to ignore. Without timber, we cannot rebuild the fleets that used to scour the seas for food. Without coal, hundreds will freeze to death this winter, and every subsequent winter. Without access to metals, our infrastructure falls ever more into decrepitude and decay. It is not a question of if we should trade with the Star Continent, but with whom. Kelsey, as a member of the Holdfast family, I would like to hear your opinion.'

Kelsey frowned. She had kept quiet up to that point, conscious of the fact that her loyalties were divided.

'I don't know,' she said. 'I have no easy answers. My mother, of course, thinks that I should be trying to persuade you all to deal exclusively with her; but, if we do that, then there will be strings attached.

Sure, she'll give us what we want without us having to send any salve to the Star Continent, but she'll expect the City's assistance if the Empress attacks our family. On the other hand, I don't trust Daimon. The Empress's new dream mage could be extremely dangerous.'

'If it comes to war,' said Daniel, 'then who do you think would win – the Empress or the Holdfasts?'

'It depends.'

'I realise that, Kelsey,' said Daniel, 'but try to give a balanced opinion.'

'Alright. The Empress has all of the soldiers, which should give them an unbeatable advantage. But, we have Karalyn and Sable. Karalyn on her own could annihilate the imperial army, if she wanted to. The question is, would she be prepared to do it? If I had to guess, I'd say no. Sable, on the other hand, would have no moral compunctions about shedding blood. If she was unleashed, then she could probably assassinate the Empress and her entire court, especially if Corthie could be persuaded to help her. But, Sable could be killed by a single stray crossbow bolt to the back of her head. She might think she's immortal, but she's not. So, you know, it depends.'

Daniel nodded. 'Do we have any forces that we could lend the Hold-fasts, Major-General?'

'I've looked into the figures, your Majesty,' he said. 'At best, we could perhaps send a mixed formation of around one thousand soldiers – a combination of Banner forces and Blades, with perhaps a few local militia. I would advise sending them from garrisons where the food supply is already critical, to relieve some of the pressure on existing stocks.'

Lady Aurelian raised an eyebrow. 'Could we not arm ten thousand starving Evaders and send them? They're used to rioting; I'm sure they would be able to fight.'

'They would be slaughtered by any disciplined force, my lady,' said Van.

'What a pity,' said Lady Aurelian, giving a gentle shrug.

'We could also think about sending the dragons,' said Van. 'Two dragons would certainly boost the capacity of the Holdfasts' forces. They could defend Colsbury against all comers.'

'I shudder at the thought of losing our two most valuable assets,' said Emily, 'and we shall need Frostback and Halfclaw to hunt down the remaining greenhide queens once Sweetmist is over. Beside, I doubt they would wish to go.'

'You might be wrong about that,' said Kelsey.

Emily frowned. 'What do you mean?'

'Frostback and Halfclaw would quite like to move to the Star Continent.'

'Why?' said Emily, her eyes reflecting hurt and surprise.

'Sorry to be the one to tell you all this,' said Kelsey, 'but the dragons don't like living on this world. They hate the weather; they hate the greenhides, and they're frustrated by the lack of space. That's why they still haven't had any baby dragons. They're holding off, hoping that I'll take them to Colsbury.'

The meeting room descended into silence.

'I must say,' said Emily, 'that this has come as rather a shock to me. I had always assumed that the dragons were loyal to the City. Did we not fight Simon together? Were it not for Frostback and Halfclaw, we would have been pushed out of Jezra long ago.'

'They didn't ask to come here,' said Kelsey, 'and they feel that they have done their bit. They've worked hard for the City, but hate living in a damp, leaky cavern. So far, I've managed to put them off talking about it, but they're bound to bring it up again sooner or later. If I told them that they could go as part of an expeditionary force, they'd be off in a heartbeat.'

'It is as I suspected,' said Lady Aurelian. 'We were foolish to believe that dragons possess any shred of loyalty. They are savage beasts, pure and simple.'

'I strongly disagree,' said Emily. 'They are noble and proud, and, now that I have been made aware of their feelings, I shall endeavour to improve their living conditions with immediate effect. The halls of the

Royal Palace in Ooste are large enough to fit two dragons. I shall arrange to have them relocated there as soon as possible.'

'Dragons in the Royal Palace?' said Lady Aurelian, her voice high.

'Why not?' said Daniel. 'It is unfit for human habitation, ever since Dawnflame burned half of it to the ground.'

'So,' said Lady Aurelian, 'the reward for the dragons incinerating the palaces of the City is that they get to live in one?'

'If we can go back to the topic of trade,' said Quill, 'perhaps a little subterfuge is in order? Could we not trade with both the Holdfasts and the Empress, but pretend that we are dealing exclusively with each party?'

Emily shook her head. 'I refuse to consider such a notion.'

'Besides,' said Kelsey, 'we'd get caught. Karalyn or Daimon would see through it in a second. What we need is a really good negotiator; someone cunning, who has experience of this sort of thing.'

'Do you have anyone in mind?' said Daniel.

Kelsey shrugged. 'Nope.'

'Dear gods,' said Van, putting his head in his hands. 'There is someone, but you might throw me out of the chamber for suggesting it.'

'Who?' said Lady Aurelian. 'I hope you aren't referring to me. I have always been straightforward in my trade negotiations; never cunning.'

'No, my lady; I wasn't referring to you.'

'Then who?' said Emily.

Van cringed. 'Naxor?'

Lady Aurelian burst into laughter. 'Oh my, Van; how droll.'

Daniel grinned, then pointed to the room's entrance. 'Right; out with you, Van. There's the door.'

'Wait one moment,' said Emily. 'Didn't Naxor handle the salve trade with Lostwell for three hundred years under the God-King's authority? He did a highly professional job, or so I am told. Should we dismiss this suggestion out of hand?'

'Yes,' said Lady Aurelian. 'That treacherous little weasel betrayed all of us to Simon.'

'I am well aware of his crimes,' said Emily. 'However, and please hear me out; we need to be thinking long-term. Naxor is a demigod; unless we execute him, then he is destined to remain in prison forever. He is also the only person in the city with experience of trading salve on other worlds.'

'I'm sorry, darling,' said Daniel, 'but you seem to be ignoring the fatal flaw in your argument. Let's say we make Naxor swear an oath. I'm sure, to secure his release, he would be only too willing to say the words required. But, we cannot trust him. Would we give him a Quadrant and a ton of salve, and then send him on his way? He would be off to Implacatus before we could blink.'

'I don't know about that,' said Emily. 'If he's desperate, then he may wish to come to an accommodation with us. I know it's hard, but place yourself in his shoes for a moment. He betrayed us – yes. Why? Because he was terrified of Simon. He calculated the risks, and decided that there was no way to defeat the Tenth Ascendant, so he made his choice. His sisters Lydia and Doria are currently residing in Port Sanders – perhaps they could be persuaded to accompany Kelsey to the dungeons under Maeladh.'

'Eh?' said Kelsey. 'What makes you think I want to see that rat again?'

'You would have to be present,' said Emily, 'to prevent him from using his vision powers once his hood and blindfold have been removed.' She looked at the disbelieving faces around the table. 'It is a risk, I grant you, but perhaps we need someone of his... particular expertise on our side. And remember, Amalia's crimes were of a far greater magnitude than Naxor's, and yet we forgave her.'

'This seems like a dreadful error,' said Lady Aurelian.

'And Naxor has only been in prison for four months,' said Kelsey. 'He's barely suffered at all.'

'Nevertheless,' said Emily, 'I think we should explore Van's suggestion. If Naxor agrees, then he could be given the burden of negotiating a deal with the Star Continent that would keep everyone happy. If he doesn't agree, then he can stay in his cell. Kelsey, I would like you to use the Quadrant to fetch Ladies Lydia and Doria from Port Sanders. Do not tell them exactly why, not just yet. Bring them here, and Daniel and I shall speak to them.'

Kelsey glared at Van. 'Next time you get an idea like that, keep your damn mouth shut.'

Four hours later, Kelsey and Van were escorting the two demigod siblings of Naxor through the dungeons of Maeladh Palace. While much of the upper floors had been gutted by fire, the basement levels had survived intact, and were being used to imprison those who had collaborated with Simon's regime. The majority of the inmates were Blade officers, but there were a smattering of men and women from the other tribes, as well as a single demigod.

Lydia and Doria had remained quiet since being told the purpose of their visit by the Queen, and their silence was beginning to annoy Kelsey.

'I thought you two would be more angry,' Kelsey said, as they walked through the damp, lamp-lit passageways.

'Why would we be angry?' said Lydia.

'Well, Naxor betrayed you, too.'

'That is not entirely accurate,' Lydia said. 'Doria and I were among those who bowed before Simon. Our brother was just a little more eager with his support. I, for example, handed over many Sanders and Evaders for the daily executions. To have done otherwise would have meant my certain death. And Naxor played no part in how poor Doria was treated. I always felt it a little hypocritical of the mortal monarchy to have released me, Doria and Amalia, but to have imprisoned Naxor.'

Kelsey shook her head. 'What about you, Doria?'

The demigod shrugged. 'Naxor is my brother, and he will remain so, long after you are dead, Miss Holdfast. What Simon did was unforgivable, but Naxor was just as frightened as the rest of us.'

'Pyre's arse,' muttered Kelsey. 'Am I the only sane one here?'

'You are a mortal,' said Lydia, 'and, hence, you think like a mortal. I have ruled Port Sanders for a thousand years; such experience gives me a longer perspective than you can possibly imagine. The winds change, and mortals come and go, but we endure.'

They reached a closed wing of the dungeon, and a young Banner soldier unlocked a sturdy wooden door. Kelsey caught his glance as he turned, and her vision clouded over. A fragment of the future leapt out at her; a confusion of noise and movement. Was she witnessing a brief moment in the midst of a battle? Soldiers were fighting under the red sky of the City, and bodies lay scattered on the ground. An armoured man charged forward, and plunged his sword into the chest of the Banner soldier; and the vision ended as quickly as it had begun. Kelsey blinked, her head spinning. More than any other type of vision, she hated seeing someone's death. Part of her wanted to tell the soldier, but what possible good would it do? Nothing would change what she had seen. Of more importance was the fact that a battle seemed to be taking place within the City, but she had no way of knowing how far into the future it would happen – months? Years? Decades? As she did with so many of her visions, Kelsey decided that she would try to forget it. She pushed it into the dark recesses of her mind, while attempting to keep her expression settled.

The young Banner soldier glanced at Van. 'Lord Naxor is the only prisoner kept in this wing, sir. He's in the last cell on the right.'

'Thank you, corporal,' said Van.

Kelsey kept her eyes down as they passed through the entrance, and then the soldier handed them a lamp, as there were none lit within the closed wing. Van held the lamp high, and led the way down the dark corridor. They passed empty cells on their left and right, before coming to the end of the passageway. Kelsey peered through the bars.

'It's not time for dinner,' said a voice from the shadows, 'therefore, I must assume that something different is about to occur.'

Kelsey shook her head. 'I see his tongue has grown back.'

'Ah. Kelsey Holdfast. This cannot be good news. Am I to be executed?'

'No, brother,' said Lydia.

'Lydia? Who else is out there?'

'I'm also here, brother,' said Doria.

Naxor laughed. 'My two surviving sisters? What is this? What's going on?'

'The mortal monarchy wishes to offer you a deal,' said Lydia. 'If you have any sense, you will take it.'

'A deal?' said Naxor. 'I'm intrigued. What kind of deal?'

Kelsey's eyes grew accustomed to the low level of light, and she caught a glimpse of the prisoner amid the shadows of the filthy cell. Naxor was sitting on a low bench, his wrists and ankles chained to an iron ring embedded into a stone wall. A thick hood was covering his head, to prevent him from using his powers.

'First,' said Van, 'you would be required to swear an oath to the King and Queen of the City, pledging to obey their orders, and to carry out any appointed duties faithfully and diligently. Are you prepared to do so?'

'In return for what?'

'In return for your freedom, demigod,' said Van. 'The King and Queen are considering handing you an important task – one they feel your skills are suited to.'

'That's a little ambiguous. I have many skills. It strikes me that, if Kelsey is here, then there is no need for me to keep this hood on. As a gesture of goodwill, would you be prepared to remove it? I prefer to conduct conversations in which I can see the other person's face.'

'Very well,' said Van. 'Remain where you are.'

Van gestured to the soldiers at the end of the corridor, and four walked forward.

'You two, keep your crossbows trained on the prisoner,' he said, pointing. 'And, you two, enter the cell and remove his hood.'

'Yes, sir,' said the corporal.

'It goes without saying, Naxor,' said Van, 'that if you try anything, I will order the soldiers to loose.'

'Naturally,' said Naxor. 'I wouldn't expect anything less.'

The young corporal unlocked the cell door, then strode in, along with one other soldier, while the other two aimed their bows at Naxor. The corporal unfastened the padlock keeping Naxor's hood secured to his head, then pulled it free. He then untied the blindfold. Naxor blinked, and smiled. The two soldiers retreated from the cell, and the door was re-locked.

'Well, this is fun,' said Naxor. 'What date is it?'

'It's the nineteenth of Namen,' said Lydia.

'Urgh. Sweetmist. I should have known. So, Major-General Van Logos of the Banner of the Lostwell Exiles, tell me more about this deal, and then I shall tell you if I would prefer to have the hood placed back on to my head.'

'Very well,' said Van. 'The King and Queen would like to trade salve with Kelsey's home world. The Star Continent has all of the resources that the City currently needs, and the Empress there seems willing to negotiate. The biggest challenge will be keeping the Holdfasts happy. They have also offered to negotiate, but they are locked in a dispute with the Empress. The King and Queen have agreed that the City should deal with the legitimate government, rather than with the Holdfasts.'

A faint smile danced across Naxor's lips. 'And what would I be expected to do?'

'Lead the negotiations,' said Van. 'But first, I would like to hear your advice.'

Naxor laughed. 'My advice? The last time we met, you wanted to kill me, Major-General; and here you are, requesting my advice.'

'You have the most experience in these matters.'

'Indeed, I do. Three centuries of trading salve on Lostwell, to be precise. This, however, is different. As far as I can see, there would be little need for extreme secrecy. No, what you are looking for is some subtle diplomacy. Fortunately for you, I am also an expert at that. It sounds as though I need to think of a way to deal with the Star Conti nent without upsetting Kelsey's delightful family.'

'We have several conditions regarding the trade,' Van said. 'First, the City must not be dragged into any war on the Star Continent. Second, the flow of goods and materials from the Star Continent must commence as soon as possible, and continue indefinitely. And third, we do not make enemies of either the Holdfasts, or the Empress.'

'Don't forget Daimon,' said Kelsey. 'He's a dream mage, and he works for the Empress.'

'A dream mage?' said Naxor. 'Like Karalyn Holdfast?'

'Aye,' said Kelsey, 'only a lot younger. He's only sixteen. I'll also be at the negotiations, but that won't stop Daimon from reading your mind.'

Naxor smiled. 'There are ways to get round that difficulty.'

'And you won't touch the Quadrant.'

'I presumed so. You have the God-King's Quadrant? I know it well. Tell me – how do you use it without vision powers?'

'With a great deal of difficulty. I've been studying maps and practising. A lot.'

'Good for you, Miss Holdfast. Would I be free to roam the City if I agreed?'

'You would be confined to Port Sanders in the first instance,' said Van. 'Lady Lydia has kindly agreed to allow you to stay in Tonetti Palace with her and Lady Doria.'

Naxor smiled. 'Thank you, sisters.'

'We few survivors of the Royal Family should stick together,' said Lydia.

'Quite. And what does our dear grandmother think of this plan?'

'Amalia's not in the City, brother.'

Naxor frowned. 'No? Where is she?'

'She's on Implacatus with Karalyn Holdfast,' said Van. 'They are attempting to rescue Lady Belinda from Cumulus.'

Several expressions flitted across Naxor's features.

'We three are the only immortals currently in the City, brother,' said Doria. 'Jade is living in the Eastern Mountains, and Aila is on the Star Continent.'

'How our numbers have thinned of late.'

'Aye?' said Kelsey. 'Perhaps if you hadn't assisted Simon, more of your family would be alive.'

'What bad form, Miss Holdfast,' said Naxor. 'I had presumed that we weren't going to mention... him. It is as well that Jade is not in the City. I feel that she would try to kill me on sight. I did go a little too far that day by the salve mine; but enough of my past mistakes. Is that it? I construct a satisfactory trade arrangement, and then you will let me go free? It seems... too easy.'

'We want you back in the fold, brother,' said Lydia. 'If the mortals wish to show clemency, then we advise you to take it before they change their minds. Only this time, be a good boy. It is time to reconcile yourself to the Aurelian monarchy.'

Naxor sighed. 'Yes, I suppose it is. With so few immortals remaining, any coup would be utterly pointless. Our time seems to have finally passed; what a pity.' He turned his glance to Van. 'Very well, Major-General; I submit to you, and accept your terms. I shall kneel before our illustrious rulers and pledge my fealty with as much sincerity as I can muster, and then I shall get to work.'

Kelsey shook her head, and suppressed a snort.

'Do you have something you wish to add, Miss Holdfast?' said Naxor. 'I realise that you probably think I am nothing but a liar, but everyone always forgets one thing about me – I love this City with all of my being. It is my home. I could have betrayed it a thousand times over to the gods of Implacatus, but I did not, and I shall not. Ever.'

'You betrayed it when you sided with Simon.'

'There you go, bandying that name around again. However, you are mistaken. I allied with... him, because he promised to leave the City after a short while. By the time I realised my mistake, it was too late, and he had the City by the throat. I will say it now – it was the worst mistake of my life. I appeased a monster, because I was scared. We were all scared. Well, all of us, it seems, apart from Jade. Who would have guessed that?'

'I will carry your words to the King and Queen,' said Van, then he gestured to the soldiers. 'Place the blindfold and hood back on to the prisoner.'

'Yes, sir,' said the corporal.

The soldiers went through the same process as before, then they stepped out of the cell, and locked the door.

'How long shall I remain in here?' said Naxor.

'That's up to the King and Queen,' said Van. 'They would like the trade negotiations to start soon, so, if their Majesties agree, then you could be released as early as this evening. Thank you for your time, Lord Naxor.'

'No; thank you, Major-General; it has been a pleasure. Lydia, Doria, I hope to see you soon in Tonetti Palace. Do me a favour, and order in some Taran brandy and a tray of fresh mussels. I like them cooked in red wine.'

Lydia laughed. 'I'm sure I can manage that. See you soon, brother.'

Van led the way, and they left the cells behind. The young corporal secured the door that led to the closed wing, then Van, Kelsey and Naxor's two sisters retraced their steps through the basement of Maeladh. They emerged up a stairwell, where a ruined segment of the ground floor provided some shelter from the torrential rain.

'Will you take us back to Tonetti, Kelsey?' said Doria.

'The Queen wants you to return to the Aurelian mansion,' said Van, 'to discuss how it went.'

'Very well,' said Lydia. 'We shall see you there.'

Lydia picked up a large umbrella from where she had left it when they had entered the palace, and the two demigods hurried towards Princeps Row.

Kelsey groaned. 'What are we doing? I mean, Naxor? Pyre's tits.'

'We're doing it for the City, Kelsey,' said Van. 'We need to put our personal feelings to one side.'

'He tried to torture Jade, and Maddie's sister; and we're just going to let him go?'

'If he does as he's told. The City can't afford to throw away a demigod with his wealth of experience. Still, I'd be a lot happier if there was someone in the City who could read his mind, to see if he intends to be loyal. Unfortunately, as Lydia said, there are only three demigods left in the City, and only Naxor has vision powers.'

Kelsey smiled. 'You've just given me an idea.'

'Yeah? What idea?'

'I think I might know two other people currently in the City who can read minds. I'll give you a clue – they'll both be eight-years-old tomorrow. And, if Kyra feels like making Naxor bark like a dog, then who am I to stand in her way?'

CHAPTER 20
TRUE TO THE END

Cumulus, Implacatus – 17th Tuminch 5255

Karalyn crouched by the ventilation duct, her shoulder brushing against the thin sheets of fine mesh that prevented vision powers from penetrating the interior of the Palace of the Almighty. A group of gods was striding past, and among them was an Ancient wearing eye-guards. Karalyn remained in the thick shadows, keeping silent. She hadn't opened her mouth to speak in... well, she wasn't exactly sure how long she had been inside Edmond's fortress. Four days? Five? With no sun to guide her, she had lost track of time. The oil lamps that lit the maze-like passageways were always burning, regardless of the hour, and people were continually on the move. No mortals were permitted inside the fortress-palace, but there were many gods and demigods living there; some working as slaves in the kitchens and laundry rooms, while others strutted around in fine robes, or swaggered in brightly-coloured stone armour.

Karalyn waited until the footsteps had receded into the distance, then she stole out from her hiding place. She had been sleeping inside the myriad ventilation shafts that provided a measure of fresh air to the inhabitants of the palace. She would carefully unfasten one of the many layers of fine gauze, crawl in, and then re-fasten the mesh sheet behind her. She never slept well, half of her mind alert to possible danger, and she always awoke disorientated.

You cannot see me. You cannot see me.

She had repeated the same four words in her head countless times since she had entered the palace, and had wandered the endless passageways like a ghost, stealing food from kitchens and rubbish middens, and spying on the gods. A voiceless wraith, haunting the fortress. She had been lost more times than she could remember. Every corridor looked the same, and there were no signs or notices to inform those inside where they were, or in which direction they were going. The walls, floors and ceilings were formed of smooth, solid granite, and the palace was like no building Karalyn had ever been inside. It was as if tunnels, stairs and chambers had been carved out of a massive, mono-lithic slab of stone, designed by a paranoid recluse. Slowly, over time, Karalyn had constructed a mental map of her surroundings, but she still found herself caught out with annoying regularity. It was impos-sible to use her powers to scan more than her immediate vicinity – the doors had seals round their edges, and no keyholes, and no internal window was without its multiple sheets of fine gauze.

In all her time within the palace, Karalyn had yet to catch a glimpse of Belinda. She had read the minds of dozens of unprotected gods, and knew that Belinda was somewhere inside the building, but none of those whose thoughts she had raided knew exactly where the Third Ascendant was located. She had seen Lord Bastion once, but he had been wearing eye-guards, and she had ducked into the shadows to let him pass. She had tried to follow him, but he had slipped away, disap-pearing through a doorway, and then using his stone powers to seal it behind him. That had been her greatest clue – and she had been lingering in the same area for many long hours since, hoping to see the sealed door open again.

Two demigods strode past her, but she was invisible to them. She scanned their minds briefly, but they were low status, and knew nothing about where Belinda was, or how to get to her. She reached the corridor where she had last seen Bastion and crouched by the narrow opening to a ventilation shaft. She pulled out a small knife, and loosened three metal screws fixing the sheet of gauze to the walls. She lifted the mesh, and crawled into the space. The shaft widened, and she turned in the cramped tunnel, and pulled the mesh down again to cover her tracks. She lay still in the warm, fetid air for a moment, tired and nauseous, then pulled the small bag from over her shoulder. She sat up, the top of her head grazing the ceiling of the shaft, and opened the bag. Inside was a chunk of rye bread, a flask of water, and a handful of grapes. She drank the water, quenching her thirst, then tore off a piece of bread and placed it into her mouth, chewing slowly.

She considered giving up. She had been unable to find Amalia, let alone Belinda, and her spirits were at a low ebb. Through trial and error, she had worked out how to return to the gateway where she had entered the palace. The gates were opened once a day, to allow supplies of food, drink and other goods into the palace. If she was careful, she would be able to slip out, and escape the claustrophobic maze of the palace; then she could return to Colsbury, defeated but alive. What was the alternative? Was she destined to wander the passageways of the Palace of the Almighty until she died?

She chewed a grape, but it seemed sour to her, as sour as her mood. She thought about everyone who was waiting for her – her children in the City of Salve, her mother in Colsbury, Sable… wherever she had gone; Cardova, Amalia, Kelsey. None of them would have the slightest idea where she was, or what had happened to her. It was the twins' birthday soon, or perhaps it had already passed? She had promised Kyra and Cael that she would spend the day with them. She shook her head. She had told everyone that she would only be away for a few thirds when she had left Colsbury to hunt for Corthie, and she had been gone for over four years. Was history repeating itself?

The sound of footsteps approached, a clack of heels on the granite floor, then low voices reached Karalyn's ears. She sat frozen, her full attention on the view through the gauze at the entrance to the shaft.

'Are you sure, my lord?' said a female voice.

'Of course I'm sure,' snapped another voice. Bastion.

Karalyn's heart raced a little faster.

'But, my lord,' the female god went on, 'how could an intruder possibly have penetrated the interior of the palace?'

'If I knew that, I wouldn't be talking to you,' said Bastion. 'Increase the patrols, and have dogs brought up from the lower levels to assist with the search.'

'Yes, my lord. Might I ask – how do we know that someone has managed to infiltrate the building?'

'There's no conclusive proof, merely a number of hints. Missing food from the kitchens, mysterious sightings, odd noises. Each on their own would signify nothing, but added together they amount to a clear breach of security. Not a word of this must leave the palace; understand? It would be wise not to reveal to the other gods of Cumulus that what was deemed impossible has, in fact, come true.'

'I won't breathe a word of it, my lord.'

'See that you don't.'

Karalyn eased herself forward, and glanced through the mesh. The opening was at ground level, and she caught a glimpse of two sets of shoes in the corridor outside the shaft.

'You are dismissed,' said Bastion. 'Report to me at once if the intruder is found.'

The woman turned, and walked away to the right. Bastion waited for a moment, then approached the sealed doorway that Karalyn had previously seen him disappear through. There was a sound of grinding stone, then silence. With no time to think, Karalyn pushed herself forwards. She wriggled through the opening to the shaft, then re-fixed the three screws to the mesh as quickly as she was able. She got to her feet and ran after the female god. She came to a crossroads, and thought she had lost her, then she saw the god's robes swish round a corner, and set off after her. She caught up with her as she was about to enter a chamber. She needed the woman to turn, before she could get away.

'Hey!' Karalyn cried, letting her voice be heard.

The god jumped, then stared around, unable to see anyone in the corridor with her. Karalyn dived into her mind, filling it with her powers.

The woman's unprotected eyes glazed over.

Go back to the sealed door and open it. Now.

The woman started to retrace her steps. Karalyn leaned back against a wall to allow her to pass, then followed her. They passed the crossroads, and approached the door that Bastion had sealed. The woman raised her hand, and Karalyn sensed her stone powers penetrate the doorway. The granite groaned as the seals were broken, and the door slid open.

Count to ten, then reseal the door and go back to work. Then, forget every-thing that has occurred in the last two minutes.

Karalyn slipped through the doorway. On the other side was an identical corridor to the one she had left. She waited, and the door closed behind her, the stonework merging as if the rock were molten. Karalyn glanced ahead. There was no sign of Bastion, but worse, there were no ventilation shafts to hide in if he reappeared. Karalyn strode down the passageway, keeping her steps light. She came to a set of stairs, and ascended, her heart pounding. If a god with eye-guards and a weapon happened to pass, it was all over, and a wave of fear surged upwards from the pit of her stomach, making her almost throw up.

She reached the top of the stairs, and gasped with relief as her eyes caught sight of a ventilation shaft. She crouched by it, loosened the screws, and crawled inside, her breathing ragged. She had been sitting there for a few minutes before she realised that she could hear a low murmur of voices. They weren't coming from the corridor, but seemed to be emanating from further down the shaft. Karalyn turned, and crawled further along the narrow tunnel. She passed another low gauze-shielded opening and peered through the mesh; and was rewarded with the sight of Bastion's boots. He was speaking to someone that Karalyn couldn't see, his tone light and friendly. The chamber where he was standing was comfortable and well-lit, with oak furniture, and Karalyn could see the corner of a wide bed.

'How are you settling in?' said Bastion.

'Very well, thank you, my lord,' said the other voice, and Karalyn realised that the Ancient was speaking to Amalia.

Karalyn almost wept with relief. At last, she had found Amalia; and even better, she seemed to be fine. Karalyn had been worried that the gods would have executed her, but no – she was alive and well.

'Is there anything you require to make your stay more comfortable?' said Bastion, his tone cordial.

'No, my lord. All I ask is that I am allowed to pay my respects to the Blessed Second and Third Ascendants; to wish them well for their coming nuptials.'

Bastion laughed. 'My, you are persistent. Very well, I think I can allow that. But first, however, I have a couple of questions. I'm sure you won't mind answering them for me.'

'Of course, my lord. I have nothing to hide. After all, you have already read my mind thoroughly.'

'I have. You know, I happened to be on Lostwell at the same time as you; what a coincidence, yes? Tell me; when you fled the City, why did you decide to go to Lostwell? It wouldn't have been my first choice.'

'Well, my lord, I was limited by the number of worlds I knew how to travel to. I could have come here, but I wasn't yet ready to surrender myself at that stage. My only other option was Yocasta, my home world, but I didn't particularly wish to live in a desert wasteland; therefore, Lostwell was the only feasible choice.'

'I see. Yes, that makes perfect sense. And then you returned to the City?'

'Yes, that's right.'

'Using the "go back" command on your Quadrant?'

'Yes.'

'Hmm.'

'You have read my memories regarding this, no?'

'I have.' He sighed, as if unwilling to bring up something awkward. 'Here's the thing, Amalia. Your memories indeed show that you did not use the Quadrant upon Lostwell. However, when I arrived on that world, I scanned the minds of the sadly-deceased Sixth and Seventh

Ascendants – Arete and Leksandr. They recall a rumour of you having been with Lady Belinda in Shawe Myre. Is that correct?'

'Yes. I was in Shawe Myre. I was hiding there, and managed to make contact with Lady Belinda. She joined me there for a while. When the Sixth and Seventh Ascendants arrived to take her away, I hid in the forest.'

'Ah. Of course. Explain to me then how it is possible that both Arete and Leksandr also remember seeing you in Yoneath, that very same day? You were part of the group that snatched Kelsey Holdfast, were you not? Arete, in particular, remembered it as clear as day. How is that you were able to travel hundreds of miles in a single day without a Quadrant?'

'No, I... I wasn't in Yoneath, my lord.'

'You have no memory of being in Yoneath; but that is not the same thing, Amalia. I know what I saw in Arete's mind, so either her memories were altered, or yours have been altered. Which is more likely, I wonder? Now, here's what we're going to do. You will tell me the truth; not the fabricated tale that you have heretofore spun, but the unadulterated truth. You used the Quadrant several times on Lostwell, did you not?'

'No, my lord.'

'And, having used the Quadrant on Lostwell, it stands to reason that you are perfectly aware of how to travel to the salve world. Tell me how to get there, and tell me who altered your memories, or I will be forced to make your next few hours exceedingly unpleasant.'

'I... I don't know what you're talking about, my lord.'

Bastion raised his hand, and Amalia screamed in agony. She fell to the floor, and Karalyn caught her first glimpse of the former God-Queen, as she writhed and shuddered, foam on her lips, and blood leaking from her eyes and nose.

Bastion lowered his hand, and laughed.

'I want you to picture something in your mind, Amalia,' he said. 'Think of the Quadrant, picture where you need to touch in order to travel to the salve world, and then tell me. Do this, and the pain shall cease.'

Amalia rolled on to her side, the flesh peeling from her face.

'I don't know what you're talking about,' she gasped.

'You are lying to me,' he said. 'Are you allied to the Holdfasts? As far as I know, only those damned mortals understand how to efficiently alter memories. Whoever was in your head has done an admirable job. It has taken me days to find a flaw; but, a flaw there is. No one's perfect, I suppose. Was it a Holdfast?'

Amalia said nothing.

'Oh, Amalia,' Bastion said, shaking his head. 'I am a very patient man. I am prepared to torture you for decades, if that's what it takes.' He withdrew something from a deep pocket. 'Do you see this? I'm sure you know what it is. That's right – it's a restrainer mask. Tell me how to get to the salve world, and I will spare you its torments.'

Amalia shuddered. 'I cannot tell you what I do not know.'

Karalyn glanced away as Bastion raised his hand again. Amalia's screams echoed through the chamber. Her skin sloughed off, and the floor was smeared in her blood as she writhed and struggled.

'I love seeing the pain of others,' Bastion said, as he crouched by Amalia's shattered body. 'You long for death; I can sense it. But believe me; the only merciful release you shall receive will be after you tell me how to get to the salve world.'

Karalyn sat frozen, paralysed by helplessness. Bastion's eyes were protected, and there was nothing she could do to stop him.

'I can do this over and over again,' he said. 'I can strip you down, and rebuild you; again and again, until your life is nothing but pain. You will crawl on your belly, begging me to end it, but I never shall – not until you give me what I want.'

Amalia didn't respond. Bastion shook his head, and stood. He lifted a finger, and partly healed the former God-Queen. Karalyn reached forward with her knife, and picked at the corner of the mesh shield, burrowing a little hole that would allow her vision through. She felt sick with the knowledge of what she was about to do, but could see no other way to spare Amalia from unending torment.

The flesh round Amalia's face re-formed, and she gasped for air.

'I will tell you nothing,' she whispered. 'The end of the Ascendants is coming, and you will all die.'

Bastion laughed. 'Really? How amusing.'

'The Holdfasts will destroy you all.'

Bastion's laughter cut short, and for a moment, fear passed over his features. 'Which Holdfast did this to you?'

Amalia smiled. 'Which Holdfast frightens you the most?'

Bastion said nothing.

'Corthie?' said Amalia. 'Karalyn? Sable?'

Bastion choked at the mention of Sable's name. He lashed out with a boot, and kicked Amalia in the face.

'You will suffer for that, you bitch!' he cried, then raised his hand again.

Amalia screamed, then Karalyn entered her head. She tried not to think about what she was doing, then she unleashed her full powers within Amalia's mind, scouring it clean, severing every connection, so that she would remember nothing; know nothing; feel nothing. No pain, or joy, no memories of Kagan or Maxwell, or of the City. Nothing. Amalia rolled on to her back and lay still. Bastion hesitated, and lowered his hand. He peered down at the still form of Amalia, remaining motionless for a long moment, as Karalyn wept in silence within the narrow ventilation shaft.

After what felt like an eternity, Bastion straightened, his eyes filled with rage. He spat on the body of Amalia, then stamped a boot down onto her head, crushing her skull. He turned and strode from the room, slamming the door behind him.

Karalyn cut through the mesh with her knife, and crawled out into the chamber, her hands and knees becoming coated in the blood of the former God-Queen. Karalyn knelt by the body, and wept over Amalia, the tears falling down her cheeks. She had remained true to her word, to the very end. She had handed herself over to the Ascendants, knowing what the consequences could mean, but she hadn't wavered, and she hadn't broken.

'I'm sorry,' Karalyn whispered.

She closed her eyes, to avoid having to see the mess Bastion had left of the former God-Queen, but her mind was filled with the horror of what she had witnessed. If only Sable had been with her. Sable wouldn't have hesitated for a second; she would have attacked Bastion, and killed him. And now, for Amalia, it was too late.

Karalyn heard footsteps outside the chamber, and she crawled back into the ventilation shaft. She had only just managed to pull down the wire mesh guard when the door opened, and two demigods walked in. Without a word being exchanged between them, they began clearing up. Amalia's body was lifted onto a canvas stretcher, then one of the demigods started to mop the floor. Karalyn retreated down the shaft, away from the scene of death. She passed other openings, each revealing an empty chamber, some lit by lamplight, others in darkness. She crawled onwards, becoming confused and disorientated as she crossed junctions with other shafts, until, eventually, she heard Bastion's voice again.

She froze, then crept up to a mesh-guarded opening in the shaft's floor. She looked down. Below her was a vast chamber, one of the largest she had seen within the fortress-palace. Bastion was kneeling in front of two thrones. In one, sat Edmond himself, the Second Ascendant. Karalyn had never laid eyes on him before, but she had seen his image inside the minds of Corthie and Sable, and recognised his features. His skin seemed to be glowing with its own radiance, and he was easily the most beautiful man she had ever seen. She gazed at him so intently, that it took her a moment to realise who was sitting on the other throne. She gasped. It was Belinda. The Third Ascendant was dressed in fabulous robes lined with jewels and embroidered with golden thread, and a crown sat upon her brow, with four large diamonds arranged along the front. Karalyn's initial relief began to fade, as she realised that something was wrong with her old friend. Belinda was gazing out into space, her eyes empty, and her mouth slightly open.

A thin line of saliva was coming from her lips, and her arms were hanging loose by her sides.

Karalyn tore a tiny hole in the gauze mesh. She had assumed that Belinda's eyes would be protected, but they weren't, and she entered the Third Ascendant's mind. What she saw there almost made her cry out. Belinda's mind was a void. At first, Karalyn assumed that she had been scoured, but she probed deeper, and sensed that Belinda's memories were intact, and stretched back to the moment she had awakened in the Holdfast townhouse in Plateau City nine years before, but her consciousness had been severed from them. All kinds of connections inside her mind had been cut, leaving nothing but emptiness. Her eyes were working, but no information from them was reaching her inner thoughts; in fact, there were no inner thoughts whatsoever.

'I am most displeased with your performance, my son,' said Edmond, an edge of anger in his voice. 'Amalia was the only connection we had to the world of salve, and you ended her life?'

'Someone had tampered with her mind, my lord,' said Bastion, his head lowered. 'Her memories had been altered, to make her appear innocent, and then...'

'Yes?' said Edmond. 'And then?'

'And then, my lord, as I was interrogating her, her consciousness ceased to exist. There was nothing left to read, and killing her was the only option open to me.'

Edmond clenched his fists. 'You mean you tortured her mind into oblivion? You fool!'

'No, my lord. I was very careful to ensure her mind was left intact. Something else caused this; or someone else. I have ordered extra patrols, to search for a possible intruder within the palace...'

'Don't be ridiculous, Bastion,' sneered Edmond. 'There are no intruders within the Palace of the Almighty. You are merely paranoid. Again. Ever since you returned from Dragon Eyre, you have shown signs of weakness. You allowed yourself to be bested by Sable Holdfast, and she has cursed your mind. Your fear of the Holdfasts has crippled you, to the extent that you went too far with Amalia, and have ruined our best chance of discovering the location of the salve world that has been presented to us since we were on Lostwell. When Cumulus runs out of salve, and my subjects begin to clamour and complain, I shall expect you to take full responsibility for this failure.'

Bastion bowed even lower. 'Yes, my lord.'

'Send for Lord Merlon,' Edmond said. 'I wish to discuss the wedding arrangements with him.'

'Yes, my lord. Might I suggest that the plans be pared down? Holding the marriage in an open area, with the eyes of Cumulus upon us, is too much of a risk.'

'Why are you deliberately angering me this day?' Edmond cried. 'The marriage of the Second and Third Ascendants should be witnessed by all! Without the evidence of their own eyes, the other Ascendants and the ranks of Ancients will start to doubt the truth. Already, I hear rumours that Lady Belinda is not here, or that she is dead. The people must see the truth for themselves.'

'Of course, my lord. Apologies, my lord.'

'Go, and order Lord Merlon to come here immediately.'

'Yes, my lord.'

Bastion rose to his feet, keeping his head down, and retreated from the chamber. Another door opened, and an old woman walked in, bearing a silver tray, upon which was a crystal glass filled with red wine. The old woman walked forward, and Karalyn noticed that, like Belinda, her eyes were vacant. Karalyn sent her powers into the woman's mind, and recoiled in disgust. The woman had been dead for a very long time, and her body was under the control of Edmond; her mind nothing but an empty receptacle for his wishes.

The old woman approached Edmond's throne, and the Second Ascendant took the glass of wine.

He smiled at the undead woman. 'Thank you, Theodora. My, your skin is starting to get a little flaky again.' He raised his hand, and a blemish on the woman's cheek disappeared. 'There,' said Edmond; 'that's better. We must have you looking at your best.'

The old woman bowed, then walked from the chamber. Edmond

took a sip of wine, then turned to Belinda.

'Don't get jealous, my beloved. Theodora made a terrible wife, but she is a useful servant. My heart belongs to you, and no other.' He leaned over, and kissed the unresponsive Belinda on the lips.

Karalyn's anger and horror rose to an uncontrollable pitch. She tried to force her powers into Edmond's mind, but his eyes were protected by the same thin guards that Bastion had been wearing. She clenched her fists. Perhaps, if she kicked out the gauze, she could leap from the ventilation hatch, and strike Edmond down before he realised what was happening. He had a sword strapped to his side, but he probably hadn't used a physical weapon in centuries, relying instead on his wide array of powers.

She would probably die in the attempt, she realised, but her tears from Amalia's death were still fresh, and, after everything she had seen, she longed to fight back. She steeled her nerves, imagining herself whipping the sword from Edmond's scabbard, and driving it into his skull. She wanted him to suffer; she wanted him to die – and if she died too, then at least she would have taken the bastard with her.

She needed to act. If Lord Merlon arrived before she had killed Edmond, then she would be cut down in an instant. She positioned herself over the hatch, and raised her boot, her mind filled with darkness.

Someone crashed into her, pushing her away from the hatch. Karalyn almost cried out, then a firm hand went over her mouth. Karalyn turned, ready to lash out, and saw a middle-aged woman in the ventilation shaft, her eyes pleading with her. The woman put a finger to her lips, and shook her head.

'Please,' she whispered. 'Don't throw your life away, Karalyn.'

Karalyn stared at her in a stunned silence. The woman began to crawl away, her clothes a collection of tattered rags, then she turned, and gestured for Karalyn to follow her. How had the woman known her name? She hesitated for a moment, then began following the woman down the shaft, heading away from the throne room. After a few turns, they reached a large alcove, where a shaft rose vertically. Glancing up,

Karalyn caught her first glimpse of the sky in days. It was almost blocked by the many layers of gauze mesh, but it was unmistakeable. A scent of fresh air reached her nose, then she slumped to the floor of the alcove and started weeping.

'It's alright,' whispered the woman, putting an arm round Karalyn's shoulder.

'How do you know me?' Karalyn said, too distraught to use her powers.

'I recognised the absence of powers surrounding you, and knew it must be a Holdfast. It's how I used to detect where Kelsey was. I knew it wasn't her, so I took a guess that it was you, Karalyn. Now that you're here, I feel hope again, for the first time in a long while. I have been crawling through these tunnels for months, trying to work out a way to free Lady Belinda, and I had almost given up.'

'You are the intruder they're looking for?'

The woman nodded. 'I've made a few mistakes, but mostly I've been too scared to act. Have you seen what they have done to my beloved Lady Belinda?' The woman started to cry. 'Those beasts.'

'I went into Belinda's mind, but I don't understand what they've done to her.'

'It's the crown, Karalyn. It has four jagged spikes on the inner rim, where the diamonds sit, and each was hammered into her forehead. It turned her into... you saw.'

Karalyn closed her eyes. 'Can she ever recover?'

'Yes, if we remove the spikes from the crown. I will help you. I would lay down my life for Lady Belinda. Let me help you, Karalyn.'

'Amalia's dead,' she whispered. 'Bastion killed her.'

'Amalia was here; in the Palace of the Almighty?'

'She was helping me try to rescue Belinda. She gave her life rather than tell Bastion anything; it was the bravest thing I've ever seen.'

The two women embraced as they wept.

'Who are you?' whispered Karalyn.

'I'm Lady Belinda's great-granddaughter,' the woman said. 'My name is Silva.'

CHAPTER 21
FIGHTING FOR ATTENTION

Colsbury Castle, Republic of the Holdings – 30th Day, Last Third Summer 534

So far, ma'am, said Weir, we have been able to assign four squadrons of Hold Fast militia to the new force, and will be transferring them to the western borders of the Holdings within the next few days.

Daphne frowned. *Four squadrons won't be enough to secure the entire coastal road from the Holdings to Sanang. That only amounts to eight hundred troopers. We shall need at least ten squadrons.*

I know, ma'am, but it's a start. Holds Smith and Clement have pledged a further squadron each, and we have meetings arranged with some of the other Holds.

It will have to do, Daphne said. Was that everything?

Not quite, ma'am, said Weir. Some in the government have urged me to ask if you are intending to return to Holdings City to serve out the rest of your term as First Holder.

When Karalyn returns, I can shuttle between Colsbury and the Holdings capital; but, for now, I need to remain close to the Plateau.

In that case, ma'am, said Weir, some are asking if it would better if you handed in your resignation as First Holder.

What nonsense. I will serve out the remainder of my term, and you shall deputise for me in Holdings City. If I resigned, there would be early elections, and we aren't yet prepared for that. Tell whoever is making these suggestions to calm themselves; there's no need to panic. The Empress has made no moves against us, and we just need to hold out until Karalyn gets back.

Very good, ma'am.

I'll speak to you tomorrow, Weir; at the same time. Farewell.

Daphne withdrew from her deputy's mind. She watched him for a moment as he sat at his desk, rubbing his temples, then she cut the vision connection. She blinked, then yawned. It had been a late night, and the dawn light was hurting her eyes. She had drunk too much whisky, and smoked too many cigarettes, and she coughed.

'Are you feeling all right?'

Daphne glanced up, and saw Thorn standing by her office window. 'I didn't hear you come in.'

'I knocked, but you were busy using your vision powers, so I decided to wait. Do you want me to heal your hangover?'

Daphne raised an eyebrow. 'How did you know I was hungover?'

'Just a guess,' said Thorn. 'I could hear you and that... pirate man, up talking in the middle of the night. You seemed to be having a good time.'

'I was. Olo'osso makes me laugh. I know he's not the most morally upstanding of people, but I haven't laughed like that in a long while.'

'Is he going to be staying here?'

'Just for a few days, I think. Leave the hangover; I can handle it.' She raised a hand to shield her eyes from the light coming through the shutters. 'You know what day it is today, yes?'

'It's Cael and Kyra's eighth birthday.'

'And where are they? This will be their first birthday I've missed. The poor twins; I hope that, wherever they are, they're having a nice day.' She shook her head. 'I feel so helpless. Karalyn could be in trouble, and there's nothing I can do about it. Believing that Sable was with her had given me some comfort, but now we know that's not the case. Why would Sable leave her side?'

'Karalyn is headstrong,' said Thorn. 'Sable wouldn't have left her unless Karalyn had commanded it.'

'And now that Sable is back on Dragon Eyre, she might never return. Is it too much to ask that the family sticks together when we need a little support? Anyway; enough of that. Did you need me for a particular reason?'

Thorn bit her lip. 'I thought you should know that Caelius is packing his bags.'

'But why? I apologised to him yesterday for what I said.'

'He knew you were up half the night drinking with Olo'osso. I don't think he liked that.'

Daphne sighed, and got to her feet. A shooting pain reached her head, and she started to regret turning down Thorn's offer to heal her hangover. But, having done so, she wasn't about to admit that she had been wrong. Better to suffer in silence.

Daphne and Thorn left the little office, and walked down the hallways of the keep. They came to Caelius's room, and Daphne knocked on the door.

Caelius opened it. When he saw who was standing outside, his expression darkened a little.

'Good morning, Caelius,' said Daphne. She glanced over his shoulder. Lying open on his bed was a large travelling trunk, half-filled with clothes and other items.

'Good morning, ma'am,' he said.

'Are you back to calling me "ma'am"?' she said. 'Oh dear. Are you planning on leaving us?'

'I think the time is right, ma'am. I have booked passage to Plateau City. From there, I think I will take a ship to Rainsby, and start exploring this world.'

'You've booked passage? In a carriage?'

'No, ma'am. I met a merchant who is taking a cart to Plateau City, and he is willing to allow me to sit on the back.'

'A cart? I see. Well, I'm not going to beg, but I would prefer it if you stayed.'

'Why?'

Daphne blinked. 'I'm sorry?'

'Why do you want me to stay, ma'am?'

Daphne paused, unsure how to reply. 'Is this about last night?'

'Who you socialise with is none of my business, ma'am; though I would advise caution. I had a few run-ins with pirates on Dragon Eyre, and have a little experience of what they can be like.'

'We were only having a few drinks.'

'Did I suggest otherwise, ma'am? Your choice of friends is your concern. Far be it from me to cast any doubt on your judgment. Take care; that's all I ask. This man has already stolen from you once; I see no reason why he won't do so again.'

'And I see no reason why I can't be friends with both you and Olo'osso.'

'I disagree, ma'am. It pains me to be in the same building as a man like that. If I stay here, then he and I will... well, let's just say that Olo'osso and I will never be friends.'

'But you don't even know him, Caelius.'

'I'm sure he doesn't know me, but I am perfectly aware of his reputation. Don't trust him, Daphne.'

Daphne said nothing for a moment, then she smiled. 'I'll leave you to finish packing.'

Caelius nodded, his eyes betraying his hurt, then he closed the door.

'Are you going to let him leave?' said Thorn.

'Yes. If he truly liked me, then he would stay, and fight for me.'

Thorn raised an eyebrow. 'Fight? You want him to fight for you?'

'It was a figure of speech. He's running away because I spent an evening in the company of another man. If he wanted me, then he would stay, not give up.' She turned, and started walking towards the kitchen. 'I need some coffee.'

'I think he might be jealous,' said Thorn, as they strode along the corridor.

'Then he's a fool. Nothing happened between me and Olo'osso.'

'Maybe, but you were clearly having more fun with him than you've had in a long time. The whole keep could hear you laughing.'

'Is that my fault?' Daphne said.

They reached the kitchen and entered. Olo'osso was standing by the stove, a fur-lined dressing gown tied at his waist, while Pechtang was sitting at the table clutching a mug of coffee. Olo'osso had his back to the door, and his arms were raised.

'Then I gave the command to loose the ballistae,' Olo'osso was saying, 'and four yard-long bolts of steel whistled through the air. One went wide, another tore through the dragon's left wing, but the last two struck home, smiting the breast of the beast. It cried out, then fell from the air, screaming its death wail as it tumbled towards us. Its scaly carcass slammed into the ocean, just yards from the starboard flank of the *Fancy*, and a wave smashed over us, drenching everyone on deck.' He raised a finger in the air. 'And that is why I was hunted down by the dragons of Wyst. I had slain one of their own, and dragons never forgive. Were it not for Karalyn Holdfast, I would still be languishing in that filthy pit.'

'Good morning,' said Daphne.

Olo'osso turned, and grinned. 'There she is, the lady of the house! Might I say that you are looking stunning this morning? Would you like coffee? Breakfast? Take a seat, and I shall attend to your needs, my lady.'

Daphne smiled, and sat. 'Coffee would be wonderful. Thank you. And one for Thorn, too.'

'Of course, my lady,' said Olo'osso. He glanced at Thorn. 'You remind me of my daughters, Empress-elect. You are the same age, and just as beautiful. I'd wager that you'd make a fine ship's captain. Have you ever been to sea?'

'I have been on a few boats,' said Thorn; 'but always as a passenger.'

'I would soon remedy that, were you upon my world.' He placed the kettle on to the stove, and prepared two mugs. 'So, what are our plans for this day? The sun is out, and it's a beautiful morning. Let me ask – are there any seaworthy vessels able to sail upon the lake? I noticed there was a little harbour at the western end of the island – is it operational?'

'The jetty is in need of some repair,' said Daphne, 'but I have grand plans for it, now that Colsbury is coming into my possession. There used to be several small fishing boats that sailed from here, but they were damaged or sunk in the siege.'

Olo'osso beamed. 'You know, my lady, it sounds as though you shall require someone to oversee the work of rebuilding the harbour. I could take a look. If you will it, I could have the jetty up and running in no time. Why hire an outside contractor, when you have someone right here with all the required knowledge and experience?'

'Do you know much about building ships?' said Thorn.

'My dear,' said Olo'osso, 'there is little concerning that subject that I do not know. I had no formal education as a child, but first went to sea when I was only seven years old. My first ship was a fast sloop, captained by the notorious…' The kettle whistled, and Olo'osso raised a finger. 'One moment.'

He filled the coffee pot with hot water, then stirred the contents.

A quiet cough from the doorway made Daphne turn. Caelius was standing there, his expression stern, and he avoided glancing in Olo'osso's direction.

'Yes, Caelius?' said Daphne.

'I came to tell you that I have finished packing, ma'am. My transport leaves at noon, but I might walk down to the village now.'

Olo'osso squinted at Caelius. 'And who is this? He has "Banner" written all over his face, and his accent gives him away completely.'

'This is Caelius Logos,' said Daphne; 'a good friend.'

Olo'osso gazed at Caelius with disgust. 'You are friends with a Banner soldier? You are a Banner soldier, are you not, Mister Logos?'

'I was a sergeant in the Banner of the Golden Fist,' said Caelius. 'Do you have a problem with that?'

'What is a Banner soldier doing on this world?' said Olo'osso. 'I had hoped Colsbury was free of such vermin.'

Caelius took a breath, but kept his composure.

'I thought you were leaving?' said Olo'osso. 'Did you not just say that you were leaving, Banner rat? And good riddance, too, if I might say so.'

'There's no need to be rude,' said Daphne.

'On the contrary, my lady,' said Olo'osso; 'where the Banner are concerned, there is every reason to be rude. Banner forces have occupied my world for nigh on thirty years, slaughtering and enslaving my people with impunity.' He smiled. 'Well, they were, until Sable started killing them all.' He laughed. 'She massacred thousands of your colleagues, Mister Logos; tens of thousands. How does it feel, Caelius, to know that a solitary woman annihilated entire regiments of your brethren?'

'I have nothing to say to a brutal murderer,' said Caelius.

Olo'osso put a hand to his chest, as if he had been mortally wounded. 'You're calling *me* a murderer? That's rich. Why don't you tell Daphne what happened to the island of Tankbar? The Banner soldiers killed every man, woman and child who dwelled there, leaving nothing and no one alive.'

Caelius clenched his fists. 'And you and your damned daughters have massacred countless numbers of unarmed sailors and merchants. You prey upon the weak, robbing and killing; and yes, enslaving them too, or had you forgotten that detail? The Ossos are one of those Olkian families who grew wealthy from capturing and dealing in slaves.'

Olo'osso glared at Caelius. 'Don't bring my family into this. Were it not for the presence of these fine ladies, I would teach you a lesson in civility.'

'What do you know about civility, you pirate piece of shit?'

Pechtang laughed. 'Are you two going to fight each other? If so, let me get my brother first; he'll want to watch.'

'There will be no fighting here,' said Daphne.

'You are quite correct, my lady,' said Olo'osso. 'A kitchen ain't a suitable place to settle differences. However, if this vile specimen of manhood is brave enough, I would be more than happy to kick his Banner ass outside in the garden.'

Caelius shook his head. 'This is Holder Fast's island, and I will not disrespect her by sullying her home with violence.'

Olo'osso chuckled. 'Coward.'

'Are you going to stand for that, Caelius?' said Pechtang.

'Stop encouraging them.' said Thorn.

'Why?' said Pechtang. 'We all know what this is really about. They both want to be with Daphne, don't they? It's her they're quarrelling over. I say let them fight it out. Best man wins.'

'Wins what, exactly?' said Daphne. 'This has nothing to do with me.'

Pechtang rolled his eyes. 'If you say so.'

'Well, Mister Logos?' said Olo'osso. 'Do you accept my challenge, or do you intend to run away and hide?'

'I am a sergeant,' said Caelius, 'not a mister.'

'You are scared; as well you should be. Very well; scurry away, little Banner man, and darken the doors of Colsbury no longer.'

Caelius said nothing, his eyes simmering. Daphne glanced from him to Olo'osso, wondering if there was any truth in what Pechtang had suggested. She found it hard to admit, but a tiny part of her hoped there was. If two men wanted to fight over her, she should let them. What was she thinking? She chastised herself; such thoughts were unbecoming of an aristocrat of her status.

Olo'osso turned his back on Caelius, and began pouring coffee into mugs. 'How disappointing,' he said. 'I had hoped to finally meet a Banner soldier with an ounce of courage, but, alas, *Mister* Logos is evidently lacking any bravery; just like all of those Banner soldiers lying dead on Dragon Eyre.' He smiled at Pechtang. 'They have no honour.'

'I accept your challenge,' said Caelius. 'However, there are rules. No biting, or kicking a man when he is down. No...'

Caelius got no further, as Olo'osso turned and hurled the coffee pot at the soldier. Caelius flinched to avoid it, and Olo'osso punched him in the face. Caelius lost his footing, and fell to the floor, clutching his jaw as he landed on his backside.

Olo'osso laughed. 'You were saying?'

Caelius pulled himself to his feet, as the others watched. Daphne knew she should step in to stop the fight, but she wanted to see what would happen next.

Caelius raised his fists. 'Now I know that you fight dirty, you won't catch me out like that again, pirate scum. Come at me like a man.'

'There's only one man in this fight,' said Olo'osso.

The pirate lifted his own fists. He lashed out at Caelius, but the soldier dodged and blocked, then he slammed his left fist into Olo'osso's nose, and then unleashed a fierce uppercut, catching the pirate square on the chin. Olo'osso staggered back a step, then Caelius took hold of the pirate's long hair with both hands and pulled down, raising his knee at the same time. Caelius's knee struck Olo'osso's face with a loud crack, and the pirate's eyes rolled up into his head. He groaned, then collapsed to the floor, unconscious.

Caelius rubbed his knuckles, as Daphne got to her feet. She glanced down at Olo'osso, then crouched by him.

'You knocked him out,' she said.

'I did,' said Caelius.

'You might have broken his nose.'

'Good.'

'Good?' said Daphne. 'You could have seriously injured him, Caelius.'

'He should have thought about that before provoking me.' He leaned over and picked up the coffee pot from where it lay on the floor. 'I'm sure one of the Sanang healers will be kind enough to fix his nose. It's a pity they can't do anything about his insufferable arrogance.' He placed the coffee pot on to the table, next to a grinning Pechtang, who was barely suppressing his laughter. 'Now, if that is all, ma'am,' Caelius went on, 'I shall take my leave. Good day.'

Daphne remained where she was, crouching by the unconscious body of Olo'osso. She wanted to tell Caelius to stay, but the words failed her. Caelius glanced at her, then turned and strode from the kitchen.

'You're letting the winner walk away?' said Pechtang. 'Bloody women. Can't you ever make up your minds?'

'He has a point,' said Thorn. 'Olo'osso was extremely rude to

Caelius, and got what he deserved. I thought the sergeant showed admirable restraint.'

'Can you heal his face?' said Daphne.

Thorn sighed. 'And what would that teach him? Perhaps he needs to learn the consequences of his actions.'

Pechtang nodded. 'Well said. That was a low trick, throwing the coffee pot like that. If I'd been Caelius, I would have stomped on his head.'

Daphne shook her head. 'This is my fault. I should have stopped them before it came to blows.'

'Yes,' said Thorn. 'Why didn't you?'

Olo'osso groaned.

'Are you all right?' said Daphne.

The pirate opened his eyes and gazed up into Daphne's face. 'My lady,' he said, 'I have been defeated twice in two days. I must say, I preferred being beaten up by your hands. Has he gone?'

'Yes,' said Daphne.

'Praise the gods for that.' He sat up, one hand on his bloody nose. 'I'll get him next time, mark my words. That was just a warm-up.'

Pechtang laughed. 'Your mouth is quicker than your fists, old man.'

Olo'osso joined in with Pechtang's laughter. 'Yes, you're probably right. At least I didn't lose any more teeth.'

Shella walked into the kitchen. She glanced down at Daphne and Olo'osso, and raised an eyebrow.

'I'm not even going to ask about what's going on here. Daffers, two flying carriages are approaching from the south.'

'Flying carriages?' said Olo'osso. 'Pray tell me, good woman, what are flying carriages?'

'Come and see for yourself,' said Daphne. 'We'll go down to the castle forecourt and watch from there.'

Olo'osso reached out with a hand, and Daphne helped him to his feet. They made their way to the stairs, collecting T'Lang and Agang Garo along the way. Daphne considered knocking on Keir's door, but thought better of it, having no desire to intrude upon her elder son's misery. They descended the flights of stairs, while Olo'osso chatted about other fights he had lost. He seemed in no way browbeaten or deflated at having been bested by Caelius, and appeared to have found the entire thing hilarious. Caelius wouldn't be feeling the same way, Daphne knew. Despite having won, the Banner soldier was probably brooding about the fight.

They emerged into the sunlight of the large castle forecourt, and Daphne glanced up. She saw the two cylindrical flying carriages, each being borne through the sky by four winged gaien.

'They look like dragons carrying ships,' cried Olo'osso, pointing. 'How do you persuade the beasts to hoist such a burden into the air? Any dragon on my world would incinerate you for making such a suggestion.'

'They aren't dragons,' said Daphne.

'They certainly look like dragons to my eyes, my lady. Although, now you mention it, they seem a little on the small side, and they are all the same muddy-brown colour.'

'The carriages have imperial markings,' said Thorn. 'Should we try to get away before they land?'

'And go where?' said Daphne. She glanced down, and noticed Caelius standing twenty yards away. He had put his trunk on the cobbles, and was gazing up at the approaching carriages.

'Ah!' cried Olo'osso, also seeing him. 'There is my foe.'

'Don't start anything,' said Daphne. 'Remain calm and dignified, and we shall see what happens when the carriages land.'

The winged gaien circled over the forecourt. It was large enough to fit half a dozen carriages, and the gaien began to descend. The two carriages were lowered through the air, then landed with a bump on the cobbles, one by the gatehouse, and the other by the entrance to the Summer Palace. Caelius walked over to Daphne as the winged gaien were untethered. The soldier said nothing, but positioned himself to Daphne's left, while ignoring Olo'osso.

The winged gaien ascended back into the sky, and large doors on the sides of the carriages dropped open. Imperial soldiers began spilling out and forming up in the forecourt, then a young woman emerged from the carriage by the Summer Palace. She glanced around, then saw Daphne and the others standing by the gates of the Great Keep.

'Holder Fast,' she said, striding forward.

'Lady Brogan,' said Daphne. 'Good morning, and welcome back to Colsbury. What can we do for you?'

Brogan gestured for the soldiers to surround Daphne and her party.

'This gives me no pleasure, Holder Fast,' said Brogan, 'but my mother has ordered the arrest of the following people – yourself, Keir Holdfast, and Thorn Holdfast. The three of you are to return with us to Plateau City.'

Olo'osso stepped forward. 'Arrest? What is this? How dare you speak to Lady Holdfast in such a manner?'

Brogan frowned at the pirate.

'Stay out of this, Olo'osso,' said Daphne. 'Let me deal with it.'

'Where is Keir?' said Brogan.

'Let me see the warrant first,' said Daphne.

'Of course.'

Brogan gestured to a junior officer among the soldiers, who stepped forward and unfolded a document. He passed it to Daphne. She scanned the words briefly, then noticed the Empress's signature at the bottom.

'Why now?' she said.

'My mother has received word from the Matriarch of Sanang,' said Brogan, 'officially recognising Thorn as the successor to the throne. The Empress feels that you have broken the promises you made the last time you were in her presence. You are to be put on trial in the Imperial Capital, for attempting to divide the empire, and for spreading sedition.'

Daphne smiled. 'Do you agree with these charges, Brogan?'

'What I think is immaterial, Holder Fast. Unlike you, I obey the orders of my sovereign ruler. I must add that, if you decide to resist,

Daimon is ready to act. He is watching us at this very moment. Where is Keir?'

Daphne said nothing.

Brogan pointed at a squad of soldiers. 'Enter the Great Keep. Keir Holdfast's room is on the top floor, in the north-eastern corner of the building. Bring him here.'

'Yes, ma'am,' cried a sergeant.

Daphne watched as the squad ran into the keep.

'This is bullshit!' shouted Pechtang. 'Lady Thorn is the true successor to the throne, not your idiot brother! What if we don't recognise your authority here?'

'Silence,' said Brogan, 'or I will be forced to arrest you also.'

'Go fuck yourself!' Pechtang cried.

'That's the spirit, lad!' shouted Olo'osso. 'We ain't going down without a bleeding fight!'

Brogan gestured to another squad. 'Take Lady Thorn and Holder Fast into custody.'

The soldiers moved forwards, and pandemonium erupted in the castle forecourt. Pechtang and T'Lang charged into the soldiers, their fists swinging, while Olo'osso yelled encouragement. A soldier tried to grab Daphne, and Caelius punched the man in the stomach, doubling him over. Groans and cries echoed up between the high walls and towers of Colsbury.

Thorn raised her hands. 'Enough!' she cried. 'I have death powers, and if I wished to resist arrest, every soldier in this courtyard would already be dead. Pechtang, T'Lang – show me some respect, and obey my commands. There will be no more violence here today.'

'But, ma'am,' said T'Lang; 'are we surrendering?'

'We have no choice,' said Thorn. 'Daimon will destroy us if we resist.'

A noise attracted Daphne's attention, and she turned to see Keir being led out of the keep by soldiers, his hands tied behind his back.

'Mother?' he said, glancing at Daphne.

'Arrest them all,' said Brogan.

'Hey!' cried Shella. 'What have I done? I only live here. And Agang didn't do anything, either. Come on, Brogan; be reasonable.'

'Fine,' said Brogan. 'Leave Shella and Agang Garo; but arrest everyone else, and get them on board the carriages.'

'Fuck that!' shouted Pechtang. 'I'm not going.'

The young man's eyes glazed over, and he stood still, as if frozen to the ground. His fists unclenched, and his arms lowered until they were hanging loose by his sides.

T'Lang stared at his brother.

'I control Pechtang's body now,' Pechtang said, his voice sounding strange. 'I, Daimon of Domm, dream mage to the Empress, order you all to surrender, or I'll destroy Pechtang's mind. You've got five seconds.'

'Don't do it!' cried T'Lang, raising his hands in the air. 'We surrender!'

The soldiers moved through the forecourt, securing everyone bar Shella and Agang, who stood to the side, saying nothing.

Daphne glanced at Shella as her wrists were tied. 'Don't worry about us,' she said. 'Karalyn will sort everything out when she gets back.'

Pechtang laughed. 'Karalyn isn't coming back, Lady Holdfast. She's lying dead on Implacatus. I'm the only dream mage left on this world, and your wee rebellion is over.'

'You're lying,' said Daphne. 'You don't know that.'

Pechtang laughed, then he blinked and glanced around, realising that his wrists were bound. Before he could react, three soldiers bundled him across the cobbles towards a carriage. T'Lang and Olo'osso were led away after him, then Daphne and Thorn were shoved up a ramp and into the other carriage. They were pushed into adjoining seats and strapped in, then Caelius was shoved into the next seat along from Daphne.

'You should have left when you had the chance,' she said to him.

'I don't desert my friends, ma'am,' he said. 'No matter what happens in Plateau City, if you need me, I will be by your side.'

CHAPTER 22
PLAYING GOD

Riggan Archipelago – 18th Tuminch 5255

Sable and Austin walked side by side along the cliff-top path.

'This might be the best idea I've ever had,' Sable said, as she glanced down at the waves striking the windswept coast.

'Then why don't you tell me what it is?' said Austin.

'I will,' she said, 'but not yet.'

'If I know you,' said Austin, 'it will involve blood and death. I don't think I can take any more of that. I did everything you asked of me during your rampage of revenge, didn't I? Please don't tell me you need me to kill again.'

'If this plan works,' said Sable, 'no one will die. I thought it up with you in mind, because I know how you feel about violence.'

Austin looked sceptical. 'You're going to stop the Wystians invading Ulna by peaceful means?'

'Exactly.' She spread her arms out. 'What do you see?'

'Nothing,' he said; 'just barren, uninhabited islands of Rigga.'

'Do you see any dragons?'

'Of course not. No dragon has ever been here – it's out of flying range. None of them can make it to Rigga.'

Sable smiled. 'It's perfect. Even better – it'll be quick. If it works.'

'If you don't need me to kill for you, why did you bring me here?

'I need to go back to Colsbury for a while, and I thought you might like to come along.'

'Why do you need to go to Colsbury?'

'Because that's where the Sextant is. Do you want to come with me, or should I drop you off in Ulna?'

'I suppose I could come with you,' he said.

Sable shook her head at him. 'I offer to take you to a world you've never been to before, and that's the best response you can come up with? I need to make a quick detour first, though, before we go to Colsbury. I have a little errand to carry out. Be warned – it will be pouring with rain when we arrive, and we shall have to run.' She took out the Quadrant. 'Are you ready?'

Austin nodded.

Sable swiped her thumb and forefinger along the Quadrant. The air crackled around them, and they found themselves in the midst of a torrential rainstorm, the sky heavy with black clouds.

'Follow me!' Sable cried, as she set off down Princeps Row.

They ran through the rain towards the mansion housing the Banner headquarters, and ducked under the cover of the entranceway.

'We're here to see Kelsey,' Sable said to the soldiers on duty. 'I'm her aunt.'

One of the guards nodded. 'You were here a few days ago, ma'am; I recognise you.'

The soldiers moved aside, and Sable and Austin entered the mansion. One of the soldiers closed the door behind them and the sound of the storm faded into the background.

'Where are we?' Austin whispered, as they dripped rainwater from their hair and clothes.

'I'm not going to say,' Sable said. 'Come on.'

She led him through the mansion, until they came to the room where she had previously seen Kelsey give lessons to Kyra and Cael. She opened the door, and saw her niece sitting on the floor with the twins. Both children had sorrowful expressions on their faces, and Kyra was crying.

Sable strode into the middle of the room. 'Happy birthday, little dream mages!'

The twins glanced up and stared at Sable, their mouths falling open.

'Did you think I would forget?' said Sable.

Kelsey smiled, her eyes tinged with relief. 'Hey, Sable.'

Sable crouched by the two children. 'I've brought presents for you.'

'You have presents?' said Kyra. She wiped her eyes and smiled.

'Of course I do. Would I come to your birthday empty-handed?' She pulled a bag from over her shoulder, set it down onto the rug, and opened it. She dipped her hand in and withdrew two long, sharp objects, each as white as bone.

'I have one for you, Kyra, and one for you, Cael,' she said. 'Do you know what they are?'

The twins shook their heads.

'They're dragon's teeth,' said Sable, as she passed them to the twins; 'real dragon's teeth. Be careful with them, or you might cut your finger.'

The twins grinned as they each held a long tooth in their hands.

'Where did you get those?' said Austin.

'I popped over to Gyle,' said Sable. 'There are plenty of dragon bones there.' She placed her hand back into the bag, removed two books, and handed them to the children.

'These are picture books from Dragon Eyre,' she said. 'They're about the history of dragons and their riders. And, I have one more thing for you.' She reached into the bag again, and took out something wrapped in paper. She laid it on the rug, and opened the wrapping, revealing two delicate little cakes, each topped with a strawberry.

'And here are your birthday cakes,' she said. She kissed each of the twins on the forehead. 'Happy birthday from Aunty Sable.'

'Can we eat them now?' said Cael.

'Of course you can,' said Sable.

Kelsey glanced at her. 'Can I have a quick word?'

Sable stood, then walked to the far end of the room with Kelsey.

'Thanks for this,' Kelsey said. 'The twins have been sad all day. I don't suppose there's been any news of their mother?'

Sable shook her head.

'Are you staying long?'

'No,' said Sable. 'I need to be on Dragon Eyre at the moment. Unfinished business; and it's where we arranged to meet Karalyn.'

Kelsey nodded in Austin's direction. 'Who's that?'

'A friend. Austin, come and meet my niece.'

Austin walked over. He shook Kelsey's hand, then frowned. 'Um...'

'Aye, I know,' said Kelsey. 'It's like I'm not there. Are you a demigod, aye?'

'Yes. From Dragon Eyre.'

'We'd best be going,' said Sable. 'I'll come back if there's any news.'

Kelsey nodded, then Sable swiped her fingers over the Quadrant. The air crackled again, and then Sable and Austin appeared in the Sextant chamber in Colsbury.

'We went all that way to give presents to two children?' said Austin.

'Yes,' Sable said in a low voice. 'They're Karalyn's twins.'

'Oh. That was... nice of you, I guess.'

'Don't sound so surprised. Now, keep your voice down; I don't want anyone to hear us. Daphne doesn't like me using the Sextant, and I'm going to try something new that might be dangerous.'

They walked over to the huge device. The Weathervane was lodged into its flank, and it was emitting a slight hum.

'Wow,' said Austin. 'A real Sextant.'

Sable placed a finger to her lips.

'Sorry,' Austin whispered.

She placed her palm onto the device.

What is your desire, Sable?

'Show me Wyst.'

Her vision blurred over, and then, in front of her, she saw a large landmass set amid a sparkling blue ocean. She gazed down at forest-covered mountainsides and deep ravines, and her memories made her shudder.

'What are you doing?' said Austin. 'Can you see Wyst?'

'Put your hand on to the glass surface,' she said.

Austin did so. 'Alright. I can see it; it's as if I was flying over Wyst on the back of Ashfall. I don't recognise anything, though. I guess it all looks different from up here.'

'Sextant,' said Sable, 'do you know how many dragons are on the island of Wyst?'

Yes.

'Can you see them all?'

Yes.

'What are you planning?' said Austin. 'Tell me.'

'A few years ago,' Sable said, 'Belinda used the Sextant to transport tens of thousands of people – all the way from Old Alea to another world. She saved their lives from the cataclysm that destroyed Lostwell. I was wondering if I could do something similar to the dragons of Wyst.'

'You want to move them to another world?'

'Nothing quite so dramatic. Rigga should do.'

'You're going to dump them all on Rigga?'

'Precisely. That way, they'll never invade Ulna, because none of them will ever be able to leave Rigga. They'll be trapped. Alive, but trapped. There's a nice symmetry to it, because that's what they did to me when they placed me into that pit.'

'Uh, Sable – you do realise that an estimated fifty thousand human inhabitants of Dragon Eyre live on Rigga?'

Sable frowned. 'That many?'

'I think so. They have a reputation for being a little backward, technologically speaking, but none of them will have laid eyes on a dragon in their lives. Won't the Wystians slaughter them? The natives don't have any catapults or ballistae; they wouldn't stand a chance against seven thousand angry and disorientated dragons.'

'This is why I brought you along, Austin – to prevent me from making these sorts of mistakes. Alright. I'll transport the natives of

Rigga to Wyst, as soon as I've moved the dragons to Rigga. We'll swap the entire populations around. If, that is, the Sextant allows me to do it.'

'Wait,' he said. 'People are still likely to die. You can't rip that many humans and dragons from their homes, and expect everyone to settle down and get on with their lives without a massive amount of disruption.'

'It's either this, or we start placing explosive devices deep within the caverns where the Wystians live. I checked the supply of pisspots on Haurn – we have enough to obliterate dozens of caverns. We could entomb hundreds, maybe even thousands of dragons. Would that be better?'

Austin's face paled. 'No.'

'Do you have any other suggestions? Any way we could prevent hundreds of Wystians from attacking Enna and Ulna? It's not a rhetorical question. I'm open to new ideas.'

'Maybe you could just remove the Wystian leadership – you know, their top one hundred dragons. We could hold them as hostages on Rigga, and demand that the others call off the invasion of Ulna.'

Sable frowned. 'I don't know how to identify which dragons are in positions of authority, and if I did, wouldn't those hundred dragons still attack the Riggans? No. It's all or nothing. My way would solve the problem permanently.'

'Could Rigga support seven thousand dragons? Is there enough food and fresh water?'

'There must be, if fifty thousand humans live there.'

Austin sighed. 'You're right – I can't think of a better suggestion. But that doesn't mean I think it's a good idea.'

'The Sextant might not allow me to do it. There is much about the device that I still don't understand.'

'Ask it.'

Sable nodded. 'Sextant, show me Rigga.'

Her vision raced away to the south-west, covering the hundreds of miles in seconds, then she saw the archipelago. Rigga consisted of one large island, and several smaller ones that clustered to the north and west. Unlike Wyst, Rigga was flat and almost completely without trees. The few that existed had trunks that had bent in the wind that scoured the archipelago. It was a barren, uninviting landscape. The human settlements all clung to the coastline of the largest island, where streams and rivers reached the ocean. Their houses were constructed from clay blocks, and were thatched with straw, and there were no roads worthy of the name. Sable caught sight of an abandoned Sea Banner base on the south coast. It had been looted by the native Riggans, and much of the harbour was lying in ruins. Of the garrison that had occupied the island, there was no sign.

'Sextant, can you see every human on Rigga?'

Yes.

'How many are there?'

Forty-eight thousand, two hundred and seventy-three.

'Sextant, if I requested it, could you transfer every dragon from Wyst to Rigga, and every human from Rigga to Wyst?'

Yes.

'Would they still be alive? Would the transfer hurt or injure them?'

The transfer will not compromise their physical integrity.

Sable took a breath. 'Then proceed.'

Nothing seemed to happen for a moment, then, in a flash of crackling and rumbling skies, thousands of dragons appeared in the air above Rigga. Many plummeted downwards, like hail falling in a storm, as lightning ripped across the sky. A few dragons crashed into the ground, but most were able to extend their wings and pull up in time. Everywhere Sable looked, confused and bewildered dragons were crying out, as terror surged through them. Old dragons, young dragons, male, female; they were everywhere, clustering in groups, or flying alone. Some were panicking, unleashing flames at their barren surroundings, while others were staring into space, shaking with fear.

'Holy shit,' gasped Austin.

'Sextant,' said Sable, 'show me Wyst.'

Her vision raced back across the vastness of the empty ocean, then slowed as it approached the landmass of Wyst. At first, it seemed unchanged, the forested mountains appearing the same as they had done when Sable and Austin had looked down upon them earlier; but moving in closer, Sable could see people on the ground. Humans dressed in primitive rags and animal hides were mirroring the reactions of the dragons who had been moved to Rigga. Some were already dead, having slipped down the sides of steep ravines; and there were bodies floating in some of the rivers that flowed down the valleys. Most, however, seemed to be in a daze, staring at their new surroundings.

'Sextant, how many humans are living on Wyst?'

Forty-seven thousand, six hundred and twelve.

Sable lowered her gaze. She had just killed hundreds of innocent Riggans, and altered the lives of the survivors beyond recognition.

'How many dragons remain on Geist, and on the islands between Wyst and Geist?'

Five hundred and ninety-two.

Sable lifted her hand from the Sextant, and her vision cleared.

'We've done it,' she said to Austin. 'Ulna is safe.'

Sable and Austin strode into the main reception hall within the bridge palace in Udall. Blackrose was surrounded by her dragon and human advisors, and they turned at Sable's approach.

'Where have you been, Holdfast?' said Blackrose, her tone angry. 'We have urgent issues to discuss. My uncle is urging a complete evacuation of Enna and Ulna, and suggests that we move everyone south to Throscala.'

'It is the only way, my Queen,' said Greysteel. 'If we do not evacuate, the Wystians shall annihilate us.'

Sable put a hand on her hip. 'We don't need to worry about any invasion. I've fixed our little problem.'

The dragons fell into silence.

'What are you talking about?' said Maddie. 'What have you done, Sable?'

'As it was I who caused this situation,' Sable said, 'I felt I should be the one to resolve it. And resolve it, I have.'

'How?' said Blackrose, her red eyes glowing. 'Have you slaughtered untold numbers of dragons?'

'No. A few died, but only a tiny proportion of the total number.'

Blackrose stared at her. 'I sense you are milking this for all it is worth. Cease prevaricating and reveal to us what you have done.'

Sable smiled. 'I sent every dragon on Wyst to Rigga, and every human on Rigga to Wyst.'

'Impossible!' cried Greysteel.

'Not if you have a Sextant,' said Sable.

Maddie gasped. 'You mean, you did what Belinda did? Just like she sent the folk in Alea Tanton to another world?'

'I'm glad someone has been paying attention,' said Sable. 'Yes, Maddie, that is exactly what I did. Seven thousand Wystian dragons are now stranded on the Riggan archipelago. I didn't get them all – there are still around six hundred on Geist, and on the little islands between Geist and Wyst; but I don't imagine that they'll be bothering Ulna any time soon.'

Blackrose glanced at Shadowblaze. 'Send messengers and scouts to Enna, at once.'

Shadowblaze tilted his head. 'Yes, my beloved. Ahi'edo, come with me; we shall personally inspect the situation for ourselves.'

'Report back as soon as possible,' said Blackrose.

'I shall, my beloved.'

Shadowblaze strode from the hall, with Ahi'edo running alongside him.

Blackrose turned back to Sable. 'Did you bring the Sextant to Dragon Eyre, Holdfast?'

'No. I went back to my home world, and did it all from there. I felt a little bit like a god, I must admit. The power of the Sextant is staggering. Karalyn has been lacking in curiosity and ambition, but I mean to rectify that. Just think of what else I could do – I could help my sister by removing every Banner soldier from Dragon Eyre.'

'Or you could help free Karalyn from Cumulus,' said Cardova, striding forwards.

Sable shook her head. 'No, I couldn't. Just as Edmond's palace is inaccessible to Quadrants, the Sextant wouldn't be able to see Karalyn; not if she's in there. Edmond's had thousands of years to think these things through, Lucius.'

Cardova smiled. 'I'm sure you could think of a way, if you tried hard enough.'

'I'm flattered that you believe me so powerful,' said Sable. 'Do you remember that I advised an all-out assault on Cumulus? The Sextant would make that easier, but Karalyn over-ruled me.'

'That sounds like an excuse to do nothing.'

Sable shook her head. 'Do you think I don't care about my niece, Lucius? Do you believe that I don't share the worry you feel for her safety? If I could rescue her, I would; but I'm not going to get us all killed on a suicide mission. I know it's hard, but we have to trust Karalyn.'

'Don't pretend that you care, Sable,' said Cardova. 'I know you've forgotten this, but it's Karalyn's children's birthday today, and here you are, swaggering around like a god, boasting about the Sextant. Karalyn promised us she would back for the twins' birthday.'

'I know.'

'You make me sick.'

Sable shrugged.

'That's enough,' said Blackrose. 'Sable, I'm not sure what to say to you. You have saved Ulna, and Enna, but at what cost?'

'At no cost to the Ulnans,' said Sable. 'The fifty thousand Riggans on Wyst may take some time to settle down, though. I would advise sending a delegation to speak to them, to tell them what has happened, and to offer assistance.'

'And the Wystians are on Rigga?' said Greysteel. 'I find this hard to take in. Seven thousand dragons, cut off from the Western and Eastern Rims; stranded in the middle of the ocean? Do they understand where they are? Might not some of them attempt to flee, without knowing that they are on Rigga?'

'Any that did so would fall exhausted into the ocean,' said Blackrose. 'Not even I could make that journey, and I am among the strongest on Dragon Eyre. The Wystians will realise where they are soon enough, and then their weeping shall commence.'

'Better them than us,' said Sable.

'I wasn't criticising your actions, Sable,' said Blackrose. 'I am in awe of what you and the Sextant have achieved. In an instant, the threat hanging over my realm has vanished into smoke; and the mightiest force on Dragon Eyre is now helpless and isolated. For generations to come, this moment shall be remembered. We owe you our gratitude, Sable. Thank you.'

'You're welcome,' said Sable. 'I think I might go down to the harbour to tell the Five Sisters the news. They should know that Wyst is once again safe for them to collect fresh water.' She smiled. 'But I guess they'll need to avoid Rigga from now on.' She glanced at Austin. 'Are you coming?'

'No, thanks,' the demigod said. 'I think I'll stay here for a while. I've been promising my aunt and mother that Ashfall will take them for a flight over Ulna, but the situation seemed too dangerous to take the risk.'

'It should be safe enough now, my rider,' said Ashfall.

'I'll come with you to the harbour,' said Maddie.

Sable raised an eyebrow. 'Any excuse to see Topaz.'

Maddie smiled. 'Yeah. So?'

'I'll come, too,' said Cardova.

'Really?' said Sable. 'I thought you loathed all pirates?'

'I do,' he said, 'but I want to talk to you while we walk.'

Sable took out the Quadrant. 'Who said anything about walking?'

She brushed her thumb over the surface of the device, then she, Cardova and Maddie appeared on the main deck of the *Giddy Gull*. The sailors and workers were so used to her coming and going that no one seemed startled by their sudden arrival. A few raised their eyebrows at the sight of Cardova, but others smiled and nodded towards Sable and Maddie.

Sable led them up onto the quarter deck. Work was continuing on the half-built cabins to the rear of the deck, but there was no sign of Lara. Sable glanced at the carpenters, looking for anyone she recognised.

'Hey, Ryan,' she said.

One of the carpenters turned from where he was measuring out some wood. He glanced up, a cigarette hanging from his lips, and grinned.

'Well, hello there, Miss Sable,' he said, standing and wiping his hands with a rag. 'What can I do for you?'

'I'm looking for Captain Lara.'

'She's on the *Flight of Fancy*, ma'am,' he said. 'Captain Ann's holding a meeting.'

Sable eyed him. 'You look like someone who struggles to keep a secret. I want you to spread the news about what I have done this day. Tell every sailor you meet. Can you do that for me?'

'For you, Miss Sable, anything.'

She smiled. 'The dragons of Wyst have departed the Eastern Rim. I sent them all to Rigga, and moved the humans from Rigga to Wyst. That should open up the northern passage back to the Western Rim.'

Ryan narrowed his eyes. 'Uh...'

'I can tell you don't believe me, Ryan. That's fine. Blackrose has sent scouts to confirm it. When they return, the entire town will hear the news. You're my favourite carpenter's mate, and I just wanted to do you a little favour. If you tell everyone before the scouts get back, people will probably laugh at you. And then, when they all learn the truth, your stock will rise immeasurably.'

'But... but how could that be possible? How could any man... or woman, persuade thousands of dragons to leave Wyst? And how could they travel to Rigga? It's beyond the range of any dragon.'

'I have my ways, Ryan,' said Sable. 'If I could kill an Ascendant, then transferring populations around the world should be easy, and it was. For me. I wouldn't recommend trying it yourself. You got a cigarette?'

'Eh, sure, Miss Sable.'

Ryan dug into a pocket, and extracted a crushed pack of cigarettes. He extracted one, lit it, and gave it to Sable.

'Thanks, Ryan. Remember to tell everyone you see.'

Cardova shook his head as he, Maddie and Sable walked back down the main deck of the *Gull*.

'Something wrong?' said Sable.

'I don't think I've ever met anyone as cocky and arrogant as you,' said Cardova. 'It's a wonder your head doesn't explode.'

'I'm just cultivating my legend,' said Sable.

Maddie laughed.

Sable stopped at the top of the gangway, and frowned. The last time she had walked along the quayside, she had been abducted by Unk Tannic agents working for a dragon.

'What's wrong?' said Maddie.

'I don't feel like walking today,' said Sable, her eyes scanning the crowds on the long quayside. 'While I was in the pit, was anything done about the Unk Tannic here in Udall?'

'Lord Greysteel held an investigation, and over twenty Unk Tannic agents were arrested and executed,' said Maddie. 'It was pretty gruesome; their heads were mounted on posts for a couple of months, until the gulls and crows had pecked them clean. The dragons used the truth spell on them, so at least I can be sure that they were all guilty.'

'All the same,' said Sable, as she grasped the Quadrant; 'I'm not taking any chances.'

She brushed her thumb over it, and they appeared on the quarter deck of the *Flight of Fancy*. Lara, Tilly and Topaz were there, sitting out on deck with Ann and Dina.

Sable smiled at them. 'Break out the gin,' she said. 'I have some good news.'

CHAPTER 23
MAKING AN ENTRANCE

Tara, Auldan, The City – 22nd Namen 3423

'Ow!' Naxor cried, clutching his leg.

'Cael,' said Kelsey, 'stop stabbing Naxor with your dragon tooth or I'll take it off you.'

Naxor feigned a smile as the twins ran down the hallway shrieking. 'Such charming little children,' he said. 'Delightful.'

'How did they get their hands on dragon teeth?' said Quill.

'Sable gave them one each as a birthday present,' said Kelsey.

Naxor rolled his eyes. 'Sable, eh? I might have known. That woman was always trouble.'

'At least she turned up for the twins' birthday two days ago.'

'I would have come along, too,' said Naxor, 'but I was still locked up in the dungeons two days ago. I am most terribly sorry to have missed Sable's visit.'

'Aye,' said Kelsey, 'I'm sure you are.'

A courtier opened the door. 'Their Majesties shall see you now.'

Naxor, Kelsey and Quill entered the royal audience chamber, where Emily and Daniel were sitting. Van and Lady Aurelian were standing close by, while Kelsey noticed that there were more soldiers than usual, presumably to guard against Naxor.

Quill bowed. 'I have fetched Lord Naxor from Port Sanders, your Majesties; as requested.'

The King and Queen frowned at Naxor, who performed a low bow.

'Your ever-gracious Majesties,' Naxor said; 'thank you for securing my release. I have spent a most wonderful day and night at Tonetti Palace with my sisters, savouring the fresh taste of freedom, along with some rather superb Taran brandy. I worked through the night, mastering the fine details of the upcoming trade negotiations, and feel that I am ready to begin. I have some immediate suggestions that I would like to lay before you. May I proceed?'

Daniel glanced at Quill. 'Has he sworn the oath of allegiance?'

'Yes, your Majesty. He recited the vow at dawn yesterday, prior to his release. I then escorted Lord Naxor to Sanders territory, as instructed.'

Naxor smiled. 'I can take the oath again, if you like.'

'That won't be necessary,' said Daniel. 'You have broken oaths in the past, regardless of how many times your lips have formed the words. Tell me – why should we trust you?'

'Because anything is preferable to sitting in a filthy dungeon for the next hundred years, your Majesty. I realise that I am on probation, as it were, and that any bad behaviour on my part would see me locked up again. It is in my interests to be trustworthy. Now, about those suggestions that I mentioned. If I am to lead the trade delegation, then I would need to make a few personnel changes. Kelsey shall remain part of the team, as she is required to nullify the powers of any so-called mages that may be present upon the Star Continent. As much as I would prefer her to stay here, it seems that I am stuck with her. Commander Quill, however, is out.'

'What?' said Quill.

'You may be a fine soldier, Commander,' said Naxor, 'but a nego-tiator you are not. The same goes for Major-General Logos. Your Majesties, what possessed you to send two soldiers to do the work of diplomats? I suggest that we enlist a fine lawyer to accompany myself and Kelsey; and, in fact, I have already found one. He is a Roser, with a wealth of experience, and one that I believe you all know.' He gestured to a courtier by a side door. 'Please allow Lady Aurelian's lawyer to enter.'

The courtier opened the door, and a man walked in, clutching a thick folder of documents.

'Nadhew?' said Lady Aurelian. 'Whatever are you doing, working for Lord Naxor?'

The lawyer bowed. 'Your Majesties, my lords and ladies – I was approached by Lord Naxor yesterday morning, and asked if I wished to be a part of his negotiating team. For the good of the City, I agreed.'

'I'm happy to see you, old friend,' said Daniel. 'You, I trust. Lord Naxor, is your revised team now complete?'

'Almost, your Majesty. I have one other suggestion. In my experience, a grand entrance is worth a thousand words, and so I request that Frostback also join us. If we wish to impress the citizenry of the Star Continent, we could do far worse than bringing a dragon along.'

'Agreed,' said Emily. 'If Frostback is happy to go, then you are free to take her along.'

'Excellent,' said Naxor. 'If that is all, then I think we are almost ready to depart.'

'I have a wee suggestion of my own,' said Kelsey; 'one that should allay everyone's worries about Naxor's trustworthiness, or lack thereof.'

Naxor frowned as she walked to the door. She opened it.

'Twins!' she yelled. 'Get in here.'

'Are they going to jab at me with their dragon teeth again?' said Naxor.

Kelsey smirked. 'You'll see.'

Kyra and Cael came running into the room, each wielding a long, sharp tooth.

Kelsey crouched by them. 'I need you to do something for me,' she said. 'I know that you've already read Naxor's mind, but I want you to go back into his head, just for a moment.'

'Why?' said Kyra.

'Because Naxor has been a bad god,' said Kelsey. 'Go into his head, and make him feel pain if he tries to do anything bad, or cruel, or wicked; or if he tries to tell lies.'

Naxor's features paled. 'But... but...'

'Shut up, Naxor,' said Kelsey. 'Will you do it, twins?'

'How much pain?' said Kyra.

Kelsey put on a serious face. 'A lot.'

'Alright,' said the girl. She raised a finger at Naxor. 'I've done it.'

'Me too,' said Cael. 'He won't be bad again.'

'Thanks,' said Kelsey.

Naxor raised an eyebrow. 'I didn't feel anything.'

'Try to do something bad,' Kelsey said.

Naxor laughed. 'Define bad.'

'I don't know,' said Kelsey. 'Try to punch Quill.'

'What?' said Quill. 'Forget it.'

'Alright,' said Kelsey, standing. 'Naxor, try to punch me.'

'I think I might enjoy this,' said Naxor, clenching his fists and walking towards Kelsey. 'Remember,' he said, 'you ordered me to do this, so don't blame me afterwards.'

He raised his right fist, drew it back, then howled in pain. He clutched the sides of his head and fell to his knees, then rolled onto the floor, shrieking and weeping. He quietened after a few seconds, and gasped for air.

'Well,' said Daniel, 'that was quite something to witness.'

'I agree,' said Lady Aurelian, a faint smile on her lips, 'though perhaps another demonstration is in order, just to be on the safe side. Lord Naxor, try it again.'

Naxor sat up on the floor. 'I'll pass, if it's all the same to you, my lady.' He narrowed his eyes at the twins. 'As I stated earlier, what a pair of delightful children.'

Cael raised a finger in his direction, and Naxor flinched, making the twins laugh.

'Alright,' said Kelsey, 'now I'm ready to go.'

'Please approach,' said Emily.

Naxor eased himself to his feet, then he, Kelsey and Nadhew walked up to the King and Queen, and bowed.

Emily reached into the folds of her robes, and produced a slim, glass vial, filled with a silvery liquid.

'Lady Jade refined this salve for us some time ago,' the Queen said. 'It is to be given as a sample to the Empress of the Star Continent, as a sign of our goodwill.' She passed it to Nadhew.

The lawyer bowed again. 'Thank you, your Majesty.'

'We shall order Lady Jade to begin refining at a larger scale,' said Daniel, 'if the negotiations are successful. Kelsey, I imagine that you will now need to speak to your dragon, to see if she is willing to accompany you to the Empress's city?'

'Aye,' said Kelsey. 'It should be fine. Frostback has been hoping to get invited back to the Star Continent. I'll nip over the Straits to give her the good news, then I'll come back to collect Naxor and Nadhew. We'll leave from Jezra.'

'I also have a little stop I need to make before we go,' said Naxor. 'Shall we meet back here in an hour?'

Kelsey nodded. 'Alright. See you all in an hour.'

A little over an hour later, Kelsey, Naxor and Nadhew were sheltering from the rains of Sweetmist inside the dragons' cavern in the cliffside next to the town of Jezra. Naxor and Kelsey were examining the Quadrant, though Kelsey was making sure it never left her hands.

'And so,' Naxor was saying, 'if you adjust your finger just here, you can vary the target destination when travelling to a different world. I had to do that many times when I went to Lostwell – I couldn't risk forever arriving in the same place; I would have been caught.'

Kelsey nodded. 'Right.' She placed a finger over an engraving. 'So, to get to Plateau City, which is about two hundred miles south of Colsbury, I would move my finger here?'

'Indeed. You are a quick learner, Kelsey. Now, ideally, we should arrive within sight of the city, so that the citizens can see us. I want to cause a stir, and I want the inhabitants of the city to feel a little awe, if possible.'

'Alright. I have an idea about that.'

'Are we ready?' said Frostback.

'Aye. I think so.'

'Then climb up onto my shoulders.'

Kelsey clambered up the leather straps of the harness, then leaned over and helped Nadhew ascend. The lawyer had a satchel filled with documents over his shoulder, but he seemed wary of the dragon, and kept glancing down. Naxor ascended last, and all three buckled themselves into the harness.

'Get ready to fly,' said Kelsey. 'I'm going to make us arrive a few hundred feet up in the air.'

'Understood, my rider. I shall unfurl my wings as soon as we reach your world.'

Kelsey swiped her fingers over the Quadrant. The air crackled, then Frostback appeared amid a cloudy sky. Below them was a vast body of water, while to their left, the sea walls of Plateau City could be seen. Frostback fell through the air, as her three passengers clung on, then her mighty wings were extended, and she soared upwards again.

'Well done, Kelsey,' Naxor said. 'This seems to be the perfect location.'

'Look at the sky!' said Nadhew, his eyes wide.

'Try not to seem over-awed by that sort of thing when we land,' said Naxor. 'To the inhabitants of this world, the fact that the sun traverses the sky each day is mundane, and nothing to get excited about. Your role today is to be an imperturbable lawyer; not someone who is easily impressed.'

Nadhew nodded. 'Understood, my lord.'

'Frostback,' Naxor went on, 'I would be most obliged if you would swoop and soar over the city walls a few times. Make a show of it, if you will.'

Kelsey suppressed a smile. Despite her feelings about Naxor, he had managed their entrance far better than the delegates had on their previous visit. Frostback soared over the Inner Sea, and crossed the city walls next to the high university spires. Everywhere, people were craning their necks to stare at the silver dragon. Traffic along the busy city streets ground to a halt so the citizens could watch her wheel and dive above them.

'I could burn this city with ease,' Frostback cried. 'Where are their ballistae? Where are their catapults?'

'The city's ballistae are gathering dust in the basement of the Great Fortress,' said Kelsey. 'The Empress has no need of them – this world is at peace.'

Frostback soared low over the southern suburbs, skimming the rooftops of the tenements in the Kellach Quarter, then she circled back and swooped over the ships in the large harbour.

'Look at the people running around,' Frostback laughed. 'Should I demonstrate my ability to breathe fire?'

'I don't think that's a good idea,' said Kelsey. 'We're to impress them, not terrify them.'

Naxor smiled. 'We need to find somewhere suitable to land. Where would you suggest, Kelsey? How about that park, down by the river?'

Kelsey pointed towards the centre of the city. 'We should go there. That large building with the garden on its roof. That's the Great Fortress. The top floors contain the Empress's palace.'

'An excellent choice,' said Naxor. 'Frostback – did you hear that? Make for the roof of the largest building in the city.'

'I heard my rider's words,' said the silver dragon, as she banked towards the Great Fortress.

'Please allow me to do the talking when we land,' said Naxor. 'You each have a role to play. Lord Nadhew shall be the silent, immovable lawyer; Frostback is the means to awe the people of this city; and you, Kelsey... well, just be yourself.'

'Remember that we can't trick them,' said Kelsey. 'Daimon might have already read your mind, Naxor.'

'My dear Kelsey,' said the demigod, 'do you take me for an amateur?

Daimon might have already read Nadhew's mind, but he won't be able to penetrate mine. What do you think I was doing while you were speaking to Frostback in Jezra? Shielding my mind is the last pair of eye-guards that exist in the City. I hid them in my old rooms under the Royal Academy in Ooste many years ago; not even Lady Mona knew they were there. Nadhew knows everything that I wish Daimon to know. I, however, shall be unreadable. The eye-guards also mean that I will not be able to enter the minds of anyone else, but, with you here, that seems a little immaterial.'

Frostback reached the Great Fortress, and circled over the roof. A few soldiers had gathered there to stare at the dragon, and they scattered as Frostback began her descent. She lowered herself, and alighted onto a large patch of grass, bordered by neat hedgerows and flower beds.

'Do not be alarmed!' Naxor cried to the soldiers. 'We come in peace. Please inform your superiors that the delegation from the City of Salve has arrived.'

Some of the soldiers were aiming their crossbows at the dragon, but a sergeant turned, and ordered one of their number to report what had happened to the imperial court. Kelsey unbuckled the straps holding her to the harness, and clambered down, her boots sinking into the soft turf. The sergeant recognised her, and signalled to the soldiers to lower their bows.

Nadhew and Naxor joined Kelsey on the grass, as Frostback gazed around at the city.

'Greetings, Miss Holdfast,' said the sergeant, striding forwards. 'I have sent word to the Empress that you have arrived. I'd be obliged if you waited here, until someone from below comes up to welcome you.'

'That would be satisfactory, my good man,' said Naxor. 'My, what a marvellous-looking city. It's a little smaller than I had expected, but few cities can compare with the City of Salve.' He smiled. 'I see that your attention is on the magnificent dragon that carried us here. Isn't she beautiful?'

A small group emerged from the stairs in a corner turret.

'That's Lord Bryce,' Kelsey said, nodding at the group.

Naxor nodded. He waited until the group had walked closer, then he gave a flamboyant bow.

'Lord Bryce!' he cried. 'My greetings to you; and my sincere congratulations. We are honoured that the successor to the throne of the Empire has risen to welcome our humble party.'

Bryce halted on the edge of the grass, his eyes narrow as he gazed at the dragon.

'I am Lord Naxor, chief delegate of the trade mission,' said the demigod, 'sent by their illustrious Majesties King Daniel and Queen Emily of the City of Salve. Might we be permitted to go below, and greet her Imperial Majesty, the renowned Empress Bridget, Holder of this world?'

Bryce frowned, as if he had been caught off-balance. 'Welcome to Plateau City, Lord Naxor. Kelsey, I already know. Who is the other member of your party?'

Naxor smiled. 'Which one, my lord? The dragon is named Frostback, one of the protectors of the City of Salve, a most noble and fine example of her kind. And this is Lord Nadhew, a man with an encyclopaedic knowledge of the laws of our City. He is here to handle the details of the business we hope to accomplish this day.'

'Where are the two soldiers who were here last time?'

'Why would I bring soldiers to a trade negotiation, my lord?' said Naxor, looking puzzled.

Bryce blinked, then chewed his lip. He gestured to the imperial soldiers on the roof. 'Clear a path for the delegates. I assume that the... dragon shall remain here on the roof while we talk?'

'I intend to savour the air while you humans discuss matters,' said Frostback, startling Bryce and the soldiers with her words. 'I may fly a little, to feel the wind on my wings.'

'Come back when we return to the roof,' said Kelsey.

'As you wish, my rider,' said Frostback. She extended her wings, ascended into the air, then soared away in the direction of the Inner Sea.

Naxor smiled, then strode forwards, the soldiers moving aside to let him pass, as Kelsey and Nadhew followed.

'What a fascinating arrangement,' said Naxor, as he reached Bryce's side. 'A palace within a fortress? How did this come about?'

'This is the third palace the city has seen,' said Bryce, as they began to walk towards the stair turret. 'The first was destroyed by warfare many years ago, and the second was deemed unsuitable.'

'Unsuitable, my lord? How?'

'It wasn't thought to be secure enough. It was a time of conflict.'

'I see. How interesting.'

They descended the stairs, and entered the hallways of the palace. Courtiers bowed as they passed, and Bryce led them into an audience chamber. Seated upon the solitary throne was Bridget, looking tired and displeased.

'Lord Naxor,' Bryce said; 'this is my mother, the Empress of the world.'

The three delegates bowed low in front of the throne. Standing next to Bridget were Daimon and Tabor. The young dream mage was frowning at Naxor, his eyes tight.

'Greetings, your Imperial Majesty,' said Naxor in a loud clear voice. 'The King and Queen of our world send their salutations to the ruler of this world. May we prosper together, in peace and harmony.'

Bridget raised an eyebrow. 'That was quite the entrance. Half the city is running around like frightened kittens, thanks to your flying beast.'

Naxor looked a little put out. Kelsey knew he was acting, but he was good.

'One does not refer to dragons as "beasts", my noble and illustrious Empress,' he said. 'However, I am sure that you did not mean to cause offence.'

'I'll call her whatever I please,' said Bridget.

Naxor bowed. 'In that case, we shall withdraw from your presence immediately. We did not come here to be insulted, your Majesty. Kelsey, Nadhew, let us return to the roof. Our business here is over.'

Naxor turned, then Bryce stepped forwards.

'Wait,' he said. 'This is a simple misunderstanding, Lord Naxor. My mother has never seen a dragon before, and they bear some similarity to a species upon this world known as winged gaien.'

Naxor smiled graciously. 'I would settle for a simple retraction, my lord. Not for my sake, you understand, but for Frostback, who would be mortally offended were she to know that she has been insulted.'

Bryce glared at his mother, who muttered something under her breath.

'Fine,' said the Empress. 'I misspoke. Have you brought the salve?'

'Indeed, we have, your Majesty,' said Naxor. 'Lord Nadhew, please bring out the vial.'

The lawyer shifted his folder of documents to his left arm, and withdrew the vial of salve from a pocket. He held it up for the court to see.

'What was once a block of raw salve as large as the throne you are sitting upon, your Majesty,' said Naxor, 'has, by our arts, been reduced to what you see before you. One tiny sip from that vial is enough to heal the most grievous wounds. In olden times, it was jealously guarded by the immortals who once ruled the City of Salve, but now its many benefits are shared by the mortal citizens; to such an extent that hospitals and physicians are barely required these days.'

Bryce stared at the vial. 'How much salve does your world contain?'

'Untold amounts, my lord,' said Naxor. 'Presently, we are mining the raw substance from a location that is both secret, and guarded by a dragon and a demigod with death powers, such is its value. On Lostwell, one ton of refined salve was enough to buy and sell an entire city, and the great wealth of my world is based upon its worth. Gods have fought wars over it, so much do they desire its properties. And yet, the august rulers of the City of Salve have chosen this world with which to trade. It will revolutionise the Empire, bringing comfort and healing to all those who suffer. Nadhew, please give the vial to Lord Bryce. This small sample is a gift, from our world to yours.'

Nadhew frowned, then passed the vial into Bryce's hands.

'We should test it,' said Bridget.

'On whom, mother?' said her son.

'Might I suggest something?' said Daimon.

Every eye turned to the dream mage.

'Aye?' said Bridget. 'Speak your mind, Daimon.'

'It breaks my heart, your Majesty,' said the dream mage, 'to see the way you suffer. You're in great pain, even though you sometimes deny it.'

Bridget scowled at him. 'That is none of your business, Daimon; and it's certainly not the business of the delegates. My health is no one's concern, but mine.'

Daimon lowered his glance. 'Apologies, your Majesty. It's just, well, you've always refused to be healed by mage powers. I thought that might be because you didn't want to become beholden to anyone. Like Thorn, for example. I can understand why you didn't want her to heal you. But, if this salve works like Naxor says it does, then you could be healed without feeling obliged to anyone.'

'He's got a point, mother,' said Bryce. 'It pains me, too, that you can barely walk these days. Let me try some first, to check it's safe.'

'There is no need,' said Naxor. 'Lord Nadhew will be happy to demonstrate its properties. Hold out your arm, my lord.'

The lawyer's eyes widened, then he did as Naxor had asked. The demigod removed a small knife from his belt, then he approached Nadhew, as everyone watched. Naxor slashed his hand down, and the blade sliced through the flesh on Nadhew's lower arm. The lawyer grunted, but didn't cry out, as blood trickled from the wound.

'Now, observe,' said Naxor. He reached out with a hand, and Bryce passed him the vial. Naxor removed the stopper, and held the vial up to Nadhew's lips. The lawyer took a tiny sip, then grimaced. The wound on his arm closed up within seconds, and Tabor gasped. Naxor wiped the blood from Nadhew's arm, revealing smooth skin.

Naxor plugged the stopper back into the vial, then basked for a moment in the stares of wonder the demonstration had provoked. He passed the vial back to Bryce.

'Take some, mother, I implore you,' said Bryce. 'Don't you want to feel healthy and whole again?'

Bridget said nothing for a moment, then she glanced at Naxor.

'Will it restore the sight to my wounded eye?'

Naxor frowned. 'How long ago was it injured, your Majesty? In order to be effective, the salve must work on damaged flesh. Sometimes, if a wound is very old, the body no longer deems itself to be injured.'

Bridget smiled. 'There's always a catch, isn't there? My eye was struck out some ten years ago.'

'Does it still hurt, your Majesty?'

Bridget nodded.

'In that case, your Majesty,' said Naxor, 'you may require more than one dose to fully restore your sight. I would recommend taking one sip every day for, let's say, three, or perhaps four days? That should suffice.'

'You'd better not be deceiving me,' said Bridget.

'If I were, your Majesty, my ruse would soon be uncovered. I am here to forge a deal that will span years; would I imperil that by making false promises?'

Bryce walked up to the throne, and handed the vial to his mother. She took it, and stared at the swirling, silver contents.

'Does it have any ill effects that I should know about?'

'Only upon those who abuse it, your Majesty,' said Naxor. 'Like any substance, if one over-indulges, then one may become emotionally dependent upon it. If administered correctly, as it is in the City of Salve, it offers nothing but well-being.'

Bridget pulled the stopper from the vial, and sniffed the liquid.

'If I keel over and die,' she said, 'let none of the delegates leave this palace alive, Bryce.'

Bridget raised the vial to her lips and took a sip. Her body began to shudder, and Bryce quickly took the vial from her so that she wouldn't drop it. He stood back, his eyes wide as the Empress convulsed on the throne. Bridget let out a cry, then opened her eye, a broad smile of relief and joy on her lips.

'I feel... amazing,' she said.

She stepped down off the throne, stretched her limbs, then laughed.

'Look at me!' she cried. 'My back, my legs – I haven't felt this good since I was twenty years old. Bryce, get the other children; I want them to witness this.'

Naxor gave a satisfied smile as Bryce hurried away.

'You shall have your deal, Lord Naxor,' said Bridget, as she strode up and down the audience chamber. 'I feel as though I could take on the world.' She halted, and rubbed the eye patch that covered part of her face. 'Even my blinded eye feels different. Three or four days, eh?'

'That is my best estimate, your Majesty,' said Naxor. 'Shall we discuss the fine details of our deal?'

'I'll leave that to Bryce,' she said, 'but you can be assured that we shall supply whatever you need.'

The doors to the chamber opened, and Bridget's five children strode in. They stared at their mother, then Brogan broke down in tears, and rushed to embrace her.

'Look what salve has done to me, children,' Bridget cried. 'Bryce, give Naxor whatever he wants.'

Naxor smiled. 'Lord Nadhew and I are ready to begin the negotiations whenever you are, my lord.'

Three hours later, the delegates were back on the roof of the Great Fortress. Kelsey was a little irritated by the smug expression on Naxor's face as they waited for Frostback to return, but she thought it best not to mention it in Bryce's presence.

'I shall be seeing you again soon, Lord Bryce,' Naxor said, shaking the hand of Bridget's son.

'I look forward to it,' said Bryce. 'The resources the City requires will be ready and waiting for your collection.'

Frostback wheeled over the Great Fortress, then came in to land.

'Are we ready to depart?' said the dragon.

'We are,' said Naxor. He bowed before Lord Bryce. 'Until next time, my friend.'

The three delegates climbed up the leather straps and buckled themselves into the harness upon Frostback's wide shoulders. The dragon soared into the air, then gazed down at Plateau City.

'It is a pity we have to leave so soon,' she said.

'We're not leaving yet,' said Kelsey. 'Naxor, were there any conditions about us going to Colsbury?'

'None whatsoever,' said Naxor. 'I enquired, of course, and Lord Bryce said we were free to travel wherever we liked upon this world. We are to make no formal alliance with the Holdfasts, but the terms of the deal do not forbid us from visiting them.'

Kelsey took out the Quadrant. 'Get ready, Frostback,' she said. 'I'm taking us all to Colsbury.'

She swiped a finger over the copper-coloured surface, and the air shimmered. Below them, the city was replaced by the high peaks of the Barrier Mountains, and Kelsey saw the lake, with Colsbury Castle in its centre.

Naxor stared downwards. 'Is that the home of the Holdfasts?'

'It's one of them,' said Kelsey. 'The last time I was here, mother was arranging to buy it from the Holdings government.'

'Now that is what I expect the residence of a great ruler to look like,' said Naxor. 'Empress Bridget, in my humble opinion, should consider building herself an edifice to match her status, rather than dwelling inside an old fortress.'

Frostback circled the twin keeps of the castle, then landed in front of the Summer Palace. A few workers were busy repairing the external stonework, but the island seemed quiet.

'A palace and a castle?' said Naxor, as he climbed down to the cobbles. 'I am more and more impressed, Kelsey. This is a fine location.'

'No one lives in the palace at the moment,' Kelsey said, joining him on the ground. 'In fact, everyone lives in the larger of the two keeps. My mother has big plans for the place, though.'

'I'm looking forward to meeting her.'

They waited until Nadhew had clambered down, then Frostback

took off, and the three humans entered the Great Keep. They ascended the flights of stairs to the upper levels, and Kelsey frowned.

'It's too quiet,' she said. 'I wonder if everyone's gone out for a walk or something.'

They reached the level where Daphne and Thorn stayed, and Kelsey knocked on the door of her mother's office. When there was no reply, she pushed the door open, and saw that the room was empty.

'Anybody home?' she cried.

Another door opened, and Shella peered out.

'Oh, Kelsey; it's you.'

'Aye, it's me. Where's my mother?'

Shella eyed Naxor and Nadhew for a moment, then turned back to Kelsey. 'She's in Plateau City, I'd imagine.'

Kelsey frowned. 'What?'

'She was arrested two days ago, Kelsey,' said Shella. 'They all were – everyone except me and Agang. They took Thorn, and Keir, and Caelius Logos; and the two young Sanang guys who were staying here. They even arrested the pirate from Dragon Eyre.'

'What?' cried Kelsey. 'Who arrested them?'

'Brogan,' said Shella; 'the Empress's eldest daughter. She arrived with two flying carriages and took Daphne and the others away.'

Naxor started to laugh.

'Do you think this is funny?' said Kelsey.

'I'm sorry, but yes,' said Naxor. 'All that time we were in the Great Fortress of Plateau City, and the Empress had your mother under arrest? No wonder Lord Bryce looked happy to discover that we wished to visit Colsbury. He knew what we'd find, and so did the Empress.'

'She played us,' said Kelsey. 'That bitch played us.'

'Quite,' said Naxor. 'It occurs to me that we have underestimated Empress Bridget. She has proved herself as ruthless as any god with this deception. We have learned a useful lesson, Kelsey.'

'We have to go back to Plateau City,' she said. 'Now.'

Naxor frowned. 'Absolutely not. By the terms of the deal we have negotiated, the City has pledged not to interfere in the internal politics of this world. If we go back now, we would be saying goodbye to the resources the City requires.'

'Then, what can we do?'

'Nothing, Kelsey. We shall return to the City and lick our wounds. But make no mistake, we shall not underestimate the Empress again.'

CHAPTER 24
HOUNDED OUT

Cumulus, Implacatus – 20th Tuminch 5255

Silva and Karalyn crawled along the narrow ventilation shaft. They were in pitch darkness, and the smooth granite was angling downwards.

'You should be able to feel an opening on your left soon,' said Silva.

'What if I lose my grip,' said Karalyn, 'and slide down the tunnel?'

'Please don't,' said Silva. 'This route ends in razor-sharp spikes. I know, because I once fell down here. It took me hours to climb back up again; I kept slipping in my own blood.'

Karalyn kept going, her knees and hands sore from the effort of moving slowly down the tunnel. The air was warm in the shaft, and sweat was rolling down her forehead and getting into her eyes. Behind her, she could hear Silva shuffling along, and Karalyn knew she couldn't stop. If the demigod bumped into her, she would most likely start to tumble down the shaft, and end her days impaled upon the spikes at the bottom. The fingers of her left hand were edging along the smooth wall, and they found a corner, where a smaller tunnel branched off.

'I think I've found it,' she said. 'Slow down.'

Silva halted behind her, as Karalyn's fingers felt their way round the new opening.

'It's too small to get through,' she said.

'It's not,' said Silva. 'It's a squeeze, but you can make it. It's only narrow for a few yards, then it opens out again.'

Karalyn hesitated. 'Are you sure?'

'Trust me,' said Silva.

Karalyn tried to control her breathing. In truth, she had no choice but to go on. The shaft was too narrow to turn in, and they would never be able to reverse their way back up the slippery slope. She braced herself, her legs pushing against the opposite wall, and shoved her arms through the small opening on the left. Her shoulders jammed against the lip of granite, and for a moment she panicked, as claustrophobia surged through her mind. She clenched her eyes shut, then pushed again with her legs, and wriggled through the gap. Surrounding her, she felt the press of the solid, smooth rock. There was nothing for her fingers to grip, and she inched along, squirming her way through the narrow tunnel. She felt her feet enter the shaft, and was able to get into a rhythm; the tread on her boots gaining a little purchase on the smooth rock.

'Take it slowly,' she heard Silva whisper behind her. 'You can do it.'

Karalyn was drenched in sweat by the time her fingers felt the shaft widen. There was a wide lip of rock where the tunnel opened out, and she was able to pull herself free of the narrow tunnel. She fell a few feet, and landed on solid granite, panting in relief. She rolled to the side as Silva squeezed through the tunnel and dropped down next to her.

'I don't know if I can do that again,' gasped Karalyn.

'We shall have to,' said Silva, 'if we wish to escape.'

'You've been here before?'

'Yes. I left a pack in this alcove on my last visit. Feel around with your hands – it should be here.'

Karalyn moved her fingers over the smooth rock. The darkness was complete, and she had no idea how large the alcove was, or whether it ended in a wall or a steep drop.

'I've found it,' said Silva.

Karalyn heard a buckle being unfastened, then the sound of a box of matches being shaken.

'Give me a moment,' said Silva, 'and I'll light a lamp.'

'Is that safe?'

'Yes. There are no grilles or openings leading off the alcove. No one will see us.'

A match was struck, and Karalyn blinked from the sudden burst of light. Silva lit a small oil lamp, and turned the flame down low. Karalyn glanced around. They were in a cube-shaped chamber, four yards square. High on the wall behind her, she saw the narrow opening they had crawled through, while three more openings were on the other side of the chamber.

Silva smiled. 'Not far to go. I stayed in this part of the palace for nearly a month, but I had to return to the area where I found you, as I had run out of food and water. We are deep in the foundations of the Palace of the Almighty, which explains why the air is so warm.'

'How did you manage to remain undetected for so long?'

'My powers helped. I can detect approaching gods before they can detect me, and that has allowed me to get away in time. The thick walls of the palace block me from seeing very far, but they also block the powers of the other gods. Getting into the palace in the first place was the real challenge.'

'Do you have any water in that pack?'

Silva shook her head. 'I couldn't find a supply of water down here. If we are unable to reach Lady Belinda this way, then we shall have no choice but to retreat in the direction we came.'

Karalyn nodded. 'What date is it, do you think?'

'I'm not sure any more,' said Silva. 'Perhaps around the twentieth of Tuminch?'

'What's that in the Holdings calendar?'

'I don't know what that is. Upon the world of the Salve City, the twentieth of Tuminch would correspond to the twenty-second of Namen. Does that help?'

'Not really.'

'Does it matter?'

'Aye, it does. I think I've missed my children's birthday. I've missed more than half of them since the twins were born. I promised them I would be there this year, and I've let them down again.'

Silva nodded. 'How old are they?'

'They'll be eight, assuming that their birthday has passed. At least my sister was there.'

'Is Kelsey caring for them?'

'Aye. I don't think she was too happy about it, but she agreed. I'll have to find a way to thank her when... if, we ever get out of here alive.'

'Are you ready for the next stage?' said Silva. She pointed at the three openings on the left hand wall. 'The tunnel on the right goes past the chamber I told you about. With your powers, we should be able to neutralise the guards.'

'And then what? We drag Belinda through these tunnels?'

'Can you see any other way?'

Karalyn shook her head.

'Climb into the tunnel,' said Silva. 'I'll extinguish the lamp and follow you.'

Karalyn pulled herself up. She walked to the far wall, and clambered into the waist-high tunnel. It was much wider than the one they had squeezed through to enter the alcove, and sloped upwards on a gentle gradient. The dim light of the lamp went out, and Karalyn was plunged back into darkness. She heard Silva climb up behind her, and they set off again. They crawled for several long minutes, the only sound coming from their breathing, and the brush of their bodies against the smooth granite. Karalyn came to a grille on the right hand wall, and halted. Beyond the grille was more darkness, but Karalyn's fingers could feel the mesh of the wire gauze that covered the opening.

Silva crawled up beside her.

'This is it,' the demigod whispered. 'This is the chamber where they sometimes bring Lady Belinda.'

'She's not here now,' said Karalyn.

Silva nodded. 'Then, we wait.'

Karalyn dozed in the tunnel, the warm air lulling her exhausted body to sleep. She awoke with a hand over her mouth as Silva shook her shoulder. Karalyn opened her eyes, and saw light filtering through the thick layers of gauze. She squinted through the grille. Beyond was a plain room, with bare walls of solid granite. A bed sat in the centre of the floor, and Belinda was being led towards it by a group of armed gods. As before, there was no light in Belinda's eyes, and she was walking as if in a daze. Two of the gods pushed her onto the bed, then another pulled a series of thick leather straps over her arms and legs, and secured her to the bed frame. A pillow was positioned under her head, and one of the gods used a finger to close Belinda's eyes. Some of the gods then left the chamber, but two remained. They sat down by a small table and began talking to each other in low voices.

'They never leave Lady Belinda alone,' whispered Silva. 'Here is where my courage failed. I was always too scared to attempt the next stage, and so I used to just lie here, watching my beloved great-grandmother sleep.'

Karalyn said nothing. She removed her small knife, and began to pick away the corner of the gauze, her movements slow and silent. When she had cut through a few inches, she folded the sheet of mesh to one side, and reached through to start unpicking the next layer. The blade of the knife nicked against the wall, and the two armed gods stopped talking. They glanced around, then one of them stared down at the grille. Karalyn ripped a hole through the gauze, and unleashed her powers upon the two gods. She went from one god to the next, obliterating their conscious minds in an instant. Their eyes rolled up into their heads, and the two gods slumped from their chairs, and toppled onto the floor of the chamber.

Karalyn sliced through the first layer of gauze, then ripped it from the grille. With the second, she was more careful. If they were going to retreat back into the network of tunnels, she wanted to conceal their escape route. She cut through the bottom of the mesh, and folded it up, creating a hole large enough to crawl through; then she entered the chamber, and stood. Silva joined her and, together, they gazed down at the body of Belinda. Silva started to weep. She reached out and took one of Belinda's hands, and kissed it.

'My beloved queen,' she sobbed. 'I'm here.'

Karalyn's glance went to the golden band affixed to Belinda's head. There were traces of dried blood under the four large diamonds that studded the front of the crown, and she grasped one of the jewels, and began to pull.

'What are you doing?' said Silva.

'I'm going to remove the spikes from her head,' said Karalyn. 'That's what you said these diamonds were. If we free them she can start to heal.'

'But she will be in considerable pain if we do that now,' said Silva. 'She might scream, or lash out at us. It will be easier to leave her as she is for now, until we are safely back in the tunnels where no one can hear us.'

Silva started to unbuckle the straps that were holding Belinda to the bed, and Karalyn lifted her fingers from the crown.

'We'll need to remove the bodies of the two gods as well,' Silva went on. 'We can hide them in the tunnels. Are they dead?'

'No,' said Karalyn. 'I wiped their minds, but they're still alive.'

Silva nodded, then she released the last strap from Belinda. The demigod turned and walked over to the two bodies. She crouched down, and slid a sword from a god's scabbard. Karalyn watched, saying nothing, then she glanced away as Silva decapitated the gods with two well-aimed blows. Blood poured from the necks of the headless bodies, pooling on the smooth floor, then Silva picked up the two heads, and pushed them through the open grille. She then dragged one of the bodies by the ankles, leaving a trail of blood smearing the floor. Karalyn suppressed her nausea, and helped Silva push the first body through the grille; then they disposed of the second in the same way.

'What about the blood?' said Karalyn. 'It leads right to the grille.'

Silva stripped a blanket from the bed, and crouched down. She tried to mop up the blood with the blanket, but it smeared over the smooth floor.

'You're making it worse,' said Karalyn.

Silva frowned. 'If you have any better ideas, I'd like to hear them.'

Karalyn heard a noise from outside the room. 'Quiet. Did you hear that?'

Silva dropped the blanket, and began lifting Belinda up by a shoulder.

'Help me,' said the demigod. 'Quickly.'

Karalyn took Belinda's other shoulder, and they moved the Third Ascendant into a standing position. Belinda's legs buckled under her, and she fell to the stone floor.

'She's still sleeping,' said Silva. 'We need to wake her.'

The door to the room opened, and two gods walked in. They stared at the scene, then one screamed.

'Intruders!' he cried.

Karalyn lifted her hand, and the two gods fell as she commanded them to sleep. Another god appeared in the doorway, and Karalyn tried to enter his mind, but he was wearing eye-guards. He raised his own hand, and unleashed a blast of death powers at Karalyn and Silva. Karalyn deflected them, shielding Silva. The god stared in disbelief, then fled from the chamber, his boots clacking off the stone floor.

Karalyn and Silva dragged Belinda's unresponsive body towards the grille. A low growling sound arose, then fierce barks echoed off the smooth walls.

'They're bringing dogs,' said Silva, her eyes gleaming with terror.

Four huge hounds burst into the chamber, each as tall as Karalyn's waist. Behind them, the god with eye-guards was urging them forwards, but they needed no encouragement. Two pounced at Silva, knocking the demigod off her feet in a frenzy of snarling jaws. One gripped hold of Belinda's foot, and began tugging her backwards, and the other leapt at Karalyn. Strong jaws took hold of Karalyn's left wrist, and she cried out in pain. She fell to the floor, then jabbed up with her small knife, burying the blade into the dog's neck. The beast struggled for a moment, then let out a whimper and lay still.

'Kill them!' cried the god.

Karalyn pushed the dead dog off her and crawled to the grille, edging backwards into the opening. She reached out, and dragged Silva towards her, but the two dogs were pulling in the other direction. Silva was unconscious, and covered in blood. One of the dogs had its jaws clenched round the demigod's throat, and it was ripped out as Karalyn pulled the body free. The other dog bit through the fingers on Silva's right hand as Karalyn pulled with all her strength. The tunnel was almost blocked with the headless bodies of the two gods they had killed, and Karalyn shoved one of the bodies against the grille, forming a barrier between Silva and the chamber. The dogs tore into the corpse, their teeth ripping through the flesh of the dead god, as Karalyn pulled Silva's mutilated body through the tunnel, and down the slope. She tumbled into the alcove, dragging Silva behind her, and they fell onto the two heads, which had rolled down from the grille. Karalyn jumped back in horror, then heard the sound of the dogs – they had entered the tunnel network. She grabbed hold of Silva, but it was too dark to see the extent of the demigod's injuries. Was she even alive?

Karalyn had no time to think. She hoisted Silva up onto her shoulder, ignoring the pain coming from her bitten wrist, then climbed up into the narrow shaft, from where they had entered before. This time, her claustrophobia was outweighed by the sheer terror she felt as she heard the dogs scramble through the tunnels behind them. Karalyn had to traverse the tight tunnel backwards, keeping one hand gripped round Silva's wrist as she pulled the demigod along. The dogs were in the alcove, their loud barks filling her ears. Keep going, she told herself, as she battled a rising wave of panic.

Her legs dangled free of the tight tunnel, and she remembered the spikes at the bottom of the slope. She eased herself into the wider tunnel, taking care to brace her legs against the opposite wall. The dogs had reached Silva's feet, and were trying to drag her back towards the alcove. Karalyn pulled, and hauled the demigod out of the tunnel. One of the dogs came with her, its jaws gripped round Silva's boot. Karalyn lashed out, and kicked the hound in the face. It opened its jaws to snap at her, then lost its footing on the steep slope, and tumbled away. Its cries echoed through the shaft, then were cut off. There was one last whimper of agony, then silence.

Karalyn began dragging Silva up the slope. There were still two other dogs in the tunnels, but, for a moment, Karalyn could hear nothing. She battled her way up the slope, then more growls reached her ears, coming from below, along with the clack of claws on the smooth granite.

You cannot see me. You cannot see me.

Karalyn knew it was probably useless, but the words kept repeating themselves inside her mind. The tunnel was in utter darkness, and she had no idea if her powers worked on dogs. Even if they did, they would still be able to sense her presence from scent alone.

You cannot sense me. I am not here.

The growling and snuffling continued as Karalyn hauled Silva up the slope. She heard paws scrabbling against the smooth granite, and took a little comfort from that fact that the dogs were not finding it easy to gain purchase. Sweat trickled into Karalyn's eyes, and she wiped them. Her arms were aching, and a fierce pain was burning on her left wrist where she had been bitten; but she kept going, dragging Silva's body foot by foot up the shaft. A glimmer of light appeared – a soft grey glow, and Karalyn knew that they were close to where they had started that day – close to an alcove with water and other supplies. It was hopeless. No matter how thirsty she was, she would have to keep going. The entire fortress-palace was probably on full alert, and more dogs would be sent into the tunnel network to flush them out.

Sextant, can you hear me?

Nothing. She had known it wouldn't work – the walls of solid granite were too thick to allow her powers to pass, but she was growing desperate. She tumbled over a lip of stone as the tunnel met a larger chamber, and crashed onto the floor, jarring her left shoulder. Silva landed on top of her, and in the grey light, Karalyn gazed at the blood-soaked demigod. Some of her wounds had healed, but several fingers were missing from her right hand, and the gaping injury to her neck was still struggling to close. If the hound's jaws had bitten deeper, they might have severed the demigod's spinal cord; but, as it was, Silva would need more time to recover.

Karalyn lifted the demigod onto her back, and carried on, just as the heads of two dogs appeared over the tunnel lip behind them. They started to bark, a loud insistent sound that echoed across the small chamber. Karalyn picked up a bag of food and tipped it on to the floor, then she scrambled into another tunnel.

More noise came from in front of her, and she veered into a side shaft, moving as quickly as she was able. Blinded by sweat, she tipped over an edge and dropped again, falling awkwardly onto her ankle. She suppressed a cry, and wiped her eyes. Directly above her was daylight. It was far away, at the end of a tall shaft, and several sheets of wire mesh were blocking the route to freedom. She noticed steps gouged from the solid rock, which formed into a ladder leading upwards. Once more, she pulled Silva's body over her shoulder, then she began to climb. She reached the first sheet of gauze as three dogs jumped into the chamber. They leapt upwards at Karalyn's feet, their jaws snapping, and Karalyn kicked one in the face. Another gripped hold of her left boot, and pulled. Hanging on to the ladder with one hand, Karalyn reached down, and unlaced the boot. It slipped from her foot, still clenched in the jaws of the massive hound; then Karalyn climbed again. She ripped a hole in the gauze, cutting her fingers on the sharp metal, and continued upwards.

'Halt!' cried a voice.

Karalyn ignored it. She reached a second layer of gauze, and tore a hole large enough to climb through.

'You cannot escape,' cried the voice; 'there is nowhere to go.'

Karalyn heard the thrum of a crossbow. The bolt struck Silva's back, and the body of the demigod juddered in Karalyn's grasp. They reached a third sheet of wire mesh, and Karalyn's bloody fingers tore at the corner. Another bolt whistled past her head, ricocheting off the smooth granite wall. Karalyn climbed again, as exhaustion sucked her energy away. She reached the final layer of wire gauze, the last barrier between her and the sky, but, before she could reach it, something tugged at her bare foot. She glanced down, and saw a soldier's hand gripping her ankle. Karalyn tried to kick him, but he was too strong. She reached up instead, and hauled herself up one last inch. Her fingernails reached out, and she picked a small hole in the mesh.

Haurn, Dragon Eyre. Go.

The air crackled, then Karalyn fell. Just as she was conscious of a blue sky above her, she slammed into the ground, winded. She rolled off Silva, and gasped. Fresh air, at last. She lay still for a moment, panting and bathed in sweat, then glanced at her surroundings. She was in Sable's old temple compound, and the air was perfumed with the scent of orange trees and the salt from the ocean. Karalyn sat up, and pulled off her jacket. She cried out in pain as the garment brushed over the bite on her left wrist. The wound was bleeding freely. Her fingers were also a mess, cut by the sheets of wire mesh, but it didn't matter. She was free.

She staggered to her feet, and saw a notice nailed to the door of the temple.

Gone to Ulna, Sable.

Karalyn noticed a wooden water trough, and ran to it. She crouched down, and used both hands to ladle water into her mouth. It was rank, but she didn't care. She heard a cough and a groan behind her, and she turned. Silva was lying with her eyes open, her throat having finally healed.

'Where are we?' the demigod whispered.

'Dragon Eyre,' said Karalyn.

'You mean... we failed?'

'Aye.'

Silva started to weep. 'You should have left me to die in Cumulus,' she sobbed. 'What use am I, if I am without my beloved queen? We were so close – so close. I held her in my arms. You should have left me and taken Lady Belinda.'

'I did what I had to do,' said Karalyn. 'There was no fighting those dogs. We were lucky to get out of the palace alive.'

'Lucky?' cried Silva. 'My queen is still a prisoner. Take me back to Cumulus, Karalyn. I beg you.'

Karalyn stood. 'No.'

Silva's eyes flashed with rage. 'You can give up, but I cannot. Take me back.'

'We're not giving up,' said Karalyn. 'We're changing our strategy. We need food, and rest; and I need to find a healer to fix my wrist. Get on your feet; we're leaving.'

Silva calmed a little, but she glared at Karalyn with suspicion.

Blackrose's palace, Ulna. Go.

The air shimmered, and they found themselves in the midst of the vast reception hall within the bridge palace in Udall. Maddie screamed as a dozen dragons turned to look at them.

'I need Sable,' said Karalyn, then she collapsed to the ground.

***

Karalyn awoke in pain, the wound on her wrist burning fiercely. She shot up, then realised that she was lying in a comfortable bed, the open shutters revealing a view of the harbour of Udall.

'Try not to move,' said Maddie.

Karalyn turned, and saw that Maddie, Sable, Cardova and Austin had crowded into the little room.

'Austin tried to heal you while you were sleeping,' said Cardova. 'If he tries again, can you allow his powers to reach you?'

Karalyn stared at him, bewildered for a moment, then nodded. Austin reached out, and placed a hand onto her left wrist, which had been bandaged. She felt his powers try to penetrate her, and she let them in. A surge of healing filled her body, and she gasped as all pain left her. She lay back down again, panting.

'We know what happened,' said Sable. 'Silva told us.'

'She's not happy,' said Maddie. 'She thinks you abandoned Belinda on Implacatus.'

'I had no choice,' said Karalyn.

'I know,' said Sable. 'I read Silva's mind. If you hadn't fled, the dogs would have killed you. Did we do the right thing, waiting here for you?'

'Aye,' said Karalyn. 'There was nothing you could have done to help me if you'd returned to Implacatus. You'd all be dead by now if you'd tried it.'

Sable turned to Cardova, and gave the soldier a pointed look.

'Did I miss the twins' birthday?' said Karalyn.

Sable nodded. 'Yes. It was two days ago.'

Karalyn felt a tear escape her eye.

'Are we going back to Colsbury?' said Cardova.

'No,' said Karalyn. 'I'm not giving up on Belinda.'

Austin narrowed his eyes. 'Even after everything you went through in Cumulus? Silva also told us about Amalia, and about the crown that keeps Belinda under control. It seems hopeless.'

'It's not hopeless,' Karalyn said. 'I was right to try my approach first, but it failed.'

'Do you have a back-up plan?' said Maddie.

'No, but Sable does.'

Her aunt smiled. 'Do you mean that? Are you going to let me lead this time?'

'Are we sure about this?' said Austin. 'I've witnessed many of Sable's so-called plans. They usually end in utter carnage and destruction.'

Karalyn gazed at the faces surrounding her. 'Maybe it's time for some carnage and destruction. Sable, will you do this – will you help me free Belinda?'

'Do I get to plan everything?' said Sable.

Karalyn nodded.

'And I'm in charge – everyone will have to do as I say?'

'Aye.'

Sable grinned. 'Then let's do it. Let's kick Implacatus where it hurts.'

CHAPTER 25
DINNER FOR TWO

Plateau City, The Plateau – 2nd Day, First Third Autumn 534

'I hate not having my powers,' said Thorn. 'I feel naked and unprotected without them.'

Daphne glanced at her adopted daughter, but said nothing.

'It was wrong of Daimon to do that to us,' Thorn went on. 'We're not a threat. Did he think I was going to strike the Empress down?'

Keir stirred from the shadows in the corner of the cell. 'Shut up.'

Thorn glanced at him. 'Not a particularly constructive suggestion, husband.'

'What did you expect?' Keir said. 'We're traitors. We're lucky they didn't string us up the moment we arrived.'

'We are not traitors, son,' said Daphne. 'We are the ones upholding the law. Do not forget that.'

Keir shook his head. 'You actually believe that, don't you? You're both utterly deluded. You think that disobeying a direct order of the Empress isn't treason. If only you'd kept your mouth shut and stayed in Colsbury; but no – you had to go to Sanang and spread your treason there, too. That's why we're here. The Empress didn't care about your views, but she cares if you try to break up the Empire.' He sighed. 'I should have voted for Bryce.'

'Why didn't you?' said Thorn.

He stared at her. 'I was trying to please you. I thought that, if I voted for you, then we might be able to move past what had happened in Plateau City.'

'You thought I'd forgive you for sleeping around?'

'Yes. The only thing you care about is gaining power. You valued my vote more than you valued me.'

Thorn said nothing.

For three days, Daphne had been forced to listen to Keir argue with Thorn, and her frustration was growing. All three prisoners had been stripped of their powers, and were unshackled within the small cell, but Daphne knew that Daimon was watching, and listening. She wondered where the other prisoners were being held. They had seen no sign of Caelius, Olo'osso, or the two young Sanang men since their flying carriage had landed in Plateau City. She presumed they were in another cell, somewhere under the Great Fortress. If they were sharing the same cell, Daphne hoped that Caelius and Olo'osso had found a way to get along without killing each other.

'I shouldn't be here,' muttered Keir. 'I didn't go to Sanang. The real reason I'm here is because the Empress still holds me responsible for the death of Brannig. Yet again, I'm getting blamed for something I didn't do.'

Thorn sighed.

'Don't look at me like that,' said Keir. 'This is all your fault. Your deranged sense of ambition has led us here. You lust after power so badly that you would do anything to sit on the throne. That's the only reason you wanted to become a Holdfast. I don't hear you deny it.'

'Is there any point?' said Thorn. 'Nothing I say will change your mind.'

Keir smiled at her. 'You're so weak without your powers; so helpless.'

'Be quiet, Keir,' snapped Daphne. 'Your constant complaining is driving me to distraction.'

'That's how you want me, mother, isn't it? Nice and quiet. A polite, submissive son who will always do as he's told.'

'Right now, I'd settle for one who occasionally shuts up.'

'I'm not going to shut up,' he said; 'not for you, mother, and not for my witch of a wife. Do you expect me to forget that it was you who kept encouraging Thorn? Your little whispers in her ear, telling her that she was destined to rule the Empire one day – don't you think you also bear some responsibility for what has happened to us? You've been planning this for years.'

A door opened in the hallway outside before Daphne had decided if she was going to respond to her son. The three prisoners turned. Approaching their cell was a group of imperial soldiers – tall, well-built Kellach Brigdomin soldiers. They stopped in front of the cell, and one withdrew a set of keys.

'Are we going somewhere?' said Daphne.

'Not you,' said the soldier. He pointed at Keir. 'Just him.'

'Why?' said Keir.

The soldiers ignored him. The door was unlocked, as four soldiers kept their crossbows trained on the prisoners, and Keir was beckoned forwards.

'On yer feet, lad,' said the soldier with the keys.

Keir stood. He glanced down at Daphne and Thorn for a moment, then walked from the cell. The door was closed and locked, then the soldiers led Keir away.

'At least we'll get some peace for a while,' said Daphne.

Thorn frowned. 'Why do they want Keir?'

'I don't know. It could be that they are planning to interview us one at a time. If so, our turns will come soon enough.'

'But,' said Thorn, 'if your suspicions are correct, and Daimon has been listening to us, then...'

'Then what?'

Thorn lowered her gaze. 'Nothing. Just foolishness.'

'Keir might not be happy,' said Daphne, 'but he would never betray us.'

'I hope you're right. He hates me.'

Daphne said nothing.

'I should have worked harder at our marriage,' Thorn went on, 'but I gave up. I gave up trying to appease his moods, and stopped pretending that he was ever going to change. I knew he was having an affair with Tilda Holdwain, and yet I allowed it to continue. I calculated that if he was going to be disloyal to me, then at least I knew where he was.'

'You can't blame yourself,' said Daphne. 'It was Keir who broke your marriage vows, not you. You are the innocent party in all this.'

Thorn nodded.

'If I'm right about the interviews,' Daphne went on, 'then you know what to do. Stay strong, and tell them the truth. We have nothing to hide.'

'If we do that, they might execute us.'

'Yes. I know. I am at peace with that. If we must die, then it would be far better to do so with truth and right on our side. Now, if you'll excuse me, I'm going to try to get some sleep. I suggest you do the same.'

Daphne lay down on her bed of straw, and closed her eyes, savouring the quiet. Thoughts of Karalyn entered her head, but she brushed them aside. She had warned her elder daughter what might happen if she left them and went to Implacatus, but Karalyn hadn't listened. Belinda was clearly more important to her than her own family. Daphne took a deep breath, shut all thoughts out of her mind, and allowed the stillness to envelop her.

***

'Be upstanding for her Imperial Majesty!'

Daphne's eyes opened, and she frowned. The Empress? It must be a mistake, as Bridget's poor health precluded her from walking down the many flights of stairs to visit the dungeons in the basement. Next to her, she sensed Thorn rise to her feet. Daphne sat up, and saw the Empress standing in front of the cell, a dozen soldiers with her. Daphne narrowed her eyes. Something was different about Bridget. A fire was in her eyes, and she was standing up straight, without the aid of a walking stick. Daphne stood.

'You took your time getting to your feet, Holdfast,' Bridget said.

'I was sleeping,' said Daphne.

Bridget smiled. 'Do you recall what I said to you the last time I had you locked up in the Great Fortress? I let you go that time, on the condition that you remained in Colsbury, or the Holdings at the very least. But no. You couldn't help yourself, could you? You had to go to Sanang and persuade the Matriarch to join your rebellion against my rule.'

'I am not rebelling against your rule.'

Bridget's eye flashed with anger. 'Do not interrupt me, Holdfast. You have ignored my laws on the succession to the throne, which is much the same thing as an open rebellion. I have been training Bryce to be Emperor since he was a child. It is his birthright, and you shall not take it away from him.'

'You're keen on the hereditary principle, are you, your Majesty?' said Daphne.

'That would seem fairly clear.'

'Then, with all due respect, you are a usurper. Guilliam may have died without children, but he wasn't without an heir. If you truly value the hereditary principle, then Sable should be Empress, as she is Guilliam's niece. Or, do these rules only apply to your family?'

Bridget laughed. 'Sable, eh? At least you haven't lost your sense of humour.'

'I'm glad you find the idea so hilarious,' said Daphne. 'I find it pretty funny, too.'

'Oh aye? And how did you become Holder Fast, Holder Fast? Did the other holders have a vote?'

'Property is different. The Empire is not your property, Bridget.'

'The Empire has no traditions, Daphne; it's too young to have become rule bound. We all know that Guilliam would have passed the throne on to any child he and Mirren bore. He would have founded his own dynasty, directly descended from the same dynasty that had ruled the Holdings before he became Emperor. All I am doing is the same thing.'

'Is it wise to model yourself on Guilliam?'

'Aye, as long as we're talking about Guilliam before the Creator entered his mind. Remind me – who was Queen of the Holdings before Guilliam took the throne?'

'His sister Miranda.'

'That's right. You were a great admirer of hers, weren't you?'

'I was. That passed when I realised that she had been conducting an affair with my father.'

'But she was still the rightful queen? Even though she inherited the throne from her father? Answer me.'

'Miranda was the rightful queen.'

'Then I am doing the same as her.'

Daphne's eyes narrowed. 'But you broke your word, Bridget. You promised to abide by the rules we established in Colsbury.'

'I didn't break my word; I changed my mind. I am the Empress. I am allowed to change my mind. I used to watch Bryce as a child. Already, he was clever and kind, and had a way that made others feel welcome and comfortable in his company. He would make a good Emperor, Daphne; and you know it.' She glanced at Thorn. 'Your little protégé, on the other hand, would lead the Empire to ruin. I knew what the two of you were planning, Daphne; I knew that you would bend and twist any vote to ensure Thorn was selected. I chose Bryce to spare the Empire that misfortune.'

Daphne fell into silence. Was Bridget speaking the truth?

'You are looking very well, your Majesty,' said Thorn. 'Very healthy.'

Bridget laughed. 'Does that upset you?'

'Not at all, your Majesty. I was just curious. I wasn't aware that you had another hedgewitch in the city.'

'There are no hedgewitches in Plateau City,' said Bridget, 'as far as I am aware.'

Thorn frowned. 'Then, how…?'

'Has my younger daughter been here, by any chance?' said Daphne.

'She has,' said Bridget. 'Kelsey was here a few days ago, along with a demigod and a lawyer from her world. Oh, and a big silver dragon. They were trying to impress us, I suppose. We negotiated a trade deal, while you sat down here in the dungeons.'

Daphne glanced at Thorn. 'The Empress hasn't been healed by any hedgewitch. She's taken salve.'

Bridget smiled.

Thorn's eyes widened. 'Salve did... this to her?'

'Aye,' said Bridget. 'And take a look at this.'

The Empress lifted the eye patch from the side of her face. Daphne had seen what had lain there before, but it had changed. Instead of nothing but an empty hole in her face, a new eye was growing. It was bloodshot, and a milky substance was seeping from the socket surrounding it. Daphne stared, her mouth opening.

'My vision is still a wee bit blurry in that eye,' said Bridget, 'but it's coming along nicely. Another couple of days is all it should take.' She withdrew a small glass vial from her robes, and swirled it round. 'Here it is. Refined salve. The stuff the gods want more than anything else; the stuff they've fought wars over. An entire ton of it will soon be coming into the Empire every third; enough to cure every illness, and enough to heal every injured soldier. Of course, with you two in custody, I doubt there will be any need for conflict. The Matriarch will back down, as will the Holdings government, once they learn that your cause has failed.'

'Why did you refer to the two of us?' said Daphne. 'There were three prisoners locked in this cell.'

'And now there are two.'

Daphne gripped a metal bar with her right hand. 'What have you done with Keir?'

'Calm down, Daphne,' said Bridget. 'Keir's fine. In fact, he's better than fine. He knelt before me and begged for my forgiveness. He swore that he wanted nothing to do with the Holdfasts any longer, and pledged his loyal service to me and my appointed heir.' She smiled. 'You should see the look on your face, Daphne. You want to believe that I'm lying, but deep in your heart you know that I'm speaking the truth.'

'Keir has betrayed us?' said Thorn.

'He has picked his side,' said Bridget. 'Daimon went into his mind, and confirmed that he was protecting me from Brannig. He saved my life. Therefore, I am prepared to overlook any other offences he may have committed, as he did not play a major role in your conspiracy to take the throne. He will be a useful addition to my court. I may even allow Tilda Holdwain to stay in the palace to keep him company.'

'I don't believe you,' said Thorn. 'Keir would not do this – you are trying to trick us.'

Bridget gestured to a soldier. 'Bring in Thorn's husband.'

The soldier saluted, then went to the door. He opened it, and Keir walked through. He was wearing the same clothes as he had in the cell, but his back was straighter, and he was keeping his chin high.

'Here he is,' said Bridget; 'the man himself. Ask him anything you want.'

Keir glanced at Thorn and Daphne, a glint of disdain for them in his eyes.

'Have you betrayed the Holdfasts, son?' said Daphne.

'It is you who has brought the family to the brink of destruction, mother,' said Keir. 'I tried to warn you several times, but you paid no attention to anything I had to say. It is I who shall be the saviour of the Holdfasts.'

Daphne stared at him. 'Is your brain addled?'

'Mock me if you wish, mother,' said Keir. 'You are a traitor, and I am no longer under your authority.' He turned to Thorn. 'As for you, your ambition will end when you are swinging from a noose, my dear wife.' He smiled. 'Did I say wife? We must correct that immediately. I do not wish to be married to a condemned traitor.' He bowed before the Empress. 'Your Imperial Majesty,' he said. 'I would beg a favour. You have the power to annul my marriage to this criminal. I humbly ask that you do so.'

Bridget grinned, and slapped Keir on the back. 'What a polite young man!' She raised her hand. 'With the authority vested in me as Holder of the World, I declare your marriage to Thorn Holdfast to be at an end, Keir. If I were you, I would select your next wife more carefully.'

'Thank you, your Majesty,' said Keir. He smiled at Thorn. 'I am free at last from your spite, and your sly cunning. I shall find a decent woman of good Holdings stock, perhaps even Tilda Holdwain, and re-marry. Together, we shall bear a family of strong, loyal Holdfasts to replace the traitors who have besmirched our good name. The title and position of Holder Fast shall fall to me.'

Thorn smiled back at him. 'I think Corthie might have something to say about that. Karalyn, too. And don't forget Sable. Any one of them could grind you into the dirt, Keir. Enjoy your moment of triumph, because it will not last for long.'

'It will last longer than the remainder of your life,' he said. 'A trial was held in your absence, and you have both been sentenced to death for your crimes against the Empire. Messengers have already been sent out to Sanang and the Holdings, telling them this. It's over; don't you understand? A rope will choke the life from you. I hope you glance in my direction when you're dangling from the noose; then you will see me laugh.'

Bridget frowned. 'Alright; that's enough, Keir. Go back upstairs, and Mage Tabor will show you to your new quarters.'

The anger on Keir's face dimmed a little, and he bowed. 'Yes, your Majesty.'

Daphne said nothing to her son as he walked from the hallway outside the cell.

'Keir won't be at the executions,' said Bridget, once the door had been closed. 'I haven't told him yet, but I don't think his presence would be appropriate.'

'Are we to be executed in secret?' said Daphne.

'There will be witnesses, but aye; it'll be done in private. I don't want your deaths turned into a grisly public spectacle. It pains me to have to kill you, Daphne, but you've left me no choice.'

'What about the rest of my family? Are you going to arrest and kill them, too?'

Bridget shrugged. 'I hope the deaths end with you and Thorn. I don't bear any grudge against Corthie, or Kelsey, for that matter. They have broken no imperial laws. As for Karalyn, my actions will be determined by her response. If she behaves herself, then she can continue to live peacefully with her children in Colsbury. I'll tell you one thing, though – if Sable crosses my path again, then aye. Her, I will kill. We should have executed that monster years ago. But, I will not hunt her down. If she lies low, and causes no trouble, then I am even prepared to turn a blind eye to Sable. I am not the villain, Daphne – you are.'

'When are we due to die?' said Thorn.

'Tomorrow morning,' said Bridget. 'I will have some decent food and drink sent down for you, and some cigarettes. Is there anything else you would like for your final evening?'

'My powers,' said Daphne.

Bridget smiled. 'Eh, no. I don't think that would be wise. Soldiers will come to collect you in the morning, at dawn. When you see me again, I shall be watching you both be executed.' She shook her head, and looked almost sorrowful. 'I truly wish it hadn't come to this, Daphne. You were a friend and an ally. I trusted you.'

'You've never forgiven me for taking Killop from you.'

'What? Do you really believe that? I've scarcely heard anything more pathetic in my life. It wasn't Killop who drove us apart, Daphne; it was your stubborn refusal to obey my commands. You swore an oath to be loyal to me, and then you ignored my every order. You put the ambitions and wealth of your family far above our friendship. Do not look to me for the source of our divisions – look to yourself.' Bridget took a deep breath. 'Farewell, Daphne.'

The Empress turned, and strode from the hallway. The soldiers escorted her out, and the door was closed.

Daphne glanced down. Some of Bridget's words had struck home. Had she chosen Bryce to succeed her, not because she wished to break the law, but to prevent Daphne from placing Thorn on the throne? She then thought back to the countless times she had ignored instructions emanating from the Imperial Capital. She could justify each one in isolation, but together, they painted a picture of disloyalty. And she had lost Keir. Even if a miracle saved them from the noose, any reconciliation with her elder son seemed impossible.

A tear rolled down her cheek, then she felt Thorn take her hand.

'Is this all my fault?' said Daphne.

'No,' said Thorn. 'You were trying to do the right thing.'

'Was I?'

'Yes. Remember what you told me a little while ago – stay strong, because right is on our side. That hasn't changed.'

'I should have allowed myself to be elected Empress in Colsbury, all those years ago. I didn't want the job, but neither did Bridget. And yet, we forced her to take it on again.'

'We chose her, because we agreed that she was the best person for the role.'

'We didn't all agree. You voted for me, if I recall correctly.'

'Yes. I did. The Empress viewed me as a rebel at the time, and I was afraid of her. I voted for you because I was worried that Bridget might try to harm me.'

'The worst aspect of this whole sorry business is that none of it was necessary. We all thought that Bridget's days as Empress were numbered, and that the succession would be happening soon. Salve has changed all that. Bridget looked healthier than I have ever seen her. She could rule for decades.'

Thorn released Daphne's hand, and sat down on her bed of straw.

'I'm single again,' she said. 'For one night.'

'Do you fear death, Thorn?'

'Not particularly. I fear dying, but that's not the same thing. I had always assumed that I would die of old age, or, if I was going to die young, then I would be burned to death like my sister Clove, or be beheaded like a god. Hanging isn't supposed to be able to kill me. But, without my powers, I will die as easily as anyone else.'

'I always wanted to die fighting,' said Daphne. 'Of course, the older I got, the less likely that seemed.'

The door to the hallway opened again, and several soldiers walked in. One was pushing a wheeled trolley, and he parked it in front of the cell.

'Her Imperial Majesty has sent this down for you,' said a soldier. 'Dinner for two. Stand back from the door, Holder Fast.'

Daphne retreated a few steps as four soldiers aimed their crossbows in her direction. The door was unlocked, and a soldier pushed the trolley into the cell. The door swung closed again, and a soldier re-locked it.

The soldiers glanced at each other, and one laughed.

'Is something funny?' said Daphne.

'The Empress thought that you might try to break out,' said one of the soldiers. 'Her Majesty told us that you might choose to go down fighting. Perhaps you aren't as brave as she thought, eh?'

The soldiers turned, and strode from the hallway.

Daphne glanced down at the trolley. It was crammed with dishes and plates, and a full bottle of whisky was sitting next to a teapot, along with two packets of cigarettes.

'Take whatever food you like, Thorn,' she said. 'I've lost my appetite.'

Daphne took the bottle of whisky and the cigarettes, and sat down on her straw bed. She glanced at the label on the bottle.

'Eighteen-year-old Severton? My, how the Empress is spoiling us.'

She unpicked the wax seal with a fingernail, then pulled out the stopper.

'Shall I get you a glass?' said Thorn. 'There's one on the trolley.'

Getting no response, Thorn turned, to see Daphne swigging the whisky from the bottle.

'I'm going to get very drunk, Thorn,' Daphne said, lighting a cigarette. 'I may weep; I may scream; I may become maudlin, and I will most likely embarrass myself. With any luck, I'll still be drunk in the morning.'

'I won't be able to cure your hangover.'

Daphne laughed. 'Somehow, Thorn, that's the least of my worries.'

CHAPTER 26
VOLUNTEERS

Udall, Ulna, Eastern Rim – 22nd Tuminch 5255

Sable stood by the railings of the unfinished *Giddy Gull*, as the predawn light grew in the east. A shadowy figure approached from the left.

Sable glanced at the sailor. 'Did you find any?'

'It took a bit of an effort,' Ryan said, 'but a guy on the *Patience* had some. Of course, I can't guarantee its quality, as I've not had the chance to sample it for myself.'

He handed over a small bundle.

'Thanks,' she said. 'Are you sure you don't want any money?'

'Nah,' Ryan said. 'All I want is your permission to tell the lads on board that I'm your exclusive supplier.'

Sable smiled.

'Well,' he said, 'do I have your permission?'

She nodded, and removed one of the weedsticks from the bundle. She held it up to her nose. The keenweed smelled a little stale, but it was hard to come by on Dragon Eyre. She took Meader's metal lighter from a pocket, and ignited the flame; then lit the end of the weedstick.

'Is today the big day, then?' Ryan said.

Sable took a draw. 'Yes. How did you know about that? Have you boys been gossiping?'

'You know what it's like. Blackrose tells Maddie; Maddie tells Topaz, and Topaz tells me. You'd better come back alive; otherwise my claim to be your weed supplier won't count for much.'

'Yeah, but if I die, you can tell people that you were the last person to supply me.'

Ryan nodded. 'I could do that, I suppose. I'd prefer you not dead, though.'

She passed him the weedstick, and he took a short draw as they leaned on the railings.

'What's going on here?' came a voice from behind them. 'Sable and my carpenter's mate, eh?'

Sable and Ryan turned. Lara was standing on the main deck, a dressing gown wrapped round her, and her hair wild.

'There ain't nothing suspicious going on, ma'am,' said Ryan.

'No?' said Lara. 'What's that you're smoking?'

Ryan passed the weedstick back to Sable. 'It's hers.'

'Ain't you got a shift starting at dawn, Carpenter's Mate?'

'Yes, ma'am.'

'Then you'd better get to it. I want my bleeding cabin finished by the end of the month.'

Ryan saluted. 'Yes, ma'am.'

Lara took his place by the railings as he hurried away.

'About today, Sable,' Lara said.

'You don't need to say anything,' Sable said. 'I just need to get through this one job, and then I can relax for a bit.'

Lara nodded, her eyes on the quayside as it was beginning to come alive for another day.

'I get the feeling that there will always be "one last job" with you, Sable,' she said. 'Just when I'm starting to get used to you being back, you're away again.'

'It's my life,' said Sable; 'for the moment.'

'Will it ever end?'

'Do I ever ask you if you'd give up sailing for me? You have the *Gull*, and I do… what I do.'

Sable took a long draw, then offered the weedstick to Lara.

'Nah,' said Lara. 'It's too early for that shit.'

'Are you upset?' said Sable.

'What a dumb question. Of course I'm bleeding upset, Sable. Why is it always you who has to come to everyone's rescue? And, this time, you're planning on rescuing someone you don't even like.'

'I'm doing it for Karalyn; she needs me.'

'Yeah, but you were always telling me that Karalyn is the greatest mage who's ever lived. If she couldn't manage it, then how come she expects you to do any better?'

'Karalyn is powerful, but she doesn't have the same range of experience as I do. You know what I'm capable of, Lara.'

'Yeah, and I know how reckless you are, too. Just concentrate on getting the job done, and don't get killed trying to impress your niece, eh? And when you get back, I'll be waiting here for you, as usual.'

Sable took Lara's hand, but the captain of the *Gull* glanced away, trying to hide the fact that her eyes were starting to well. Sable hesitated. She wanted to say something, but she had left Lara so many times in the past to risk her life on some operation, that she had nothing left to say. She squeezed Lara's hand.

'Good luck,' Lara whispered.

Sable withdrew her hand, turned, and strode away. She crossed the main deck, then walked down the gangway and on to the long quayside. She thrummed her powers, allowing her battle-vision to take in her surroundings, but no one on the quayside seemed threatening. Still, it was a pointless risk to take and, as soon as she was out of sight of the *Giddy Gull*, she placed her hand into a pocket, and brushed her thumb over the surface of the Quadrant. The air shimmered, and she appeared in the bridge palace. She walked into the huge reception hall. No dragons were present, but Cardova and Karalyn were there, sitting together on the edge of the high platform, smoking cigarettes and drinking coffee.

They glanced up as Sable approached.

'We're not due to meet for another hour,' Karalyn said.

'Am I disturbing you?' said Sable. 'Don't worry; I'm not staying. I just came to tell you that I'm heading to Salve City, to collect a few things.'

'Are you getting some more salve?' said Cardova. 'Amalia had the vial that we brought last time, and it was lost with her.'

Sable frowned. 'Should I tell everyone in the City that Amalia is dead?'

'Maybe I should come with you,' said Karalyn. 'I want to see the twins.'

'No need,' said Sable. 'The twins are one of the things I'll be collecting. You stay here and relax, and I'll bring the twins to you. Blackrose and Maddie can look after them while we're gone.'

Cardova laughed. 'Do they know this yet?'

'No,' said Sable, 'but I'm looking forward to telling them.'

'My poor children,' said Karalyn; 'getting passed around from person to person. Once this is over, I won't be leaving Colsbury again – not for a long while.'

Sable took out her Quadrant. 'See you soon. I'm about to get wet.'

She swiped her fingers over the copper-coloured surface. The air crackled, and she appeared in Princeps Row in Tara, the rain pouring down from the dark skies. Sable sighed, becoming drenched in seconds, then she walked towards the Banner headquarters. The soldiers at the door moved aside for her without any questions, and she entered the large mansion, dripping water onto the rug.

'Good morning, Miss Holdfast,' said an officer. 'Are you here to see Kelsey?'

'Yes. And Van, if he's available.'

'Kelsey and the major-general are eating breakfast in the drawing room, ma'am,' he said. 'Would you like to get dried first?'

'No, thanks. The weather in Dragon Eyre will dry me off soon enough.'

The officer flinched slightly at the mention of Blackrose's world, and Sable continued past him. She knocked on the drawing room door, then opened it. Van and Kelsey were sitting by a small table, while the twins were lying on the floor, reading the picture books that Sable had brought them for their birthday.

'Mind if I join you?' said Sable.

The twins glanced up.

'Hello, my little eight-year-olds,' said Sable.

'Sit yourself down, Miss Holdfast,' said Van.

Sable smiled as she took a seat at the table. 'When did I become "Miss Holdfast"?' She looked down at the selection of City food on the table, and decided to skip breakfast. 'I'm taking the twins to Dragon Eyre. Karalyn's there, and she wants to see them.'

'Karalyn's back?' said Kelsey. 'What about Belinda? Is she there, too?'

'No. The operation didn't go as planned. Belinda is still on Implacatus. Karalyn did bring back a demigod called Silva, though.'

'Silva?' said Van. 'I'm glad to hear that she's safe. She was a good friend to the City during Simon's reign.'

Sable nodded. 'Amalia didn't make it. Bastion killed her.'

Van and Kelsey glanced at each other.

'Shit,' muttered Kelsey. 'Poor little Maxwell. Should I go and break the news to Kagan? I know how to Quadrant to the estate in Roser territory where he and Maxwell live.'

'You won't have time,' said Sable.

Kelsey squinted at her.

'You're coming back with me to Dragon Eyre, niece,' Sable went on. 'I need you.'

Kelsey sighed. 'Let me guess – you want me to look after the twins?'

'No, Kelsey. I need you to lead a dragon assault on Cumulus.'

Van spat out his drink. 'What? No way.'

'We're going back to Implacatus,' Sable said. 'There will be two strike teams – one on the ground, and one in the air. Kelsey, you will be commanding three dragons in the aerial strike team. You'll need Frostback. I shall supply the other two dragons.'

Kelsey stared at her aunt. 'Me?'

'Yes, Kelsey. You.'

'You want me to lead?'

'Yes. Why is this so hard to understand?'

'But... no one ever asks me to lead anything.'

'You have the skills; you have the brains; and you have the experience. You led an assault over Alea Tanton that killed an Ascendant. Fancy a crack at some more?'

'Hold on a moment,' said Van. 'An aerial assault on Cumulus? Are you out of your mind, Sable? Thousands of gods live on Cumulus, and, out of them, hundreds have death powers. It's insane – you'll get yourselves all killed.'

'No, we won't,' said Kelsey. 'We can do it. I can shield three dragons from any powers, as long as we stick close together.'

Sable smiled. 'You'll do it?'

'Aye. I want to do it.'

Van stared at her. 'But...'

'I don't want to hear it, Van. I'm touched that you'll worry about me, but don't try to stop me.'

'I wouldn't try to stop you,' he said, 'but you don't even like Belinda. Neither of you do.'

'We're doing it for Karalyn,' said Sable. She turned, and glanced down at the twins on the rug. 'Hey!' she said. The twins looked up. 'Do you want to see your mummy?'

'Aye!' cried Cael.

'Mama forgot our birthday,' said Kyra.

'She couldn't help that,' said Sable. 'She was locked in a castle.'

'Like a princess?' said Cael.

'Yes,' said Sable. 'But she escaped, and she wants to give her children a big hug.'

Kelsey got to her feet. 'I'll start packing. Feel free to eat my breakfast, Sable.'

'Thanks, but I think I'll wait until we get to Dragon Eyre.'

'Do they have coffee on Dragon Eyre?' Kelsey said.

Sable nodded.

'Thank Pyre for that,' said Kelsey. 'Right; I won't be long; and then we can fetch Frostback.'

Kelsey rushed from the room, and Van turned his gaze to Sable.

'Keep her alive,' he said.

'My niece can handle herself,' said Sable. 'You should know that by now.'

'I know she can. But Cumulus? Dear gods, Sable – I hope you know what you're doing.'

'So do I.'

He stood. 'Wait here for a moment.'

Sable watched as he left the room, then she knelt down by Cael and Kyra. She played with the twins for a few minutes, reading from the books, and smiling whenever they caught her eye. Van walked back into the room, carrying something. He held it out.

'This is a loan,' he said. 'It belongs to the King and Queen. Make sure you bring it back.'

The air crackled, and Frostback appeared in the skies over Udall. Upon her shoulders, Kelsey and the twins were strapped to the harness next to Sable.

'What a glorious vista!' cried the silver dragon. 'This is everything Blackrose said it would be – the sun and the islands.'

Sable smiled. She had been wary about climbing onto the dragon's back, but had suppressed her feelings, as it was the most efficient way to transport everyone at once. Still, she didn't like it. Flying on a dragon's back made her think of Badblood, and the memories were churning her stomach.

A couple of dragons rose up from the bridge palace, and flew towards them.

'Remember to announce yourself as Ashfall's sister,' Sable said to the silver dragon.

'Is my sister well known here?'

'Yes. She's a hero, and she has a rider.'

Frostback laughed. 'My sister has a rider?'

The two other dragons circled round Frostback.

'What is your business here, stranger?' said one of the dragons.

'I am Frostback of Lostwell,' the silver dragon said, 'and I wish to speak to Queen Blackrose. My sister also lives here, I believe.'

'And who is your sister, Frostback of Lostwell?'

'Ashfall, daughter of Deathfang.'

The two dragons tilted their heads towards her.

'Then you are our honoured guest,' said one. 'Follow us to the palace.'

The three dragons soared down, and the twins whooped with joy as the wind blew their hair into tangles. The lead dragon aimed for a wide platform nestling amid the domes and towers on the roof of the palace, and they alighted.

'Is it always sunny here?' said Kelsey.

Sable smiled. 'Nearly always. There's no winter, either – it's like this all year round.'

Kelsey laughed. 'Simon got one thing right, at least. He used to brag about creating this world; but he seems to have done a decent job.'

'Too decent,' said Sable, as she unbuckled the harness straps. 'That's why the Ascendants want to seize it for themselves.'

They climbed down from Frostback, and then one of the other dragons led the way down a wide ramp. They entered the palace, the twins running along next to the dragons. The vast reception hall was packed, and one of their dragon escorts approached Blackrose through the crowd.

'Your Majesty,' the dragon said; 'we have a visitor – Frostback of Lostwell.'

Blackrose turned.

'Frostback!' cried Maddie, her eyes lighting up.

'Greetings,' said Blackrose, 'and welcome to Ulna, my realm.'

Ashfall pushed through the crowd, and faced the silver dragon.

'Sister,' said Ashfall. 'Are you well?'

'I am,' said Frostback.

'Why are you here?'

'To fight gods,' said Frostback. 'Will you fight by my side, sister?'

'Wait a moment,' said Sable, raising her hands. 'That's what we're here to discuss. First, though; where's Karalyn?'

'I'm here,' she said, squeezing between two dragons. She saw her children, and ran across the marble floor towards them. She crouched down onto one knee and embraced them both.

'I'm sorry I missed your birthday,' she said.

'Aunty Sable came,' said Cael. 'She brought us presents and cakes.'

Karalyn glanced up, and caught Sable's eye. 'Why didn't you tell me this?'

Sable shrugged.

Kelsey raised her hand. 'I'm here, too, sis.'

'Hi, Kelsey,' said Karalyn. 'Are you here to look after the twins?'

'No,' said Sable. 'I have other plans for Kelsey.' She turned towards the platform. 'Queen Blackrose,' she said, 'may I please address the dragons of your realm?'

Blackrose tilted her head. 'You may.'

'Thank you,' said Sable. Her eyes scanned the huge occupants of the hall. 'Dragons of Ulna,' she said, 'Today, I am going to assault the home of the gods.'

Every eye turned to watch her, and Sable smiled, a hand on her hip.

'There will be two strike teams,' she went on. 'I shall lead the first, with Karalyn; and Kelsey shall lead the second, with Frostback. I need two more dragons to volunteer. Who wants to kill some gods?'

'If my sister is going,' said Ashfall, 'then I shall not be left behind.'

'I was hoping you would say that, Ashfall,' said Sable. 'Thank you – you're in.'

'Ashfall's not going without me,' said Austin.

Sable nodded to him. 'You won't be able to use your death powers.'

'That's fine by me,' the demigod said.

'Who else?' said Sable. 'We need one more.'

'Are you truly going to attack Implacatus?' said Greysteel. 'Three dragons against a thousand gods?'

Sable smiled. 'Yes.'

She looked around, but no other dragons were stepping forward.

'You didn't mention my name,' said Cardova. 'Do I have a role in this?'

'You will be with me and Karalyn, Lucius,' said Sable.

The soldier nodded.

'Who else wants to come?' Sable said.

No one responded.

'Can I speak?' said Kelsey.

Sable turned to her niece and nodded.

Kelsey took a step forward. 'There's something I need to tell you, Sable; and you, Karalyn, that might affect things. I was in Plateau City a few days ago, negotiating with the Empress about trading salve to the Star Continent. Old Bridget took some salve, and she's all sprightly again. Anyway, after that, we went to Colsbury.' She chewed her lip. 'Um, mother's been arrested. They all were, pretty much – mother, Thorn, Keir, Caelius; even a guy called Olo'osso, though I have no idea why he was in Colsbury. Shella told me that they were flown off to Plateau City. Should we do something?'

Karalyn frowned. 'Does the Empress have them?'

'Aye,' said Kelsey. 'That's what Shella told me.'

'How many days ago was this?' said Sable.

'Um, three? I think.'

Sable glanced at Karalyn. 'What do you think? We could delay the assault on Implacatus, but the wedding between Edmond and Belinda is due to take place in Cumulus today, and my plan depends upon that. If we postpone, I could come up with a new plan.'

Karalyn lowered her glance. 'If we wait until after the wedding, then Belinda will be locked up inside the Palace of the Almighty again. Can we risk leaving mother and the rest of them in the Empress's custody for one more day?'

'Would the Empress execute them?' said Sable.

'I doubt it,' said Karalyn. 'Bridget might sentence them to lengthy spells in prison, but I can't believe that she'd have them killed.'

'Then we can probably take the risk,' said Sable. 'If we're agreed, then we'll hit Cumulus today, and deal with Daphne afterwards.'

Karalyn nodded. 'Alright.'

'Are you still looking for a volunteer?' said a quiet voice.

Sable and Karalyn turned. At first, Sable couldn't see who had spoken, then a small blue dragon pushed her way through the crowd.

'Deepblue?' said Sable. 'Are you sure about this?'

'Millen and I have discussed it,' said the little dragon. 'We want to help.'

Greysteel laughed. 'Implacatus is not the place for such small dragons.'

'She may be small,' said Sable, 'but she has enough courage to step forward, and I don't see anyone else volunteering.'

'Do you understand the risks, Deepblue?' said Blackrose. 'You will be flying into a torrent of flames and death.'

'I understand, your Majesty,' said the blue dragon. 'I want to do my part.'

'Then you have my permission to go.'

'But, your Majesty,' said Greysteel; 'surely a more powerful dragon would be better suited to such a task.'

'And are you willing to take her place, uncle?'

Greysteel looked away.

'It's settled,' said Sable. 'Deepblue and Millen are in. Queen Blackrose, may I ask if there is a chamber where I can speak to all those coming on the operation? My plan is not for everyone's ears.'

Blackrose gazed at her. 'Of course. Is there anything else I can do to assist you?'

'There is, as a matter of fact,' said Sable. 'Could you and Maddie look after Cael and Kyra while we're gone?'

The black dragon's red eyes glowed, and, for a split second, Sable thought she was going to refuse.

'It would be an honour,' said Blackrose. 'Karalyn may have betrayed me in the past, but for you, Sable, I will do it.'

Sable led her volunteers to another chamber. It was smaller than the reception hall, but was easily large enough to fit the three dragons and the small collection of humans. Sable stepped up onto a platform, and glanced at everyone. Ashfall and Frostback were side by side, and Sable could see how much Frostback had grown since they had last been together on Lostwell. Ashfall remained the taller of the two, but Frostback was almost the same size as her sister. Next to them, Deepblue looked tiny. In front of the dragons sat the humans, and Sable frowned as she saw someone who hadn't been invited.

'Silva,' she said; 'why are you here?'

The demigod gave Sable a cold stare. 'If you think I'm staying in Ulna while you attempt to rescue my beloved Queen, then you are much mistaken.'

Sable nodded. 'Fine. You can fly on Frostback with Kelsey. You can be her navigator. Kelsey, pass me your Quadrant.'

Her niece pulled the bag from her shoulder, and handed the Quadrant to Sable.

Sable crouched next to her. 'Watch where I place my fingers. Here, here and here. That will take your strike team to the skies directly above Cumulus. Got it?'

Kelsey nodded, and Sable returned the Quadrant to her. Sable stood again.

'The three dragons will attack from above. Burn everything you see. Gods, palaces – burn everything. But, and this is crucial – do not stray more than a hundred yards from Frostback. If you do, death powers will knock you from the sky before you can blink. You must remain under Kelsey's protection. She is in command, and you will obey her orders. If things get too rough, use the "go back" command on the Quadrant, and return here. Millen, you'll be on Deepblue, and Austin will be on

Ashfall. Kelsey will take Silva with her on Frostback. Silva knows the geography of Cumulus; listen to her advice, Kelsey, but the tactics will be up to you. The purpose of your team is to act as a giant distraction, while my team snatches Belinda. Any questions?'

'When shall we leave?' said Frostback.

'Kelsey will trigger her Quadrant two hours after my team departs. It is unlikely that the different teams will make contact with each other while on Implacatus; each will do their job and get out again.'

'You mentioned a wedding?' said Ashfall.

'Yes. The Second Ascendant is planning to marry the Third,' said Sable. 'It will be out in the open, in one of the central plazas of Cumulus, though I'm not sure which one. You might see it from the air. If you do, try to focus your destruction away from it. I want you to draw the enemy forces towards you, and away from Edmond. Anything else?' No one spoke. 'Alright. Good luck, and we will see you all back here.' She turned to Karalyn and Cardova. 'Are you two ready?'

'What about weapons and armour?' said Cardova. 'You can't expect us to walk into Cumulus unprotected.'

'I've taken care of that,' Sable said. 'We're going to Haurn first.'

She stuck a hand in her pocket, and thumbed the Quadrant. The air shimmered, and they found themselves in Nan Po Tana.

'I'll be coming back here a lot over the next couple of hours,' she said.

'Why?' said Karalyn.

'Walk with me, and I'll show you.'

Sable led Karalyn and Cardova along a path through the orange grove. Fruit was hanging heavy from the branches, and much of it had fallen to the ground and was starting to rot.

'This place could do with some work,' said Cardova.

'You should have seen it when the locals lived here with us,' said Sable. 'Perhaps, one day, I will come back, and make another go of it.'

Cardova smiled. 'Are you aiming to be a farmer like Corthie?'

'No, but I would quite like to sit here while others do the work. I'll supervise, from under the shade of an olive tree.'

'Listen, Sable,' he said; 'I want to apologise for giving you such a hard time recently.'

'Forget about it, Lucius,' she said. 'It's fine.'

'Why were you giving her a hard time?' said Karalyn.

'I wanted Sable to take us back to Implacatus,' he said, 'so that we could look for you. She told me it was a foolish idea, and that we should wait, but I didn't agree; and I lost my temper with her on a few occasions.'

Karalyn narrowed her eyes at him. 'You would have gone to Cumulus for me?'

'Of course,' he said. 'I felt as though I had abandoned you there. I couldn't stand it.'

Sable halted at the doors of a large out-building. She glanced over her shoulder, and saw Karalyn and Cardova standing on the path behind her, each caught up in the other's gaze. Sable smiled, and gave a gentle cough. 'Here we are.'

Cardova took Karalyn's hand, and they turned back to face Sable. She removed the chain from the doors, and swung them open. They entered the timber structure, and Sable opened several shutters to let in the light.

'By all the gods,' Cardova gasped, as he stared at the racks of explosive devices. 'Where did you get these, Sable?'

'I retrieved them from Ectus before I blew up the factory,' she said.

'What are they?' said Karalyn.

'Bombs,' said Cardova. 'Banner-made explosive devices.'

Karalyn walked up to the nearest rack.

'Be careful,' said Cardova. 'If the tapered end gets knocked, they explode.'

'Are we going to be using these today?' Karalyn said.

'We are, indeed,' said Sable.

'Do you understand how they are made?'

'No.'

Karalyn glanced at Cardova. 'Do you know?'

He shook his head. 'They were manufactured in secret. Only authorised personnel were allowed to access the factory on Ectus. If Sable destroyed it, then she might have killed everyone who knew how to construct them.'

'Some of the Unk Tannic know,' said Sable; 'but I blew up their headquarters on Na Sun Ka as well.'

'Should we keep one aside?' said Karalyn. 'We could take it back to the Star Continent, and see if we can figure out how to make more.'

Sable raised an eyebrow. 'I didn't think you were so bloodthirsty, niece.'

'I'm not, but if mother has been arrested, then we might need a little leverage.'

'Alright,' said Sable. 'We'll preserve two, and take them to Colsbury. The rest of them can add some colour and noise to Edmond's wedding celebrations.'

They walked on, passing the rows of stacked-up explosive devices, until they came to a door. Sable opened it.

'In here,' she said, 'are all the weapons and armour we could possibly need. Kit yourself up, Lucius. There will be leathers in there that will fit you, too, Karalyn. Put on a set.'

Cardova walked into the storage room. He picked up a hardened leather cuirass, smiled, then he put it down and lifted a heavy mace.

'Most of this equipment is Banner-issue,' he said.

'I think the native inhabitants of Dragon Eyre were fighting each other with spears before the gods invaded,' said Sable.

'What are you taking?'

Sable smiled. 'I already have a weapon.'

Cardova nodded. 'May I see it?'

Sable pulled back her cloak, and revealed the item that Van had loaned her.

'Where did you get that?' Cardova said, his eyes wide. 'Please don't tell me you stole it from the City of Salve.'

'Van is letting me borrow it,' she said.

She drew the sword from its scabbard, and its black blade glimmered in the light.

'What is it?' said Karalyn.

'A Fated Blade,' Cardova said. 'The sharpest sword I have ever held.'

Karalyn peered at it. 'It looks like the Weathervane.'

'I think they were both forged from the same type of metal,' said Cardova. He shook his head. 'And now Sable has it.'

Sable smiled. 'Let's kill some gods.'

CHAPTER 27
AERIAL ASSAULT

Udall, Ulna, Eastern Rim – 22nd Tuminch 5255

Kelsey glanced at the human members of her team, as they sat and waited for the two hours to pass. She had met Millen briefly in Lostwell, and had a vague memory of him. Of the two immortals, she knew very little of Austin. Only Silva was familiar to her, but the demigod had barely said a word, her gaze dejected and sorrowful.

'I used to sit and watch Austin disappear with Sable all the time,' Millen was saying; 'and I was jealous, if I'm honest.'

'Why?' said Kelsey. 'I thought Sable was in love with a pirate.'

'I wasn't jealous about that,' Millen said. 'I wanted to help Sable fight the occupation, and I hated having to wait in Haurn, making the dinner and doing all of the menial jobs.'

'Sable didn't choose me,' Austin said, 'because of any great friendship we shared. She needed my powers. I can kill, and I can heal. I can also heal myself. Sable knew that if I got injured, I would survive.'

'But you got to see all the action,' Millen said. 'I wanted a taste of that.'

Austin shook his head. 'Well, you've got your wish. Personally, I would have preferred to stay behind in Haurn. Do you think I enjoyed being a part of Sable's mad rampage? The things she did... they'll live with me forever.'

'It wasn't just that time,' said Millen. 'When Sable and Blackrose left Haurn to search for Maddie, they left us behind – me and Deepblue. They said Deepblue was too small to fly to Gyle.'

'Meader and Badblood were killed on that operation.'

'I know,' said Millen. 'Maybe, if we'd been there, things might have turned out differently.'

'Or, maybe you'd be dead.'

'Would you two be quiet?' snapped Silva. 'I am trying to think.'

'What about?' said Kelsey.

'Sable's plan. I should be with her team, not flying about on dragons. Sable seems to care more about killing gods than she does about rescuing my beloved Queen. I don't think Karalyn should have relinquished command to such a person.'

'Is that what's been bothering you?'

'Yes, Kelsey; that, and the death of Amalia. The former God-Queen of the City had her flaws, but she was my friend. She had a habit of doing a dozen wicked things before finally doing the right thing, and to think that she died to protect the City she loved – it breaks my heart.'

'Is that why Bastion killed her?'

Silva nodded. 'He was torturing her, trying to force her to reveal the location of the City, but she refused to give him what he wanted. Tell me, Kelsey – will anyone in the City mourn her sacrifice? Will anyone care?'

'I think you know the answer to that,' said Kelsey. 'Emily will care, and the handful of Amalia's grandchildren who still live in the City – they might care. The inhabitants of Medio? Not so much. And why should they? She tried to annihilate them when she opened the gates of the Middle Walls to the greenhides. Does one noble sacrifice balance out everything else she did?'

'I think it does,' said Silva. 'If Amalia had yielded to Bastion, Banner soldiers and gods would already be preparing to invade the salve world.

The City barely survived Simon; it would not survive Edmond and his legions.'

'Can I ask you something?' said Austin.

'Yes?' said Silva.

'Your self-healing powers,' he said; 'I could sense them before Kelsey arrived, but they didn't seem to be working properly. I can't quite figure out why.'

'I am still suffering from the damage Simon inflicted upon me,' Silva said. 'I was given several extremely high doses of anti-salve to quell my powers; and then I was nearly beaten to death. It might be years before I have fully recovered. When I was attacked by dogs in Cumulus, it took far longer for my injuries to heal than should be the case. Karalyn had to carry me.'

'Anti-salve?' said Austin.

'A prince called Montieth invented it,' said Kelsey. 'He experimented with salve for a thousand years.'

'And it removes the powers of the gods? Does this substance still exist?'

'There might be a tiny amount left,' said Kelsey. 'Montieth is dead, and I don't think anyone else knew the secret of how to make anti-salve.'

'That's a pity,' said Austin. 'It strikes me that it might be quite useful, especially on a day like today.'

Kelsey smiled. 'Aye. We could slip some into Edmond's wine, then watch his face.'

'Jade might know,' said Silva. 'She must have witnessed her father's experiments over the centuries. Perhaps you could ask her.'

'She'll be busy refining salve for the Star Continent,' said Kelsey. 'One ton every month. But, I'll ask. You know what she's like, though. She'll probably tell me to piss off.'

'Does she live by the salve mine?'

'Aye, with Dawnflame. Halfclaw has taken Maddie's sister out to the mountains to see her a couple of times, but apart from that, I don't think she's had many visitors. She prefers it that way.'

Deepblue's head peered through the doorway. 'The two hours have almost passed. Shall we prepare to leave?'

Kelsey got to her feet. 'Aye. Are Frostback and Ashfall with you?'

'Yes,' said Deepblue.

Kelsey gestured to the others, and they walked into the neighbouring cavern, where the three dragons were standing.

'What are our orders, Holdfast?' said Ashfall.

Kelsey walked into their midst. 'When we tried this in Lostwell,' she said, 'the three dragons – Frostback, Deathfang and Halfclaw, all stuck very close together, but we only had one target: Edmond. This time, we'll be trying to burn a much larger area, so we'll have to be more flexible. Frostback will remain in the centre, but the other two dragons can range about a bit, as long as they never go further than a hundred yards from me. Use your own judgement to select your targets; don't wait for me to point them out. If you see the wedding, let the others know, and we'll steer away from it.'

'I would like you to take me directly to Queen Belinda, Kelsey,' said Silva. 'If we see her, fly me to her.'

'No,' said Kelsey. 'That's not the plan. Sable and Karalyn will deal with Belinda.'

'Sable gave command of this team to you,' said Silva, 'and told you to take the decisions. She also told you to listen to my advice.'

The three dragons glanced at each other, and Kelsey frowned.

'I've made my decision,' she said. 'We will distract the gods, as ordered, and leave Belinda to the team on the ground. If you don't like it, you can stay here.'

Silva glared at her, but said nothing.

Kelsey glanced at the dragons. 'Let's get ready to go.'

She walked over to Frostback and began to clamber up the straps trailing down from the harness. She pulled herself into the saddle, as Silva climbed up after her, saying nothing. The demigod strapped herself in next to Kelsey.

'Do you know the street layout of Cumulus?' said Kelsey, as she waited for Austin and Millen to settle into their dragons' harnesses.

'Cumulus has no street layout, Kelsey,' said Silva. 'The city is built upon a high column of rock, and consists of palaces and towers, all set amid the rough ravines and crags of the mountain. There are a few open spaces where the gods can congregate, but this is rare. Usually, the gods remain sealed up within their fortified homes. If they wish to travel somewhere, they build a bridge by using their stone powers.'

'Any juicy targets?'

Silva glanced at her. 'Every palace is a mighty castle, and the homes of the Ascendants tower above those of mere Ancients.'

'How many Ascendants are in Cumulus?'

'There is Edmond, of course. He lives in the Palace of the Almighty, with his eldest sons – Bastion and Merlon. Queen Belinda is their prisoner.'

'That's two. What about the others?'

'There are four others. With the deaths of Leksandr, Arete and Kolai, their palaces are probably lying empty, if they haven't been taken over by some of the more powerful Ancients. The Ascendants who remain are Albrada, Tamid, Lloyd and Esher. They detest each other, but they loathe Edmond most of all. I imagine all four will be present at the wedding. To refuse would have invited Edmond's wrath.'

'Perhaps we should visit the wedding,' said Frostback. 'I crave the opportunity to strike at another Ascendant.'

Silva smiled. 'I agree.'

'It is time to leave,' said Ashfall.

Kelsey took the Quadrant from her shoulder bag. She gazed at the engravings, then glanced up.

'We'll be arriving high in the sky,' she said. 'Expect to see towers and castles, but no roads. We'll soar down, and hit the closest big target we can see.'

Ashfall tilted her head, while Deepblue looked terrified, as though she was only now beginning to realise what she had agreed to.

Kelsey swiped her fingers over the Quadrant, and the air crackled as the three dragons and their riders appeared in the skies over Implacatus. Clouds surrounded them and, for a moment, Kelsey couldn't see

Ashfall or Deepblue. She almost panicked, worrying that she might have accidentally left them on Dragon Eyre, but then she saw Ashfall above her, while Deepblue was circling to her right. Kelsey looked down. The cloud and mist continued, but she could see clusters of towers, spires and domes appearing through the murk like islands in the ocean.

Ashfall swooped close to Frostback.

'I know where we are,' cried Austin, from Ashfall's shoulders.

'I don't see any plazas,' said Kelsey.

'They're a little further to the east of here – on your right,' he said. 'Below us is the home of Lord Esher, the Ninth Ascendant. Do you see the golden domes, and the group of four spires? That's his palace. He lives on the western side of Cumulus, close to the fortress that borders Serene.'

Kelsey frowned, wishing she had Austin sitting next to her rather than Silva.

'We'll strike there first,' said Kelsey. 'Frostback, lead the way.'

The silver dragon began to dive, her slender grey sister soaring by her side. Behind them, Deepblue started to lag behind, and Kelsey kept an eye on the growing distance between her and Frostback. Below them, the golden domes of the Ninth Ascendant's palace loomed up towards them. There appeared to be no defences on the roof, and Kelsey saw no sign of anyone. Frostback opened her jaws, then Ashfall did the same, and the two dragons spewed flames over the domes and spires. The roof of the palace was soon engulfed in fire, then Frostback went a little lower, aiming her jaws at a long series of balconies that jutted out from the palace exterior. The flames burst through the glass balcony doors, then smoke belched out. Ashfall joined her sister, and together, the two dragons poured fire into the interior of the palace. Kelsey glanced up, trying to see Deepblue, then noticed her circling above the golden domes.

'What's wrong with Deepblue?' she said.

'She is frightened,' said Silva. 'She should not have come here.'

'We should burn the border fortress next,' Austin yelled, from

Ashfall's back. 'I'm not sure anyone will have noticed us attacking Lord Esher's palace, but they won't be able to ignore an assault on the fortress.'

'Alright,' cried Kelsey.

'Point the way, Austin,' said Frostback, breaking off her torrent of flames.

Austin raised his arm and pointed to their left. In the distance, Kelsey could see dark battlements and fortifications rise out of the banks of cloud. Frostback turned, and began to speed towards the west.

'Wait for Deepblue,' said Kelsey.

'Where is she, my rider?' said Frostback, slowing. 'It is her responsibility to keep up with me, not the other way around.'

Deepblue descended, and swooped under Ashfall.

'You must stay closer,' Frostback called out to the small blue dragon. 'If you stray out of range, and are struck with death powers, you will have no one to blame but yourself.'

'Sorry,' Deepblue said.

Frostback sped up again, and the three dragons soared towards the huge fortress on the western edge of Cumulus. They formed into a line as they neared the battlements, and Kelsey saw the masses of soldiers up on the walls, or standing upon the roofs of the many square towers that punctuated the main wall. The three dragons opened their jaws, and flames burst out over the top of a fortified tower, incinerating the Banner soldiers stationed there. Another squad of soldiers was trying to load a ballista that had been positioned atop a neighbouring tower. Ashfall turned her head, and a roar of flames engulfed the bolt-throwing machine. Alarm bells pealed, and soldiers were running around the forecourts in the centre of the fortress. The three dragons flew over the wall, and Kelsey looked down. At the base of the high wall, there was nothing, just a sheer drop leading into a dark abyss. A hundred yards ahead of them stood the cliffs of Serene, but there were no bridges connecting the two cities. The dragons wheeled in the sky, and came round for another pass at the fortress. Flames and smoke were already rising from the two towers that had been hit, and the dragons veered a little to the north. They unleashed their combined fire at a section of wall, and dozens of soldiers fell, their bodies burning as they toppled back into the wide forecourt. A ballista bolt whistled past Ashfall, and Frostback aimed her flames at the tower where the machine sat, incinerating it, and its crew.

'Thank you, sister,' said Ashfall. 'It is an honour to fight by your side.'

'The honour is mine, sister,' said Frostback. 'This day, let us gain vengeance for our slain father.'

'For Deathfang!' roared Ashfall, then she and Frostback soared over the fortress, blasting fire down into the forecourt. Screams rose up as the massing soldiers were caught in a conflagration. Deepblue was lagging behind again, as the sisters rushed ahead, and by the time the small blue dragon had reached the forecourt, there was nothing left of the soldiers but smoking carcasses.

Kelsey sensed death powers, and vision, and she looked around for the source. One of the fortress's keeps was on their right, and three robed figures were standing on the roof, their arms raised.

'Over to the right,' Kelsey called out. 'There are gods on the roof.'

'We seem to have attracted their attention at last,' said Frostback, banking. She and Ashfall swept round in a tight turn, and re-joined Deepblue as she was coming from the other direction.

'Deepblue,' cried Frostback. 'Watch out for ballistae as Ashfall and I send these gods to their deaths.'

The two sisters rose up, as Deepblue began to circle. Frostback and Ashfall ascended above the keep's roof, and directed a great burst of fire down onto the three gods. The immortals wailed and cried out, their flesh consumed by the inferno. They were healing themselves, but not as quickly as the flames were devouring them. One fell to his knees, then collapsed onto the roof, as the two dragons kept steady, their flames unceasing. One of the gods seemed almost to melt, her last cries lost as she turned to ash before their eyes. The last god fell, and still the two dragons kept burning, until nothing remained of the three immortals but ash and bone, lying amid the red-hot stone blocks of the roof.

Silva shuddered in the harness next to Kelsey.

'Let's move away from here,' Kelsey yelled. 'We'll attack from a different direction, to confuse them.'

'We should go to the plazas,' said Silva. 'Sable might require our assistance.'

'We'll take a quick look,' said Kelsey; 'but that's all – just a look.'

Deepblue ascended to their level, and the three dragons soared back to the east. They passed Esher's palace, which was still burning, and sped through the thick formations of cloud that hung over and around Cumulus. Kelsey glanced over her shoulder. Black smoke was pouring upwards in waves from the border fortress, while a thin plume of grey smoke was rising above the palace of the Ninth Ascendant. So far, the plan was working. She could hear the loud peals of the many bells that were ringing throughout the city. They couldn't all be for the wedding, she thought. She wondered if any of the gods were worried. Were they aware that they were under attack? Over to her left, she caught a glimpse of the largest building she had ever seen – larger even than the Great Racecourse in the Circuit, which was over a quarter of a mile long.

She pointed at the massive, solid-looking slab of granite in the distance. 'Is that the Palace of the Almighty?'

'Yes,' said Silva. 'At all cost, we must prevent Lord Edmond from taking my beloved Queen back into its interior.'

'There is a plaza ahead,' yelled Austin.

Kelsey turned. She looked down, but saw nothing amid the clouds. Silva tapped her arm, then gestured for her to raise her glance. Kelsey looked straight ahead, and saw a four-sided, raised building with an enormous flat roof.

'The plazas here are raised up on platforms,' said Silva; 'otherwise they would be lost in the clouds.'

The demigod fell silent as she and Kelsey stared at the plaza. It was packed with thousands of people, who were all facing the same direction – towards a section that had been raised higher than the rest of the roof. Upon this inner platform stood hundreds of gods in armour, who were surrounding a massive throne of gold. A smaller throne sat next to it, but both were unoccupied.

'This is the place,' said Silva. 'My poor, beloved Queen.'

Kelsey peered into the massed crowds. In the centre of the armoured gods, a procession was taking place. A path had been cleared that led to the two thrones, and a multitude of coloured banners, flags and standards were flying in the breeze.

Silva started to weep. 'I see her! My Queen! My Queen!'

Some of those in the huge crowd were turning to glance up as the dragons approached.

'What should we do, my rider?' said Frostback.

'Take me to Queen Belinda!' cried Silva.

'No,' said Kelsey. 'Frostback, swoop over the edge of the crowd and burn a few gods, then we'll head back the way we came.'

'As you will it.'

Frostback, Ashfall and Deepblue formed into a column, and soared down by the edge of the enormous plaza. They opened their jaws, and three streams of fire exploded onto the massed crowds. Kelsey grimaced at the sight, sickened at the orders she had given. Thousands of people in the plaza panicked, stampeding to flee the flames and the dragons, while robed gods were pointing into the air, but to no avail. Kelsey sensed the death powers that left their hands, but nothing reached the dragons. The plaza erupted into chaos. People fell, and were trampled under those trying to escape.

'That's enough!' cried Kelsey. 'Back to the west.'

The three dragons banked to the left and soared away, leaving hundreds of smouldering bodies in their wake.

'Pyre's bawsack,' muttered Kelsey.

'Most of those who have been burned will recover,' said Silva. 'Every person in that plaza is a god, Kelsey.'

'What?' said Kelsey. 'They're *all* gods?'

'Yes. No mortals are allowed in Cumulus, excepting the Banner soldiers who garrison the fortress we burned at the border with Serene.

You should have taken me to Queen Belinda. We might not get another chance like that.'

'We're doing the job that was given to us,' said Kelsey; 'and we're doing it well. The entire city must know that three dragons are here.' She glanced over to Ashfall. 'Austin, pick another target.'

'The Palace of Theodora lies ahead,' the demigod shouted back.

'I thought Theodora was dead.'

'She is, Kelsey. Powerful Ancients have lived there for centuries.' He pointed ahead and a little to their right. 'Do you see the black tower?'

'I see it,' said Frostback.

'Wait!' cried Deepblue. 'Someone else is flying; look!'

Kelsey turned in the saddle, and glanced around. Over to their right, black specks were rising into the sky. At first, there were only a few, then more ascended, until dozens were approaching the three dragons.

'What are they?' Kelsey yelled. 'More dragons? Do dragons live in Cumulus?'

'I've never heard of any,' Austin shouted back.

'They are indeed dragons,' said Ashfall.

'Something seems wrong with them,' said Frostback, as the three dragons slowed, and turned to view the approaching threat.

'I am going to move out of Kelsey's range for a second,' said Ashfall, 'so that my rider can strike them down.'

'I'll have the Quadrant ready,' Kelsey yelled; 'just in case.'

Ashfall ascended into the sky, travelling upwards to move away from any gods who might be on the ground. Kelsey pulled the Quadrant from her bag, and tucked it under her left thigh, as she stared ahead at the large formation of flying beasts racing towards them. She frowned. They were definitely dragons, but they were flying in a strange manner, and some had wings that appeared ragged and torn.

'Their odour is all wrong,' said Frostback.

Kelsey looked up. Ashfall was over a hundred yards higher than Frostback. Kelsey looked down again, expecting to see the bodies of the approaching dragons start to fall from the sky, but nothing happened.

'Shit,' she muttered. 'It's not working.'

'What shall we do, rider?' said Frostback. 'There is no time to flee to Serene; they are almost upon us.'

'Fly up to Ashfall,' Kelsey cried; 'then we'll get out of here.'

Frostback beat her wings, and soared up into the sky, Deepblue racing after her. The first of the approaching dragons reached Deepblue, and lashed out with its talons. The small blue dragon dived out of its reach, and Kelsey caught a glimpse of her pursuer's face for a split second. Her eyes widened, and her mouth fell open.

'They are dead,' gasped Frostback. 'Every one of those dragons is a flying corpse.'

Ashfall was descending at the same time as Frostback was ascending, and they met, high above Cumulus.

'I used my powers on them,' Austin cried, 'but they don't work. They've been reanimated; I can't kill what's already dead.'

Ashfall sent a burst of fire at one of the undead dragons as it raced towards them. Its wings erupted into flames, and it fell from the sky.

'Some of them have riders,' said Frostback.

'The riders are gods,' said Silva. 'They are there to control the creatures. It is time to leave. We cannot fight a hundred undead dragons.'

'I agree,' said Ashfall. 'In a few moments, we shall be surrounded. Kelsey – trigger the Quadrant.'

'Wait,' Kelsey said; 'where's Deepblue?'

'Damn that fool,' cried Frostback, turning her neck to look. 'I cannot see her.'

'I thought she was with you, sister,' said Ashfall.

'She was. She was following me as I rose up to meet you.'

They all glanced down. Below them, the sky was filled with undead dragons, who were ascending in waves towards them.

'We can't leave them,' said Austin.

'We have no choice,' said Silva. 'If we do not leave now, we shall all die.'

Everyone turned to Kelsey, waiting for her to take the decision. She swallowed. Frostback twisted in the air, then unleashed a burst of flames, and one of the undead dragons fell, its wings on fire; but dozens more were getting closer with every second.

'Bollocks!' Kelsey cried, then she swiped her fingers over the Quadrant.

The air crackled, and the two dragons appeared in the clear blue sky over the bridge palace of Udall.

Kelsey clenched her fists. 'Damn it all; bastards... damn it!'

'You should have taken me to Queen Belinda,' said Silva.

'Be quiet, demigod,' said Frostback. 'My rider – this tragedy is not your fault. We did not know that the gods had a legion of dead dragons under their control. If we had, our tactics would have been different.'

Kelsey put her head in her hands. 'I've killed Millen and Deepblue. The first time anyone's put me in charge of anything, and I fucked it up.'

'My sister is right,' said Ashfall, hovering alongside Frostback. 'You led us well, Kelsey, and we fulfilled our part of the operation. Deepblue was supposed to keep up. She knew the risks; as did Millen.'

'This is going to break Maddie's heart,' said Austin.

'We should go back to Implacatus,' said Kelsey.

'To what end, my rider?' said Frostback. 'To join Deepblue in death? Those abominations now control the skies over Cumulus.'

'We don't know that Deepblue and Millen are definitely dead,' said Kelsey. 'They might have got away in time.'

Ashfall and Frostback gazed at her, but said nothing.

'I'm sorry, Kelsey,' said Silva, 'but Deepblue and her rider were surrounded by dozens of undead dragons. They are dead. The blue dragon should never have come with us. This is Sable's fault, for she allowed Deepblue's naïve desires to overcome her common sense. She should have selected a mighty dragon, one with great strength and speed. Poor Deepblue. Her heart was pure and good, but she should never have been in a place like Cumulus.'

'We shall have to tell Queen Blackrose and Maddie,' said Ashfall.

'I'll do it,' said Kelsey. 'Deepblue and Millen were my responsibility. Take us down to the bridge palace, Frostback.'

CHAPTER 28
GROUND ASSAULT

Cumulus, Implacatus – 22nd Tuminch 5255

Karalyn and Cardova lay on the narrow ledge overlooking the enormous plaza, as they waited for Sable to return. Thousands of demigods and gods, along with hundreds of Ancients and a handful of Ascendants were gathered below them, filling the raised plaza from end to end.

'Can you see Belinda?' Cardova whispered.

'Not yet,' said Karalyn, 'though there's no doubt that this is where the wedding will take place. I can see Bastion; he's up on the platform, standing just in front of the two thrones; and I think I can see at least two Ascendants. They're wearing eye-guards, so I can't be sure, but everyone is bowing to them.'

Cardova glanced up at the sky. 'We left Ulna two hours ago, by my reckoning. The dragons should be arriving soon.'

Karalyn kept her gaze on the high platform in the centre of the plaza. She was using her vision to scan the faces of those gathered there. Rows of throne-like chairs had been positioned in front of the two real thrones, and Ancients in robes were sitting there, while demigod servants fanned them, and kept them supplied with drinks and food. At the rear of the high platform was a ramp, and Karalyn noticed a line of carriages waiting by its base. She tried to push her vision into the interiors of the carriages, but each one had been sealed, their windows shielded by the same thin wire gauze that had been inside the Palace of the Almighty. Hulking gods in full battle armour were surrounding the carriages. Some were carrying swords with blades that were at least four feet in length, while others had enormous battle axes. Karalyn shifted her position. The ledge was an uncomfortable place to be, but it had a perfect view of the plaza; and was sheltered on three sides, protecting them from receiving any unwanted attention.

Cardova nudged her, and pointed to the west. 'Is that smoke?'

Karalyn frowned. She could see a tiny patch of grey hanging over Cumulus a few miles away, so she sent her vision out. She sped her sight over the domes and spires of the city, then halted. A palace was burning, its upper floors alight. She glanced around for any sign of the three dragons, then saw them. They were racing away further to the west, towards the huge fortress that protected the western flank of Cumulus.

'I see the dragons,' she whispered. 'They've set fire to a palace, and are heading towards a fortress.'

'How can you see them?' Cardova said. 'I thought Kelsey was shielding them; preventing them from being seen.'

'I can't sense her powers, and she's stopping me from sensing the powers of Silva and Austin; but, and here's the difference between me and ordinary vision powers – I can see her if I happen to be looking in her direction. Gods can't. Kelsey isn't invisible. If she was standing in front of a god, they would see her with their eyes, but they can't see her with their powers. Does that make sense?'

'Not really,' said Cardova.

'It makes sense to me,' came a voice next to them.

Cardova nodded. 'I thought you might have got yourself lost, Sable.'

'I had a lot to do,' Sable said, 'but it's all done. Karalyn, did I overhear you say that you have spotted Kelsey's team?'

'Aye,' she said. 'Over to the west of here.'

Sable nodded, then glanced into the plaza. 'No one down there has noticed them yet. We'll wait until they do. We have twenty minutes.'

'Twenty minutes before what?' said Cardova.

She smiled at him. 'Before the bombs go off.'

The soldier frowned. 'I don't understand. Have you invented some kind of timer?'

'I guess you could say that,' Sable said. 'Thirty bombs, thirty... timers. Yes, let's call them timers.'

'I still don't understand.'

Karalyn bit her tongue. She knew how Sable had arranged the bombs to go off at a certain time, and the cruelty of her aunt's methods made her feel a little nauseous. Sable had done the same thing on Dragon Eyre, persuading 'volunteers' to carry the explosive devices and then set them off after a predetermined interval.

'Just focus on the operation, Lucius,' Sable said, her eyes fixed on the plaza. 'Leave the ugly details to me. Karalyn, have you seen the row of carriages by the ramp?'

'Aye,' she said. 'We should presume that Belinda is in one of them.' She glanced at Sable. 'I know that I asked you to lead, but are we doing the right thing? Shouldn't we just snatch Belinda the moment she emerges from a carriage?'

'We could,' said Sable, 'but we would have wasted a perfect opportunity to strike fear into the hearts of the Ancients and Ascendants. The dragons, the bombs, us – the purpose of this operation is not only to save Belinda; it's to ensure that the gods are too terrified to ever attack the Star Continent, or Dragon Eyre, for that matter. The more immortals we kill, the better.'

Karalyn frowned.

'If it gets too dangerous,' Sable went on, 'then we can always abandon my plan, grab Belinda, and get out of here as quickly as possible. But, if I can reach Edmond, the Ascendants might never be a threat to us again.'

Cardova pointed. 'The carriages are moving.'

Karalyn sent her powers back down to the plaza, and watched as the carriages were pulled up the ramp onto the high platform by horses. Armoured gods made way for them, and the carriages lined up in front of the rows of seats. A side door opened, and Lord Edmond appeared, dressed in the purest of white robes, with gold chains around his neck, and a crown on his head. The seated gods rose to their feet and cheered, and Edmond rewarded them with a wave. He descended to the platform, and strode to the second carriage, flanked by enormous warrior-gods, while Bastion walked to their rear. Edmond opened the side door of the second carriage, and reached in with a hand. A moment later, Belinda appeared. Her wedding gown was so large that it filled the interior of the carriage, and courtiers hurried forwards to ensure that it didn't snag as the Third Ascendant stepped down to the platform, her left hand held by Edmond. The crowd roared as they caught sight of Edmond's bride-to-be, none of them seeming to notice that Belinda's eyes were blank.

'She's still wearing that crown I told you about,' said Karalyn.

'I see it,' said Sable. She shook her head. 'Belinda.'

'Let me guess,' said Cardova; 'the last time you met, you were trying to kill each other.'

'Of course not,' said Sable; 'that was the second last time we met. The last time, we fought side by side with Corthie, to defend the Sextant from the Ascendants. We still hated each other, but we put that to one side, in order to deal with the greater threat.'

'You did fight her, though, before that?'

'Yes.'

Cardova eyed her. 'Who won?'

'She did. The bitch kicked my arse. Despite that, I still managed to rescue Maddie, so I'm calling it a draw.'

Karalyn glanced away from the plaza, and peered into the west.

'More smoke,' she said. 'A lot more smoke. The dragons are burning the fortress that flanks Serene.'

'Excellent,' said Sable. 'With any luck, they'll kill a few gods and attract some attention.'

Karalyn frowned. 'I'm not comfortable with Kelsey being in danger.'

'You put me in charge of the operation.'

'I know I did. I'm here, following your orders, Sable; but if anything happens to my sister...'

'She has a Quadrant; she'll be fine. Tell me; why does the rest of the family always underestimate Kelsey? It puzzles me.'

'I guess it's because Kelsey never seemed to care about the Holdfasts. When she was younger, she did nothing but mock the family, and criticise everything we did.'

'Yeah, but she's changed a lot. Lucius, tell her.'

'I didn't know Kelsey when she was young,' Cardova said, 'so I can only go on what I knew of her in the City. Van and I, and Queen Emily, would trust Kelsey with anything. She has proved herself countless times. I don't want to speak ill of the Holdfasts, but I admit that it grates a little when I see the way her mother speaks to her.'

'My feelings are less complex than my mother's,' said Karalyn. 'I hated Kelsey when we were younger, but I love her now, and I don't want her to get hurt. That's it; it's as simple as that.'

'Look,' said Cardova; 'the dragons are flying towards the plaza.'

Karalyn and Sable glanced up, and saw the three dragons. Deep-blue was easily recognisable by her size, but, at that range, Frostback and Ashfall were indistinguishable.

'What are they doing?' said Karalyn. 'I thought they were supposed to stay away from the plaza.'

'They were,' said Sable, 'but nothing they've done so far is causing much of a distraction. Trust your sister, Karalyn; and get ready to move. This could be our opportunity.'

The three of them watched as the dragons soared down by the far end of the plaza. They formed into a column, then fire burst out from their jaws, cutting a swathe through the panicking crowd. Gods screamed as the flames devoured them, and others were falling in the stampede to escape. Chaos took hold, and every eye turned to see what was happening. Up on the higher platform, even Edmond turned to look. He had been escorting his bride between the ranks of armoured gods, but the screams had made him glance round. He whispered something to Lord Bastion, who nodded then hurried away.

The dragons banked in the air, and turned away from the devastation they had caused on the plaza, heading back towards the west.

'Let's go,' said Sable. 'Remember, your entire purpose is to shield me. As soon as we reach Belinda, we leave, and get our arses back to Dragon Eyre. Stand up.'

The ledge was narrow, and Karalyn clung on to the wall behind her as she got to her feet. She glanced down, but the base of the building was shrouded in thick cloud.

Sable turned to her. 'How close do I need to stay to you to remain invisible?'

'A few yards,' said Karalyn. 'It won't work on any gods with eye-guards.'

Sable drew the Fated Blade from its scabbard. 'Lucius,' she said, 'keep a count for me.'

Cardova gripped his shield with both hands and nodded.

Sable put her free hand into a pocket, and the air shimmered. They appeared in the plaza, surrounded by screaming and panicking gods.

You cannot see us.

Sable exploded into action. She swung the Fated Blade, and the sword slashed through the closest god, cutting him in two at the waist; then she leapt up and decapitated a hulking warrior. His helmeted head flew through the air, and landed amid a group of demigods. More screams took hold in the crowd, as the unseen Sable advanced. Cardova had his shield raised to protect Sable's back, and Karalyn sheltered behind it, keeping pace with her aunt.

You cannot see us.

Sable hacked down another god, the dark blade slicing down from her shoulder to her waist. Blood spattered across Sable's leather armour and face, and she laughed. A warrior god lunged out from the left. Sable was invisible to him, but he knew someone was there. He raised his sword.

Karalyn pointed at him. *Sleep.*

The warrior clattered backwards, taking two smaller demigods with him as he toppled to the ground.

Karalyn pointed again, to a group of gods to their right.

Sleep.

A dozen fell, their eyes closed, as Sable reached the base of the ramp. Two enormous soldier-gods in brightly-coloured stone armour were guarding the way up to the higher platform, but the Fated Blade cut through their armour as if it were paper. Sable was moving like lightning, her body twisting, ducking and dodging, as her sword arm swung over and over again. Cardova gasped at the sight and, despite the carnage, Karalyn felt a twinge of pride. Sable leapt up the ramp, getting out of range of Karalyn for a split second, and the gods saw her.

An Ancient pointed, and screamed. 'Holdfast!'

Pandemonium erupted on the upper platform, as warriors rushed to form a thick line between Sable and the Second and Third Ascendants. Spears were hurled, and crossbows loosed, and a bolt grazed Sable's left thigh. Karalyn and Cardova bounded up the ramp, jumping over the bodies of the slain, and Sable disappeared from the sight of the gods.

Edmond, however, could still see her; and he wasn't alone. Several huge gods were also wearing eye-guards, and they drew their weapons as Sable slashed her way through the crowd.

'A palace for the one who brings me the head of Sable Holdfast!' Lord Edmond cried out. 'Powers are useless against her. Use swords, and cut her down!'

The gods wearing eye-guards urged the others to draw their weapons, and a mass of them charged Sable's position. Cardova raised his shield, and a crossbow bolt struck it, then he moved, his feet skipping as he deflected a powerful sword blow that would have taken Sable's head off. Cardova grunted, sweat trickling down his face. Karalyn kept pace with him, terror burning a hole in her heart as the gods surrounded them.

Sleep.

Another ten gods fell. Ahead of them, Edmond was pushing

Belinda back towards the carriages, as more huge warrior gods moved between him and Sable. The Holdfast woman seemed untiring, unstoppable, her sword dealing death with every swing, but she was now facing those who could see her. They were throwing themselves at Sable, their bodies piling up into a barrier, sacrificing themselves so that the blessed Second Ascendant could make his escape with Belinda. Sable leapt up onto the armoured body of a dead Ancient, as their enemies pressed around her. Cardova hefted his shield, protecting her rear, but to Karalyn's mind, it was starting to seem more like a last stand, rather than a rescue attempt. She raised her hand, and more gods fell to the ground, unconscious. She could sense death powers swirling from a dozen locations, all aimed at the figure of Sable, and Karalyn was deflecting each one, creating a bubble of protection around Cardova.

Sable pointed her sword at Edmond, and smiled. The Second Ascendant flinched, despite the dozens of gods who stood between him and the Holdfast woman; then the moment passed, and more gods charged at Sable, their massive swords and maces swinging. Sable moved, jumping down from the Ancient's corpse. She moved out of Karalyn's invisibility range again, heedless of the danger, and charged into the melee. Karalyn readied her powers, preparing to transport herself and Cardova to Belinda's side. Sable was proving again how reckless she could be, and it was time to snatch the Third Ascendant and get out of Cumulus.

Shadows flickered overhead.

Karalyn ignored them, as she and Cardova tried to catch up with Sable, then a dragon swooped down, its claws out. Sable saw the danger in time, and rolled, the claws missing her by inches.

'Look out!' Cardova cried. 'Dragons; dozens of them!'

Karalyn glanced up, then raised her hand at the closest beast.

Sleep.

Nothing happened, then Karalyn realised why. Every one of the dragons above them was already dead, their bodies preserved by the powers of the gods. A few dragons had Ancients riding on their harnesses, there to control the flying beasts. Another dragon soared down, its claws raking their way through the crowd towards Sable. Several gods were decapitated or torn in two, then the dragon's claws grasped hold of Sable by the waist. It ascended into the air, and Edmond raised his fists in triumph.

'Take her to the Palace of the Almighty,' he ordered. 'I will deal with her there.'

The dragons called off the attack, and soared back into the sky, the lead dragon bearing Sable away. Cardova's eyes widened. He looked exhausted, and was panting.

'Drop the shield and crouch down,' Karalyn whispered.

Cardova flung the damaged shield to his side, and they took cover next to a heap of dead gods.

'We're still invisible to most of them,' Karalyn went on, her voice low. 'I think they were too busy staring at Sable to notice us.'

'We need to rescue her,' Cardova gasped.

'One thing at a time,' Karalyn said. 'We might be able to get Belinda before Sable reaches the Palace of the Almighty. Follow me.'

They crept along the pile of bodies, and Karalyn glanced at the crowds on the upper platform. Bodies lay everywhere, both dead and sleeping. Some of the gods were weeping as they stared at the blood and carnage, but Edmond looked victorious.

'Clear the bodies,' he said. 'The wedding shall go on; we shall not cower or hide from mere mortals.'

'But, my lord,' said Bastion, 'there might be more Holdfasts in the city. They had dragons, and...'

'Silence, Bastion,' said Edmond. 'Quell your childish fears.'

Bastion nodded, his head bowed. He looked terrified, and Karalyn remembered that Sable had manipulated the Ancient's mind in Dragon Eyre.

'Apologies, my lord,' he said.

Amid the chaos, Belinda was standing still. Her eyes were glazed over, and she had streaks of blood staining her magnificent white wedding dress.

'There's nothing we can do,' whispered Cardova. 'We should save Sable and get out of here.'

The first bomb went off.

A roar of noise and a flash of light erupted from the base of a building a hundred yards away. The tall, slender tower groaned, swayed, then toppled over, sending tons of rock falling to the ground in an explosion that deafened Karalyn for a moment. The screams rose up again from the plaza, then everything went mad as twenty-nine other bombs went off at once. One had been placed in the centre of the plaza, and body parts were flung out from the cloud of rising dust and debris. Others had been positioned in several neighbouring buildings. Roofs collapsed, walls were blown out, and the ground rumbled and shook. The noise was more than Karalyn could bear. She clutched her hands to her ears and closed her eyes as if the world were ending. Cardova huddled down next to her, an arm over her back. Karalyn glanced up, as her ears rang. The closest bomb had been detonated next to the carriages, and had transformed them into a smoking tangle of smouldering metal and splintered wood. Bastion was lying on the ground, his face a mask of blood; and a large shard of metal from Edmond's carriage was embedded into his chest. Even Edmond looked shaken, his robes in tatters as he stumbled his way through the carnage. It was hard to see in the dust and smoke, but then Karalyn saw Belinda. She had remained frozen to where she had been standing, and her left arm was covered in blood, her gown ripped and coated in dust. Edmond staggered up to her.

'My beautiful queen,' he gasped, his voice hoarse and wavering. 'What have those villains done to you?'

Karalyn grabbed hold of Cardova's arm. 'Let's go.'

They ran through the clouds of dust, avoiding the dazed and wandering gods.

You cannot see us. We are not here.

They dodged between two hulking warrior gods, one of whom had lost an arm, and ran towards Edmond and Belinda. Just another few yards, Karalyn told herself, then they could be back in Dragon Eyre.

Edmond glanced up, saw Karalyn, and his features froze. 'Protect us!' he cried.

A fist swung out from the crowd, and punched Karalyn in the side of the face. The force of the blow knocked her into Cardova, and they both lost their footing and tumbled to the ground. Within seconds, they had been surrounded, and a huge array of weapons was pointing down at them – crossbows, swords, battle axes, spears; and the gods holding them were staring down at Karalyn with violent hatred. Karalyn lifted a hand to her face, and her fingers came away covered in blood. She tried to summon her powers, but her head was spinning.

'Who struck the blow?' said Edmond, striding forwards.

'It was I, my lord,' said a god in black robes, bowing.

Edmond reached the front of the crowd surrounding Karalyn and Cardova, and smiled.

'Well done, Lord Merlon,' he said; 'my faithful son. Today, for this act, you have risen above Lord Bastion in my affections.'

Merlon smirked at his brother, who was sitting up, and trying to remove the shard of metal from his chest.

Edmond glanced down at Karalyn. 'If they move, kill them.'

'You heard the blessed Second Ascendant,' said Merlon. 'Keep your weapons trained on the Holdfast woman. She is extremely dangerous.'

Karalyn felt far from dangerous as she lay on the ground. Her jaw felt as though it had been dislocated, and the pain was burning through her.

Sleep, she gasped, but only two of the gods around her fell.

Edmond laughed. 'Congratulations, Holdfast. You and Sable are to be commended. No one has ever breached the defences of Cumulus the way you two have done this day. Imagine what I could achieve if I had a dream mage on my side. Your execution shall mark the high point of the wedding celebrations.'

A slight frown creased Merlon's lips. 'Are we still intending to press ahead with the marriage, my lord?'

'Of course we are,' said Edmond.

Bastion got to his feet. He had removed the metal from his chest, and was wiping the blood from his eyes.

'But, my lord,' Bastion said, 'the plaza has been devastated. Might I suggest that we retire to the Palace of the Almighty until everything has been cleared up?'

'Why?' said Edmond. 'This moment marks my greatest triumph. For too long we have cowered from the very mention of the Holdfasts, and upon this very day they have come to us. We have Sable, and now we have Karalyn.'

'We should execute them both immediately, my lord,' said Merlon.

'Karalyn shall be executed,' Edmond said, 'as soon as the Third Ascendant and I have exchanged our matrimonial vows. Sable, though, I think I will take my time over. Lord Bastion needs to witness her being broken, I feel; otherwise her grip on his mind might never recede. Lord Merlon, have the prisoners brought before my throne. I wish to see them kneel before my majesty.'

Merlon gestured to the warrior gods. They leaned down, and Karalyn and Cardova were hauled to their feet.

'Who is the mortal?' said Merlon. 'My eye-guards are preventing me from reading his mind.'

Cardova spat in the Ancient's face.

Karalyn flinched, expecting the gods to strike Cardova down, but Merlon merely laughed, and wiped the spittle from his cheek. She and Cardova were bundled across the upper platform. The clouds of dust and smoke were starting to lift and, although hundreds had fled the plaza, and hundreds more were lying broken and motionless upon the ground, there remained thousands of gods in attendance. Karalyn glanced at them, feeling sick. Merlon was careful not to let her get too close to Belinda, and they were guided to the base of the largest throne. Her head was pushed down by an armoured god, and she was forced to her knees, Cardova next to her.

Edmond mounted the throne, and Belinda was led up to the other throne, her eyes still glazed over.

'Lord Merlon,' he said; 'it is time. Let the wedding commence.'

Merlon bowed low, then turned to face the crowds, who stilled.

'Today,' Merlon proclaimed, raising his hands, 'our gracious and beloved leader, the Blessed and Honourable Second Ascendant, Lord Edmond of Cumulus, King of Serene, destroyer of Lostwell; the noble lord who vanquished Yocasta and subdued Dragon Eyre; the first of the gods, our lord and saviour, creator of worlds and slayer of dragons; today, our Sacred King takes the hand of the mighty Third Ascendant, Lady Belinda, to be his obedient and loyal wife. At the feet of the golden throne kneels a proud Holdfast, defeated and in misery. Gaze upon her, you noble gods of Cumulus – the Holdfasts' reign of terror is over. Sable and Karalyn Holdfast have been humbled; their wicked plots come to naught. Before this day is over, the head of Karalyn shall be displayed for all to see, and her body will hang upon the battlements of the Palace of the Almighty, next to that of the traitor Nathaniel.'

Karalyn started to ignore Merlon's words, as the Ancient launched into a list of Edmond's achievements. Next to her, Cardova was silent, his eyes closed as they knelt before Edmond's throne. Karalyn glanced sideways. Bastion was standing to Merlon's left, a look of fierce displeasure on his face following his humiliation by his father. Blood was streaking his cheeks, and his robes were ripped across his chest, where the shard of metal had pierced him.

His left eye-guard had slipped.

Without thinking, without hesitating, Karalyn bored her way into his mind. It was in torment. He had been terrified when Sable had been cutting her way towards the carriages, and he had allowed his father to witness his fear. Karalyn could see what Sable had done to his mind. It was powerful, and enduring.

You hate your brother, she whispered in his head. *Your father favours him more than he favours you. You should be leading the wedding ceremony. You are the elder, and Merlon is the younger. Feel the anger and jealousy course through your mind, Bastion. Feel it consume you.*

Bastion started to tremble, his eyes staring at Merlon.

Karalyn kept a strand of power inside Bastion's head, then entered the mind of Cardova.

Get ready, Lucius. Get ready to charge at Belinda's throne.

I am ready to die, Karalyn,' he responded.

She had no time to reply. Instead, she returned to Bastion's mind.

Strike your brother down! Stop him from claiming your birthright. Merlon loathes you, Bastion. Strike him down. Now!

Bastion drew his sword, gripped it in both hands, and swung. The blade flashed out, catching Merlon mid-sentence, and cleaving his head from his shoulders. Edmond shrieked, his eyes wide, as his son's head bounced across the ground. Karalyn launched herself upwards, throwing herself towards Belinda as the assembled gods stared at Merlon's decapitated body. She sensed Cardova next to her as they charged toward the smaller throne. Crossbows thrummed, and Cardova took a bolt to his right leg, then another bolt struck Karalyn's left arm, lodging itself in her wrist. She cried out in pain, and reached the base of the throne.

Bridge palace, Udall. Go.

Karalyn clattered to the floor of the huge reception chamber, colliding with the limb of a massive dragon. The bolt in her wrist snapped, and she howled in agony, almost oblivious to the cries and shouts echoing around her.

'Austin,' shouted a voice, 'get over here!'

Someone pulled the bolt from her wrist, then she felt a hand on her brow. She allowed the demigod's powers to reach her, and she spasmed, then the pain ceased. Her breath rasping, she opened her eyes. Austin was crouching by Cardova, who was sprawled on the ground two yards away, while a crowd had gathered round the motionless body of Belinda, her wedding dress tattered and covered in blood.

The twins rushed to Karalyn's side, and she reached out for them; then Kelsey ran over.

'You did it!' Kelsey cried, her boots skidding to a halt on the floor slabs. 'Um... where's Sable?'

Karalyn burst into tears as she embraced her children. 'Dead dragons...' she gasped. 'They took her.'

Kelsey put an arm over her sister's shoulder as the hall quietened. Cardova grunted, and got to his feet, the wound in his leg healed.

Blackrose's head loomed out of the shadows. 'There has been more than one loss this day, Karalyn Holdfast. Deepblue and Millen did not return from Implacatus, either. I hope you consider Belinda to be worth this sacrifice.'

Austin fell to his knees, tears falling down his cheeks. 'Sable's dead?'

'She was carried away,' said Cardova. 'Edmond told us he wanted to break her before he kills her. That was his plan, before we snatched Belinda. It might have changed.'

'I'm going back,' said Karalyn, sobbing. 'I'm not leaving Sable there. What she did to Bastion's mind saved us. I can't leave her.'

'I'll come with you,' said Kelsey.

'No. I must do this alone.'

She got to her feet, and walked over to where Belinda was lying. Austin was kneeling next to the Third Ascendant, weeping.

'Help me remove the diamonds from the crown,' said Karalyn, 'then do what you can to heal her.'

Austin stared at her, uncomprehending.

Karalyn crouched down, and gripped one of the diamonds that were arrayed along the front of the crown. She braced her feet, then heaved upwards, and a long barbed spike came away from Belinda's forehead, trailing blood and brain matter. A few voices gasped, and Maddie put a hand to her mouth. Karalyn reached down and gripped the second diamond, and Austin grasped hold of another one. Together, they pulled, and two more spikes emerged from Belinda's brain.

'I think I'm going to be sick,' said Maddie.

Austin took hold of the fourth and final diamond, and pulled it free. Without the spikes to hold it in place, the golden crown fell from Belinda's brow and clattered onto the floor. Austin placed his hands on to Belinda's bare arm, and closed his eyes. Belinda screamed, and writhed on the ground. Karalyn felt more tears spring from her eyes as she helped pin the god down. Cardova joined in, holding the Ascendant's legs as she struggled and squirmed. The four holes across her forehead closed up, and Belinda lay still.

'I've done what I can for now,' said Austin, as everyone in the hall stared down at the Third Ascendant.

'Is she better?' said Maddie.

'It will take a while,' said Austin, 'but her mind is starting to repair itself.'

Belinda opened her eyes, and Karalyn gazed down at her.

'Where am I?' the Ascendant whispered. 'My sight is blurry. Am I on Lostwell?'

'You're on Dragon Eyre,' said Karalyn, as tears fell down her cheeks.

'Karalyn?'

'Aye. It's me. And Kelsey, and Blackrose. You're safe.'

Belinda closed her eyes again, and sobbed. She reached out with her arms and wrapped them round Karalyn's shoulders, pulling her close.

'What happened to me?'

'Something terrible,' said Karalyn, 'but it's over.'

'Don't leave me, Karalyn.'

'I must. Sable was captured trying to save you. I have to help her. You stay here and rest.'

'Sable? Sable was trying to help me?'

'Aye. We'll all go back to Colsbury once I've fetched her.' Karalyn raised her head. 'Can we put Belinda somewhere she can sleep? Her self-healing powers are weak, and she needs food and rest.'

'Of course,' said Blackrose. 'Maddie will find the Ascendant some suitable accommodation. However, Karalyn, I must advise against returning to Implacatus. Our losses this day are already enough to break my heart – please, I ask you, do not add to them.'

'I have to.'

'But you must also eat and rest. You are in no fit state to rescue anyone.'

'I will accompany Belinda to her rooms,' Karalyn said, as the Ascendant continued to cling on to her shoulders like a child, 'and then… then I will do what I must.'

CHAPTER 29
THE GALLOWS

P lateau City, The Plateau – 3rd Day, First Third Autumn 534

Daphne felt her shoulder being nudged. She groaned from the pain in her head, and rolled over on to her side. Just a bit more sleep...

The hand touched her shoulder again. 'It's dawn.'

'I don't care.'

'The soldiers will be coming for us soon.'

'Let me sleep.'

'You asked me to wake you up at dawn. I can let you sleep, but do you want the soldiers to drag you out of here when they come?'

Daphne opened her eyes. The cell was thick with shadows, but she could see Thorn crouching beside her, her blue dress marked with stains from the damp and dirty straw she had been sleeping on. Daphne's glance went to the bottle of whisky. She had passed out after drinking most of it, and the sight of what remained made her want to vomit. Why had she thought that drinking herself into oblivion had been a good idea? Fierce pains were shooting through her stomach, and her head was pounding.

Thorn passed her a mug of water. Daphne didn't respond, so Thorn set it down on the floor next to her.

'Damn it,' Daphne muttered. 'I smoked all of the cigarettes last night.'

'I saved you one,' said Thorn. 'I stole it from the packet when you weren't looking.'

Daphne felt a flash of interest. She pulled herself into a sitting position, and leaned back against the wall of the cell. Thorn reached under her straw mattress, and withdrew a single cigarette. Daphne took it without a word, and sat hunched over as she lit it with the last match in the box. The first draw made her feel even worse. She coughed, and almost threw up, then her nausea settled a little, and she smoked more of the cigarette, her right hand shaking.

'You look terrible,' said Thorn.

'Did I do anything crazy last night?'

'You tried to set fire to the cell,' Thorn said, 'but the straw was too damp, and the blankets wouldn't catch the flame.' She picked up a woollen cover, and showed Daphne the corner, which was blackened and scorched. 'You went through most of the matches trying, though. I'm not sure what would have happened had you succeeded. No guards came to visit us, and I don't know if they would have heard anything.'

Daphne balanced her half-smoked cigarette on the edge of her bed, and picked up the mug of water. She took a sip, then drained it. She coughed again, then swapped the mug for the cigarette.

'What did you do?' she said.

'I ate dinner.'

'I meant, what did you do while I was trying to burn down the cell?'

'Nothing. I sat in the corner and watched. You were in no mood to be contradicted, so I let you get on with it. After you couldn't make the blanket burn, you started to cry, and then you passed out.'

'What was I crying about?'

'Keir, mostly. About how you should have been a better mother, and about how you regretted...'

'Enough,' said Daphne. 'I get it.'

Thorn reached under her mattress again, and took out a chunk of bread. 'I also saved you this. You should try to eat it.'

'Why?'

'So that you will feel better.'

'We're going to be dead in a couple of hours; what does it matter?'

Thorn's eyes tightened a little. 'I'm not giving up, not until I'm swinging from the noose. Part of me refuses to believe that the Empress will go through with our executions.'

'She hates us. She'll go through with it.'

'Will she? The Empress hates me, but she must still have some feelings of friendship towards you. But, even if she doesn't, she must be aware that executing us will have serious consequences. Sanang and the Holdings will not take our deaths kindly, not when we haven't actually done anything to act against the Empire. We've talked, but we haven't acted.'

Daphne finished the cigarette and stubbed it out on the floor. 'She's gambling that a display of ruthlessness will quell any opposition to her plans for the succession. Who will any potential rebels rally around if we both die? Will anyone step up to take your place, Thorn? I doubt it.' She paused as the pain in her head surged.

'The salve she's taking has also given me hope,' Thorn said. 'The Empress will feel that she will be able to reign for another few decades. That means the succession is no longer an immediate problem. She doesn't need to kill us any more. Why make martyrs of us when she could keep us in prison?'

Daphne gave a grim chuckle. 'I'm glad one of us is feeling optimistic.'

The door to the exterior hallway opened, and a squad of imperial soldiers entered. They strode up to the cell, and an officer nodded to the soldier holding the keys.

'Open the cell,' he said.

The soldier stepped forward, while the others kept their crossbows ready. The door was unlocked, and the soldier swung it open.

'On yer feet,' said the officer. 'It's time.'

Thorn stood, her hands clasped in front of her. Daphne groaned, then tried to get up. She gripped a bar with her right hand, pulled, then fell back down to her mattress. She clutched her stomach, and panted.

The officer eyed the bottle of whisky, and laughed. 'I think Holder Fast might be feeling a wee bit worse for wear, lads. Grab her shoulders and help her along.'

Thorn stood to the side as two soldiers entered the cell. They seemed wary at first, as if it might be a trick, then, as soon as they realised that Daphne was in no fit state to resist, they hauled her up by the shoulders.

'Watch her left arm,' said the officer. 'The Empress told us to be gentle with them.'

'Are we going up to the palace, Captain?' said Thorn.

'No, ma'am. The plan has been altered. You are to be executed down here, in the basement.'

Thorn frowned. 'Do you know why?'

'Between you and me, ma'am,' the officer said, 'I think her Majesty wants as few witnesses as possible. Too many folk in the Great Fortress would see you if we took you up all those stairs.' He glanced at Daphne, who was being supported by two soldiers. 'Let's move.'

Daphne shrugged off the soldiers as she started to walk. Her feet were unsteady, but she couldn't bear the added humiliation of being carried into the execution chamber. The soldiers released her, but stayed close, watching as she staggered forwards. The officer led the way, and they left the dungeons. The underground passageways were lit with oil lamps, and the walls were streaked with damp. Apart from the prisoners and their escorts, no one else was around, and their footsteps were making the only sound Daphne could hear. They stopped at a door, and one of the soldiers opened it, revealing a large chamber. They entered, and the soldiers led the two prisoners between a few rows of seats towards a low platform, upon which sat a gallows. Daphne glanced up at the wooden beam that would hang them. A rope with a noose was dangling from the end of the beam, with a stool placed directly below it. The officer gestured to the seats in the front row, and the prisoners sat down.

'We'll wait here,' he said, 'until everyone has arrived.'

'Do you have any cigarettes?' said Daphne.

The officer glanced at his squad. One of the soldiers reached into a pocket, and withdrew a crumbled packet.

'Thank you, private,' said the officer, taking it and passing it to Daphne.

'And matches?' said Daphne.

The soldier tossed a small box over to her. Daphne lit a cigarette, and settled into her seat. She was starting to properly wake up, and the fears that she had blotted out with the whisky were returning. She avoided looking at the gallows, but the fact that there was only one was bothering her. Who would go first? Would the other person have to watch? Which was worse?

'We arrived in Plateau City with several men, Captain,' Thorn said. 'Are they well?'

'They are in custody, ma'am,' he said, 'but they're being fed and watered.'

'What's going to happen to them?' Thorn said. 'They are guilty of nothing more than trying to defend us. They don't deserve to hang.'

'I have no answer for you, ma'am. Perhaps you can ask the Empress when she arrives.'

'Will she be long?'

The officer shrugged. 'Her Majesty is due here any moment, ma'am, along with some of her children.'

'I hear them coming now, sir,' said one of the soldiers.

Daphne listened, and caught the sound of approaching footsteps. The soldiers stood to attention as the door opened. Lord Bryce strode in, accompanied by his sister Lady Brogan. Neither sibling looked at the prisoners. Following them, the Empress staggered in, swaying.

'Let's get this fucking over with,' the Empress shouted, her voice slurred.

Thorn and Daphne glanced at each other.

'You're drunk, Bridget,' said Daphne.

'Aye? So what?' the Empress said. 'It's not every day you have to hang an old friend.'

Bridget collided with a chair as she stumbled forwards, sending it clattering across the stone floor. Bryce took a seat in the second row, his eyes lowered, while Brogan tried to assist the Empress.

'Get yer hands off me,' Bridget cried. 'I can fucking walk on my own.'

'Where's Daimon?' said Daphne. 'I thought he would be here for this.'

Bridget laughed as she fell into a seat. 'That wee bastard? I got him drunk last night. Ye should have seen it; it was hilarious. He vomited all over Bryce's shoes, and soldiers had to carry him to his bed. That lad cannae handle his drink.'

'You practically forced the whisky down his throat, mother,' said Brogan, taking her seat.

'Aye? Well, he was annoying me. He had the damn cheek to tell me that I shouldnae be drinking. It's none of his business what I do. I'm the Empress, not him. The wee radge.' She looked up at the gallows, and then glanced at the prisoners. 'And he was a bit too keen to see ye both swing, and I didnae like that.' Her face contorted for a moment, and Daphne thought that she was about to start weeping.

'Thank you for not bringing Keir,' Daphne said.

Bridget nodded. 'I'm not a monster.'

'Shall we proceed, your Majesty?' said the captain.

'In a minute,' Bridget said. She leaned forward in her seat, and hung her head. 'Why is my fucking eye sore? It's tearing a hole in my head.'

'They're healing pains, mother,' said Brogan. 'The salve heals more every day, but it's bound to hurt a little bit. You're growing a whole new eye, after all.'

'It's giving me a bastard of a headache,' Bridget muttered, 'and I cannae think straight.'

She reached into her robes, and took out the vial of salve.

'You're only supposed to take one small dose a day, mother,' said Bryce. 'That's what Lord Naxor told us.'

'Shut it,' Bridget said. 'If I dinnae take any now, ma head'll fucking explode.'

She pulled the stopper out and raised the vial to her lips, but nothing came out. Bridget stared at the empty vial.

'Fuck!' she screamed, then she hurled the glass tube at the wall. It smashed against the stone blocks, then she turned to Bryce, as rage flashed across her face. 'When's that Naxor wanker coming back? I need more salve.'

Bryce stood, his eyes wide. 'You've finished the entire vial?'

'Aye. So?'

'You were only supposed to take one tiny sip a day. The rest of the vial was supposed to go to the city infirmaries.'

'Ye never answered ma question. When's Naxor coming back?'

'We didn't set a precise date, mother,' Bryce said. 'It could be any time in the next ten days or so.'

'Ten days?' Bridget cried. 'How am I supposed to last another ten fucking days?' She slid a finger under her eye-patch and scratched. 'Somebody needs to get me more whisky. I need a drink to watch Daphne swing.'

Brogan frowned. 'I think you've already had quite enough, mother.'

'Shut yer face.' Bridget glanced at a soldier. 'You. Bring me another bottle.'

The soldier saluted, and hurried from the chamber.

Bridget turned to Daphne. 'Any last words before the rope goes round yer throat, Holdfast?'

'Yes,' said Daphne. 'Caelius Logos, Olo'osso, Pechtang and T'Lang are somewhere down here. Please let them go free.'

'I was gonnae do that anyway,' said Bridget. 'Have ye nothing to say to *me*?'

'What can I say? You have ordered the execution of myself and Thorn. Do you want me to beg for my life?'

'As if ye would do that, Daphne. Ye've always been a stubborn cow.' She shook her head. 'Ye should have taken the throne when ye had the chance. Why the fuck didn't ye? I would have been happy to fade into obscurity; do ye think I enjoy this?'

'You were the best person for the job.'

'Then what happened? When did ye stop respecting me? I did ma best. I tried. I wanted to be yer friend, but ye kept pushing me away.' She started to cry. 'Killop loved us both. You were his partner, and I was his best friend. What would he think, if he could see us now?'

Daphne said nothing. The Empress was in pain, she could see that clearly. A battle was raging in her mind, between what she wanted to do, and what she felt she had to do.

'You don't have to go through with this, your Majesty,' said Thorn. 'You could show mercy, and change our sentence from death to imprisonment.'

The Empress lowered her head and sobbed, and the chamber fell into silence, the only sound coming from Bridget's tears. A few of the soldiers glanced at each other, but none moved. The door swung open and the soldier who had left to fetch more whisky returned, a bottle clutched in his hands.

'I advise you not to drink that, mother,' said Bryce.

'Fuck off,' Bridget mumbled. She took the bottle, pulled out the stopper, and drank. Whisky spilled down her chin as she swallowed. She swayed in her seat. 'Right. Thorn first. Get the rope round her pretty wee neck.'

Thorn stood as two soldiers approached. 'I do not require any assistance,' she said. 'I can walk to the gallows on my own.'

The soldiers stood back a little as Thorn held her head high.

'Your Majesty,' she said. 'I wish you a long and fruitful reign. We might have had our disagreements, but know that I hold you in great respect. You have been a true leader of the Empire, and I am sorry that we must part this way.'

She walked up onto the low platform and stood by the dangling rope. The two soldiers stepped up next to her. One extended his hand, and Thorn took it, then climbed up onto the stool. The other soldier took hold of the noose, and slipped it over her head. He adjusted the knot, and tightened the rope round her throat. The soldiers then turned to face the Empress, waiting for her orders.

'I love you, Thorn,' said Daphne. 'Be strong.'

'I love you, too, mother,' said Thorn.

A tear rolled down Daphne's cheek, but she refused to look away.

'Wait,' said Bridget, her voice choking as she wept. 'Thorn, tell me ye renounce yer claim to the throne. Just say the words, and I'll let ye live. I swear it. Just say the fucking words. Please.'

'I cannot,' said Thorn. 'I was selected to be your heir. I am your heir.'

Rage flashed over Bridget's face. 'You stupid bitch!' She rose to her feet, swaying, the bottle of whisky grasped in one hand. 'Do ye want to die? Is that it? Ye want to be a fucking martyr? Yer pride is the reason yer standing with a noose round yer neck. That's all it is, Thorn – pride.' She raised a finger, and pointed it at Thorn, her face red with anger. 'I've had all I can take of yer bullshit. Do ye think I want to do this? Do ye think I want yer blood on ma hands?' She gasped, and put a hand to her chest.

'Maybe you should sit down, mother,' said Brogan, her eyes wide.

'Fuck off. I... I...'

Bridget's eye rolled up into her head. She made a horrible choking noise, then collapsed onto the stone floor, the whisky bottle rolling away, its contents spilling over the boots of her children.

Bryce leapt to his feet, staring at his mother.

Brogan pushed him aside and crouched by the Empress. 'We need a doctor!' She glanced at Thorn, the rope still round her neck. 'Help her!'

'I can't,' said Thorn. 'Daimon took my powers.'

Brogan burst into tears, her hands clasping her mother's face. Daphne crouched next to her, while the soldiers did nothing, their eyes fixed on the Empress. The captain ran from the room.

'I'll get help,' he shouted.

Daphne felt for a pulse, and found nothing. She lowered her gaze.

'She's dead. The Empress is dead.'

'You're lying!' Bryce cried.

Daphne edged back, then she whipped a sword from a soldier's scabbard, and held the blade to Brogan's throat.

'Everybody back off,' Daphne said. She stood, forcing Brogan to her feet, as the sword traced a line of blood on her neck. Daphne glanced at the two soldiers on the platform. 'Release Thorn from the noose.'

The soldiers did nothing.

'Do it,' Daphne cried, 'or I'll kill Brogan.'

Bryce looked close to hysteria. 'My mother's dead, and you're threatening my sister?'

'Yes,' said Daphne. 'Do you want to lose two relatives today? Thorn and I will be leaving now.'

'You heartless bitch!' Bryce yelled.

No one moved, then Thorn reached up and removed the noose from her throat. She stepped down from the stool.

'What should we do, sir?' said one of the soldiers.

'He's not "sir", any more,' said another. 'Lord Bryce is now the Emperor.'

Daphne frowned. 'Allow me to disagree. Lady Thorn is your new Empress. You should be kneeling before her.'

'Sir? Your Majesty?' the first soldier said to Bryce.

Bryce stared at the blade being held against his sister's neck. 'Let them leave.'

'I want my friends released,' Daphne went on. 'You; yes, you with the keys to the cells. Take us to where Caelius and the others are being held.'

The soldier glanced at Bryce.

'Do it,' he said, 'but if they kill Brogan, show them no mercy.'

The soldier with the keys rushed from the room, and Daphne went after him, shoving Brogan along with her, as Thorn followed. Behind her, Bryce and the remaining soldiers kept close, their eyes never leaving Daphne.

'Don't let them escape, brother,' Brogan gasped, as she was pushed along a passageway. 'Our mother is lying dead in that chamber, and all Daphne cares about is getting away.'

'Don't speak about matters you don't understand,' Daphne said. 'Your mother was my friend. Bridget...' She paused, suppressing the tears that threatened to come. She couldn't afford weakness; she had to be resolute.

'Bridget was a great empress,' said Thorn, finishing the sentence for her. 'The entire Empire will mourn her passing; but she tried to kill us. How do you expect us to act?'

'Shut your mouth, you evil witch,' Brogan cried. 'You'll pay for this.'

The soldier with the keys stopped at a cell. Behind the bars, Olo'osso jumped to his feet, while the other three men stared at the sight of Daphne holding a sword to Brogan's throat.

'Holder Fast!' Olo'osso cried. 'My heart races to see you, my lady. Have you come to grant us freedom?'

'Open the door,' Daphne said to the soldier.

The soldier fumbled with the keys. He found the right one, and unlocked the cell door. Olo'osso pushed it open and strode out. He walked up to the soldier, and slid the sword from the man's scabbard.

'I'll take this, I think,' he said, a smile on his lips.

Caelius joined them in the passageway, then the two young Sanang men followed, and each took a weapon from the soldiers, as Bryce said nothing.

'Should we kill these bastards?' said Pechtang, raising his sword.

'No,' said Thorn. 'I want no more deaths this day.'

'More deaths?' said Caelius. 'Who has died?'

'The Empress,' said Daphne. 'She suffered a heart attack, I think. Her body is lying a few yards from the gallows where she intended to hang us.'

Olo'osso gave a grim smile. 'That sounds just. She tried to kill you, my lady, and found her own death instead.'

Brogan struggled, her eyes enraged, and T'Lang took over from Daphne, grabbing Bryce's sister and shoving his blade against her neck, while Pechtang gripped her arms.

'Where's Keir?' said Caelius. 'Is he still locked up somewhere down here?'

'My son has made his choice,' said Daphne. 'He shall not be coming with us.'

'Lord Bryce,' said Thorn; 'lead us out of the Great Fortress. Do not try to trick or betray us. My Sanang friends are not as merciful as Holder Fast and I. Remain calm, if you wish your sister to survive.'

'Don't do it, brother,' Brogan said, her arms twisted behind her back. 'They are traitors. You are the rightful Emperor. If they get away, they'll spread rebellion against your rule.'

'I'm not risking your life, sister,' Bryce said. 'With mother gone, you mean more to me than anyone else. I'm not going to lose you today.' He glared at Thorn. 'Follow me.'

Bryce turned, and set off down a long, damp corridor. The soldiers trailed behind, while T'Lang and Pechtang kept a tight grip of Brogan.

They ascended a set of stairs, and Daphne recognised where they were. Ahead of them were the original entrance gates to the Great Fortress, which led out into the Old Town. A squad of guards on duty turned at their approach, and their hands went to their weapons.

'Nobody move,' Bryce cried. 'My sister is a hostage.'

The soldiers, all of whom were Kellach, stared at Daphne and the others with anger in their eyes, but no one drew a weapon.

'Open the gates,' said Bryce.

One of the soldiers ran forward, unbarred the gates, and swung them open. Daphne blinked from the sunlight, then gestured for the others to leave the Great Fortress. Thorn led the way, followed by Olo'osso and the two Sanang men, who bundled Brogan over the threshold. Caelius remained where he was, guarding Daphne's back.

'If you kill my sister,' Bryce said, 'no power on this world will save you from my wrath.'

Daphne nodded her head to him, then ran through the gate, Caelius by her side. The fugitives raced down the steps by the front of the gate, then sprinted into the warren of streets. Flanked by tall tenement blocks, they turned into a deserted alleyway, and ran until Daphne felt as though she was about to throw up.

She slowed to a walk, and the others did the same.

'I hate you,' Brogan said, tears streaming down her face.

'I know,' said Daphne. She glanced at the two Sanang men. 'Release her.'

'Should we not keep her a bit longer?' said Pechtang.

'No,' said Daphne.

The Sanang men glanced at Thorn.

'Do as Holder Fast says,' Thorn said. 'She is now the Herald of the Empire. Treat her orders as if they were issued from my mouth.'

T'Lang withdrew his sword from Brogan's throat, and Pechtang released her arms.

Brogan rubbed her neck. 'This isn't over.'

'I know,' said Daphne. 'Go back to the Great Fortress and tell your brother to renounce his claims to the Empire. It is the only way to avoid open conflict.'

Brogan spat on the cobbles by Daphne's feet. 'Go fuck yourself, Holdfast.'

She turned, and ran back down the alleyway.

'What now?' said Caelius, his hand still gripping the hilt of a sword.

'The harbour,' said Daphne. 'We'll catch the next boat to Amatskouri, then take a carriage to Colsbury from there.'

Pechtang frowned. 'A boat? I'm not getting on any damn boat.'

'Yes, you are,' said Thorn. 'Follow me.'

The large ship was heaving with people as it slipped away from the long pier. Most passengers were Rakanese, but there was a sprinkling of Holdings and Kellach on board, and even a few Sanang. Daphne and Thorn stood by the railings, anonymous amid the crowd of onlookers. Gulls shrieked and called out above them, circling round the sails and perching atop the highest mast.

'We'll be in Amatskouri in a couple of days,' Daphne said. 'Daimon won't be able to track us, not with no powers to sense.'

'By the time we arrive,' said Thorn, 'Bryce will have been

proclaimed Emperor.'

'Yes. We can do nothing about that. In fact, we can do nothing until we reach Colsbury. Once there, we shall hold a coronation of our own in the Summer Palace, and proclaim you as the true sovereign ruler of the Empire. Then, we'll need to raise an army.'

Thorn frowned. 'What army?'

'Let me worry about that.'

Daphne glanced at the faces of the other passengers. The news of the Empress's death had not yet filtered out from the Great Fortress, and she wondered how the citizens would react.

'I'm going down to our cabin,' she said.

'Are you sure?' said Thorn. 'Don't you get seasick?'

'I'll be fine.'

Daphne moved away from the railings. The ship was turning in the wide harbour, aiming its bow towards the open waters of the Inner Sea. Daphne squeezed past a crowd of Rakanese, and descended a steep flight of stairs. She followed a passageway to the cabin that she and Thorn were sharing, and unlocked the door. The cabin was tiny, with two hammocks and a single chair. Daphne sat, and lit a cigarette, her right hand shaking.

She started to cry, as the death of Bridget finally sunk in. Her sobs were quiet and slow at first, then all of the pent-up emotion burst within her, as if a mountain dam had been breached, and she wept until her chest ached.

Bridget had gone. They had known each other for thirty years, and had suffered so much together – Slateford, the mad Creator, Agatha, Killop. They had loved each other, but they had hated each other, too, and their relationship had been filled with as much anger and sorrow as there had been joy and laughter. Despite everything, Daphne already missed Bridget; missed knowing that her old friend was in charge; missed her easy ways, and her smile. There remained nothing but struggle; a struggle for the soul of the Star Continent.

Daphne wiped her eyes.

The Empress was dead. Long live the Empress.

CHAPTER 30
FROM THE DEAD

Cumulus, Implacatus – 22nd Tuminch 5255

The air whipped past Sable's face as the dead dragon grasped her in its talons. Her right hand was still clutching the Fated Blade, but her shoulders and arms were being compressed by the dragon's grasp, and she couldn't move her elbow. Dozens of other dragons were soaring around them, escorting the Holdfast prisoner towards the Palace of the Almighty, and the dark, monolithic slab of granite was looming closer with every second. Sable attempted to force her powers into the dragon's mind, but its dead eyes rebuffed her. She could feel a corner of the Quadrant jab into her left side; it was safe, but out of reach. She might have an opportunity to touch it once the dragon had landed, but if it took her into the windowless palace, then it would already be too late.

An explosion tore through the air to the dragon's right, and a tower began to topple, its foundations blasted away. Sable frowned. Why had one of her bombs gone off early? She had timed them all to... All thoughts were driven out as every other device detonated at the same time. The sky above Cumulus filled with noise and light, then smoke, and the squadron of dead dragons was buffeted by the shock waves.

One crashed into the side of a castle keep, and another dropped from the sky like a stone, disappearing into the thick banks of cloud that swirled beneath them. The dragon carrying Sable banked wildly, its wings ripped by flying debris as a dense cloud of smoke and dust enveloped them. The talons round Sable's body loosened a fraction, and Sable aimed upwards with her sword, plunging it through the scales and into the beast's right forelimb. The dragon made no sound, or perhaps its roar was drowned out by the cacophony of noise assaulting Sable's ears. It began to spiral, plummeting from the sky as it spun. The smoke intermingled with the low cloud cover, and she lost sight of the city; then the dragon hit something as it fell. Sable caught a brief glimpse of a dark cliff face, then the dragon continued to drop, deeper into the thick clouds. It crashed into the bottom of a ravine, and skidded along the ragged rocks, its neck bent back, and its giant head crushed by its own weight. It ground to a halt amid the impenetrable clouds, and Sable lay still for a moment, still clutched within the grasp of the beast's claws. She wriggled and pushed her way out from the talons, then fell four feet onto the broken ground. She glanced around, but could see almost nothing through the cloud. Part of the dragon was visible, along with a sheer wall of the ravine, and the rocky ground under her boots; but all else was lost in the murk.

Sable stood in silence, listening, the Fated Blade grasped in her hand. She had to get back to Karalyn; her niece couldn't fight, and Belinda had been surrounded by armoured gods wearing eye-shields. Sable considered using the Quadrant, but she had become disorientated within the clouds, and wasn't sure of the direction or distance. She needed to move to higher ground, somewhere out of the clouds, so she could get her bearings.

'Holdfast!' cried a voice.

She turned, and saw a god climbing down from the body of the motionless dragon.

'Stay where you are,' the god said, a battle axe in his right hand.

Sable laughed. 'Did you not see what I did to your immortal friends in the plaza?' she said. 'Are you so keen to join them in death that you're challenging me?'

'The dragons will be hunting you, Holdfast,' the god said. 'I need only delay you; there is nowhere to run.'

'You're starting to bore me,' Sable said.

She clicked her fingers. *Sleep.*

The god's eyes went hazy and he collapsed to the rocky ground. Sable walked over to him. She raised the Fated Blade, then decided to read the god's mind before killing him. He might know their location, she thought. She opened his right eye with her fingers, and entered his mind.

He was a dragon rider, the commander of a squadron, responsible for controlling six of the dead beasts, including the one that had snatched Sable from the plaza. He was also an Ancient, who had lived in Cumulus for over a millennium, watching as Implacatus slowly decayed and died. There was a great fear buried deep within his consciousness – one that overshadowed his terror of Edmond and Bastion. His greatest fear was that Implacatus did not have long. The toxic wastelands that had spread over the world were constantly threatening to encroach upon Serene and Cumulus; and if the Ascendants and Ancients did not find another home soon, a catastrophe was inevitable. The immortals had been pinning their hopes on Dragon Eyre, but Sable had ruined their plans. Next to that disaster, even the failure to find the salve world seemed insignificant – they could live without salve if they had to, but if Implacatus became uninhabitable, they could all die. Sable found a recent memory, when Bastion had spoken to a group of Ancients. The Ancients had been angry with Lord Bastion's retreat from Dragon Eyre, and several had demanded that he return, taking the reserves of Banner soldiers that remained in Serene with him to finish the job. To their surprise, Bastion had refused. He had given them a speech about waiting for the right time to strike, but something about his tone had disconcerted the other Ancients. Bastion was afraid. Such a thing would have seemed impossible before he had gone to Dragon Eyre – for what could frighten Bastion? His return had changed him, and his fear had confused and scared the other Ancients. Worse, his fear had a name.

Holdfast.

Sable smiled, then slashed down with the black-edged sword, slicing the Ancient's head from his shoulders. She placed the Fated Blade back into its scabbard, then began to clamber up the side of the cliff face. Cloud engulfed her like fog, and she lost sight of the crashed dragon as she climbed over boulders and loose scree. A flash of flames burst far off to her right, then another, but Sable had no idea what was burning. She reached a high ledge, and pulled herself up onto it. Another flash of flames appeared, and she realised that she was watching a god with fire powers at work. Were they trying to flush her out? If so, they were targeting the wrong location. She scaled a tall boulder, and came to a gap in the cloud cover. The dragon carrying her had crashed into a deep crevice, where the clouds were particularly thick, and she saw the broken landscape of Cumulus on either side of the ravine. Smoke and flames were rising from over a dozen places. She couldn't see the plaza, and tried to guess where it was, as her fingers went into the pocket where her Quadrant lay. She turned her head, and saw several dead dragons circling in the sky to her right, above the place where the god-rider had been sending down fire bolts. The sound of dogs reached Sable's ears; a fierce barking from the location beneath the circling dragons.

From the sound the dogs were making, they had found something. Sable hesitated. She needed to get back to Karalyn, but she didn't want to abandon whoever the dogs were attacking. She judged the distance to a rocky outcrop that was poking above the clouds, and brushed her thumb over the Quadrant. The air shimmered, and she found herself standing next to the outcrop, the noise from the dogs increasing tenfold. Sable hurried down the steep slope and back into the cloud, following the growls and barks. Her steps slowed as she peered into the murk. A dark shadow lunged at her, and she reacted, holding out her sword as a shape emerged from the fog. A huge black hound leapt at her, impaling itself on to the Fated Blade. It cried out, whimpering, then slid off the blade and disappeared into the murk.

Another animal noise reached her ears. Not a dog, but an animal in pain. More shadows became visible – smaller shapes prowling round a larger one; attacking and retreating. Sable charged forward, and the hounds broke off their attack to leap at her. The Fated Blade flashed out, cutting through anything it met, and Sable's leathers became drenched in blood. Every dog that leapt at her was cut down as she raced through them, her feet dancing on the rough ground. She turned, and heard nothing. She peered through the murk, ready for more attacks, but none came.

'Who is there?' came a weak voice.

Sable blinked. 'Deepblue?'

'Sable?'

She crept forwards, and saw blue scales appear, dripping with blood. The small blue dragon had rolled into a ball, and was covered in wounds.

'I cannot fly, Sable,' the dragon whispered. 'Save Millen and leave me here.'

Sable placed her left palm on to the side of the dragon's neck, and Deepblue's head appeared from where she had been hiding it beneath a ripped and tattered wing.

'Frostback and Ashfall have gone,' the small blue dragon whispered. 'I wasn't fast enough.'

A fire bolt ripped past, illuminating the murk as it crashed into a cliffside twenty yards to their left.

'They know you killed the dogs,' Deepblue said, her voice weak. 'Go, quickly, and take Millen with you. I am sheltering him within my forelimbs.'

Sable scanned her surroundings. The cloud cover was too thick for her to be able to calculate direction and distance. The Quadrant was still usable, but not to travel anywhere within Cumulus; the risk was too great. Karalyn needed her, but so did Deepblue, and she hesitated.

Another burst of flames penetrated the clouds, landing just a few yards from Deepblue's right flank.

'Shit,' Sable muttered. She would need to be quick.

She brushed a thumb and two fingers over the Quadrant, and the air crackled as more fire bolts tore through the air. Deepblue covered Sable with a wing as they appeared at the base of the bridge palace in Udall, next to the wide, brown river. Sable touched the Quadrant again, and they found themselves inside the bridge palace.

'You're safe now,' Sable said to the blue dragon. 'Stay here. I need to return to Implacatus.'

Deepblue collapsed onto the marble floor, and Millen spilled out, released by the blue dragon's forelimbs. He rolled onto the ground, unconscious.

'Hello, Aunty,' said Cael.

Sable looked up, and saw the boy standing a few yards away.

'Deepblue and Millen need help,' Sable said. 'I'll bring your mother home.'

'Mama is already here, Aunty. She's going to look for you.'

Sable blinked. 'What?'

'Mama's going back to Implacatus.'

'Tell her to stop!' Sable cried.

The boy nodded, then his eyes glazed over for a moment. The air shimmered, and Karalyn appeared in the vast hallway. She stared at Sable, then saw Deepblue and Millen.

Sable put a hand on her hip and smiled. 'You got back before me?'

'I'm sorry I left you, Sable,' Karalyn said.

'You didn't leave me; I was carried off by a dead dragon. Did you... get Belinda?'

'Aye.'

'We did it?'

'Aye, Sable. We did it.' Karalyn turned, 'Maddie!' she shouted.

The dragon-rider appeared in the entrance to the reception hall, then others also emerged from the hall. Maddie cried out at the sight of

Deepblue and Millen, and the hallway became crowded with people and dragons.

Maddie threw her arms round Sable. 'You rescued Millen and Deepblue. I think I love you, Sable.'

Austin got to work, crouching down next to Millen, as Cardova and Kelsey joined Maddie and Karalyn by Sable.

'Well, Lucius?' Sable said. 'How many did I get?'

Cardova laughed. 'You must be joking, I lost count at twelve.'

'Thank you for bringing Deepblue back,' said Ashfall, her long slender neck angling down so that her head was level with Sable.

'And Millen,' said Maddie.

Austin moved on to Deepblue. He knelt by the dragon and placed his hands on to the blue scales. Deepblue shuddered as the demigod healed her. Millen got to his feet, his clothes ragged and covered in blood. He embraced Deepblue's head, and sobbed.

Another figure shuffled forward. Sable stared at the woman. She looked terrible, as if she had been ill for months.

'Belinda,' Sable said.

'Sable,' gasped the Ascendant. 'Thank you.'

'You should be lying down,' Karalyn said, reaching out with an arm to support Belinda. 'You need to rest.'

'Listen,' said Sable; 'I learned something from an Ancient before I got away.'

The others fell into silence.

'Austin was right,' Sable went on. 'Implacatus is dying, and the gods are afraid. They don't know how much longer they'll be able to preserve Serene and Cumulus from the poisonous wastes that surround them. They might try to return to Dragon Eyre, or, they might choose somewhere else to conquer.'

'We shall not concern ourselves with the worries of the gods,' said Blackrose. 'If Implacatus dies, it shall be no more than the Ascendants deserve, and, if they come here, we will be ready for them.' She raised her head. 'Now is the time to celebrate this great victory. The carnage unleashed by the Holdfasts and the three dragons this day will live long in the memory. If Edmond feared you before, Holdfasts, he will be doubly terrified of you now. He has lost his son, and his bride.'

'His son?' said Sable. 'Is Bastion dead?'

'Bastion killed Merlon,' said Cardova.

'I forced him to do it,' said Karalyn. 'What you did to Bastion's mind made it easier, Sable. For all we know, Bastion might also be dead, struck down by his father.'

'The gods will be weeping and wailing in torment,' Blackrose cried. 'Oh glorious day! I am proud of you all, my friends. Let us feast!'

Kelsey frowned. 'Um, sorry to spoil the mood, but shouldn't someone do something about mother?'

'I'll go,' said Sable. 'I'm in the mood to tangle with Empress Bridget.'

'Thank you,' said Karalyn. 'I would go, but Belinda and the twins are here, and...'

'You don't have to explain anything to me,' Sable said. 'Kelsey, are you coming? You can shield, and I'll wave the Fated Blade around. If Daphne and Thorn are there, we'll get them out.'

'And Keir,' said Karalyn. 'Don't forget him.'

'Lara is on her way up to the bridge palace,' said Maddie. 'What will I tell her?'

Sable shrugged. 'Tell her I'll be back soon.'

She brushed her fingers over the Quadrant and the air crackled. Sable and Kelsey appeared amid the garden on the roof of the Great Fortress in Plateau City, and Sable glanced up at the clouds. It was nice to have them far above her head again, rather than being lost among them.

'Can you sense Daphne or Thorn?' she asked Kelsey.

'No, but that doesn't mean anything. They might not be using their powers just now.'

There was no one else on the roof, so they walked to a corner turret, and descended the steps into the palace.

'Your front is covered in blood,' Kelsey said, as they reached the plush hallways of the palace.

Sable nodded. 'It's been a busy day.'

'I thought I'd made a mess of everything,' Kelsey went on. 'I thought I'd got Deepblue and Millen killed.'

'You did a great job,' said Sable; 'it was exactly what we needed, at precisely the right time.'

'Are you sure? I thought, you know, maybe…'

'Stop doubting yourself, Kelsey. If I ever need a lieutenant, you would be my first choice.'

Kelsey smiled.

'Halt!' cried a voice.

Sable looked up. Ahead of them, two Kellach Brigdomin soldiers in imperial uniforms were blocking the passageway.

Sable raised a hand. *Sleep.*

The two soldiers toppled over like felled trees, their armour and weapons clattering off the floor.

'That will have woken up a few people,' Sable said. 'Give me a moment.'

She sent out her powers, and rushed them through the palace. In a room just to their right, she located Keir, who was sitting alone, his head in his hands.

Sable cut the connection and turned to Kelsey. 'I've found your brother, and guess what – he's not in the dungeons.'

They walked forward, and Sable opened the door.

Keir glanced up, and his eyes widened. He opened his mouth, as if he was about to scream.

Sable dived into his mind.

Hush. You will tell me what I need to know, quietly.

'Where's Daphne?' she said, keeping her powers inside Keir's mind.

'I don't know,' he said.

Sable frowned. 'Why not?'

'She escaped. So did Thorn and the others from Colsbury.'

'They left you here?' said Kelsey.

Keir glanced down. 'Yes. The Empress is dead.'

Kelsey gasped. 'Pyre's arse. How? Did mother…?'

'It wasn't mother,' Keir said. 'Or Thorn. Daimon took their powers.

The Empress had a heart attack, and… she died. Lord Bryce said she had too much salve, and he's blaming you and Lord Naxor for poisoning her. You need to leave, before they get here.'

Sable stared at him. 'Bridget's gone?'

'What aren't you telling us, brother?' said Kelsey. 'Why is it safe for you to stay here?'

Keir's face flushed. 'I… I had no choice. I only wanted to do the right thing. Thorn should never be Empress; you don't know her like I do. She would destroy this world; she…'

Kelsey raised a hand. 'And what? Are you telling me that you sided with Bridget over our own mother, Keir? You betrayed the Holdfasts?'

'Mother and Thorn are traitors against the Empire,' Keir cried. 'They held Lady Brogan hostage and ran from the palace. And now… now, Daimon can't find them, because he removed their powers.'

Sable felt another presence appear in Keir's mind. It was so powerful that her own vision skills were pushed out of his head. Sable flinched, and an ache began to form behind her temples.

She stared at Kelsey. 'Daimon knows we're here.'

'But he can't detect me,' said Kelsey.

'He doesn't need to; he's in Keir's mind.'

Sable reached for the Quadrant as the door burst open. Daimon strode into the chamber, followed by Lord Bryce and a dozen armoured Kellach soldiers.

'More damn Holdfasts?' cried Bryce.

'We came here for my mother,' said Kelsey, edging backwards.

Daimon raised a hand, and Sable's hand froze an inch from the surface of the Quadrant.

You will not escape, Sable, said a voice in her head.

Sable strained to resist the voice, but its power was flooding her mind. Was that what it felt like, she wondered, whenever she forced someone to do something against their will?

'What are you doing, Mage Daimon?' said Bryce.

'Sable is trying to flee, your Majesty,' Daimon said. 'She has a Quadrant in her pocket.'

Give me the Quadrant!

Sable felt her resistance start to crumble. Her hand went round the device and gripped it, then she withdrew it from her pocket.

'That's it, Sable!' Daimon crowed. 'Your powers are strong, aye! But not as strong as mine. You will give me the Quadrant, and then you will show me how to use it.'

Sable grunted, as her will was bent. She felt Daimon pierce her memories, looking for information about the Quadrant, and she was powerless to stop him. Kelsey stared at her in horror.

'Take it, Kelsey!' she cried. 'I can't resist Daimon.'

'Stop them!' Bryce shouted.

Kelsey snatched the Quadrant from Sable's fingers as the soldiers charged. Her fingers brushed the copper-coloured surface, and the air shimmered. They found themselves in the Sextant chamber in Cols-bury, and Sable collapsed to her knees, panting. A bead of sweat trickled down her forehead, and she closed her eyes.

'He's as powerful as Karalyn,' she gasped. 'I couldn't stop him. A few more seconds, and I would have given him the Quadrant.'

'Should we go back for Thorn and mother?' Kelsey said.

'They could be anywhere by now,' Sable said. 'In a carriage; in the tunnels under the Old Town; on a ship. Without powers to home in on, we could be searching for days. They'll come here, if they're able.'

Kelsey collapsed into an armchair. 'I can't believe Bridget's dead. What happens now? Is Bryce Emperor; or is Thorn the new Empress? And Keir? I knew he was a numpty, but I never thought he'd betray us. Are you going back to Dragon Eyre?'

Sable pulled herself to her feet. 'We'll have to. Karalyn and the others are there.'

'That's not what I meant,' Kelsey said. 'Once we've brought them all back here, to Colsbury, are you going to live on Dragon Eyre with Lara?'

Sable lowered her gaze. 'What about you? Are you going back to the City?'

'I don't know any more, Aunty. What if mother needs us here? What if Karalyn needs us? I don't want to brag, but we both have powers that the others can't do without. I mean, if Daimon's coming after the family, they'll need all the help they can get.'

'Maybe we should fetch Corthie, too.'

'Aye, maybe. Shit. I wonder if Van would agree to stay here for a while. Lara might move here, you know, if you asked her. Look; we don't have to decide everything right now. Let's get back to Ulna, and we can talk about it later.'

She held out the Quadrant, and Sable took it.

'Where's yours?' Sable said.

'I left it on Dragon Eyre.'

Sable smiled, and shook her head. 'You need to stop carrying it around in a bag, Kelsey. Find some clothes where you can keep it close to you at all times.'

Kelsey raised an eyebrow. 'You're lecturing me, after I saved your arse?'

'I'm your aunt; I'm allowed to lecture you.'

Sable flicked her fingers over the Quadrant, and they appeared outside the vast reception hall within the bridge palace in Udall. They strode into the hall, to find it packed with dragons and humans. Karalyn was sitting on the edge of the platform with Cardova and the twins. Karalyn stood when she saw them approach.

'Greetings,' said Blackrose. 'How did you fare?'

'Not very well,' said Sable. 'We were chased out of the Great Fortress by Daimon.'

'The Empress is dead,' said Kelsey.

Karalyn staggered back a step.

'Bryce thinks it was the salve that killed her,' Kelsey went on. 'Mother and the others escaped, though. Well, not all of the others. Keir has switched sides.'

'Slow down,' said Karalyn. 'That's a lot to take in at once.'

'We should go back to Colsbury,' said Sable. 'Kelsey and I are thinking of staying there for a while, to help.'

'I'd like that,' said Karalyn. 'Thank you.'

Lara pushed her way through the crowds until she was facing Sable. 'What did I just hear?' she said. 'Are you leaving me again?'

'My home world is about to descend into turmoil,' Sable said. 'I need to help my family.'

'Just one more job, eh?' said Lara. 'When will it end? Will we ever get a chance to be happy?'

'I warned you that my life was like this,' Sable said.

'Yeah, but you also promised me that you would settle down, once the gods had been kicked out of Dragon Eyre. And then you had to rescue Austin; and then you had to rescue Belinda. There's always going to be something else, ain't that right?'

Sable glanced down. 'Probably.'

'Is that it, then?' said Lara. 'Have I been wasting my time?'

'Come with us,' Sable said. 'Stay with me in Colsbury. That's where your father will be heading; he's with Daphne.'

'What about my life here? What about the *Gull*? I can't just leave.'

'It won't be forever.'

Lara said nothing.

'I'm not going to beg,' said Sable, 'but I would like you to come. Try it. If you hate it, I can bring you back here.'

Tilly approached, and put an arm over Lara's shoulder. 'If nothing else, sister,' she said, 'it'll be an adventure. I'll look after your crew for you.'

Lara's eyes narrowed. 'Promise me you won't let Dina captain the *Gull*.'

'I wouldn't let Dina captain a rowing boat, sister.'

'Alright,' Lara said, her gaze on Sable. 'I'll try it.'

Blackrose raised her head. 'Might we get back to the celebrations? There is food; there is wine; and you are all my guests.'

'I'm going back to the *Gull* to pack my things,' said Lara. 'Don't leave without me.'

'We'll be here,' said Karalyn.

Austin approached, and pushed a glass of wine into Sable's hands.

'I've decided to stay in Udall,' he said. 'My mother and aunt like it here, and Ashfall wants me to help her get rid of the last greenhides hiding on the island.'

'Thanks for everything,' Sable said.

'I have no regrets,' he said. 'You pushed me hard, but I didn't break.'

Sable smiled. 'Well, you cried a few times.'

He laughed. 'So did you.'

They embraced, then Sable felt a hand touch her shoulder. She turned, and saw Belinda standing behind her. The Ascendant was leaning on a walking stick, and she looked as ill as before.

'Are we friends now?' said Belinda.

'I don't know,' said Sable. 'I thought you hated me.'

'I used to. Some of my memories have returned. We fought side by side with Corthie in Old Alea. Didn't we?'

'We did. Do you remember anything after that?'

'Just flashes,' Belinda said. 'I think I was put into a restrainer mask for a while, but it's all a blur. Karalyn told me that I was almost married to Edmond, but I have no memory of that. I would like to see Corthie again.'

'I'm sure we can arrange that,' said Sable.

Karalyn and Kelsey joined them.

'We kicked some arse today,' said Kelsey. 'The Holdfast girls together.'

Karalyn smiled. 'We made it out alive; that's all that matters to me.'

'We kicked arse,' said Sable; 'that's true. But then we went to Plateau City, and we got our arses kicked by Daimon. I thought I was strong enough to resist him, but I'm not. He almost made me hand over my Quadrant.' She lowered her voice. 'Blackrose might think it's all over, but it's not. Without Bridget to restrain him, who knows what Daimon will do? He'll have Bryce wrapped round his little finger; if he can manipulate my mind, then he'll have no problem doing the same thing to Bryce, or Keir.'

'So, what do we do?' said Kelsey.

'We're Holdfasts,' Sable said; 'we stick together.'

Kelsey rolled her eyes. 'Pyre's arse, Sable; you're beginning to sound like my mother.'

Sable smiled. A comment like that would have stung only a short while before, but a strange new feeling was quelling any annoyance at Kelsey's words. She wondered what the feeling was for a moment, then she realised. For the first time since she had discovered she was a Holdfast, she felt part of the family, and the feeling made her giddy. At last, she was no longer the outcast; no longer alone.

She belonged.

AUTHOR'S NOTES

NOVEMBER 2022

Thanks for reading God Restrainer – I hope you enjoyed it.

Seeds that were planted all the way back in the Magelands Epic are now finally coming to bloom – the ambitions of Thorn, the crimes of Sable's past, and the tension between Daphne Holdfast and Bridget ae Brenna. Weaving them into the threads of the City, Implacatus and Dragon Eyre was the main challenge of God Restrainer, but it was a book I loved writing. Of the four final instalments of the series, it was by far the easiest to draft, and the one that gave me the fewest sleepless nights!

RECEIVE A FREE MAGELANDS ETERNAL SIEGE BOOK

Building a relationship with my readers is very important to me.

Join my newsletter for information on new books and deals and you will also receive a Magelands Eternal Siege prequel novella that is currently EXCLUSIVE to my Reader's Group for FREE.

www.ChristopherMitchellBooks.com/join

ABOUT THE AUTHOR

Christopher Mitchell is the author of the Magelands epic fantasy series.

For more information:
www.christophermitchellbooks.com
info@christophermitchellbooks.com

www.ingramcontent.com/pod-product-compliance
Lightning Source LLC
Chambersburg PA
CBHW060724190726
48285CB00001B/55